I0691681

JAKE C. WALLACE

DARE TO LOVE FOREVER

Published by
DREAMSPINNER PRESS

5032 Capital Circle SW, Suite 2, PMB# 279, Tallahassee, FL 32305-7886 USA
www.dreamspinnerpress.com

This is a work of fiction. Names, characters, places, and incidents either are the product of author imagination or are used fictitiously, and any resemblance to actual persons, living or dead, business establishments, events, or locales is entirely coincidental.

Dare to Love Forever
© 2016 Jake C. Wallace.

Cover Art
© 2016 Reese Dante.
http://www.reesedante.com
Cover content is for illustrative purposes only and any person depicted on the cover is a model.

All rights reserved. This book is licensed to the original purchaser only. Duplication or distribution via any means is illegal and a violation of international copyright law, subject to criminal prosecution and upon conviction, fines, and/or imprisonment. Any eBook format cannot be legally loaned or given to others. No part of this book may be reproduced or transmitted in any form or by any means, electronic or mechanical, including photocopying, recording, or by any information storage and retrieval system, without the written permission of the Publisher, except where permitted by law. To request permission and all other inquiries, contact Dreamspinner Press, 5032 Capital Circle SW, Suite 2, PMB# 279, Tallahassee, FL 32305-7886, USA, or www.dreamspinnerpress.com.

ISBN: 978-1-63477-715-5
Digital ISBN: 978-1-63477-716-2
Library of Congress Control Number: 2016911388
Published September 2016
v. 2.0
First Edition published as Dare to Love Forever: New Vampire Justice Book by Amber Allure, 2014.

Printed in the United States of America
∞
This paper meets the requirements of
ANSI/NISO Z39.48-1992 (Permanence of Paper).

Readers love *Soul Seekers*
by JAKE C. WALLACE

"…I couldn't rip myself away from the pages and kept reading until the wee hours of the morning… The story was cleverly worked so that it kept me guessing who was good and bad.
—Sinfully Gay Romance
Book Reviews

"*Soul Seekers* by Jake C. Wallace is a phenomenal tale of survival and triumph. With fast paced action and heart stopping discoveries on every page, this is one you will not want to miss."
—Joyfully Jay

"Quite literally, the intricacy and detail of this novel blew me away in the best possible way. Between the character developments, the mystery, and the world building, I was hooked."
—The Novel Approach

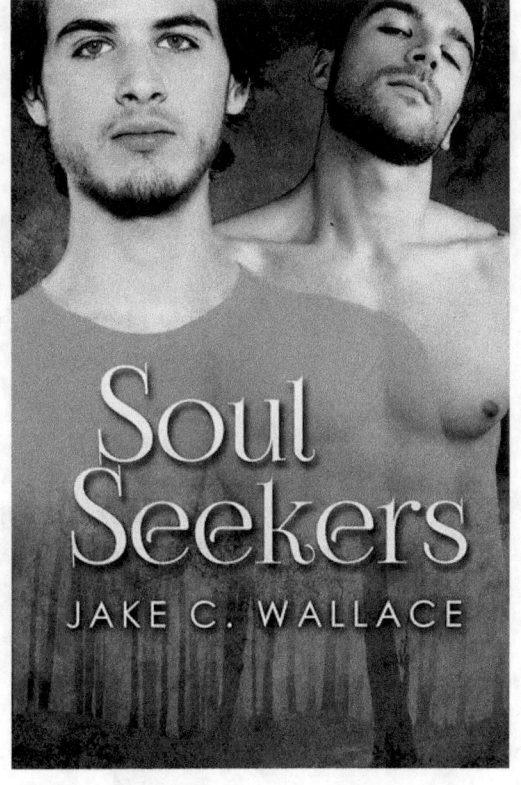

"There were enough twists and turns that I didn't want to put the book down just so I could find out what would happen next."
—Scattered Thoughts and Rogue Words

By Jake C. Wallace

Dare to Love Forever
Soul Seekers

Published by Dreamspinner Press
www.dreamspinnerpress.com

When you venture into unknown territory, having a guide who knows the lay of the land can ensure you don't get lost. My guide in the land of M/M publishing has been Julie Lynn Hayes. She found this clueless and wayward soul, took me by the hand, and showed me the path. She has answered endless questions, edited tens of thousands of words, and had my back. She is tireless, selfless, and a true friend.

Julie, this story is dedicated to you.

A special thank-you to Raine O'Tierney because you will always be my favorite.

CHAPTER 1

CARSON LOCKE was starving. Thoughts of veins and warm blood flowing through arteries clouded his thinking. His stomach had hollowed. His bones protruded, and his muscles shook from weakness. His self-control, held by a fragile thread, stretched to the breaking point. When it snapped he'd turn into the monster he'd avoided becoming for over twenty-three years.

He needed food. He needed blood.

Now.

The cold wind bit at Carson's thin skin, even though he crouched behind a dumpster. Ten days. Ten days since he last ate. Ten days too long for a young vampire. Ten days since he fled his home. Ten days since his mother and brother and uncle were slaughtered and he ran for his life. They were all dead because of what he was. He choked back a sob, forcing his focus on the back door of the building he'd been watching.

This was his last chance. If he couldn't get the blood he needed, that last thread of self-control would snap, and he'd attack someone. The memory of the last time he was forced to bite—the screaming, the wide, vacant, staring eyes, the nothingness—still haunted him. Carson squeezed his eyes shut and drew in several deep, steadying breaths. His task was too important to mar with past horrors he couldn't rectify.

He jumped as the door opened. A large dark-haired man and two women bundled against the cold exited the building. As the women shuffled off to their cars, the man punched numbers into a keypad, securing the door. Carson clenched his fists as the man pulled out a cigarette and patted his pockets, no doubt searching for a lighter.

"Just leave," Carson said in a pleading whisper.

Cigarette finally lit, the man moved toward the parking lot. Carson held his breath until he disappeared around the corner. A siren blared in the distance, startling Carson. He clenched his teeth, drew air in through his nose, and blew it out through his mouth. The beating of his heart threatened to fill the night air. He was terrified, but he was more hungry than scared.

He pulled his parka up over the lower half of his face, crept out from behind the dumpster. He jumped and grabbed the bottom rung of the fire escape and struggled to pull himself up. His arms shook with the effort. Sweat broke out on his skin as he managed to get a foot on the rung. The idea that vampires possessed superhuman strength was a myth, but damn, he was about as strong as an eight-year-old. He just had to climb to the roof, drop through the small window, get the blood, and get out. Then he could worry about bigger issues.

He climbed over the ledge of the old brick building on shaky legs, propelled by adrenaline. Without that extra push, he would be flat on his face with exhaustion. The previous night he was in this same spot on the roof and jimmied the lock on the old wood-framed window. Before he could enter, the sound of a door slamming somewhere scared him off. Being caught trying to break into a Vampire Blood Market would bring certain death, but that had to be better than slowly starving.

Seeing the window was still unlocked, Carson sighed with relief. His hands were so cold that jimmying the lock again would be impossible. With both hands he pushed up on the frame of the window, which resisted moving. Gaining leverage with his legs, he slowly inched the window open. His entire body shook, not just from his struggle with the window, but knowing once he entered the building, there was no turning back. His stomach cramped, reminding him there was no other choice. He had to eat now.

Feet first he shimmied into the dark room on the third fLoor, unsure what he would find there. During his three-day stakeout, he hadn't seen any lights on that fLoor. Still, he crouched as soon as he was inside. Despite the corners of the small room being dark, he could tell the room was empty—except for the creepy cobwebs hanging everywhere. He shuddered, knowing that meant spiders.

"Focus."

He pulled a flashlight from his jacket pocket and surveyed the room. The door was ten feet across from him. Knowing the direction to go, he shut off the flashlight to avoid calling attention to anyone who would alert the NVJ. In many of the movies he'd seen and books he'd read, vampires could see in the dark. Nope, no night vision, no superhuman strength, no ability to glamour people. Same as humans in every way, except vampires needed blood to survive.

Reaching for the rusted knob, blood roared in his ears, and his heart sped up as if preparing to explode. Of course the wood door *would* creak. He slipped into a dark hallway and turned on the flashlight. On each side of the hallway were several closed doors, but no windows. Within the corridor the sounds of the surrounding city were faint. The same layer of dust on every surface and cobwebs overhead spoke of the vacant nature of the entire floor. Beneath his boots the constant hum, like that of an engine running, vibrated up his legs. At the end of the hallway, the beam of light illuminated a steel door, the kind that would lead into a stairwell. He needed to move. The longer he spent wandering only increased his chances of being caught.

He crept to the closed door. Beads of sweat ran down his face. He swiped them away with the back of his hand. What if someone was behind that door, ready to kill him? Breathing through his nose to stop the scream pushing into his throat, he placed his palms against the cold metal bar.

"No one is in the building." Still his mind wasn't buying it.

He shoved open the door, hoping if someone were there he'd knock them over. No one was there. He chuckled and wiped at his forehead and face. As he shined the light, the beam fʟashed over the edge of a railing. Stairs going down were to the left. After descending the first fʟight, he came to another door, and then opened it with more confidence. Boxes filled the small space. Blood needed to be refrigerated, so he continued down the stairs.

The flashlight flickered as he descended farther, and he froze. The beating of his heart filled his ears. A knot of dread expand in his gut. Gods, if he'd had anything in his stomach, he would have thrown up. He needed the blood only the VBM could provide. His fangs had only ever sunk into a vein once, and the nightmare of that moment was locked away because dealing with the memory would no doubt drive him insane. Vampire bites hurt like a bitch, and had become the sport of pain sluts and adrenaline junkies who visited the legal bite clubs. No vampire drank human blood to survive, or at least legally they couldn't. Synthetic blood came from VBMs and had been supplied to Carson his entire life.

He had to feed himself now. Without money that meant stealing what he needed, or else….

No. He wouldn't let that happen.

At the bottom of the stairs, he peered through the small window in the door leading into the market. Walls of illuminated refrigerated cases held blood in containers similar to milk jugs. Unfortunately stealing blood didn't hold the same consequence as stealing milk.

His fear dissipating, Carson grasped the door handle. What he feared would be locked opened freely. Inside the large market, the refrigerated cases hummed. Cool air hit his face. Carson's mouth watered as his stomach clenched. He rushed to the nearest case and threw open the door. He tore the top off the closest white container. He lifted the jug, prepared for that first drop of lifesaving liquid to hit his tongue.

"Freeze!"

The lights came on. Carson dropped the container. His heart pushed into overdrive. His breaths barely escaped his throat. He gaped at the three men and two women dressed in black uniforms, pointing guns at him. Guns with bullets. Carson tried to remain still, but his feet moved him backward.

"Freeze or we'll shoot!"

A man with shorn black hair, who appeared to be larger than a truck, leveled his gun at Carson's head. The man could end all of his pain. One well-placed shot. One bullet could erase the fear, the hunger, the uncertainty, the agony of losing his family. Just charge at the giant or slip his hand into his pocket as if he had a gun, and the bullets would do the rest. But Carson ran into a wall and his muscles seized. He was going to die no matter what he did.

"Down on your knees and hands on your head!"

Carson went down hard, obeying the man's orders. The hunger along with the terror of what would come next muddled his thinking. His legs shook. It was all he could do to remain where he was. He closed his eyes and thought of his younger brother, Caden, and his mom. He just wanted it to be over quickly.

"Strip him," he heard the giant command.

"What? Why?" A short blond-haired officer wearing glasses, standing behind the man, frowned.

The giant's face twisted in anger, but his eyes never left Carson. "Because I'm lead and that means I call the shots."

The short officer rolled his eyes and lowered his weapon. He lifted his chin to the red-haired officer next to him. As they approached, Carson's chest locked up. His parka was pulled off, and then his sweater and T-shirt went over his head. The chill of the room sent a shudder through his emaciated body.

Please, make it quick.

The officers held Carson by his upper arms, as if he might try to resist. Any self-preservation he had when entering the VBM had vanished. Tears burned his eyes like acid. Gods, his life had sucked so far. This was the perfect ending.

The large officer stepped forward. Carson dared to look up at him. Not as large as a truck, but still massive. His heavy black boots scraped the floor. NVJ in large white letters crossed his chest. *New Vampire Justice*. There because Carson had tried to steal blood, an act punishable by immediate death.

"You've been caught in the act of stealing blood from a certified Vampire Blood Market, an act punishable by death according to the Vampire Justice Act of 1975. Under the jurisdiction of the New Vampire Justice code number 456.5, as an enforcement officer for the city of Utica, I hereby pass the sentence of death. Do you have anything you wish to say before this judgment is carried out?"

The gruff voice barely penetrated the cottony fog filling Carson's mind. He managed to shake his head. Panic rushed through him like a fast-acting drug. His muscles shook uncontrollably. A foot away the contents of the jug he spilled across the industrial tiled floor had begun to coagulate in the cold room. Carson looked away before the temptation caused him to act on his hunger.

"Dennison, have you lost your mind?" one of the female officers asked, disbelief covering her face.

Ignoring her, the lead officer stepped closer and pulled a dagger from his belt. The steel blade glinted in the fluorescent lights. Carson swallowed against the rock forming in his throat. If he'd any energy left, he might have cried for the tenth time that day. He was going to be marked as a thief before they killed him.

"Dennison. You know you have to wait for the commander." The brown-haired woman glanced warily to the officers on each side of her. They all lowered their weapons. Uneasiness showed in their faces. "You know that law is never carried out anymore. What happens next is the commander's call."

They wouldn't kill him?

His would-be executioner stopped with her warning. The lines around his mouth and eyes deepened, which told Carson scowling was most likely his permanent expression. "Only if there are circumstances creating doubt, Wright." His eyes never wavered. His intent to carry out the sentence shone bright in his hard gray eyes. Carson swore he saw… enjoyment? He said he was in charge. Gods, he was going to kill Carson despite any protest, and enjoy every minute of it. "He was caught red-handed. There's no doubt here."

"Dennison, quit being an ass," the short officer holding Carson's right arm said. "You know that even without doubt, the archaic vampire statute has only been carried out in two different cases of blood theft in the past five years."

Carson squeezed his eyes shut, hoping that was true.

"Look at him. He looks so… young," the other female officer said.

Dennison licked at his lips, grinning. A pang of fear greater than his impending death shot through Carson. This man was going to make it hurt.

"He's still nothing more than a lowlife thief."

Carson swore his heart stopped as the giant raised the dagger, and before Carson could utter a sound, the tip of the knife sliced across his chest. He felt nothing, until the searing pain ran through his chest and expanded through his torso. His vision grayed, and he prayed to pass out.

CHAPTER 2

LINCOLN SAMUELS climbed out of his car at the end of Fowler Street. NVJ and Utica PD cruisers had blocked off the area. Fuck, he was tired and wanted to be back in his warm bed, wrapped tight around Devon. Or was it Derek? Whatever his name was. Lincoln shouldn't have been out at half past midnight on a Friday night because some asshole decided he didn't have to pay for blood.

He wove through the police cruisers. Utica city police handled crowd control, which was in everyone's best interest. Patrons from the bars on the strip had surged into the street to get a glimpse at why the NVJ was there. With racial tensions between the non-blood-drinking humans, or Nons, and vampires rising across many areas of the country, a crowd of drunk humans and vampires was a riot waiting to happen. Just one asshole, human or vampire, saying the wrong thing to the wrong person, and punches would fly. Utica hadn't fallen into what amounted to rising violence against vampires that had been seen in many of the larger cities. That didn't mean they were immune.

Human pushback against vampires attempting to gain equal rights had both sides tense. The argument was stupid. Vampires were identical to humans in every way, except for elongated, pointed canines, which never disappeared, and the need to supplement their food consumption with a steady diet of blood. Not human or—yuck—even animal blood. The synthetic stuff was sufficient.

And still they were third-class citizens.

Even having migrated into human culture over a hundred years ago, living peacefully among Nons, they were still denied many rights. Were barred from joining the military, could never hold public office, or even be treated by Nons doctors. In some cases animals had more rights than vampires. For just that reason, in the eighties, New Vampire Justice was formed. Vampires policed vampires because many Nons' law enforcement would rather shoot first and ask questions later. Racist assholes.

As HE strode to the entrance of the VBM, Lincoln passed Utica police officers, who cut him a wide berth. Most of the Utica force had ended up on the wrong side of Lincoln's temper on crime scenes that involved vampires. The one exception to that rule currently barked out orders to his officers. Sergeant Dwayne Simpson didn't wear the superior attitude many members of the Nons police had when dealing with vampires. Dwayne and Lincoln had been friends since Lincoln moved to Utica four years earlier.

As Dwayne caught sight of Lincoln, he smiled, dimples hollowing his cheeks. More than once Lincoln had thought, if only the burly, dark-skinned cop were gay, they'd be more than friends. Unfortunately Dwayne was happily married with a loving wife and three great kids.

"Hey, Commander." Dwayne shook Lincoln's hand. "I was wondering if they'd drag your sorry ass out here tonight."

"One of the pitfalls of the job, Dwayne. These jerks have to wait until I'm in bed to pull this shit." Lincoln shook his head.

Dwayne snorted, his expression one of disbelief. "Yeah, I imagine you were actually asleep in bed. Who's the flavor of the week?"

Lincoln waved his hand. "Starts with a D."

A laugh erupted from Dwayne. "That's more than you usually know."

Lincoln narrowed his eyes, but Dwayne didn't even flinch.

"So someone got caught stealing blood for a midnight snack, yeah?" Dwayne asked with an expression of distaste.

"Looks that way."

Harsh penalties—even those not as permanent as death—had sharply decreased the theft rate of blood in the last ten years, but every once in a while, someone had to try.

"I know you need to drink that shit to live, but damn, just thinking about taking a big swig of…." Dwayne's face soured, and he let out a sign of disgust.

Lincoln huffed. Despite being a synthetic counterpart to human blood, many Nons couldn't stomach the idea of drinking the thick red liquid. That just reminded humans vampires could drink their blood.

That along with stories and movies portraying them as monsters had caused many Nons to fear vampires, even though they weren't a violent race.

Or species, as they'd been labeled in the past.

Lincoln shook off that thought, or he'd definitely be looking to rip someone's head off.

"It's just food, like those Bloody Marys you drink at brunch on Sundays. Like I said, try it, you might like it. Though I recommend the real stuff." Lincoln smacked his lips, then grinned.

"Fuck off, Samuels. That's cannibalism." Dwayne shoved Lincoln's shoulder. Their laughter caught the glares of a few cops.

Fuck 'em.

Dwayne glared in their direction. "Don't you need to get in there?"

Lincoln leaned against the wall of the VBM. "Nah. I think I'll just hang here for a while. I'm sure Kincaid has a handle on everything."

Dwayne's smile faded. His face sombered. "Did you see the shootings in Detroit on the news yesterday?"

Lincoln pursed his lips. Fucking senseless. So many vampires dead for no reason other than being vampires. Eight dead and four critically injured after a gunman opened fire on a VBM. A five-year-old and a teenager were among the dead.

"Info coming through says the human was just released from prison for violent crimes against vampires." Lincoln looked around. The closest Nons cop was over twenty feet away. Lincoln leaned closer to Dwayne and whispered, "I got a look at the initial report from Detroit NVJ. The Non claimed a vampire had bitten one of his family members."

Dwayne looked at Lincoln with disbelief. "No way."

Lincoln leaned back. "Exactly. If that had actually happened, the entire world would have known within an hour, and we'd be dealing with dozens of vampire deaths by now. No vampire is stupid enough to bite a human and bring that wrath down upon us."

"Do you think this latest shooting and the fact this guy is a repeat offender against vampires will push the hate crime bill through this time?"

"Until a human is killed because of someone targeting vampires, the politicians don't give a shit what happens to us. If they did they'd lose all of that hate money contributed to their campaigns from fuckheads like the Coalition for Human Purity. They fund some of the worst vampire hate groups in the country and deny it." Lincoln shook his head morosely. "Humans like that are just biding time until some vampire fucks up, and then it'll be open season on anyone with fangs."

"Not all humans hate vampires. Surely they would—"

A scream came from inside the VBM.

"Ah fuck." Lincoln raced through the door.

Gasps and sobs came from the back of the market. A group of Lincoln's officers surrounded what looked to be a kid kneeling on the floor. They were all shouting at Dennison. Not surprising, given the man's attitude and recklessness.

Lincoln focused on the kid. His head hung low. Long black hair hid his face. Blood streamed from a deep gash across his bare chest. Had to be Dennison. The fuckhead had marked the kid.

"John Dennison, stand down!"

Dennison turned toward Lincoln with that shitty I-rule-the-world scowl. Man had a real problem with authority. Too bad Lincoln outranked him.

"Hey, Lincoln. There was no need for you to drag yourself off your latest twink. I've got this under control." Dennison sneered.

Lincoln stepped up, bumping chests with Dennison. He'd most likely been waiting for the chance to fuck with some vampire stealing blood. "That's Commander Samuels to you. What makes you think you can sidestep my orders? All level-one cases require that I'm contacted immediately. As lead that was your first responsibility. Luckily someone here was smart enough to call it in."

The muscles in Dennison's jaw clenched as he scanned the room, no doubt looking for the guilty party. He huffed. "I was just trying to scare the kid, get him to realize what could have happened."

Dennison was close to getting his ass kicked. "I don't care what kind of scared-straight program you thought you were running. You follow procedure, or I'll have your ass and your job. Got it?"

When he didn't speak, Lincoln knew Dennison had bitten back his retort to Lincoln's "I'll have your ass" comment. Probably Dennison's usual one about his asshole being exit only. Turning to the kid, Lincoln suppressed his grin as he cataloged ways to deal with his rogue officer later.

Officer Taylor Myers and Lieutenant Max Kincaid each secured an arm of the vampire kneeling between them. His pale skin had that translucent quality that developed when a vampire went too long without blood. His ribs and collarbone were visible, his stomach concave, and not an ounce of fat covered him. Max's fingers wrapped around the entire circumference of the vampire's biceps. The belt holding the kid's too-large pants had been notched way past the last hole. Either the belt wasn't his, or he'd recently lost a crapload of weight.

The vampire was starving. At that advanced stage of emaciation, the synthetic shit wouldn't cut it. He needed the real deal fast to come back, if it wasn't already too late.

Lincoln nudged the kid's knee with the toe of his boot. The suspect flinched but didn't look up. Lincoln crouched and lowered his voice. "Hey, kid. What's your name?"

Every muscle in the too-thin body shook. There was no answer. From the scream he'd let loose, Lincoln surmised he could talk. He touched the kid's shoulder. Still he didn't move, but his shaking ramped up a couple of notches.

"I'm not going to hurt you. You're safe now." Lincoln turned to his officers behind him. Of course Dennison was the only one with his gun still drawn. "Holster your weapon, Dennison."

Dennison hesitated, not bothering to hide his disdain. Lincoln raised his brow. Dennison huffed, then did as he was ordered. Lincoln turned back to the kid. "The guns are put away."

The kid raised his chin and cocked his head, peering past the dark hair covering his eyes. Large brown eyes, filled with despair, sucker punched Lincoln in the gut. He surveyed the vampire's sharp cheekbones and jawline, sunken eyes and hollowed cheeks, and… the reddest lips that contrasted with his pale skin. Blood rushed to Lincoln's groin, and his cock pressed against his jeans. Shit, it was forever since he'd gotten hard on sight. A warm mouth on his dick was generally required before anything stirred below—the hazards of a fuckton of one-night stands and a dead heart.

Damn.

"When was the last time you ate?"

The young vampire stared at Lincoln, and then, as if he'd decided to trust him, answered. "T-ten days ago."

After ten days the kid should have been attacking every vein in sight, even if he'd never drank straight from a human. He had a shitload of self-control, especially with blood pooling on the floor next to him.

Lincoln looked to Max, who didn't need for Lincoln to tell him how dire the situation was. He released the kid. He swayed but stayed upright. Max pulled off his jacket and rolled up his sleeve. It was dangerous to allow a starving vampire near a vein, but someone had to feed the kid right then. Lincoln couldn't be the donor, even if he wanted. He'd have to make sure the guy didn't drain Max. Of everyone on his team, Max was the most levelheaded. No doubt he was the one who called in the level-one situation. Lincoln trusted Max with his life, and vice versa.

Lincoln tentatively set his hand on the vampire's shoulder. Power, immense and nearly uncontained, emanated from the kid, unlike anything Lincoln had ever felt. His cock hardened further. Those brown eyes. Fuck.

Lincoln cleared his throat. "I'm sure I don't have to explain the effects of blood deprivation on a vampire. You're already past the point where synthesized blood will help."

The kid's brown eyes widened, and he shook his head violently. "N-no. I can't!"

That fear came from only drinking blood from a cup his entire life. Didn't mean he couldn't drink from the vein. The thought terrified most vampires who'd never sank their fangs into flesh. Lincoln recalled his first bite at a certified bite club his uncle brought him to. He was sixteen. Humans desiring the bite were able to meet vampires who wanted to drink their blood. Lincoln had been scared shitless. The wrong placement of fangs or sudden jerk of the donor could severely injure the Non and possibly kill them.

For Lincoln, drinking from a human woke some primordial, animalistic need. The human blood was like an aphrodisiac. Without even taking his cock out of his pants, he'd orgasmed, same as the Non guy he chose. That first bite unearthed a need Lincoln was unable to ignore, bringing him back to the clubs every couple of months.

"I know you've probably never done this before, but it's not that hard. Feel for the pulse with your tongue. That's where you want to place your fangs. Bite down firmly, but don't go too fast. Stop once the blood starts to pool on the skin. Pull out and suck."

Restless movements from his team told Lincoln they'd probably never seen a vampire bite someone as well.

"You're going to feed him? What the fuck? He broke the law!"

Leave it to Dennison to object. Lincoln clenched his jaw and ignored the rant. Max raised his wrist to the kid's mouth, but his reaction surpassed fear alone. He yanked against the hands holding him. Terror-filled eyes were glued to Max's wrist. A war of need and fear raged in the depths of the kid's eyes.

"I can't! Get away from me!" The kid gasped and fought for breath as if some horrible monster stalked toward him. "You... d-don't... under... s-stand!" His adrenaline-fueled state increased his strength as he tried to escape the wrist before him. He was going to hurt himself.

His useless fight annoyed Lincoln. "Calm down, kid! No one's going to hurt you."

"Put him out of his misery," Dennison muttered.

The vampire's struggle ceased as his entire body stiffened. His eyes flashed white as they rolled up into his head. He slumped forward and was out cold.

"Dammit, lower him to the floor."

Max and Taylor laid the kid on his stomach. That's when Lincoln saw the symbol tattooed at the base of his spine.

"Fuck me!"

Things had gone from bad to worse in a split second.

CHAPTER 3

THE FOGGY web in Carson's head cleared as he woke. He was tired but warm, and the gnawing hunger that had been trying to eat his stomach was gone. He moved his arms and legs and found resistance.

He was tied down.

Shit.

Panic quickly cleared any of the fog left. His eyes popped open. White walls and a tiled ceiling with fluorescent lights did little to tell him where he was, but he knew they'd found him. The ones who wanted to use him, make him do shit he didn't want to do, use him as a weapon. Why hadn't they killed him? He didn't care that they were NVJ. He didn't trust them or anyone. He was too dangerous to live now that he'd been captured.

The straps cut into his skin, but his need to escape was second to the pain. An alarm blared from a machine next to the bed, catching his attention. The wires from that machine were clamped to white pads stuck to his chest. A bandage covered the gash the large officer had slashed across his torso. An IV pushed blood into a vein in his arm. That explained why he wasn't hungry anymore. Of course they'd feed him. He wouldn't be any good to them dead.

Muffled footsteps and shouts sounded outside the closed door to the room, and then the door burst open. Two of the officers who were at the VBM entered, still in uniform. Carson ceased his struggle as they both looked him over.

The officer with the blond hair and glasses stepped forward. "It's okay. Just calm down." Carson recognized him as the vampire who'd offered up his wrist.

"L-let me go. I have to get out of here!" He had to run. If they used him…. He wouldn't do that again.

"I'm Lieutenant Max Kincaid, and this is Officer Taylor Myers of the Utica NVJ. You're safe here."

They didn't get it. He struggled harder. "Let me go!"

"Get Lincoln," Officer Kincaid said to Officer Myers, who promptly left.

Carson could take Max if he could just get himself out of the restraints. His wrists burned from the friction of the straps, but he couldn't stop until he was free.

The door opened, and *he* walked in. Oh gods, the one with the bright-blue eyes and neatly trimmed dark beard, dressed in the same NVJ uniform as the others. He walked with an air of authority right up to Carson's bed. He hit a button on the machine, which ended the annoying sound.

"I'm Commander Lincoln Samuels, chief enforcement officer of the Utica NVJ. You're in the medical wing of our headquarters. You're not in any danger here, I promise, so just calm down." His whiskey-soaked voice strummed over Carson's nerves.

He ceased struggling, not sure if it was because of the commanding tone or the momentary flicker of kindness in those eyes.

"Please, I have to go. You don't understand. *Please*," Carson whispered. He wasn't above groveling.

Commander Samuels furrowed his brow and remained silent. He'd appeared much taller when Carson was kneeling on the floor, but compared to Carson, he was tall. Commander Samuels had wide shoulders, a thick neck, and large biceps. Stubble covered his square jaw. Beyond that was power, raw and unyielding, surrounding him and stretching out to Carson. He was sensitive to the power in other vampires, possibly an ability of his kind. He didn't know for sure, given he'd found little information on Tabulae Rasae. Carson sensed nothing from the other two officers, indicating they weren't one of the half-dozen different kinds of vampires. Empathics, healers, those with telepathy, precognition, and the most dangerous and rare, those with the ability to wipe minds. A sixth kind of vampire rumored to exist was last reported in the 1800s.

The power emanating from the vampire captivated Carson, resonated deep in his bones. The resulting hum, the arousal, the high, was nothing short of intoxicating. He wanted to feel more. Feigning the need to shift his body, he moved closer to the bed railing, closer to Commander Lincoln, wishing for a touch, even if only on the arm.

"You need me to do anything, Lincoln?" Officer Kincaid asked.

Lincoln.

The strong name fit the formidable man.

"I got this, Taylor."

Carson's breath caught as Lincoln leaned forward, bracing himself on the metal side rail. "You're severely malnourished. This is your third pint of blood, and you'll need several more. Another day and you could've been dead. Leaving anytime soon isn't an option."

The harsh words cut deep. Carson wanted the soft-spoken man back.

"You don't know what I am," Carson blurted out. If his hands had been free, he would have slapped one over his mouth. He bit his lower lip instead. His uncle had continually chastised Carson for not thinking before he spoke. *Shit.*

Lincoln pursed his lips. "Yes, I do, Mr. Locke."

Carson shifted away. Any need he thought Lincoln could fulfill fled.

"You know my name? Did you kill my family too?" Carson lunged forward, but the restraints caught him. "What the fuck do you want? Why did you kill my mom and my brother and my uncle?" He struggled and screamed. "They never hurt anyone! I would have gone with you if you'd just asked!"

Their eyes widened, but no one moved. Whatever energy Carson had gained from the three pints of blood quickly waned. He was so weak, but if his hands had been free, he would have tried to kill them all. Tears burned his eyes again as the end of his adrenaline-fueled ten-day flight brought forth the mourning he'd avoided. The only members of his family were dead, and he was alone.

Why hadn't they killed him too?

"I'm sorry about your family."

Carson sniffed. Lincoln sounded sincere.

"We aren't responsible for their deaths. I know your name because I looked in your wallet. I know what you are because I saw the symbol on your back. When I found your name and address, I checked to see where your family was, and know there was an incident in your house."

Carson's body shook as he fought his tears. He wasn't going to cry in front of three strangers. He jumped as Lincoln patted Carson's shoulder in an awkward gesture of comfort. What the touch did was open a conduit between them. Carson shivered as the foreign power infiltrated his body, causing his muscles to twitch. His limbs lightened.

Heat suffused every cell, every nerve, flushing his skin. Carson's gaze snapped up to meet Lincoln's. Did he feel it too? Lincoln looked down on Carson with confusion.

Lincoln yanked his hand away as if Carson were an animal ready to bite. The connection broke, leaving a tingling reminder zinging through him. Nothing he'd ever experienced came close to the pull he'd felt, as if the power wanted to combine with his own.

Or possibly take over.

Staring at one another, Carson felt as if Lincoln was someone he could trust. Maybe he could even regain some feeling of safety. Carson had to force himself to look away. He frowned deeply with confusion. Truthfully he just needed the nightmare to end.

"Hey, Max, give me a hand here." Lincoln worked to remove the restraint from Carson's wrist as Officer Kincaid worked on the others.

"Why did you restrain me?"

Lincoln moved down and started on Carson's ankle restraint.

"You were thrashing about, and your IV kept getting pulled out. Doc didn't have a choice."

Carson's other wrist was freed, and he rubbed the raw skin. "Thanks, Officer Kincaid."

"Call me Max." He smiled wide.

Carson couldn't smile back. Being free brought on his tears. Sobs wracked his chest as he tried to breathe. Any minute his entire body would scatter on the wind. He curled into a tight ball and hid his face.

"Gods, someone killed them all."

Despite the whisper Lincoln heard him. "You're safe here."

There was hesitancy in Lincoln's voice. Having to deal with someone who was crying most likely made him uncomfortable. Again Lincoln used that awkward pat of comfort. The power flooded Carson. Still, a man touched him, even if only to give comfort. A snort broke through Carson's sobs. Of course he had to be wailing like a baby in front of a good-looking man. His life sucked. What would he do now? Where would he go? His mother's final words spoke to him.

In the box on my dresser. Get the letter. Find Jameson.

That letter had told him to find Jameson Merrick if Carson ever needed help. Just being a Tabula Rasa vampire put their lives in danger every single day. His mother had known, and prepared for the inevitable.

Before he mentioned the letter, he stopped himself. Perhaps Lincoln had played him to earn his trust and cooperation. If they had Jameson's name, they'd know where he would head if he needed to escape. Although if they searched his coat, they would find that letter. Gods, he had to man up, stop crying, and feign cooperation.

Sitting up, he leaned his back against the cold metal of the side rail. Lincoln's blue eyes caused an uneasy feeling in Carson's gut. He looked down at his lap as a blush crept across his cheeks. How much more could he embarrass himself?

"Sorry," Carson mumbled, wiping his tears and snot with the back of his hand. His uncle had always tried to toughen him up, teach him to protect himself. Never really worked.

"Here, try these." With a helpful smile, Officer Kincaid set a box of tissues on the bed.

Carson grabbed one. "Thanks." He tried to return the smile but was unsure if he was successful.

"Mr. Locke, can you tell us what happened to your family?" The authoritative tone had returned.

Carson blew out a breath. "My mom and uncle and my… l-little brother." Caden had only been eighteen. Carson failed to protect him, failed them all.

The silence as the officers watched Carson made him uneasy. Did they want more?

"Tabula Rasa vampires are very rare and highly sought after. You know what a Tabula Rasa is, don't you?" Lincoln raised his brow with his inquiry.

What the fuck kind of question was that?

Carson lifted his chin and scowled. "Of course I know what I am. Tabula Rasa translates into 'blank slate.' Because of *what* I am, I was never allowed to leave the grounds of the compound, never had a life outside of an acre of land. I took medications that curbed my instinct to bite until I learned to control those urges. Apparently the need to bite goes along with what I am. Those meds made me sick and weak. But what's worse, my family was killed because of what I am." The last sentence barely made it past his lips.

What he equated to was a monster—a vampire who could wipe clean minds with one bite. Left behind was a programmable machine, mindless follower without conscience, without remorse, without fear. The perfect army, the perfect killing machines. His uncle warned him relentlessly how dangerous he would be in the wrong hands. They probably should have drowned him at birth.

Neither officer showed a hint of emotion on their face.

"Registration for Tabulae Rasae is NVJ law, but there is no record of Carson Locke in any database," Lincoln said.

Carson could only shrug. He didn't know much about the NVJ or their laws except the one condemning a vampire caught stealing blood from a VBM to death. All vampires were schooled in that fact. Just when they'd stopped that practice had escaped Carson's attention. He also knew a lot about vampires and Tabulae Rasae. Since he was old enough to understand he was different from other vampires, how dangerous he truly was, he'd scoured every source for information on his kind. There wasn't much.

"Why didn't your parents register you at birth?" Lincoln crossed his arms.

"To protect me."

"From what?" Max asked, now standing next to Lincoln.

Carson leapt to his knees, clenching his hands on the bed rail. "What the fuck do you mean, protect me from what? People like the ones who killed my entire family."

They stared at Carson as if he were some dangerous animal ready to attack. If any of this were funny, Carson would have laughed out loud.

Carson narrowed his eyes menacingly. Carson didn't falter, and it had nothing to do with how beautiful he thought Lincoln's eyes were. By his expression Carson could tell Lincoln was ready to serve up some harder questions. He didn't look like the sort of person who had issues being blunt.

"Have you ever bitten anyone?"

The words slammed into Carson, and time seemed to stop. He fell back onto the bed. He couldn't breathe, couldn't speak. His lungs refused to take in air. He grasped the sheets in his fists. The memories. He squeezed his eyes shut, shaking his head. *Justin.* His head spun and his stomach roiled. He'd blocked out the worst day of his life for so long that eventually he'd convinced himself it never happened.

"Carson?" The voice echoed as if they were in a tunnel.

Carson tried to answer, but the world tilted sideways. His brain was unable to keep up with the information flooding his synapses.

"What's wrong with him?" another muffled voice asked.

"Get Doc," he heard Lincoln say, and then Carson shut down completely to stop remembering.

CHAPTER 4

LINCOLN RUBBED his face as he viewed reports from the Gifford PD. He sipped at the swill Myers tried to pass off as coffee. He'd been up for over thirty hours. Doc's only choice was to sedate Carson after his breakdown, and he was still out. The look of horror on the man's face (definitely not the kid Lincoln mistook him for) had etched itself into his mind. Something in Carson's past terrified him, and he definitely hadn't dealt with it yet.

Lincoln rubbed his chest. What he'd experienced when touching Carson's shoulder was… electric, and exciting, and arousing —and the power. Fuck, the power in Carson was amazing, running into the very depths of his being. And that well of power seemed to be endless. Maybe Doc could tell him something about it. Very little information was available for Carson's kind. Less than four were currently registered around the world. Carson's lack of registration had Lincoln wondering how many there really could be. The thought of those dangerous vampires being unknown to the NVJ was scary.

From a folder he removed a packet of crime scene photos. Losing your entire family in one day. How did someone ever come back from that? Would the shock ever truly go away? Would Carson ever enjoy life again? Currently he was in survival mode, still in flight. When no longer in danger, Carson would have to deal. Unsure why, something about him tugged at Lincoln's gut.

Someone knocked. "Enter."

Max pushed the door open, holding a box in his arms. He looked as worn out and at the ass end of his rope as Lincoln felt. Strands of his shoulder-length hair floated around his head, having escaped his ponytail. His glasses were askew, and his normally jovial grin had turned into a hard, thin line. He dropped the box onto the couch and then flopped into the chair next to the desk.

"What've you got?" Max asked.

Lincoln sighed. "A mess. Gifford PD reports don't line up with what Carson told us. The mother is definitely dead, found in the living room stabbed to death." He tossed a crime scene photo across the desk.

Max picked it up, then raised his brow.

"Yeah, nasty. No less than ten stab wounds to the chest. Cause of death is exsanguination."

Max placed the photo on the desk. "This looks personal. Someone was pissed or wanted to make it look that way."

Lincoln nodded. "No signs of the uncle or brother."

"Well, that definitely doesn't jibe with his story."

Lincoln sat back in his chair, fingers steepled. As an officer one of first things you learned when investigating a crime was not to ignore the obvious suspect, which would be Carson. Why did that seem wrong, even when the evidence was stacking against the guy?

It wasn't Carson.

But Lincoln had to stick to the facts and not follow that gnawing feeling about the gorgeous—

"I'll bet you a beer at Nail Creek Pub that you're thinking what I'm thinking."

"Huh?" Lincoln looked to Max.

"Your theory about who didn't do this?" Yeah, Lincoln wasn't falling for that bet. He grinned and shook his head. "I already owe you three beers. I'm not adding a forth."

Max shrugged. "What can I say? I'm rarely ever wrong."

"I'm thinking what even first-year rookies would see. Facts point to Carson. He grew up totally secluded, never allowed to leave home. No friends. Couldn't go to school or do anything like a normal kid. Man, to grow up knowing that if you bit someone even once, you'd essentially kill who they are? That's a hell of a lot of pressure on a kid. It would drive anyone off the deep end, but—" Lincoln clenched his fists. "I don't know why, but I'm not feeling it."

Max pushed his glasses up his nose. "I may be right about a lot of things, but when it comes to your gut, you tend to be dead-on. But don't let the guy cloud your judgment." The tone of warning caused Lincoln to pause. He'd been friends with Max since they were kids. He knew Lincoln better than anyone, and sometimes that pissed Lincoln off.

"What's that supposed to mean?" Lincoln leaned forward, elbows on the desk, and let his irritation show.

Max leaned forward as well, unaffected by Lincoln's attempt to intimidate him. While he might be small, he was fearless.

"You like him. When's the last time you tried to comfort someone or gave a shit about how they felt?"

Lincoln feigned ignorance. "I only put my hand on his shoulder. He lost his entire family." Max had read something from him in that room.

Again that pissed him off. He crossed his arms.

"You don't touch me, and we've been best friends since we were kids. If you touch someone, they might get past that shield you've put between you and everyone else. Gods forbid if that happens. It's why you keep dragging those boys home from the bar."

"They're not boys." Max might be his best friend, but he was one sentence away from getting punched in the mouth.

Max huffed. "They might be legal, but they certainly aren't relationship material, and that's how you like them."

"Jesus." Lincoln fell back into his chair and pinched the bridge of his nose. "Not the relationship crap again." Fucking broken record. If he wanted a relationship, he'd have one. He liked his freedom. His job averaged eighty hours a week, and he didn't need someone dictating his life.

Max pointed his finger at Lincoln. "Yeah, that 'relationship crap' again. It's been three years, Linc. You're going to be thirty, and the longest relationship you've had since Luke is with your online porn provider. Time to get over it and move on."

"I am over it." Lincoln went back to shuffling through reports. "Can we focus on work and not my love life?"

Max snorted. "What love life?"

Like a broken record.

Lincoln shook his head and threw a folder at Max. "Shut up and be helpful."

Max fumbled the file and threw Lincoln an expression telling him the subject wasn't closed. Sitting, he opened the file. Lincoln turned his attention back to the report, but large brown eyes plagued his thoughts.

WHATEVER DOC had given Carson would knock him out for about twelve hours. Enough time for Lincoln to go home to an empty bed and a note telling him not to bother calling. He grabbed a quick nap, showered, and scarfed down a sandwich. He was back at the office by seven Saturday night.

Lincoln swiped his key card in the electronic lock, and then entered the building. He had to pass through three checkpoints to get to his office. Lincoln took security seriously. As he walked by Dennison, he knocked his knuckles on the top of his desk. "My office. Now."

Dennison went, followed by the snickers from Maggie Wright and Tia Warez. Lincoln made a beeline for the coffeepot. Dennison could stew in Lincoln's office for a few minutes Make their meeting more exciting.

He grabbed his *All Hail the Commander* mug, a gift from Max when Lincoln was appointed to his current position. He inhaled deeply as he filled his cup. Doc came down the hall and grabbed a mug.

"Save some for me."

Lincoln lifted the pot, and Doc held out his mug for Lincoln to fill. When Doc dumped enough sugar and creamer in for three cups, Lincoln shook his head but said nothing.

"Your Tabula Rasa is awake and—"

"You mean Carson?" Sometimes Doc could be too clinical.

He nodded but didn't say the name. "I've given him a mild sedative, so he'll be a tad groggy. Even after giving him enough to knock out a horse, he still tossed and turned all night. He's malnourished, and the emotional stress of the past two weeks has taken a toll. I haven't been able to wean him off the human blood. After even one pint of the synthetic, his vitals fall, he throws ketones, which means he's burning what little fat is left in his body. His body can't process the synthetic blood." Doc raked his fingers through his graying hair. "I'm not sure his body has the ability to heal the damage from going so long without blood."

Lincoln tightened his hand around his mug. He hated being used, hated what he was, but Carson needed it.

Lincoln put his mug down before it busted in his hand.

"I wouldn't ask if it wasn't crucial to his recovery. He's mourning his entire family. They were all he had. The mind has a large role in recovery, and his mental health isn't stable. It's interfering with his body's ability to heal. In his weakened state, he's also highly susceptible to infection. The flu virus would probably kill him right now. If he can't get a handle on the psychological side, I'm afraid he might not...."

What happened the last time he donated his blood couldn't happen again, could it?

"But what if—"

"The chances of that happening again are astronomically small."

For Lincoln it was a huge gamble, and the last time cost him dearly. If he had to go through it all again, he wasn't sure he'd survive.

He swallowed hard. He'd do what he had to and not dwell on the what-ifs.

"I have to meet with Dennison and ream him out for a while."

"I heard he went off in the VBM. He's a bit of a loose cannon. You sure you want him on your team?"

Dennison was an act first and ask questions later guy. And what he did to Carson was inexcusable. But he was fearless, quick thinking in tight situations, a crack shot, which were all assets to Lincoln's team. He needed to put Dennison on a shorter leash and, Lincoln snickered, maybe sensitivity training.

"Unfortunately he's got some good skills that are invaluable to the NVJ."

Doc only shook his head.

"About Carson. Before I decide whether or not to let you relieve me of my blood, I need to talk to him. How long do we have before it's... too late?"

Doc rubbed his chin. "Hard to say. He's stable on the human blood, but as I said, the issue is his immune system. He couldn't fight off a cold at this point. I've decreased visitors to his room and am only allowing staff who show no signs of illness near him. I don't want someone near him, even if they only have a tickle in their throat."

That gave Lincoln some time with Carson, to get to know him. Even with the astronomical odds, if history decided to repeat itself, Lincoln wanted to know something about Carson. Lincoln nodded and headed to his office. When he entered he found Dennison lounging on the couch.

"What's up, chief?" His shitty tone was close to insubordination, but Lincoln wouldn't be dragged into a power struggle.

Lincoln sat on the corner of his desk, crossed his arms, and leveled a steely gaze at Dennison. Time to cut to the chase.

"You deliberately ignored protocol in a level-one situation. You led a vampire who was close to starving to death to believe that you were going to execute him for stealing blood. You marked him as a thief with a silver dagger. A scar he will carry forever. You want to tell me why I shouldn't fire your ass right now?"

Dennison sputtered. "He looked perfectly healthy to me. How was I supposed to know the thief was dying?"

Lincoln growled, grinding his teeth. "Because you're not an idiot, John."

The use of his first name took some bravado from Dennison.

"You did this to one of the rarest kinds of vampires protected by NVJ law. You've been distracted lately, off your game, angry, and snapping at everyone. You're a good officer, but you're heading down a real slippery slope. As it stands I have to suspend you for two weeks without pay. Push me and I'll make the suspension permanent. Time to get your head out of your ass."

The muscles clenched in Dennison's jaw, his body taut and appearing ready to attack. He was pissed. Well, Lincoln was even more so. If Dennison had accidentally killed Carson, it would have been Lincoln's ass strung up on a pole.

Dennison stood. "Anything else, Commander Samuels?"

Lincoln eyed him, hoping their chat had sank in. "No. Dismissed. Go home, John. Spend some time with the family. Come back ready to work."

Dennison stormed from his office and slammed the door. Some days Lincoln hated his job.

CHAPTER 5

CARSON STARED at the wall, drifting through a medication-induced fog. His body was calm and still, but his mind was a hive of activity, never turning off, never letting him forget. He missed his family, even his uncle who was gruff and distant. Carson's mom was always there—protecting, teaching, and loving Carson. And Caden… they'd been close. When he was younger, Caden always hung around the house to keep Carson company. They played basketball and video games, watched movies, and sometimes just hung out. Caden had given up much of his normal life for Carson.

A sob worked into Carson's throat. He swallowed hard, trapping the sound. The endless crying had caused his eyes to swell and his head to ache. He'd even cried in his sleep, waking with his pillow wet and covered in snot. Wasn't pretty.

His life was in the gutter, his will to live depleted, his hope gone. Lying in that tiny room, Carson was content to never move again. Just rot where he lay. What was the sense in going on? His family was gone. What did he have to live for?

Everything.

That's what his mother had told him whenever he felt sorry for himself. Her outlook for his future was brighter and happier than his. No matter what Carson was, how limited his life had to be, she always wished a beautiful life for him. A few months after Justin, she told him of a day that would come in the future, just when he believed he had nothing left, and he'd find love. One person who shone brighter than everyone else, who would speed up his heart, whose voice like a melody only he could hear, would appear. A man who would love him completely.

Love is life, my sweet boy. When you find love, then you will truly live.

His mother was a hopeless romantic, but he so wanted to believe he'd love again. Live.

...one who shines brighter than everyone else... speeds up your heart... voice like a melody....

Lincoln.

Carson groaned. Apparently he'd inherited that streak of romance from his mother. Handsome officer swoops in and saves the damsel, or should he say "mansel" in distress. He didn't even know Lincoln. For Christ's sake, Carson had committed a crime—for the second time in his life. Lincoln's job was to arrest those who broke the law. Carson had done just that and would probably go to jail for life. He was tarnished while Lincoln was noble, strong, and probably wasn't dragging around baggage that was stuffed full.

While Carson understood the impossibility of his fantasy, something about Lincoln twisted Carson's gut. Life and power thrummed beneath the surface, barely contained within Lincoln. Even that power was immensely attractive to Carson, but that didn't matter. He didn't deserve to be happy. The thought of Justin, his first and only love, brought the tears again. Justin, beautiful and alive and happy, but never again.

The door to his room opened. Carson buried his face in the pillow. Probably Dr. Reynolds, who told Carson to call him Doc. Every few hours Carson could count on Doc to come and check vitals, ask questions, and poke and prod. Doc was nice enough, but his bedside manner sucked.

Carson held his breath and listened closely as someone approach the bed. Still no sound. His fears took over, convincing him someone was ready to attack. Tentatively he peered out from beneath the blanket. Not Doc. Lincoln stood next to the bed, eyes intent on Carson, hands clasped behind his back.

Carson bolted upright and managed to stay that way despite the room spinning around him. Damn, he wanted to puke. Lincoln's stony expression would have made a mannequin appear lifelike. Carson tried to imagine what Lincoln would look like laughing. Would he get those lines by his eyes? Would the blue lighten even more? Would Lincoln have dimples? If Carson had it in him, he would have cracked a joke. As it was, if he spoke, he wouldn't know what to say.

As their gazes met, Carson lowered his eyes. Silence passed between them. Carson wanted to ask why Lincoln was there but feared he might leave. Carson wasn't sure why, but he didn't want him to go. He was lonely.

"How're you feeling?" Lincoln finally asked.

"I'm fine," Carson said quickly.

The assessing look from Lincoln told Carson he didn't believe him. "I'm sorry about your family. I'm pulling reports from Gifford PD, working on catching who did this. Since there is no NVJ presence in that area, they fall under our jurisdicion anyway. We have two main teams here at the NVJ and then a group of lower-level grunts, I mean, officers that both teams supervise. The beta team received your case, but I used some favors and took over."

Carson's eyes widened, his breath hitched. *Your case.* As in he was a suspect. "I didn't do it. No. I couldn't... I wouldn't hurt—"

Lincoln frowned and raised his hands. "Currently you aren't a suspect."

Carson couldn't believe that. Actually he made the perfect suspect. The only one left alive, and he'd run. Then he was caught stealing blood. Oh gods. He groaned and buried his face in his hand.

"Mr. Locke?"

Carson chuckled morosely and scrubbed his palms over his face. "Could you call me Carson, please? Every time you say that, I think that my uncle.... Well, that was my uncle. Not me."

"Sure. You can call me Lincoln."

Seriously? It thrilled Carson to be on a first-name basis with him.

"I guess it doesn't matter if I'm charged with murder, right? I'm sure stealing blood is a life sentence since the death sentence is gone." He was fucked either way. Would he even survive in prison? Wait, he was a rare vampire. They'd probably sequester him somewhere alone. He snorted. His life had managed to whittle him down to just himself.

Pity party for one, please.

"You aren't being charged with the theft of blood."

Carson could have imagined hearing that statement. He drew his brow down. "You know that officer—I think he's called Dennison—was a jerk, but he was right. I was caught red-handed. I broke in to steal blood." And why didn't he just confess to everything he'd ever done wrong while he was at it? What was it about Lincoln that made Carson strive to be truthful?

Lincoln's face appeared to soften, the harsh authoritarian mask falling off. The ramrod posture relaxed. He exhaled. "We don't punish vampires for trying to survive. This isn't Nons law where survival is a crime and gets you a prison sentence. You didn't hurt anyone, which would have challenged even the right to survive."

Yeah, then by that definition, he was a criminal. That guilt pooled on the surface of a well he'd thrown it down long ago. Carson had survived, but at the price of someone else.

"Vampires in need can go to the care centers for help with almost anything, but given your situation, I'm sure you weren't aware they existed. Even if you had known, going there could have been dangerous."

No, he wouldn't have gone.

"So I'm not under arrest?"

"No, you're not."

When Lincoln immediately looked away, Carson knew something else was up.

"I can't leave here, can I?"

Lincoln shook his head. "No. You're an unregistered Tabula Rasa. You have no support system in place, which is required to live in the community."

At least he didn't say Carson didn't have any family. Having to stay there should have been more upsetting, but Carson liked the feeling of safety. What kind of support system could he possibly get? Better question was "need."

"I can't stay here forever."

"No. Once you're better, we'll bring in a social worker to help you locate a place to live that provides the level of supervision needed for a Tabula Rasa."

It was too much to think about. Carson sighed and rubbed at the bridge of his nose. When Lincoln stepped closer to the bed, a shudder ran through Carson.

"Doc says you won't eat."

Carson looked at the bag of blood hanging on the pole next to the bed. A tube of bright red ran from the bottom of the bag and disappeared under the tape on his arm. "I don't have much choice."

He scowled at the excessive tape. Twice during his drugged state he'd ripped the IV out, ready to die. Doc wrapped almost an entire roll of white tape around the site where the needle penetrated his skin. It would take Carson hours to unwrap that tape. Once the sedative wore off, so did his desire to die and his appetite for food.

Lincoln gave him a stern look. "You know you have to eat solid food."

Carson crossed his arms. "I'm not hungry."

A smile tugged at Lincoln's lips, startling Carson. "Is that so?"

"Yeah, so unless you're going to stuff it down my throat or puree it and shove another needle into my arm, you're out of luck."

Lincoln's gaze tried to intimidate Carson and force him to give in. Carson held his stare. It was exhausting feigning strength and bravado.

Lincoln sighed. He grabbed a chair and set it by the bed, then sat and got comfortable. His stony expression had softened further and the intensity in his eyes had lessened. "Relax. You look exhausted. Lie down before you fall over."

Carson *was* exhausted. Pressing the button on the bed, he raised the head and then lay back.

"The reason I'm here is to go over what happened the day of the attack."

Carson narrowed his eyes. "Why?"

"Because you're a witness, and possibly something you tell me could help."

"I wasn't in the house when it happened. I was at the back of the property. I didn't hear anything or see anybody. When I went back, I f-found my mom." He so didn't want to talk about this. Deep breath. "I wasn't supposed to leave the house without telling her or my uncle where I was going, as if I could go far. Sometimes I just wanted to get out without anyone knowing where I was." The remorse of not being there had been eating him alive.

Lincoln rested his forearms on the side rail of the bed. "If you'd been there, they would've taken you or killed you."

He wished they *had* killed him.

"Did you see anyone suspicious hanging around the house before that day, or see anything odd?"

Carson couldn't recall anything different or strange. Except….

"I heard my uncle arguing on the phone that morning. He was in his office, and whoever he was talking to was making him angry, but that was nothing new. He had a temper."

Lincoln cocked an eyebrow. "Really? How so?"

Carson didn't like the look of suspicion. "My uncle *didn't* do this, if that's what you think. He may have been a cranky asshole most of the time, but he took care of us, made sure we had everything we needed. He was the only one in our family who stuck around after they found out what I was."

"Did he ever hurt you? Make you do something you didn't want to do?"

"No! I told you my uncle took care of us." Carson trusted his uncle. He never would hurt Carson's mother or Caden.

"Okay," Lincoln said. "Your brother, Caden. He was younger than you?"

Was.

Carson nodded.

"What was he like?"

"He was my little brother. He was awesome, and he tried to make me feel normal, and I *won't* let you drag him down." Carson squeezed his eyes tight against burning tears.

"What about your father?"

Carson shrugged. "I never knew my father. He died in a car accident when I was about three months old. My mom raised me with my uncle."

"What about Caden's father?"

Too many questions. "He lives in Gifford. My mom was only with Henry for a short time. He was a nice guy, but it's hard to have a relationship when you have a Tabula Rasa for a son, especially when he's not your biological kid."

"Does he ever see Caden?"

"Caden goes...." He choked on the present tense. "Caden went there some weekends, and they'd do stuff together. But the past few years, they'd grown apart. I think it's because Caden was trying to spend more time with me."

"Did Caden's father or anyone who came to the house ever get into a fight with your mother or uncle? Anyone who had a grudge against them?"

"Not to the house. Like I said, my uncle sometimes yelled when he was on the phone."

"Did your mother or uncle owe anyone money that you know of?"

Carson shrugged.

"Have the police ever been called to your house?"

"A few times when the alarms were tripped, but it usually ended up being an animal. A couple of times my uncle called them because he'd seen someone suspicious walking on the road by our house or found footprints around the fence on our property. Nothing ever came of that either."

"What was your relationship with your mother like?"

Carson's chin quivered as he recalled her beautiful smile, her lyrical laughter, and how she gave him a life as normal as possible when nothing was normal.

"I loved her. She was caring and sweet, baked the best apple strudel, made sure my life was full and I was happy. She always had a project going that we all worked on." Carson smiled. He had such great memories of growing up. "We built a life-sized tree bark canoe. It floated and everything. And a solar-powered scooter, but that only held enough energy to ride for a few minutes. Every year she took us on vacation somewhere we'd be safe. She had people who helped her make it happen. I don't know who they were."

Carson was glad he kept himself from crying. When he looked to Lincoln, he listened intently, a wistful expression on his face.

"But do you want to know the best thing about my mom?"

Lincoln nodded.

"She never resented me for ruining her life, for causing her to be alone all of those years. There were a few guys, including Caden's father, but they never stayed. She should have hated me for that alone."

Lincoln leaned forward intently. Carson couldn't look away, enthralled by his open and sincere expression, his relaxed body, the fluidity and calmness of his energy. "She was your mother. I can't imagine she would blame you for something you had no control over. She sounds like she wanted you to have as normal of a life as was possible."

Carson couldn't believe she was gone. Or Caden. He furrowed his brow deeply as the pain of that continual realization threatened to drown him.

Lincoln appeared to contemplate something and then sat back. "I have to ask you another question, and if you don't want to talk about it, you don't have to. I've raked you over the coals pretty hard today." A half smile followed.

Carson's heart fluttered as Lincoln's eyes crinkled at the corners. Carson was sure he'd agree to anything at that point. "Okay."

"Who's Justin?"

Like a punch to the gut. Why were they so insistent on reminding him of the worst time of his life? Well, the worst until now. "How do you know about Justin?"

"I don't. Doc said you were saying his name in your sleep. Do you have another brother?"

Carson bit down hard on his lip. The pain helped to focus his attention, which tried to fly off elsewhere. His mind didn't want to deal with this, never had.

"I know something happened to Justin, something you don't want to talk about. But maybe it would help to get it out."

Carson wanted to confess everything, free himself of the burden, but such a confession would pull his head under the water. And then Lincoln, everyone, would see him for the monster he was. He should've been arrested long ago, had wanted to go to the NVJ at the time and confess, but his uncle and mother hadn't let him.

"Is he a friend?"

"He was."

"He isn't anymore?"

He wasn't much of anything anymore. Carson shook his head. What if Lincoln arrested Carson and the sentence for such an act was a death sentence? Escape one sentence, only to be dealt another?

Lincoln raked his hand through his hair. "Okay. Has anyone ever tried to take you before? You're twenty-three. Plenty of people would covet something so valuable, try to grab you."

Shit, was Carson's brain feeding him a script of just what to ask?

Carson nodded. When he closed his eyes, Justin's smiling, freckled face appeared, quickly replaced by his terror-filled forgiving eyes just before Carson was forced to....

Another shudder ran down his spine.

"Are you cold?"

"No. Can we talk about the rest later?" Carson couldn't tell right then.

"Tired?"

Carson shrugged. "I get tired easily, but I just need some time before we talk about Justin." *Time to get to know you more.* "So what kind of vampire are you?"

Lincoln narrowed his eyes. "What do you mean?"

Damn, was that an inappropriate question? "I'm sorry, I didn't mean to be rude."

"You're not. I meant why did you think I'm one of the kinds?" Lincoln's suspicion had gone.

"I don't know why, but I can feel power in other vampires. It's strange. It's like a concentration of energy, like a force field around their bodies. But it's not just vampires. I can feel it in the Nons too. If I get the chance to touch them...."

Carson sat up. He reached and touched the back of Lincoln's hand, large in comparison to his. A muscle in Lincoln's hand twitched, but he didn't move away. Lincoln's power was different than any he'd ever experienced. Hot, tingling, calming. Carson couldn't deny his attraction to Lincoln. Carson had done more than touch Justin. They'd kissed and groped and sucked each other, but they didn't fuck. Carson had never been penetrated with anything more than his own fingers. Twenty-three and a virgin.

The entire touch lasted less than five seconds, but time seemed to stretch and expand. When Carson dared to look up, Lincoln's narrowed eyes, his exaggerated breathing, flipped Carson's gut.

CHAPTER 6

CARSON PULLED his hand away, waiting for Lincoln to comment on the unsolicited touch. When he didn't say anything, Carson relaxed on the bed, as if he hadn't been so bold.

Lincoln appeared to have chosen the "nothing happened" route as well.

Carson pulled his knees to his chest. A shudder ran through him as the energy expanded in his body.

"Anyway, sometimes I see a colorful aura surrounding a particularly powerful vampire or Non. I've only met a few like that. When we were on vacation one time, I met a wiccan priestess. Her aura was a mass of swirling colors surrounding her. Anyway, I can feel that you have power."

"Do I have an aura?"

"No. But your power is…. It's strong." He couldn't tell him how affected he was by Lincoln's power, how it was unlike anyone he'd ever experienced.

"I'm a Sanatore."

"The healer. I've read a little bit about the healing properties in the blood of the Sanatore." Carson wouldn't say why he'd searched for that information, or they'd be back to talking about Justin.

"Oh yeah? Where did you read that?" Lincoln appeared genuinely interested.

"Books my mother and uncle brought me. Internet archives. Mostly I was searching for information about my kind, but there wasn't much. There's tons more information available about the other kinds of vampires."

"We Sanatore aren't plentiful, but there're enough of us that I've met several during my life. Truthfully we're quite unremarkable except for our blood."

Carson sat up. "Are you kidding? You can heal other vampires with your blood."

"Doesn't always work."

Carson thinned his lips. "Yeah, I read that. Doesn't work on humans either."

"Nope. And sometimes the outcome isn't worth the risk."

Carson cocked his head. "I read an article by some researcher in France... and to get it I may have had to.... I probably shouldn't tell you."

Lincoln raised his brow. "What?"

"I, um... hacked into three servers to get it." Nothing like admitting to a crime in front of a NVJ commander. Compared to what Carson could admit, this was nothing.

Lincoln's eyes widened. A smile broke across his face, and he belted out a hardy laugh. And he didn't stop there. He laughed hard. The sound did all kinds of things to Carson's insides.

Get a grip. So not the time to think of picking up a guy, even if your heart and gut and groin don't agree.

"You think it's funny I hacked a network?" Carson frowned although he wasn't angry.

Lincoln was red in the face and gasping for air, with no sign of stopping. He nodded and managed to say, "Yes.... Me... officer...."

"Ahh, you're laughing because I now qualify for one of those world's stupidest criminal shows?" On the flip side, was being a smart criminal anything to be proud of either?

Lincoln shook his head and raised his hands. "No.... It's... it's j-just...."

The door opened and Carson jumped. Max peered in, eyes narrowed at Lincoln, who wiped his tears. Max pointed to Lincoln and looked at Carson. "What did you do to him?"

"What? No. I didn't do anything. I told him something, and then this happened."

"Hey, Linc? You okay?"

Lincoln laughed with less intensity, still gasping and unable to answer.

Max looked to Carson and, in all seriousness, said, "I think you broke him. Last time he laughed was 2012 when John Dennison tasered himself in front of a group of high school students."

That ramped up Lincoln's laughter. Carson chuckled at the image of the asshole officer tasering himself. Max frowned at Lincoln falling apart at the seams. And hell, did seeing Lincoln smiling wide, blue eyes shining, cause warmth to pool in Carson's chest.

"What exactly did you tell him?"

Lincoln gasped for air, pointing to Carson and shaking his head. "He… told me…."

Max raised his brows, waiting for Carson.

Carson shrugged. "I told him I read this unpublished article about Sanatore vampires that I had to hack into three networks to get."

Eyes wide, Max looked to Lincoln, who nodded. "Are you kidding me? Just like that guy!" Lincoln nodded, appearing to know who Max was thinking of. And then Max joined Lincoln on the crazy train.

No way could Carson get angry for being the crux of the joke along with some other guy. Not with Lincoln turning that dazzling smile his way. Took his mind off his growing headache as well.

Again the door opened and Doc entered, his gaze on the two men falling over one another laughing.

"What did you do?"

No way was Carson getting Doc going as well. "Absolutely nothing."

Doc shook his head. "Wrap it up, guys. I've got a patient here."

That seemed to bring them around. They both wiped at their eyes.

"Can you tell me what was so funny?" Carson asked, ducking from Doc and his flashlight.

Doc grasped Carson's chin and turned his head. "Later. How're you feeling, minus the sideshow by the immaturity squad?" Doc flashed his light in Carson's eyes and pain shot into his head. He drew his brows together and closed his eyes.

"Did that hurt?" Doc asked.

Carson nodded.

"Any pain in your head?" Doc palpated around Carson's jaw and neck.

"Got a headache. Kind of tired."

Doc moved away from the bed. The laughter had ceased. Max still looked highly amused. Lincoln wore a slight smirk, his face still bright. He hung back.

"Everything okay, Doc?" Lincoln asked.

Returning to the bed, Doc ran a cup-shaped piece of plastic attached to a handheld device over his forehead. After the beep he said, "Temperature's a little elevated, but nothing to be alarmed about. BP is good. I think your headache is from listening to these numbskulls making fools of themselves. I'm going to give you something for the pain and it'll help you to sleep. You need some good rest."

Carson didn't want to sleep. For a short time, he'd forgotten how alone he was in the world. He'd laughed. He couldn't remember the last time he found anything worth laughing about since….

Doc pushed a syringe into Carson's IV. The clear fluid disappeared, and Carson knew he'd be asleep within minutes. His gaze met with Lincoln's. Carson's eyes tried to close. He blinked to keep them open awhile longer. Lincoln had an odd expression on his face, possibly curiosity or confusion?

Sleep took hold. As he closed his eyes, Carson whispered, "Thank you."

He drifted off to dream of things that he couldn't have.

LINCOLN WATCHED Carson sleep. He'd thanked Lincoln for something, but he wasn't sure what. Not turning him in for hacking a few networks to get a research paper? Could be some type of scientific espionage? He snorted. Something about Carson just felt….

A hand touched Lincoln's shoulder. Doc motioned them both to follow.

Max rolled his eyes, no doubt expecting the same tongue-lashing from Doc as Lincoln did. They deserved to be scolded if they'd done anything to harm Carson.

Lincoln closed the door quietly, followed Doc down the hallway and into his office. He rounded his desk. "What the hell was that back there?"

Lincoln raised his eyebrow and looked to Max, who shrugged. Visions of them from their childhood came to him, the two them standing before the principal's desk, being asked pretty much that same question.

"Laughing." Still Lincoln wanted to smirk.

Doc snorted. "You haven't laughed since John tasered himself in 2012."

"Jesus Christ. I've laughed since then. That joke is getting way old." Made him sound like an uptight asshole.

"Not like that." Doc leaned on the desk with both hands, eyes intent on Lincoln. Made him feel as if Doc was assessing him.

Lincoln just wanted to head out of there. "Listen, Doc, we won't let it happen again—"

"Yes, you will."

"Huh?" Max scratched his head, appearing as confused as Lincoln felt.

"We will?" Lincoln asked.

Doc stood. "Yes, you will. If Carson sits in that room every day alone and thinks of everything he's lost, he won't improve. I told you the mind plays a large part in healing. There's truth to laughter being the best medicine."

Doc wiped his hand over his mouth, and Lincoln could see something was wrong. His breath caught. He shook off the fear threatening to make him feel something for someone he'd just met. Carson was just a vampire who needed help. Nothing more.

"You're not saying something."

"It's all speculation. There's something abnormal in his blood tests. He's stable for now, but improvement has been slow. It could have something to do with him being a Tabula Rasa. I'm looking further into his kind."

No mention of Lincoln's blood. No pleas or long, drawn-out explanation to change his mind. Lincoln appreciated Doc wasn't pushing yet. Lincoln couldn't ignore the cost of that quick decision to heal another person. The entire event thoroughly traumatized him. He'd come close to being put down.

"What can we do?" Max asked.

"You can keep him company when he's awake. Watch funny movies, tell stupid stories, get one of those video game consoles, whatever. And when he needs to talk, listen. We'll see how it goes over the next week."

"We'll get him anything he wants," Lincoln said.

Max nodded in agreement.

Doc picked up a folder from his desk. "Good. Now go somewhere. I've got work to do."

Lincoln followed Max from the office and stuffed his hands into his pockets.

Max mirrored the action. "I was trying to call you. That's why I came into Carson's room. What were you doing before you busted out laughing?"

Lincoln's cheeks heated. Was he fucking blushing because Carson's touch had flipped his stomach? The need to touch him soaked every cell his body? Jesus. "He was awake, so I was questioning him."

Max cocked his head and was silent for a moment. "Find anything?"

Lincoln rubbed the back of his neck. He was tired, hungry, and horny. Had to be because he'd missed his weekend fucks. Whenever he had a Friday or Saturday free, he cruised the bars, found some guy about half his size because that was his thing. He liked them easy to handle, easy to dominate. Take a guy home for the night and send him on his way in the morning. Back out on Saturday night. Rinse and repeat. He was perfectly happy to go on like that forever, so why did that life seem pathetic now? Dammit. What changed?

Lincoln shook off the uneasy feeling that threatened to choke him when he thought of touching someone else. Someone who wasn't Carson. "He was at the back of the property when the murders occurred. Didn't see or hear anything. Couldn't name a reason why someone would want to harm his family. The mother had only had a few past relationships. Longest resulted in the brother, Caden. The uncle sounds as if he was a hard-ass, but I couldn't get Carson to say a negative thing against him." Lincoln rubbed his chin. "He did mention hearing his uncle arguing on the phone earlier that morning."

Max's eyebrows rose above the frames of his glasses. "You think whoever he argued with came in and took care of the mother, grabbed the uncle, maybe the kid too?"

"But why? Why not kill the mother and brother and take just the uncle?"

"Leverage? Get the uncle to comply?"

Lincoln nodded slowly. "Would explain the absence of their bodies. Still doesn't explain why Carson says they were dead when they weren't on the property." And Lincoln held back with the hard questions, something he'd never done in the past.

"I'll get the phone records for the landline and the cell phones for everyone in the house." Max punched at the screen of his phone.

"Pull some strings and get a rush on that. If your theory is correct, then Carson's entire family isn't dead, but they might be soon." If he brought back at least part of Carson's family, he'd probably get better without Lincoln's blood.

"Will do." Max headed down the hall.

Lincoln walked a few feet when he noticed he headed in the direction of Carson's room. He dropped his head as he corrected his direction. He didn't even feel like himself anymore. Caring about the guy, wanting to be near him, learn everything about him, laughing, that fucking strange feeling in his gut. If he had to label it....

No. He wasn't interested. He needed to get laid. Tonight he'd head out and pick up a quick fuck. Better yet, he'd go to a bite club. Then he could get on with his life.

CHAPTER 7

CARSON FELT the walls and ceiling closing in on him, ready to crush him with bone-weary boredom. While he slept often, there were hours he'd just lie there, trying not to think. He had a stack of books from Taylor that covered an odd array of subjects. From Doc came a stack of magazines. Carson wasn't bored enough for *Physician's Weekly*. He'd been through all of the crappy channels on the TV three times and then given up.

He appreciated their thoughtfulness to help cure his boredom. He missed his books and computer. He missed his room and the smells from the kitchen. He even missed the square acre of land that had imprisoned him. Would he return home after he healed and the killer was caught? How would he survive? He didn't have any money or any job skills. He knew about networks and hacking. Maybe an online job?

But how could he return home with everyone gone, with the memories of his mother lying in a pool of her blood in the entryway? The old wood floor no doubt had soaked in the blood, never allowing him to forget. If not home, then where? Would the NVJ boot his ass out the front door with a "Thanks for coming. Don't come back"?

Just as his panic revved up, there was a knock. Doc and the nurses never knocked. Neither did Lincoln, so no reason to get excited.

"Come in."

Max entered, pushing a cart. He was dressed in a gray T-shirt and jeans, his hair tied back. "Hey, there's our favorite patient. What're you up to?"

"Feeling sorry for myself," Carson mumbled.

Max wheeled the cart stacked with food and what looked to be games, movies, and possibly a video game console up to the bed. Carson was sure he smelled pizza.

"What was that?" Max asked.

Carson forced a smile. "Becoming an expert at boredom."

Max smirked and nodded. "Don't I know it. I've spent a lot of time in hospitals. They definitely are the opposite of fun. Well, I'm your cure for boredom for at least the next couple of hours, that is, if you aren't tired and are actually interested."

"Yes, please. Anything's better than counting the number of brown dots on the ceiling tiles."

"That's beyond bored. I have the antidote. Board games, movies, an Xbox with some games, playing cards, *Uno*...." He crouched and looked at the lower shelf. "To eat we have pizza loaded with all the necessary food groups: bacon, pepperoni, sausage, and ham. Three kinds of chicken wings, nachos, chips and dip, pepperoni and cheese, and of course, apple pie."

Carson laughed. "Planning a party? You've got enough food for about ten people."

Max chuckled. "I was just covering all of the bases. So anything you see tickle your fancy?"

Carson searched the cart. "You know how to play rummy?"

"It's been a while, but I think I remember."

Carson sat up, making sure he kept himself covered with his flimsy hospital gown. "If we put the railing down, we can play on the bed. You can sit at the foot and I'll push back. Should give us enough room."

"Good idea." Max lowered the railing. "You don't need this anymore. Want me to put the other one down?"

"Yeah. I feel like I'm either a prisoner of this bed or a two-year-old. Doc doesn't want me going out into the public areas. He's afraid of germs."

Max laughed out loud. "I had to shower with antibacterial soap and let him take my temperature before I could set a foot in here. While he's a tad neurotic, it's only because he wants you to get better."

"I know."

Max hopped onto the bed and shuffled the cards. Carson grabbed a can of soda. Maybe he'd start there and see how his stomach handled it.

"Not hungry?" Max dealt the cards.

Carson took a sip of the ginger ale. "Not really. I'm hoping my stomach doesn't reject this." He set the can down and picked up his cards. Not a bad hand, but not great.

They quickly got into the rhythm of the game, picking cards from the deck, setting down three and four of a kind, sequences of face cards. Carson got bolder and started some smack talk, which Max gave right back. Not long into the game, Carson shouted "rummy," laying his last card down and winning the first hand.

Max frowned. "Hmm, don't get too cocky over there. It's all coming back to me now."

"I'm shaking in my boots." Carson dealt the cards.

Max grabbed a nacho chip loaded with meat, cheese, and sour cream. "Sure you don't want anything? This is so fucking good."

"I'm sure. I'm sorry I'm not eating after you got all of this food."

"Don't worry. It won't go to waste around here. The minute it hits the kitchen, the vultures will descend in a frenzy of carnage unseen by most. Animals, I tell you."

Carson laughed while sorting his cards. An ace. Lucky. "Earlier you said you'd spent a lot of time in hospitals. Were you sick?"

Max's body tensed, and his expression turned grim.

Carson shouldn't have asked. "Sorry. I'm prying."

"It's okay. My wife, Grace. She had an aggressive form of ovarian cancer and was already stage four when she was diagnosed. Lots of chemo and radiation. And when that didn't work, experimental treatments at the Upstate Cancer Center in Syracuse and Dana Farber in Boston."

Those were hospitals for humans. Carson had assumed Max's wife was a vampire. Interracial marriages between the two races had only become more common in the past few years. Not without backlash. In certain areas of the country, there were Nons who vehemently frowned on the union, many religious fanatics going as far as calling it bestiality. Just crazy.

Max shook his head, staring at his cards. "After five months her body gave up. That was two years ago."

"I'm really sorry to hear about your wife."

"Thanks. She was so beautiful. I knew within thirty minutes of meeting her at a coffee shop that I wanted to spend the rest of my life with her. Took Grace a bit longer, but eventually she realized I wasn't going away."

Carson sighed. "Sounds romantic."

"It was. She's been gone for two years, but I guess it's getting… easier? I don't know. I'm at the point where I'm not only remembering her when she was sick. Now the memories are more about our lives together, mostly the good parts." He smiled weakly.

Carson picked a card. No matches. "I know what you mean."

Max didn't take his turn, looking with curiosity at Carson. "What?"

"You said you understood. What did you mean?" Max's gaze was intense.

Shit. He had no filter lately. "When I was sixteen, I met a…." How would Max react to hearing Carson was gay?

"What? A vampire? A human? A platypus?" Max chuckled.

"A guy." There, he said it.

Max widened his eyes and tilted his head. "Aaaaand was he a vampire or a human?"

Seriously? Max didn't care about the guy part? "Human."

"Grace was a halfie."

That explained her access to human doctors. A halfie was the offspring of a vampire and human and had a 50 percent chance that blood wouldn't be required in their diet. Also their canines tended to be shorter, many matching human size. Those halfies could live as Nons.

"How did you meet this guy? Did he visit your house?"

Carson lifted the corner of his lips. "He climbed over the fence into my yard. Said he just knew there had to be something special on the other side. We became friends first, then got more serious." Carson folded the cards in his hand. "He died. I remember feeling the same way you described."

"Hey, man, I'm sorry. He was young?"

Max's eyes showed his sincerity. Carson chastised himself for even mentioning Justin. He was yanking stuff from a pit better left alone. It was just hearing Max describing feelings and thoughts Carson had experienced, ones he'd never spoken about with anyone. He refused his mother and Caden, even his uncle, to have any of that part of him, that guilt.

"Sixteen. He died six months after we met." Carson blew out a breath.

"What happened?"

Carson couldn't answer, couldn't even come up with a decent lie. He raked his fingers through his hair.

Max dropped his cards. "Man, we sure know how to have a good time, don't we? I came here to give you some fun, a distraction, and I do the opposite."

Carson was grateful Max let his lack of answer stand. "No, this is great. It's fun and just what I need. Thanks."

And he'd gone a whole hour without thinking about Lincoln. His crush had been running away with his imagination. He had them set up in a nice little house with a dog where no room was safe from their copulating. At that point he'd grabbed the first book on the pile. *The Mating in the Wild.* Just from the title, Carson knew the universe was out to get him.

Max gathered the cards. "My pleasure. Besides, I'd only be home sacked out on the couch while infomercials ran on the TV."

Carson let his head fall back and closed his eyes. "Gods, even that sounds better than my life. That's pathetic."

Max huffed. "It's all about context."

"Are you and Lincoln friends?" Darn, where had that come from?

Max hesitated for a moment. He'd probably say it was none of Carson's business, but he smiled. "Since we were kids. Grew up together. Went to the NVJ academy together. Came to Utica together. I can't get rid of him."

Carson chuckled. "You seem so different. You're easygoing, less serious."

"That's an understatement. But even if he seems like an unfeeling hard-ass, that's not the real Lincoln. He went through something a few years ago that was…. It was hard for him. Anyway, once you get to know him, he's a different person."

"I know."

Max gathered the cards into a pile. "Another game?"

Carson shook his head, and Max put the deck away. "So is Lincoln working tonight?"

Max averted his eyes. "No, he's not working." The way he avoided looking at Carson confused him. Maybe….

"Is he married?" Of course he was. Men like that weren't single. Why hadn't Carson even thought of that?

"Why do you ask?"

"No reason. Just a question." But one that could stop his growing obsession.

Max smirked and cocked his head. "He's not married."

"Oh."

"His last relationship was Luke. That was that hard time I mentioned. There hasn't been anyone permanent since."

Carson quelled his reaction.

"No matter what I've tried, I haven't been able to get him to move on. I think it's gonna take someone special to break through that wall." Max gave Carson a sideways glance. Then stood. "So what next?"

Carson looked at the cart, his mind too busy processing what Max had said. He needed distraction. "How about a movie?"

LINCOLN GROWLED and yanked off his uniform hat, chucking it into his office as he passed. His night out was totally fucked. Before he headed out, a call came in from the Utica PD asking for assistance on a domestic disturbance call across town, a Non and vampire couple, which meant the NVJ had to be there. He was about to send Max and Taylor, then found out that Max was hanging with Carson. Lincoln's first thought? He could keep Carson company while Max went out. Then Lincoln kicked himself in the ass for that stupid idea and went instead.

And he wanted to believe all of that was the reason he hadn't gone out. It wasn't the fact he'd gone to his truck, sat for over thirty minutes, unable to even put the key into the ignition. Couldn't have been a dark-haired vampire with big brown eyes.

Now he was headed to medical, convincing himself he had to check in with Doc. He wasn't going to Carson's room. Nope. Or maybe he'd just pop his head in. Standing before Carson's door, Lincoln heard laughing. Max was still in there. Over two and a half hours? Lincoln gritted his teeth. He lifted his hand to knock, then scrubbed his hands over his face. When had he become so indecisive, so besotted?

The moment a vampire looked up at you and grabbed hold of something inside of you, that's when.

He had better control than that. Pushing the handle down, he entered without knocking. What he saw stopped him. Carson and

Max. Reclining side-by-side on the bed. Eyes focused across the room on the TV. Smiling. Laughing. Lincoln clenched his fists at his sides. Something violent reared its ugly head in Lincoln's gut. Carson was his.

What the fuck?

CHAPTER 8

LINCOLN LET the door close behind him as he focused on Carson, his body so close to Max, so close to touching. Had they been touching? Max wasn't even gay.

Hearing the door, they both pulled away from whatever they were watching to look at him.

"Lincoln." Carson sat up, and the smile he gave Lincoln dried his mouth and snapped a tight band around his chest. The feeling was too much. He had to get out of there.

"Hey, just checking in. Looks like you're busy, so I'll just—"

Max rolled off the bed and stretched. "No. I have to head out anyway. I've got to be here bright and early tomorrow." Max looked to Carson. "My boss is a real slave driver."

Lincoln rolled his eyes and crossed his arms. He noticed Carson wasn't as pale as earlier, his eyes livelier, his face less gaunt, lips still red. They were locked in a stare that caused Lincoln to turn his focus to Max. He unloaded what looked to be games and movies onto the side table.

"Linc, you hungry? Got enough food for an army, or Taylor." Max chuckled.

Lincoln shook his head. He'd follow Max out. Whatever was happening whenever he was close to Carson had to stop. He couldn't go down that road again. Then Max fucked him over.

"Thanks for the good time, Carson. I'm sure Lincoln will hang out and spend some time with you. Maybe watch a movie?" Max gave Lincoln a sideways glance and that fucking smirk. He was so dead. "I'll stop in tomorrow."

"Thanks, Max." Carson waved.

Lincoln stepped aside to let Max out of the room.

"See ya, Linc."

"Yeah." Lincoln wandered to the bed. "So what were you guys watching?" The credits were rolling on the screen.

"*The Hangover*."

Out of the corner of Lincoln's eye, Carson fidgeted on the bed, chin resting on his knee. Being in the same room didn't have to be so awkward. Lincoln knew how to have a good time. "How about a movie with lots of explosions and shooting?"

Carson's face brightened. "Okay. That sounds good. Let's me see what we have." He shuffled through the pile Max had left and then held up a case, nodding. "Gerard Butler kicking some Persian ass? Yeah?"

"Sounds good." Lincoln took the case, ejected the previous movie, and then loaded the new one. He sat in the chair next to the bed.

Carson worked the remote, going straight to the menu, and started the movie. Lincoln had seen *300* before, but it had been a while. He kicked his booted feet up onto the footboard of the bed and leaned back in the less-than-comfortable chair. Probably the reason Max had ended up sharing the bed.

"You're wearing your uniform. Max said you weren't working?"

"I wasn't supposed to, but I went out on a call to a domestic disturbance. Vampire and human couple were going at it. The wife was a spitfire. She was punching the crap out of the husband on the front lawn when Myers and I arrived. Took both of us to cuff her."

"Wow. What was the fight about?"

Lincoln raised his hands and dropped them. "It was a he said, she said kind of deal. Something about money and the kids, and as the woman put it, some fucking whore-bag slut."

Carson laughed. "Sounds like fun."

"Loads. She's chilling in one of our holding rooms. He's down at Utica PD. Our liaison is meeting with the Nons liaison to work out what to do next."

Carson lifted his brow and crinkled his nose in the most adorab—

Shit. Lincoln wiped his hand over his mouth.

"Sounds messy."

"Can be."

Lincoln looked at the TV, but who was he kidding? He was too distracted by that pull deep in his gut, the need to get closer. He recognized that feeling. First and last time was with Luke, who bartended at one of the gay bars Lincoln frequented. Within seconds of Luke asking what he wanted to drink, Lincoln had been caught by his seductive eyes, the dimple in his chin. He fought the attraction by running away, fucking just about every guy in sight. But that did nothing to suppress his attraction to Luke.

Lincoln regretted wasting those three months. Was he heading down the same path? Gods, he never imagined feeling that attraction to anyone again, wanting them past one night of fucking. Didn't come close to a hot guy catching his attention and wanting to fuck him hard. Luke was everything, and Lincoln had been happy. Then he made a decision Luke couldn't live with.

Four years later another vampire sucker punched him, a vampire he wasn't even sure felt anything for him. He shuddered as he thought of Carson touching his hand. The spark flowing between them when Carson touched him had burrowed under his skin. If he wanted to run, now was the time. He could still head out and pick up someone.

"What the hell is that?" Carson's voice startled Lincoln.

"What?"

Carson pointed to the screen. "That huge thing with the fangs as long as my hand. Wait… did he just call it a wolf? Fucking big-ass wolf. You could ride that thing into battle."

Lincoln laughed at Carson's wide-eyed expression.

"Seriously. Although he's kinda dumb for getting stuck in between those rocks."

Lincoln sat forward. "Actually the entire movie is beyond the realm of believability. There's a guy on YouTube who makes videos pointing out what he calls 'cinema sins' or what's wrong in movies."

"Really? I love seeing mistakes in movies, like when something in a scene disappears and then reappears. Or something modern shows up in a period movie like an airplane flying by before airplanes existed."

"You'd like these videos. They tend to call out the plot or something in a scene." Lincoln paused, and because he didn't want Carson to lose that damn eager, authentic joy on his face, Lincoln said, "I can show you, if you want."

But Carson's expression did falter. "There's no computer in here, and I can't leave the room."

Lincoln stood, and Carson's gaze followed. "What Doc doesn't know. There's a computer in a vacant office close by. I've snuck in there myself when I needed to get some shit done but no one would leave me alone. No one else goes in there. And Doc has the entire medical wing sanitized for everyone's protection daily. Not a germ could survive."

Carson's smile returned. Lincoln's heart skipped a beat. Carson was gorgeous.

"Doc will kick both of our asses if he catches us."

Lincoln could see a mischievous glint in Carson's eye, and Lincoln knew Carson was in.

"He won't know. I just need to know if you can handle walking, or do I need to get a wheelchair? I won't let you get tired and sicker." Lincoln showed Carson he was serious.

Carson nodded enthusiastically. "I promise I can walk. I just might need to go a little slower." He looked down. "But I don't have any clothes. And even though I'm wearing underwear, my butt's hanging out of this so-called gown."

Lincoln gritted his teeth, his imagination showing him Carson's round, pert globes peeking out of the gown, enticing him. He let out a stuttering breath.

"Lincoln?" Carson gave him a questioning expression.

"Sorry. Let me show you a trick." He looked through the drawers of the side table. "Aha. Here. Put this on backward." He tossed Carson another gown. He slipped off the bed, then pulled it on.

"Looks good. Let's go."

Carson was both excited and nervous as hell as he followed Lincoln on their clandestine mission. Lincoln confused him, vacillating between gruff and moody to smiling and easygoing, as if someone had wound him up too tight and then let him go. Carson knew he shouldn't read anything into Lincoln's behavior.

As they walked from the room, Carson's legs were weak. His breaths were short and labored. "Close by" now had a whole new meaning to Carson.

Lincoln stopped at a door around the corner. He pulled a ring of keys from his pocket, chose one, and slipped it into the door. "Master key for the master." He waggled his eyebrows.

Carson rolled his eyes with great exaggeration. He followed Lincoln inside, closing the door behind him. The office wasn't too large. A desk with the promised computer sat in the center, a file cabinet to the left, a small couch to the right. Lincoln rounded the desk and sat in the chair as he powered up the computer. In a bold move, Carson sat on the top of the desk, bringing his bare leg into close contact with Lincoln's arm. As if an electric current crossed the short distance between them, sharp prickles raced over Carson's skin.

Lincoln typed on the keyboard, his body visibly tense. Carson swore Lincoln swallowed hard. As he moved the mouse, Lincoln's arm bumped repeatedly into Carson's leg. His gut clenched, and his breath caught with each touch. Carson moved just a half an inch closer, and Lincoln's elbow ran over his skin. Carson shuddered.

Lincoln frowned deeply.

I knew this was a bad idea. What were you thinking?

He moved his leg away so they were no longer touching. That was when Lincoln rested his hand on Carson's thigh. He sucked in a breath, the muscle in his thigh jumped, goose bumps rose on his skin. He'd never been as nervous as he was right then. Carson didn't know what to do. His heart rattled his ribs, his stomach flipped, and he could possibly throw up.

When Lincoln pushed his fingers under the fabric of his gown, Carson's cock filled in seconds flat. Adrenaline hit hard. His hands shook. His respirations increased. He looked up and gasped. Staring intently, lips parted, face flushed, Lincoln's mesmerizing gaze was unyielding. His lips…. Carson wanted to kiss him.

Lincoln stood, moving his palm up Carson's thigh, under his gown. Carson shuddered. Lincoln stepped between Carson's legs, eyes never wavering, his chest visibly rising and falling. Time had stopped, it must have, because Lincoln was motionless. Anticipation had stolen Carson's ability to speak, but he heard what he wished to say in his head.

Kiss me.

Breaking out of his inert state, Lincoln ran his tongue over his lower lip, catching Carson's attention. His cock throbbed against the forearm he used to keep his rock-hard cock from tenting his gown.

Lincoln removed his palm from Carson's leg, then cupped his cheek. He exhaled as if he'd been holding his breath his entire life, waiting for that moment. Heat expanded, radiating across his chest.

"I need to kiss you," Lincoln whispered.

Even before their lips touched, a whimper rose out of Carson. Sharp tingles electrified his skin, and then their lips touched. A small moan escaped from Lincoln. He moved his hand to the nape of Carson's neck, bringing him closer. Parting his lips, Lincoln's tongue met Carson's for their first taste of each one another. Add in the intoxicating, musky scent in the air, and Carson was ready to pull Lincoln on top of him and rut like an animal.

Carson ran his fingertips over Lincoln's chest, his black T-shirt stretched tight over his pecs. Lincoln jumped as Carson found Lincoln's nipple. Rubbing the hardened nub elicited a groan deep in Lincoln, and he intensified the kiss. He tightened his hand on Carson's neck while he wrapped the other around his waist, crushing them together.

Oh fuck. The new position trapped Carson's cock between their groins along with Lincoln's impressive bulge. Carson wrapped his arms around Lincoln and gripped his ass. Carson wriggled and ground against Lincoln, who moved his hands to the top of Carson's ass. Their panting filled the air as the kiss broke. Carson would cum soon if they continued their erotic grinding.

Carson looked into Lincoln's eyes as he raked his fingers through Carson's hair. "So beautiful."

"I need you to touch me." Carson couldn't believe he'd asked, but he needed to cum with Lincoln touching him.

Lincoln reached between Carson's legs, closed his hand around Carson's shaft through his underwear, and squeezed gently. Pleasure unlike any he'd ever experienced contracted Carson's stomach muscles. He cried out, his control held by a fragile thread.

"Need you so bad," Lincoln said on an exhale.

He covered Carson's mouth with his, another kiss that ramped Carson up further. He rocked his hips, thrusting into Lincoln's tight fist. So good. He squeezed Lincoln's hard cock, eliciting a rumbling groan from deep within his chest. Lincoln rolled his hips as he pushed against Carson's hand. He needed more. Needed to explore every part of Lincoln. Needed to feel Lincoln's hands on his skin. Needed to taste Lincoln.

Their frenzied movements filled the space between them. Carson worked to open Lincoln's belt, which now seemed to be a complicated task. Lincoln kneading Carson's balls made thinking that much harder. Finally the belt opened, leaving the button.

Lincoln bunched Carson's gown up on his stomach. He hooked his fingers in the waistband and, in one motion, the underwear was off and dropped onto the floor. The cool air made Carson's cock twitch, needy for any stimulation.

"Let me." Lincoln took over Carson's fumbled attempt to open his pants. Unbuttoned and unzipped, Lincoln pushed his pants to his knees.

Carson grasped Lincoln's cock and pumped. When Lincoln did the same, Carson grunted. "I'm gonna… cum." He couldn't catch hold of the thoughts swirling in his head. He never imagined… hadn't thought....

"Yeah, you are." Lincoln yanked his cock from Carson's hand, then dropped to his knees. Took Carson's cock deep into his mouth. He moved his hand to Lincoln's head. Tangled his fingers in his hair.

"Oh shit! That… feels so good."

Carson leaned back, bracing himself with his arm. His head fell back. The heat of Lincoln's mouth, the sensation of his tongue gliding over the head of his cock, the slide of his mouth from base to tip, overwhelmed his nervous system. It was too much. Tears filled his eyes. He couldn't catch his breath, couldn't halt the rush of adrenaline spiking and pushing into his balls. His muscles contracted and twitched. His balls clenched. The power to form words, to warn Lincoln he was close, failed Carson. Pulling gently on Lincoln's hair only resulted in a moan. The resulting vibrations raced down Carson's shaft.

"Oh… oh gods."

Carson arched his back, his chest locked, and his stomach clenched. Suspended within the building orgasm for a few blissful seconds, the pressure built to an unbearable level, and cum exploded from his cock. His entire groin and ass spasmed as Lincoln worked to swallow Carson's seed.

His eyes went wide. A whimper escaped his throat as Lincoln continued to swallow and nurse on his cock. The breath trapped in Carson's chest whooshed out. He closed his eyes, forcing the few tears that had formed from the intense experience. His arms and legs felt lighter. He floated until he felt Lincoln move away. Carson opened his eyes. Lincoln stood over him. The look on his face…. Gods, it was all kinds of confused and remorseful and maybe panicked.

"You okay?" Carson asked, realizing he was naked from the waist down. He sat up and pushed the gown down, a foreboding feeling growing in his gut.

Lincoln pursed his lips. He'd just given Carson the most amazing orgasm ever, and his over-the-top reaction kept Carson from returning the favor. But Lincoln's cock was no longer hard. Lincoln's cum had splattered on the carpet and the front of the desk. Fuck, that was hot.

But that look—was that fear?—made Carson certain that Lincoln might have reached the regret stage. *Just as well.* There could never be anything more between them.

Carson decided it was only fair to give Lincoln an easy out. He feigned a yawn and slipped from the desk. The head rush was immense but passed without clueing Lincoln in. He heard Lincoln's zipper, then the jingling of his belt. Carson stepped into his underwear, his sensitive cock brushing against the fabric.

When they returned to his room, he'd lie down and fake falling to sleep. Then Lincoln could leave without needing to say something. That thought brought a sharp pain to Carson's chest.

Don't fall for someone you can't have.

Too late.

CHAPTER 9

"ARE YOU okay? Did I hurt you?" Lincoln's voice had an undertone of panic.

Was that what he regretted? "You're afraid you hurt me?"

"I shouldn't have pushed myself on you. You're sick, and I'm supposed to protect you, not make you sicker."

Carson closed his eyes, his chin quivering minutely. Lincoln rubbed his shoulder. Carson looked at him. "You're supposed to protect me?"

Lincoln looked away and shifted. "I'm an NVJ officer. That's my job."

"Ouch." Carson slapped his hands over his heart and smirked. Why had the mood become so serious?

Lincoln narrowed his eyes. "What does that mean?"

"Seriously?"

"Of course seriously."

"You told me that I'm your job."

"That wasn't what…. I didn't…. I don't do what we just did with anyone who…."

Carson sighed and sat back against the desk. "Who may have murdered his entire family?"

Lincoln's expression softened. "You didn't do that."

Carson cocked his head. "Why should you believe me? You don't even know me." Didn't know what Carson had done.

Lincoln's assessing gaze ratcheted up Carson's nerves. Why couldn't he just keep his mouth shut?

"No. I don't know you, but I trust you. It's a gut feeling I can't ignore." Lincoln looked down, raking his fingers through his short hair, shifting foot to foot like a nervous schoolboy. "I just…. I don't know. This is all new to me." Said as if this were the hardest thing he'd done so far in his life. But when he looked into Carson's eyes, there wasn't a hint of a shy boy. Only confidence. "This is only the second time in my life that I've wanted to get to know someone better."

That had to be the most perfect thing Carson had ever heard. He smiled. "It's new to me too. And everything is so fucked up. My.... I lost everything, and dealing with that is so fucking hard. When I'm alone the silence of the room is overwhelming. I can hear my mother and Caden, even my uncle's voice in my head. I forget, you know. And then bam, I'm sideswiped and cry so hard I can't breathe." He rubbed at his forehead. Karma had come 'round and kicked his ass. He was the one who should have died. What he did, and his family were the ones to pay for his sin? Who would pay next for Carson?

Lincoln touched Carson's arm. "You look exhausted. If I don't get you back, Doc will skin my hide. Let's go."

Lincoln took Carson's hand and led him back to his room. Luckily no one noticed they'd left. Lincoln motioned Carson to the bed. He climbed in. Lincoln pulled the covers up and arranged them as if tucking Carson in, then kissed him on the forehead. He ran his hand down Carson's arm. Carson felt his exhaustion in every muscle, but his mind raced relentlessly. Lincoln had kissed him. Brought Carson to an orgasm that nearly stopped his heart. Wanted to get to know him.

... only the second time in my life that I've wanted to get to know someone better.

Which meant knowing everything, including the dark secret he'd carried for the past six years. Panic rose with an intensity that dug down deep. The urgency to confess hit hard because, without doing so, it would tarnish anything they could have—or crush the life from it in a split second. The moment Carson allowed his heart to open again, that guilt spilled out and had him in a stranglehold. Lincoln didn't know what kind of monster Carson could be.

Carson grabbed Lincoln's arm before he could move away. He had to know....

"I bit Justin."

Lincoln's hand stilled. He slowly stood. Carson didn't want to look into his face and see anything but want, knowing the absence might tear his soul apart. Carson focused on a spot across the room and detached himself from his emotions.

"Justin was my boyfriend. We were sixteen. I didn't go to school… didn't go anywhere, so meeting guys was impossible. No one was allowed to come to the house. Caden wasn't allowed to bring friends home."

Lincoln didn't make a sound or move, so Carson continued.

"I used to go to the farthest points on the property. An acre is really small when it's your entire world, but I found places where I couldn't see the house. A six-foot-high barricade fence surrounded the property. Near the back was a large stand of trees. In the summer the brush grew up thick and the trees were covered with leaves and blocked the house. I went out there a lot and pretended I was somewhere else, on some other soil, hundreds of miles away from my prison. Gods, I was so lonely. I was a teenager, and I was under lock and key."

With that statement Lincoln shifted, and Carson knew why.

"I wasn't literally under lock and key. I just knew I couldn't leave. I understood the implications of what I was and what would happen. I played by the rules… until I didn't."

Carson rubbed his fingertips over his temple, where a pulsing headache was forming. "One day I was at the back of the property reading some book when I heard someone walking around on the other side of the fence. No one should have been there, so I sat quietly and waited for them to leave. Instead someone grabbed the top of the fence and pulled himself up, and jumped over." The most beautiful guy Carson had ever seen. Sandy-red hair, peachy skin tone, bright greenish-hazel eyes.

"Justin?"

Carson nodded, relieved Lincoln spoke. "Yeah. As if scaling fences was an everyday thing, he just jumps down and looks around, saying he wondered what was on this side of the fence and decided to check it out."

Carson smiled at the memory of their first meeting. It would be the first of dozens of covert rendezvous. For the first time in his life, Carson made a real friend, not just someone in an online chat room, but someone to talk to and laugh with. It was all so *normal* in a life filled with the abnormal. He remembered when their friendship turned into something more, when their touches became more intimate, their first stolen kisses in the brush, then frotting and blowjobs. Carson's life, for once, was bright and sparkly and amazing.

"We got really close and spent time together almost every day for six months, and I...." Carson almost said he'd fallen in love, but he caught himself. "Anyway, I made a mistake. I told Justin what I was. I mean, he knew I was a vampire, and he was cool with that. He said he had friends back where he used to live who were vampires. But I told him my secret and he said he'd keep it forever... promised and swore."

Carson stopped to take in a deep breath. His hands shook. The throbbing in his head grew.

"He told someone, didn't he?" Carson heard the accusation in Lincoln's tone.

Carson nodded and pressed his fingertips hard into his temples. The pain was like a tightening vise around his head. "He told his mother. I know he didn't think anything would happen. It was his mother, right? He wanted to tell her he'd met me, that we were close. They lived with his grandfather. Justin believed he overheard them talking. His grandfather was a gambler and a con man, trying to make money anywhere he could." Carson shuddered hard and huffed. "He told a guy who hunts rare vampires where to find me for a large amount of money. When Justin found out what his grandfather had done, he snuck out to warn me."

Carson closed his eyes. Memories sharp as razors descended on him, as if it were happening all over again. "The hunter must have followed him. He took us both. I found out later that he'd taken Justin for proof of what I could do. He had a buyer, some rich foreign guy, and the man wanted *proof.*" The shaking filled his body, and a sharp pain shot through his head. "They m-made me.... They held guns to our heads.... Told me to bite him, but I refused. I couldn't do that, you know? I knew what would happen to Justin if I did, but then they s-shot him in the leg." Carson could hear his screams piercing his ears, the hole in his thigh, the helplessness that nearly drowned him.

"I begged them to stop, to let him go and I'd go with them, do what they wanted. He was my best friend. I loved him." Carson's chest heaved, and there wasn't enough air. "Then they... they shot him in the the other leg." The screaming filled his head with a sharp pain. His skin dripped with sweat, but he shook as if the room were freezing cold.

"You don't need to tell me anything else. I understand." Lincoln ran a hand gently over Carson's arm. The touch was too much, and he pulled his arm away. He didn't deserve consoling, didn't deserve to be cared for. He didn't even deserve pity. He was a monster, a creation of the devil himself. Sooner or later he'd hurt anyone who chose to love him. "It wasn't your fault."

Carson squeezed his eyes shut as he remembered leaning over Justin, tears blurring his vision, and Justin's pain-filled voice, saying over and over, "It's okay, Carson. They're going to kill me anyway. It's okay." Worse, they made Carson drink from him, and he had to choke down the blood that burned like acid down his throat. When they finally let him stop drinking, everything he swallowed came back up when he dropped to his knees.

A sob broke through, and Carson wanted nothing more than to crumble into dust and blow away. When Lincoln sat and pulled Carson to his chest, he struggled to get free. He deserved to have his life ended as Justin's was. Justin, who loved Carson, forgave him before he even sank his fangs into Justin's neck. Carson could never forgive himself, never.

"Carson, please relax. Your heart is beating so fast. You're going to hurt yourself," Lincoln murmured, trying to hold him still.

Carson pushed at Lincoln's chest to get away. "I killed him! He loved me…. I loved him… and I killed him!" The pain and heartache were loose, and he couldn't handle the hidden emotions bubbling to the surface.

He whimpered as the pain in his head increased, sure his skull would collapse under the pressure.

"Carson, what's wrong?" Lincoln asked, his voice nearing panic. "Carson?"

But Carson refused to answer, even if he could, because if his death had finally arrived, he would welcome that relief with open arms.

LINCOLN FOUGHT to hold Carson until he started to tire. Carson's fight faltered, but he shook relentlessly, holding his head. Things were getting worse. Gods, what was Lincoln thinking, taking advantage of Carson?

Lincoln reached up and hit the call button for help. "Carson, please talk to me, honey. What's wrong?" He cringed at the use of the endearment, which came out too easily.

"My head hurts," Carson whispered.

Lincoln ran his hands over Carson's back in soothing circles. "I called Doc. He'll give you something to help."

"Don't. Want to die." The weak, defeated voice stabbed at Lincoln's self-control. Carson had been through hell twice. Lincoln knew a bit about hell, but this was worse than anything he'd ever been through. He had to save Carson.

"You're not going to die. Everything's going to be okay. I promise." Lincoln rubbed his chin over Carson's head and then placed a kiss in his hair.

Where was Doc? Carson was going to shake out of his skin. With that thought the door opened, and Doc strode into the room. He frowned slightly, seeing Lincoln holding Carson, but Lincoln didn't give a shit.

"It's about time," Lincoln growled.

Doc ignored the comment. "Hey, Carson. What's going on?"

"Head… hurts."

The meek voice was painful to hear.

Doc nodded. "Anything else?"

"Shaky."

Lincoln let out an exaggerated sigh. "Can you just give him something?"

Doc scowled. "Mind if I play doctor for a few minutes?"

Lincoln bit his lip as Doc pulled out his stethoscope and listened to Carson's heart. He examined Carson's eyes, felt around his neck, then his stomach. Without a word, Doc walked to the cart on the opposite wall. Lincoln ran his hands over Carson's shaking body. He'd quit fighting Lincoln and held his shirt in a death grip. Carson felt so right in his arms. A perfect fit. Lincoln was so screwed. He could just hear Max now.

Doc returned with a syringe. He swabbed the port of Carson's IV, pushed the needle in, and pushed the plunger. "That'll help with the pain and the shaking."

Lincoln gave Doc an imploring look, but he turned away and disposed of the syringe.

The shaking subsided. Carson's grip on Lincoln's shirt eased as the drug worked its way through his body.

Carson murmured into Lincoln's chest. "I'm sorry, Justin. Didn't want to do it."

Lincoln rocked him gently. "It's okay, Carson. Just go to sleep. When you wake up, you'll feel better." Lincoln rested his cheek against Carson's head and closed his eyes, breathing deep. A throat clearing brought Lincoln back. He opened his eyes. Carson slumped against him.

"He's asleep," Doc said.

Lincoln gently lowered Carson, then stood and tucked the covers around him. He missed holding Carson, wanted to crawl in next to him, keep him safe from any nightmares that might wake him.

Doc motioned for Lincoln to follow. Reluctantly he trailed behind Doc out into the hallway. Doc ran a hand over his short, bristly hair. He looked every bit of his forty-nine years. He was good at what he did, and the apprehensive look he gave Lincoln unnerved him.

"He's getting worse."

"But why? He looked better when I came in tonight." Doc had to be wrong.

"The latest blood tests say otherwise. I don't know if it's because he's a Tabula Rasa, which I know shit about, along with the rest of the vampire medical community. It could be something organic or—" Doc threw his hands up. "Gods, I've done every test I know and then some. I don't know what's going on. This is beyond going too long without blood and mourning his family."

The frustration was evident. It was rare Doc didn't have an answer. Lincoln remained quiet. He knew what he needed to do, and damn the consequences.

As if reading his thoughts, Doc turned to Lincoln. "You're getting close to him."

It wasn't a question, but Lincoln didn't know what to say to that. He knew what to do. "In the morning I'm heading to the lab to donate, and then I'm going to find who made him…. Find the person who caused all of this." Someone was going to pay.

As he turned to leave, Doc stopped him. "Be careful, Linc."

Lincoln headed down the hallway and muttered, "Little too late for that."

CHAPTER 10

LINCOLN PUSHED open the door to the lab bright and early the next morning. Casey Daley, resident lab technician, danced around the lab table to the music playing through her earbuds. She was oblivious to Lincoln's presence. He leaned against the doorjamb and stuffed his hands into his pockets, grinning. With a twirl, she froze when she spotted Lincoln. She yanked the earbuds out, eyes wide, cheeks reddening.

"Lincoln!" She threw the pencil she held at him. He laughed as it missed its mark. "Quit sneaking up on me." She put her hands on her hips.

Currently Casey had an on-again, off-again relationship with Max. If he were smart, he'd make sure it was permanently on.

"You're the one blasting music in your ears. A bomb could go off, and you wouldn't hear it."

She narrowed her eyes, but then her face softened. "You're here to donate, aren't you?"

Lincoln nodded. He rolled up his sleeve as he walked to the chair and sat. He didn't want to talk about the past and what could happen. He laid his arm on the small table attached to the chair. He raised his chin confidently as Casey pulled on a pair of gloves, then gathered the supplies she needed. Casey had witnessed the results of Lincoln's last donation. She bit on her lower lip, no doubt stopping herself from saying something fruitless. Once Lincoln decided something, he didn't back down. If he wanted to get to know Carson, see if there really was something there, he had to live. Lincoln could give that to him.

Casey swabbed his arm, then wrapped a tourniquet around his biceps. Before she pushed the needle into his skin, she hesitated and gave him a telling sideways glance. Lincoln stared ahead, his face neutral. As the needle penetrated his skin, he couldn't back out now even if he wanted to.

LINCOLN RETURNED to his office, forcing his feet to stay on course and not to return to Carson's room. Doc assured him Carson would sleep for a few more hours. When he woke, Doc would introduce Lincoln's blood into Carson's body.

When Lincoln entered his office, he found Max leaning over the desk, perusing more files.

"Did we get anything else?" Lincoln asked.

He headed to the minifridge and pulled out a bag of synthetic blood. Donating had made him light-headed and hungry. He poured the blood into a mug and drank it cold. The thick sludge coated his tongue and throat, but he sucked it all down. A vein right about then would have fed his hunger better. The feeling of a warm body beneath him, Carson grinding against him, the thrumming of blood through veins, the salty taste of the skin, that resistance before his fangs punched through Carson's skin, the first splash of warm, coppery blood, the orgasm....

"Earth to Linc."

Lincoln sucked in a deep breath. Carson had become the star of all of his erotic thoughts. After what they did last night, he was sure that wouldn't end. He shook his head. "Sorry, what did you say?"

"Well, first I asked how you could drink that shit cold." Max made a sour face.

Lincoln shrugged and put down the empty mug. "Not so bad." Even he didn't believe what he was saying.

"Whatever," Max said with a sigh. That sigh didn't bode well.

"What's up?" Lincoln joined Max at the desk. Files were spread out and sitting in some kind of order only Max understood.

"We received more reports from Gifford PD. First off they have an APB out for Carson for questioning."

Lincoln nodded. "That's expected given they were first on the case. Even if they turned lead over to the NVJ, they don't trust us subhumans to catch anyone. Tell them we have Carson in custody. All parties involved are vampires, so tell them thanks but no thanks to any further help." Lincoln huffed. Most Nons police didn't trust vampires to police their own. Too bad it was federal law; they had to butt out.

Max's eyes darkened. "They have the murder weapon."

Just the hesitation in Max's voice told Lincoln what he needed to know. "And Carson's prints were on it, right?"

Max nodded. "His bloody prints."

Lincoln pursed his lips. Carson didn't do this. He was a wreck over losing his family.

Max walked around the desk and snatched up a sheet of paper. "It's incriminating. But something's off. Carson said he found his mother lying in the doorway between the living room and entry. Forensic reports limit the crime scene to that area. They found a boot print in the blood. I checked the shoes Carson wore when we brought him in. It's not a match."

Lincoln ran his fingers through his stubble. He hadn't bothered to trim in days. "Could be from the brother or uncle."

Max shrugged. "It could be, but as of now, they're on the missing list. APBs are out for them as well."

"You think after this long, they're still alive?" Lincoln couldn't imagine they were.

"I don't know. The possibilities are endless. Say the uncle killed the mother and fled with the brother. Where are they now? Why did they leave Carson behind? Carson couldn't have killed the uncle or brother anywhere else since he never leaves the property. Forensics didn't find anything in the surrounding area or in the two vehicles parked on the property."

"That leads us back to our first theory. Someone killed the mother and took the uncle and brother, but why? You'd think the target would have been Carson. He was on the property, so he wouldn't have been hard to find, and he actually went into the house shortly after the mother was killed. Carson says he was really close to his brother. The uncle has been in the picture since Carson was born. I guess the mother could have argued with the uncle and it got out of hand, but it still doesn't fit. Carson's the key. I know it." Lincoln shook his head. "Maybe the brother and uncle were dead and someone removed the bodies to frame Carson for her murder." Even that didn't fit.

"Did you ask him if he actually saw the uncle and brother dead?"

Lincoln rubbed at the back of his neck. "I can't right now. He's pretty fragile. Doc had to sedate him last night."

Max frowned, seeming to throw accusations at Lincoln with his glare. "But he was fine last night when I left the room. What happened between the time I left and his need to be sedated?"

So much had happened that Lincoln couldn't share. That tangled mess wasn't unraveling anytime soon, and he needed time to think, plan. "His head hurt and got worse pretty fast. Doc doesn't have a clue what's keeping his body from healing. Carson's biggest issue when he came in was his lack of blood, but even the real deal isn't helping anymore. Doc says something in his blood is off."

Max sat in Lincoln's chair, looking every bit as exasperated as Lincoln felt. "We need to find the uncle and brother. Maybe it would help if Carson knew they were still alive. All of this has to be too much for him to handle. Could help turn him around."

Before that would happen, Lincoln's blood would heal Carson. Looking to Max, Lincoln wondered if their friendship would survive his decision? If Max knew Lincoln planned to heal Carson, there would be an argument. Max wouldn't understand. For now the more Lincoln could keep his mind off Carson, the better. Doing his job would accomplish that.

"Get the team together and comb through this info. Dig deeper into the background of friends, family, neighbors, business associates, anyone even remotely connected. Look for anything that might point to where the uncle and brother could be. Someone has seen them if they're out there. No one just disappears. There's always a trail."

Lincoln needed one thing from Max, and he was sure he'd agree.

"Uh-oh. You have 'but' face." Max gave him an innocent, questioning look.

"That's as funny as the one about the last time I laughed." Lincoln tried for a stern look, but why bother? Max never feared Lincoln, even in high school when Lincoln was twice his size.

Max waved his hand. "Yeah, yeah. Save that look for the rookies. Just tell me."

"For now we have to keep Carson out of this."

Max sat forward, elbows on this knees. "You know, I've spent time with Carson. I really like him and don't think he did this, but he might have more info that could help. If we don't continue to question him, the others on the team might start to ask questions."

"I know. I've thought about that, but he just needs more time."

Max chewed on his bottom lip, no doubt weighing the consequences. When he nodded, Lincoln let out the breath he'd been holding in.

"Thanks, Max."

Max rose and rounded the desk. "I'll get the team together." When his hand was on the knob, he stopped for a few breaths, then turned. "I've seen the way you look at Carson and how he looks at you. It's been a long time since I've seen that look in your eyes, Linc. It's none of my business, but it's good to see. Just wanted to let you know that."

Lincoln nodded, then Max left. Lincoln perused the files and papers laid out on this desk. Gods, what a fucked-up situation made even more so by his attraction to Carson. Shit, who was Lincoln trying to kid? It was more than attraction at this point. Max and Doc saw it. If that relationship interfered with his job, he'd have to pull himself from the case, and then he couldn't protect Carson. Lincoln had a larger question to answer. He'd let the team deal with the murders and finding the uncle and brother. Lincoln wanted more information on the kidnapping of Carson and Justin. Possibly the kidnapping and murder were related. What happened to the monsters who forced Carson to essentially kill the first person he ever loved?

"FUCK," LINCOLN said to the air. Two hours of scouring NVJ records and Nons police databases and he hadn't found a single mention of the kidnapping. The only reference to Justin Masters was in records from the high school in Gifford. He transferred in at the beginning of ninth grade, and after tenth, he disappeared.

In more ways than one.

A search of tax records showed Herman Masters owned the land adjacent to the Locke property for over twenty years. Then in 2006 taxes weren't paid. None in the next three years. In 2009 the property was auctioned off for taxes. Carson was sixteen in 2006, the year he claimed the kidnapping occurred. Everyone who would know anything about the kidnapping were either dead or missing… or had their mind erased.

Where was Justin now? Was he even alive? The bite no doubt reduced him into a mindless drone, only retaining the most basic functioning. Beyond that the information about the victims of a Tabula Rasa bite wasn't out there. The last reported bite by a Tabula Rasa was in 1925. The eleven-year-old victim, a girl, was bitten by her younger Tabula Rasa brother. She disappeared soon after the incident, along with her brother and parents. Records for the family after that were nonexistent. What came from the awful incident was the start of the required registration to calm the fears of the Nons. So why wasn't Carson registered?

The questions never stopped.

The door to his office flew open. Tia rushed in, followed by Maggie with her scarlet-red hair. Last month her locks were traffic-cone orange. The officer was anything but dull. In her hand she carried a plastic evidence bag containing a piece of paper. Stopping at the front of the desk, she held it out for Lincoln.

"This was in Carson's pocket. Maybe it's our next lead," Maggie said.

Lincoln reached for the plastic sleeve. Tia stuffed her hands into her pockets and rocked silently. Shit, this was something big if she was silent. Very rarely happened.

Lincoln cringed. Bloody fingerprints covered the edges of the handwritten letter. Lincoln had to push the vision of Carson's bloody hands out of his head. He perused the letter. A quick glance at the bottom showed it was signed by Carmen Locke, Carson's mother. The paper didn't appear to be very old, the edges only slightly worn.

My dearest Carson,

If you are reading this letter, then something has happened to me. I regret having to leave you, but I've done my best to instill in you strength and self-confidence and the ability to care for yourself. You have grown into a brilliant, handsome young man. You, my dear, are incredible. Your inner strength, your ability to live the life you've been given, is nothing short of amazing. Please take care of your brother. Your uncle is a good man and will provide for you both, but I'm afraid he may be unable to give you the nurturing environment you both need.

There is so much you don't know about your origins and your kind. I know you have continually searched for this information, and there may be something I can do to help you discover more. There is a shaman, Jameson Merrick, who predicted your birth as a Tabula Rasa and was present at your birth. He marked you as a Tabula Rasa, but warned us not to register you and keep your existence a secret because you are a very special vampire destined for great things. That's what Jameson told us after your birth. That is why I am not afraid for your future. Show this letter to your uncle. Find Jameson, and he will tell you what you need to know.

Please know that I love you and Caden with all of my heart, and I will always be with you. Both of you are my pride and joy, my greatest gift. I love you both. Mom.

Jameson Merrick? That name sounded familiar.

Tia finally spoke. "Jameson Merrick is a shaman in Sauquoit."

"That's only about ten miles from here. That must be where Carson was heading."

Why didn't he tell Lincoln about the shaman? *Because he's not stupid.*

"Here's his address." Maggie held out a sheet of paper with directions to the residence of Jameson Merrick.

Lincoln took the sheet. Vampire shamans always creeped Lincoln out, with their rituals, spirit walks, and talk about souls and predictions. Didn't matter how Lincoln felt. This was their first lead. Maybe a good lead. The letter raised more questions than it answered. Yet Lincoln couldn't ignore the twisting in his gut.

"You want us to go and talk to him, or bring him in?" Tia asked, ready to jump on the lead.

Lincoln put the paper down. "No. Get me more info on this man before we visit. I want to know everything, including his connection to Carson and his family. I want the upper hand if I can get it."

Had Lincoln heard of Jameson Merrick before and forgotten where? Possibly the gnawing foreboding feeling was unfounded and the shaman harmless. Lincoln wouldn't dismiss his instincts, which had served him too well in the past. When he visited Merrick, he wanted a mountain of facts behind him in case the shaman had a part in what happened to Carson's family. Catching people in their lies was what Lincoln did best.

Tia and Maggie both nodded and left. Lincoln would be the one to speak with Jameson when the time came. Within the hour Doc would use Lincoln's blood and try to heal Carson. Lincoln had to be there. While Doc placed the odds of a reoccurrence of what happened with Luke at astronomical, Lincoln had a premonition Doc was wrong. He would be okay with that. It was the outcome he wanted to be different this time.

CARSON'S EYES couldn't open. He floated in dark, numbing waters, struggling to break free of something, he wasn't sure what. Images assaulted him, battering him in his semiconscious state. Caden… his mother… his uncle. His mother's blood. The knife he pulled from her chest. That awful gurgling sound as she forced herself to speak. Her final breath. The perpetual nightmare snared him and gripped him tight. Through it all those blue eyes appeared repeatedly, yet whenever Carson reached out to Lincoln, he faded away.

He heard the door to his room open and then snick closed several times. Muffled voices floated around him, their words jumbled in his head. A hand touched his leg, the palm rubbing over his bare skin. Warmth rushed through his arm, suffusing his body. Any residual hunger was sated. His body made quick use of whatever source of nourishment coursed through his veins.

Power.

Familiar, comforting.

Lincoln.

What was Lincoln doing to him?

Heat swelled and burned in his core. Outside his sphere of consciousness, something waited, looming in the darkness, bringing with it foreboding of an enormous magnitude. What it was and what it wanted, he didn't want to contemplate. He tried to retreat farther into his mind, find a corner to hide in, but it was as if he were in the middle of a field stripped of vegetation, exposed and in the open. A shudder racked his body as his muscles contracted. The cold air of the room disappeared as soon as it reached his heated skin. His arm throbbed, and he tried to pull away from the source, but whenever he tried to move, he couldn't, as if hands held him down.

In the distance a guttural groan made of pure pain rose. The desolate and mournful sound was just awful. He prayed the person found relief so their wailing would cease. He wanted to cover his ears and block it out, but there was no hiding, no retreating, no hope.

Again he wished to die.

LINCOLN PACED the small confines of the room as his blood ran into Carson's arm. The moment Casey had hooked the bag to Carson's IV, his gut had knotted. So much could still go wrong. The properties of his blood would accelerate Carson's healing, physically and emotionally, but there could be side effects—for both of them.

Carson thrashed on the bed. Sweat beaded on his skin, flushed red, the agitation, the pitiful moaning, all spoke of Lincoln's blood doing what it should, what it shouldn't. Already the bond reached across the room, wrapping tendrils around Lincoln, binding to Carson on a molecular level. Bonded to Carson. He couldn't be upset. Deep down it was what he'd wanted to happen. If Carson weren't suffering, Lincoln's elation from being given a second chance to bond with another would have soared.

Way too soon to be happy. Carson had to accept.

Lincoln spun around as the door to the room flew open. Max rushed in, his eyes wild as he focused on Doc, on Casey, on the bag of blood. When he again turned to Lincoln, he grabbed handfuls of Lincoln's shirt and pushed him hard into the wall.

"What the fuck do you think you're doing?" His voice filled the room. A scowl twisted his face. The pain in his green eyes belied the anger raging on the surface.

Lincoln didn't have an answer, and that seemed to piss Max off more.

"Max, let him go!" Casey yelled, but Max continued to push hard into Lincoln's chest.

"This is a patient's room!" Doc kept his eyes on the monitors showing him Carson's vitals. "Max. Get your ass out!"

Lincoln grasped Max by the forearms, a nonthreatening gesture to calm him, show his sincerity. "I'm sorry. It's already done. I had to save him."

Max pushed away, pacing in a circle. "How could you do this? I know you feel something for Carson, but what about the mess with Luke when you healed him? Fuck, that nearly killed you. What if this goes wrong? I can't… I can't lose you this time."

Lincoln hated that he had to explain himself and wouldn't have bothered if it were anyone other than Max. "I couldn't save him only to let him die."

Max raised his chin defiantly. "I told you to be careful."

"Shit, Max. This isn't about being careful. He was dying. What kind of a person would I be if I just stood by and let it happen?"

If looks could kill, Lincoln would be a pile of dust. Fuck him and his big mouth.

"Yeah, but that didn't stop you from letting Grace die."

Before Lincoln could reply, Max was gone, the door slamming behind him. Casey looked to the door, then Lincoln. "Who's Grace?"

Lincoln rubbed his hand over his face. He wasn't going there. "That's up to Max to tell."

Lincoln forced Max's reaction from his mind. This was about Carson. He went to the side of the bed. Casey stepped back and let him pass. Doc continued to monitor a dozen machines that all measured the success of Carson's healing. Lincoln clenched his teeth, seeing Carson writhing in pain, his body going through the healing process. Lincoln yearned to run his hand over Carson's forehead, soothe whatever torment he experienced. He clenched his hands at his sides, choosing not to share the nature of his relationship with Casey and Doc, which was ridiculous.

Carson's color improved. The blue veins once highly visible beneath his skin disappeared. The gaunt appearance of his face lessened. While he appeared to be improving, something wasn't right. Lincoln could feel Carson's body fighting something in the blood. Lincoln took in a shaky breath. Luke's healing hadn't been as tumultuous. His body had been more accepting. This… this was almost like rejection.

Doc's mouth was pinched, his brow furrowed, his expression one of confusion and concern.

Shit.

"What's happening, Doc? This isn't right." Panic wrapped steely fingers around Lincoln's chest and threatened to take over.

Doc shook his head, surveying the readings of the machines. "His body is responding to the blood and healing, but…." Doc studied the paper flowing from the EEG machine. "His brain waves are contradicting one another. The delta waves show he's in a deep sleep, where he needs to be to heal. But… his gamma waves are nearly off the charts. Considering the level of the delta waves, the gamma waves shouldn't be this high. Levels this high are associated with learning, memory processing, higher activity. It's almost impossible."

Carson's agitation only increased as the moaning returned. "Fuck it." Lincoln's need to comfort Carson overruled keeping his hands off.

He laid his palm over Carson's forehead. His skin was sweaty, clammy, and burning hot all at once. On the monitor his temperature reading hit 105 degrees. Lincoln was about to say something when Carson's body went completely still. His chest quit moving.

He wasn't breathing.

Alarms went off. Doc yelled to Casey to get a crash cart. Doc pushed a red button on the wall. A nurse rushed into the room seconds later. Chaos ensued. Lincoln froze. His hand remained on Carson's forehead. An unbelievably icy loss flooded his veins. The bond faltered, leaving a vacuous hole in Lincoln's chest. Blood rushed from his head, leaving behind a cold unreality.

This can't be happening.

Bonded, only to have his bond mate die before his eyes. He shook his head as Doc ripped the bandage off that covered the cut Dennison carved into Carson. What had been a raised, red line had faded, barely visible. Healed. Then why wasn't he breathing?

Doc pushed the paddles against Carson's chest, ready to shock his dead heart. Just as he called out, "Clear," Carson's eyes popped open in a wide, unseeing gaze, his pupils dilated. They all jumped back. Carson sucked in air, filling his chest to capacity and then exhaling. Another breath, and then another. The machines continued to beep out their warnings. The EEG spit out paper covered with jagged, scribbled peaks. His heart rate was over two hundred beats per minute. He was going to have a heart attack or stroke out.

Doc turned Carson's head to face him. Shining his penlight in his eyes, he shouted, "Carson? Can you hear me? Carson." Not even a blink. "Ten milligrams lorazepam, stat!"

The nurse scrambled to prep a syringe, then pushed the medication into the IV. Thirty seconds and nothing changed. "Another ten milligrams."

Lincoln's fear squeezed its icy hands around his throat. He was suffocating. He was going to lose Carson, and he couldn't do anything. A helplessness he hadn't experienced in a lifetime claimed him. "Doc, do something! He's going to die."

Doc gave Lincoln a sideways glance. "What the fuck does it look like I'm doing?"

The door flew open. Max rushed in, eyes wide. "What the hell's going on? Alarms are going off all over the building!"

Max's eyes widened more, and he gasped, seeing Carson struggling to live. Lincoln was sure his own face displayed pure terror. He tried to say something... anything... to Max, tried to move, but he couldn't.

Carson turned, his eyes focused and aware, fixed on Lincoln. Carson's chest continued to heave. His exaggerated breaths were barely audible over the alarms.

"Carson! Can you hear me?" Lincoln needed him to answer. "Please!"

A perplexed look crossed Carson's face, his eyebrows furrowed, and then his eyes widened.

A scream unlike anything Lincoln had ever heard erupted from Carson's mouth. Everyone clamped their hands over their ears. Carson's body convulsed, his screams unyielding. He flopped so hard Lincoln feared he'd bounce off the bed.

Lincoln and Max held him down as Doc tried to push a needle into the IV port. Giving up, he stuffed the needle straight into the tubing. Carson's strength was amazing. And Lincoln couldn't keep him from coming off the bed with each convulsion.

"Let go of him! Get back!" Doc took a step back.

Max grabbed Lincoln and yanked him away from the bed as Carson's endless screams tormented every cell in Lincoln's body. Carson's skin turned scarlet red, mimicking a severe sunburn. The veins in his neck and arms popped out. Machines went haywire and many stopped working altogether.

An overwhelming need ran over Lincoln's skin, through his muscles, winding its way into his organs. Against the odds the bond had formed, except Carson's reaction was wrong. Something was tearing Carson apart inside. Tears stung Lincoln's eyes as Max held him with an arm wrapped around Lincoln's chest.

"I have to go to him, Max. I think he's dying." He didn't struggle to get away. "It's killing him. This is all my fault."

Every wide eye in the room was on Carson, none of them able to do anything but stare, even Doc. Carson's relentless screaming tore chunks from Lincoln's heart. He'd done this to Carson.

"What the hell is that?" Casey pointed to Carson.

Along Carson's torso and arms, black marks surfaced on his skin. Gasps filled the room as foreign words and symbols solidified like tattoos. Carson's body stilled. His chest rose and fell in a steady rhythm. The red covering his skin faded. His muscles, which moments ago were rigid, relaxed. He appeared to be sleeping. Lincoln's ears still rang with the phantom noise of that gods-awful screaming. He'd never forget that sound.

The indecipherable words and symbols decorating Carson's skin once again brought silence to the room. Lincoln couldn't look away. It was unlike anything he'd ever seen before. Had his blood caused that, whatever *that* was?

The door flew open and Wright and Dennison rushed in.

"What the hell's going on? We were locked out of the building, then heard the alarms." Wright stopped short upon seeing Carson. "Oh my gods. What the hell is that?"

Dennison approached the bed. "Well, that's interesting."

Max dropped his arm from around Lincoln's chest. Even though he was free to move, Lincoln remained where he stood. He recalled Dennison was supposed to be on suspension, but couldn't have cared less at the moment.

Doc rushed to the bed. "Get me some new machines in here. I want a full workup and a CAT scan and an MRI. And get me a shaman, 'cause I have no clue what this shit is."

That got the nurse moving out the door.

"What language is that?" Max stepped tentatively closer to the bed.

Lincoln shook his head. Conversation ensued around him, but he blocked them out. He moved forward, the pull to be close to Carson too great to give him any other choice. *Bonded.* For the second time. He neared the bed and reached to touch Carson's newly tattooed skin. Already he knew how the touch would feel electrified. Yet as his fingertips touched Carson's skin, the foreign script glowed a fiery red with the illusion of hovering above Carson's skin, as if in 3-D.

Lincoln snatched his hand away, and the writing faded to black.

"What the fuck did you do?" Dennison's accusatory tone wasn't anything Lincoln needed right then.

Lincoln looked around the room and was confronted with looks of suspicion. "Nothing. I-I just touched him."

"You're bonded, aren't you?" Casey asked with an exasperated sigh.

Max moved to the foot of the bed. "Even if they are, this—" He waved a hand at Carson. "This doesn't have anything to do with bonding."

Dennison pointed at Lincoln. "Are you fucking crazy? You bonded with him! A fucking Tabula Rasa. Wasn't the chaos you caused last time enough? What happens when he rejects you and you lose it—again?"

"I didn't think that this would happen again." The lie passed over his lips easily. He tried to move around Max to get to Dennison. Max pushed Lincoln back to keep him separated from Dennison. "Doc said it wouldn't."

"I said the odds were astronomically low that it would happen again. Not that it *couldn't*. You're all missing the important shit here. Bonding is the least of our worries."

"You're a fucking idiot!" Dennison yelled.

Lincoln charged him. "Get the fuck out of here! You're supposed to be on suspension!" He was going to kill Dennison with his bare hands.

Wright grabbed Dennison's arm and yanked him toward the door. "John, stop! Come with me and cool down." John jerked his arm from her grip and lunged at Lincoln. Wright stepped in front of him, trying to hold back what amounted to a raging bull.

Lincoln struggled against Max when someone said his name.

"Lincoln? What's going on?"

Carson stared at Lincoln, who didn't think this could get any weirder. "Holy shit," Lincoln muttered.

Carson's irises had turned blood red.

CHAPTER 11

CARSON HATED how everyone stared at him. He pushed back against the headboard. Last thing he remembered was being in Lincoln's arms, feeling as if he were dying, and now…. Why were they all looking at him?

"Lincoln?" Carson tried to cover the panic in his voice but failed. Lincoln looked shell-shocked, not moving, possibly not breathing. "You're kind of freaking me out." The nervous chuckle did little to change Lincoln's expression.

As he waited for Lincoln to say anything, something materialized between them, like a connection. Carson gasped as the pull intensified and tugged at him to move toward Lincoln.

Doc approached the bed as if Carson were a rabid animal. "Hey, Carson? How do you feel?"

Carson ignored him, instead focusing on Lincoln. Why wasn't he speaking or moving? Was this regret for what they'd done? Must be, and he didn't want Carson to expect anything more. Well, fuck him. Carson didn't need him… but he did. He ached inside to touch Lincoln. The flare of heat and desire and need was undeniable.

But Lincoln didn't want him.

Carson felt Doc place his stethoscope on his chest. The cold against his heated skin caused Carson to suck in a deep breath, drawing his attention to his chest.

"What the fuck?" Carson scooted back on the bed, pushing up against the wall. Black writing and symbols covered his chest, his stomach, and his arms.

"Carson, calm down. You're okay," Doc said, but Carson wasn't buying it. Someone wrote all over him while he was sleeping!

"Fucking calm down? You calm down! Who wrote this shit all over me?" Carson looked to Lincoln again, certain their shocked expressions mirrored one another. "Say something!"

Lincoln flinched, knocking him out of his daze. Approaching the bed, his tentative movements caused Carson to snort. What was Lincoln so afraid of? Could be the weird-ass fucking writing, or….

"Everything's okay." Lincoln didn't look as if he believed a word of that. Why should Carson?

"What's okay?" That fallacy seized his chest with panic, pushing the air from his lungs.

"No, it's not." Dennison's voice shook. "He's got some funky-ass writing popped out all over him, and his eyes are fucking red!"

Carson lifted his hands to his eyes as the air whooshed out of him. "My eyes…."

"Fucking hell, Dennison! Get your ass out of here!" Max pushed Dennison from the room.

"Casey, can I get two milligrams of lorazepam?" Doc pulled out his penlight.

Practically catatonic as she stared at Carson, she nodded slowly and moved to the cart.

"No! No more drugs!" Carson looked to Lincoln, and his skin crawled with the need to touch Lincoln, to…. "Lincoln, please… I need you to…." Shit, he didn't know.

Carson pulled his knees to his chest and wrapped his arms around his legs. In about two seconds, he was going to lose it. Inside, something foreign battled at the core of his being, something trying to emerge. Carson squeezed his eyes shut, concentrating on forcing whatever wanted to surface to remain hidden and unknown.

A voice chanted, "No… no… no… no…." The words were coming from him.

"Carson?"

Lincoln leaned over the side of the bed, his close proximity calming Carson. He pulled his arms tighter around his legs to prevent himself from jumping on Lincoln. It was as if every cell in his body needed Lincoln, cried out with desperation for his body, his touch… his soul. *I'm cracking up.*

"Hey."

Carson shivered from that deep voice and closed his eyes.

"Don't touch him."

Carson's eyes popped open at the command. Lincoln's hand hovered over his arm, but his attention was on the entrance to the room.

An older man dressed in a colorful serape with salt-and-pepper hair and a long braid draped over his shoulder stood in the doorway. Beads flowed from the hair that wasn't caught up in his braid. Strands of colorful beads adorned his neck. Tattoos crawled up from under the serape, hinting at a larger design below. His skin was dark bronze, possibly indicating Native American descent or too much sun. Carson couldn't be sure. What made Carson's jaw drop and his eyes widen was the colorful aura surrounding the man, like a rainbow fog.

Lincoln reacted quickly. He moved his hand to his back and, in a move Carson almost missed, had a gun trained on the strange man. "Who the *fuck* are you, and how did you get in here?"

The man smiled—smiled with a gun trained at his head. Carson's world was quickly spiraling out into a parallel universe.

Lincoln stepped closer.

"Lincoln, put your gun away, son," the man said.

Lincoln blinked. He looked confused and then scowled. "I asked, who the fuck are you?"

The man stepped toward the bed, his focus now on Carson. Looking into the gray-blue eyes, Carson recognized something ancient, something powerful, something beyond anything he'd experienced before. He pushed farther back against the wall.

"Freeze! Stay away from him!"

The commanding tone in Lincoln's voice stopped the man's forward movement. Doc moved closer to Carson in a somewhat protective gesture. He wasn't sure what protection was needed. This diminutive man looked like a stiff wind could blow him away.

"I assure you I'm not here to hurt Carson." Shit, he knew Carson's name too. "I'm Jameson Merrick."

The self-satisfied grin on the man's face was a bit.... Wait... Jameson? *Find Jameson.*

"M-my mom said to find you," Carson whispered, an unexpected wave of fear and excitement crashing into him.

"How did you know he was here? And how in the hell did you get in here?" Lincoln asked, leading Carson to believe people couldn't just walk into the building.

The rising tension in the room kicked into overdrive. The hairs on Carson's body stood on end.

"I'm very sorry about your mother, Carson."

"That's enough!" Lincoln's voice echoed through the room.

The door was pushed open, and an army of agents swarmed in with their weapons drawn, led by Max.

"Lincoln, he just walked in. Opened locked doors as if they weren't locked and somehow disabled the alarms," Max said, the fear apparent in his eyes despite his stony, all-business exterior.

"You care to explain that, Mr. Merrick?" Lincoln's jaw ticked, but other than that movement, he was still.

"Gentlemen, ladies. Please lower your weapons. They'll have no effect on me. I am a Manashan shaman." A few gasps filled the room. "The powers I possess are unfathomable."

Carson looked to Lincoln for his reaction, but his face held that expressionless mask.

"I knew where to find young Carson here because I predicted this day would come, just as I predicted his birth." Jameson stepped around the bed, to stand opposite of where Lincoln stood.

Every gun in the room followed his movements. Carson hated guns, but if they stopped this lunatic, he was all for them. Doc moved closer to Carson.

Jameson looked to Doc. "Don't worry, Simon. I won't hurt Carson. I knew this would happen, and it's marvelous."

Carson frowned. "Marvelous for who, buddy? You aren't the one sporting some weird-ass tattoos and red fucking eyes!" Were they totally red, or just the irises? And why?

Jameson reached out, about to touch Carson's hand, when a loud growl echoed through the room. Lincoln's expression seemed to dare Jameson to touch Carson, who knew the result wouldn't be pretty.

Jameson stopped short of touching Carson. He cocked his head and raised his hands palms up, one toward Carson and the other toward Lincoln. He closed his eyes. A humming tone rose from his throat.

He opened his eyes and dropped his hands. "That's one of the strongest bonds I've ever encountered. Not surprising given that your blood has evolved Carson into what he is now."

Carson sucked in a breath. Lincoln's face paled from the words. Lincoln did this to Carson?

"And what is he?" Doc asked, assessing Carson with a critical eye.

"A phenomenon created from the union of two of the most powerful kinds of vampires to exist. There's no definition for his power and abilities. What you see here is more than a new kind of vampire. Carson is a savior, straight from the Great Spirit. His purpose is to unite the vampire world."

Carson sucked in as much air as he could while the room spun around him. This wasn't happening. He'd always believed his life couldn't get much worse, and then Justin happened and his family was killed, and now....

His vision grayed at the sides. He bent over, his mind bobbing in a sea of fear because this was all too much to handle.

LINCOLN PACED the observation room located outside of Interrogation Room B. Max leaned against the wall, watching Lincoln pace. Through the one-way glass, Lincoln caught glimpses of Jameson sitting at the table, a relaxed, joyful expression on his face. His eyes were closed, and he appeared to be meditating or something.

This was one fucked-up mess. Nothing made sense. Carson had apparently changed into something never seen before in vampire history. Jameson claimed he predicted the event, and that's why he showed up. The note left by Carson's mother told Carson Jameson knew what he was. Lincoln wasn't buying Jameson predicted this would occur. No. Something strange occurred when Lincoln's blood mixed with Carson's. Strange, but not an ancient prophecy.

Lincoln punched the wall. He let the pain race through his system, pumping the adrenaline he needed to confront Jameson.

Tia Warez, a member of Lincoln's team, entered the room. "You called, boss?"

"Max and I are going to interview Jameson Merrick. He's a suspect in the murder of Carson Locke's mother. He's also a shaman. Keep an eye on him. If he pulls anything and tries to escape, shoot him."

Tia's deep-brown eyes lightened. "Seriously?"

"Seriously. Let's go, Max."

He stepped into the interrogation room followed by Max.

Jameson's eyes popped open. He retained that relaxed and peaceful demeanor that made Lincoln itch to punch him. Or maybe it was because his claims messed with Carson. Lincoln sat across from Jameson. Max dropped a folder he'd been carrying onto the table. He went to the video camera set up in the corner and pressed record.

"This meeting will be recorded on video, Mr. Merrick. Do you have any objections?" Lincoln asked as Max sat next to him.

"Am I under arrest by the NVJ, Lincoln?"

"You may call me Commander Samuels, and this is Lieutenant Kincaid. For now you aren't under arrest. You're being questioned in a murder investigation."

Jameson continued his creepy calm demeanor. "Just like the Nons police. How wonderful."

A miracle would occur right in that room if Lincoln didn't beat the man before the end of questioning. If Jameson had any hand in what happened to Carson, Lincoln would.

He opened the folder. He pulled out the crime scene photos and laid them before Jameson. "Carmen Locke. Stabbed a total of fourteen times."

A slight cringe and then Jameson was back to his original irritatingly bright expression. "Tragic. A lovely woman. Carmen loved that boy."

"You knew Carmen Locke?" Lincoln wanted to know what else he knew.

"Of course I did. I predicted Carson would be a Tabula Rasa at birth, just as I predicted the event that came to pass today."

"What do you mean predicted?" Max asked.

Jameson ran his braid repeatedly through his hands. "I have the gift of foresight. Future events of great magnitude don't just occur. They take great amounts of power and energy built up over time. Nothing just happens by the snap of a finger. Every event must be arranged and built upon, actions and thoughts, elements of nature. That building of power and energy can be felt by certain people, but you must have the ability to interpret that energy, the intentions, the location, when that energy and power will unfold. Wars, murders, catastrophic events of nature. To obtain these goals, the buildup starts months or years"—he leaned forward—"or millennia before the actual event. Carson's transformation started hundreds of years before his birth, set in motion in the far reaches of the world."

Jameson's irises were a mesmerizing mixture of colors unlike anything Lincoln had ever seen. His stare didn't waver. Lincoln swore he felt something physical, like a nudge. Had it come from Jameson? He snorted at his foolish thought and held his ground.

"You're a Sanatore vampire. Rare in your own right. I'm surprised you gave your blood to heal Carson after what happened the last time."

Lincoln ground his teeth and growled. How did Jameson know about Luke?

"You Sanatore are a touchy lot when you're bonded. You're a statistical anomaly, Commander Samuels. Bonded twice in one lifetime. Unheard of since bonds are rarely ever broken." Jameson cocked his head. "Exactly why was your first bond broken?"

Lincoln slammed his fist on the table. "None of your fucking business!" The interrogation was running away from him. *Get back on track.* "Where were you on October eighth? Can anyone account for your whereabouts on that day?"

Jameson smoothed his hand over his Technicolor serape. The shaman was so peculiar. "No. I was on a three-day retreat in the Adirondack Mountains. I don't have anyone who could corroborate that. I do, however, have toll and gas receipts."

Max scribbled on the pad. "Where in the Adirondacks?"

"Near Blue Mountain Lake. There's a wide nexus of energy in the area. I spent three days in meditation."

Lincoln stood as the incredible pull to Carson crawled under his skin. He couldn't focus. Luckily Max stepped in. "You said you knew Mrs. Locke. When did you meet?"

"I contacted her when I received the prediction of Carson's birth."

Lincoln huffed. He believed in predictions as much as he believed in the Easter Bunny. Regaining control, he circled behind Jameson. Lincoln smirked, seeing the unease that caused the shaman. "What was your role in his birth?"

"I was present at the birth. I examined the baby, and he was indeed a Tabula Rasa. I tattooed him, as is the customary rite. I also schooled the family on living with such a dangerous vampire."

"Did you know the uncle?" Lincoln continued pacing as the ache to return to his bond mate painstakingly wormed its way through his body.

Jameson shook his head. "No. He came into the picture after I was personally involved."

"Do you know where the uncle and the brother are?"

Jameson blinked. His peaceful demeanor morphed into an expression of puzzlement. "You don't?"

Lincoln reiterated through gritted teeth, "Do you know where the uncle and brother are?"

"No."

Lincoln looked sideways at Max, wanting to ask about Justin and their kidnapping, the bite. No one beyond the room could know Carson's secret. Whether or not he was coerced, he'd be elevated from prized possession to public enemy number one. People persecuted out of fear. Even Lincoln had a healthy awareness of Carson's abilities.

He had to know and would have to trust Max to keep quiet. Lincoln went to the video camera and pushed stop. Max raised an eyebrow but remained silent.

Returning, Lincoln leaned on the table, his hands resting on the edge. Pain from the sharp edge helped clear his head. "What do you know about Carson's kidnapping?"

Max sat forward.

The twitch in Jameson's eyes said he knew something. He shifted in his chair, his first hint of discomfort during the interrogation. "How did you know about that? There's no record of the incident."

"And why is that? Why is there no record of the kidnapping of a Tabula Rasa and the human he bit?"

Max sucked in air and abandoned his professional neutrality. "Carson bit someone?"

Lincoln watched Jameson for any sign of deception.

"Because Carson *bit* someone." Jameson looked to Max. "Was coerced to bite, actually. If that had become public knowledge, Carson would have been destroyed."

A shudder ran down Lincoln's spine. If he had, he never would have met Carson, never bonded with him. Already the coupling felt natural and right.

Jameson lifted his chin. "Tell me, will this bonding go the way of the last? I was only privy to the aftermath. You're a cunning and dangerous man, from what I hear, Commander Samuels."

Lincoln straightened and crossed his arms as a reminder to keep his hands to himself. Wouldn't do them any good if he hurt their only suspect. He wasn't falling for Jameson's attempt to distract him with the past. Max eyed Lincoln critically, no doubt recalling the entire epic failure of his bonding with Luke. Max was the one who saved Lincoln. He owed Max his life.

"Just know this, Commander. If this bonding fails, you're not just dealing with another vampire. Carson is more powerful and dangerous than anything you've ever seen or experienced. You may have been the one to lose control after your failed bonding, but if Carson does, not only will you pay, but the world as well." Jameson sat back, a little too smug in his predictions.

Before Lincoln could question him, there was a frantic knocking on the door. Lincoln nodded to Max, who rose and opened the door. Casey hurried in, eyes wide and chest heaving as if she'd sprinted a mile.

"Lincoln, you have to come now. Carson needs you!"

"What's—"

Sweet little Casey pointed at Lincoln and scowled. "Just get your ass to his room now!"

Shit! Lincoln pushed past her. "Warez, lock this door and don't let him leave. Shoot him if he tries."

"10-4."

Lincoln sprinted to Carson, turning corners, narrowly missing unsuspecting hallway pedestrians. Footsteps pounded behind him as Max and Casey followed. As Lincoln neared Carson's room, he heard the screaming.

"I want Lincoln! Lincoln! Get the fuck away from me!"

Max rushed into Carson's room. Before Lincoln could enter, a hand snagged his arm. Lincoln growled and yanked away, ready to ream the fucker out.

He found Jameson behind him. "You didn't complete the bonding yet?"

Casey gasped, seeing Jameson, and backed against the wall.

"What the fuck? You were locked in the interrogation room!"

"Yes, locks and guards." Jameson chuckled and shook his head. "Don't worry. Your officer is unharmed. She's merely napping. Now answer my question."

"Casey, get someone here now to lock him up." Casey nodded and raced down the hall.

Lincoln wasn't answering anything the freaky shaman asked. Again Jameson grabbed his arm and stopped him going to Carson. His screams continued to penetrate the door and tried to suffocate Lincoln.

"Commander, you may think I'm your enemy here. I'm not. But what I am is the best resource for bonding you have at the moment."

A loud crash echoed into the hall, startling Lincoln. *Jesus.* Doc yelled for Lincoln.

"You didn't complete the bonding yet, did you?" Jameson asked with exasperation.

"We have at least forty-eight hours. And besides that, it happened just before you popped in."

Jameson shook his head. "Carson isn't just a vampire anymore. His need to complete the bonding is on a level even you've never experienced. He's going to be strong, and if you go in there, he's going to get what he needs."

That pretty much boiled down to Lincoln was going to get fucked into next week.

CHAPTER 12

LINCOLN CONTEMPLATED his options as Max stepped out of the room, closing the door behind him. "They're barely able to hold him down. He's beyond strong." Upon seeing Jameson, Max frowned. "What the hell's he doing here?"

"Apparently he can walk through fucking walls."

Max opened his mouth, but Lincoln spoke first. "I'm going in."

"Wait." Lincoln glared at Max. "Linc, you can't go in there. He's going to tear you apart." The concern on Max's face was appreciated, but this was happening to Carson because of Lincoln's decision. He had to step up. He didn't think Carson would hurt him—hopefully.

"We don't have much of a choice," Casey said, returning with Dennison of all people. "Doc has given him enough sedative to knock out an elephant, and it's not working."

Dennison stepped up behind Jameson, who voluntarily put his arms behind his back, allowing himself to be cuffed. Lincoln snorted, thinking that would last for about five seconds.

"Lincoln!"

Another crash and Doc ran from the room, a small cut dripping blood across his forehead. Casey rushed over and placed her sleeve over the cut. Doc shook her off. "I've got six guys in there, and they can barely contain him."

"Put him down before he kills someone," Dennison said as he led Jameson away. Lincoln turned to lunge at Dennison, but Max and Doc held him back. Why was he still there? He suspended the asshole.

"Focus on Carson," Max said. "He's just going to get worse. We have two choices. Either you go in there or we do put him down."

Lincoln shoved Max back as the fear of losing Carson took over. "No one touches him!"

He pushed past Doc and entered the room. Six officers worked to hold Carson on the bed, but he continually freed his arms and legs. They were going to hurt him.

"Carson!" Lincoln barked.

Immediately his struggle stopped. Carson focused on Lincoln. The black of his pupils ate up the red of his irises. Shit, he was pretty far gone with the need to bond. Carson's chest heaved as he licked his lips. The tangibility of Carson's lust and desire pulsed within the room. Lincoln's cock filled instantly. His breaths increased. He scented the bonding pheromone, and his focus narrowed to Carson.

Lincoln growled low in his throat at the men touching what was his. Hearing the sound, Carson leapt up, breaking free of the men. One moment Carson stood on the bed, the next he practically flew through the air at Lincoln and knocked him to the ground.

"Get out!" Lincoln roared.

The men scrambled out the door, and it slammed shut. With one rip, the front of Lincoln's shirt was gone.

"Lincoln." A low, throaty moan came from Carson as he reached for Lincoln's belt.

"Carson, I know the need is strong…."

Carson destroyed Lincoln's belt and then popped the button and separated the zipper, continuing to rip Lincoln's pants apart until his entire groin was exposed.

"Need you so bad. Can't take it anymore. It hurts." Carson panted.

Their union wouldn't be about sharing or tenderness. Carson was claiming Lincoln. Once the bond was completed, their energy entwined, dependent on one another, the bond unbreakable, unless….

Carson nipped at his neck. Every touch flamed across Lincoln's skin, heated and expanding. His cock had never been so hard. He writhed beneath Carson, who ground his erection into Lincoln's groin in a steady rhythm. Pants and whimpers and groans competed with the thrumming rush of blood in Lincoln's ears.

Lincoln ran his hands over Carson's smooth skin. He reached up and pulled the tie on the hospital gown. Carson humped harder. The friction was agonizing and wonderful. Carson latched his teeth on to Lincoln's nipple. He cried out, arching his back, almost bucking Carson off. An almost feral sound came from deep in Carson's chest. The pain in his nipple and the pleasure in his groin mixed in a swirling mass of sensations, overloading his neural pathways, shorting out his ability to think.

Carson pushed himself up onto his knees, scooted down, then ripped Lincoln's underwear and pants down his leg. Lincoln's shaft slapped against this stomach. He wanted to stroke himself, desperate for any kind of relief. When Carson knelt beside him, Lincoln thought maybe....

Carson pushed his hands under Lincoln's shoulder and hip. In one motion Lincoln was flipped onto his stomach. He gasped as the cold floor pressed against his cock. His thighs were kicked apart. When Carson slid his tongue over Lincoln's hole, he yelped. Carson circled his hole with his tongue, teasing, then finally pushing in, ripping a moan from him. Relentlessly, without remorse or control, Carson made love to Lincoln using his mouth and tongue.

"Oh gods," Lincoln groaned, raising his ass as Carson worked him open.

Lincoln lowered his shoulders to the floor and stroked his shaft. Shocks sparked in his groin as he pulled from root to top. Precum leaked, coating his fingers. Drops fell in long strings that reached the floor. Carson dug his fingers into Lincoln's flesh. The action would leave bruises. So hot. Lincoln had never been so turned on.

He needed to be fucked.

A terrifying thought given he'd never been penetrated by a cock before. But Lincoln *needed* Carson to sink into him. Now.

The air crackled around them. Vibrations filled every cell in Lincoln's body, ready to burst. Carson's sweet, probing tongue, Lincoln's hand on his cock, stroking and pulling, the energy combined from their wanton bodies, a blanket of electricity covering their skin, pushed Lincoln to the edges of ecstasy. Black pushed into the edges of vision.

Carson pulled away. The cold air caused Lincoln to shiver. Lincoln only felt the head of Carson's cock against his hole for a second before it was buried balls deep in his ass. He stiffened, opening his mouth in a breathless cry. Burning pain shot through his ass. Tears stung his eyes. Air escaped his lungs, and he panted as the initial pain subsided. Still fucking hurt.

Carson started with quick, sharp thrusts. Lincoln moaned, never having felt so full. His hole stretched wide around Carson's shaft. Carson shifted his hips higher, pushing down into Lincoln.

Stars burst in Lincoln's field of vision. Pleasure blossomed, mixing with the pain, expanding into his groin and balls. Blissful. Immense. Mind shattering. Amazing. No slow build, no caresses, no kisses, no connection. Hollow and utilitarian.

Kind of like all of those one-night stands.

The difference? Lincoln's heart belonged to Carson. And he knew that would lead to love.

Carson lay on Lincoln's back and wrapped his arms around Lincoln's chest. Panic sent a shudder through Lincoln as Carson brushed his mouth against his ear. *Tabula Rasa.* What if Carson lost control and bit Lincoln? Helplessly pinned beneath Carson, Lincoln wouldn't stand a chance.

One well-placed thrust and Lincoln's thoughts dissolved, leaving the growing ball of pleasure in his cock and balls. His grunts filled the air. Carson's breathy moans spiked Lincoln's arousal. He forgot the threat of a bite, forgot the fact he was being fucked for the first time, forgot his blood had changed Carson into… something. His limbs were weightless, his mind spinning. His vision turned white as his orgasm built.

"I… I can't… I…."

"Come on, baby." Carson increased his pounding, then rubbed his cheek against Lincoln's in an overtly intimate gesture.

"C-Carson," he gasped out with a ragged breath.

Erratic thrusts, harsh breaths, and Carson tightening his arms around his chest told Lincoln that Carson was close. The thought that his bond mate's seed would soon solidify their bond tightened Lincoln's throat and stung his eyes. He spiraled until a painful spasm clenched his balls. His chest constricted, his stomach muscles seized. Blood rushed to his head. The need to come was immense. Growing, tingling, expanding until he screamed. Cum exploded from his cock, pulsing shot after shot. His hole spasmed around Carson's cock. Lincoln's body vibrated and shuddered, suspending him within a mass of firing neurons.

One last thrust and Carson shoved deep into Lincoln. A strangled cry from Carson and then his shaft pulsed against Lincoln's hole over and over. A never-ending orgasm triggered aftershocks in Lincoln. Cum ran out of Lincoln's ass and down his legs. Perfectly sated, Lincoln let his eyelids flutter shut. He collapsed under Carson's weight.

Carson covered Lincoln's body with his, nuzzling his neck. Lincoln laid his head on his folded arms. The hard institutional floor cooled his front while Carson's heat caused his back to sweat even more. He closed his eyes. *Just for a minute.* He wanted to suggest the bed, but his mind had disconnected from his body and they no longer communicated.

He drifted into the hazy outskirts of sleep, his normal state of internal chaos calm. *Bonded.* He thought of Luke and the fiasco of their bond. That was a Sanatore bond between two vampires, but with Carson.... What Carson was, even Jameson didn't know. What if Carson rejected the bond as Luke did?

As Lincoln fell deeper into sleep, he knew if Carson rejected him, they'd have to put him down. Already the strength of the bond far surpassed anything he had with Luke. He went half-mad when Luke rejected him. The pull with Carson drew on Lincoln's very essence, on his soul. If Carson rejected him, Lincoln's officers would have no choice but to lock him away.

CARSON RUBBED circles over the hard plane of Lincoln's stomach. Carson kept his initial terror of being unable to wake Lincoln at bay, shifting his focus to the gentle rise and fall of Lincoln's chest. Two hours after their bonding, and he still hadn't woken. Doc said that was normal. And that's *all* he said. Normal.

Nothing about that shit show was normal. Carson had so many questions and no one to answer them.

First question: what had caused his trip to Dominationville with a layover in Psychoville? He still couldn't process the magnitude of the drive that took over with a single pinpoint of need.

Lincoln.

Carson's cock had never been so hard. He had never wanted to fuck anyone so badly, as if his life depended on it. The only option for relief was to fuck Lincoln, or Carson would have hurt someone.... Everyone.

Vivid, visceral memories of their copulation haunted him. Was he even human in that state? Desire magnified times a thousand crowded out his humanity. Primal. Feral. Did male animals feel that drive when scenting a female in heat? And Carson fucked Lincoln—large, muscular, commanding, alpha Lincoln. Had he ever had a cock up his ass? Had Carson raped him? His list of crimes was growing exponentially.

What did it all mean? Carson last remembered sitting on the desk, head thrown back as Lincoln sucked him off and blew his mind. But that didn't even touch the energy, the raw power that passed between them. Colossal, enormous, massive…. An event of cosmic proportions. Not just a joining of two rare vampires. A bond that tethered Carson and Lincoln together by invisible strands. His blood, meant to heal Carson, triggered some latent… thing within him. Even now he could feel whatever *it* was lying dormant, waiting…. But waiting for what? Some other freaky event to yank it to the surface? That flipped his panic switch on. He swallowed down hard on those fears. Any more freak-outs and Doc would have him on a Thorazine drip.

Lincoln stirred in his sleep, but his breathing stayed steady and even, his expression peaceful and calm. Much different than the twisted, pained contortion of his face when he first stepped into Carson's room. Guilt overwhelmed the part of Carson's humanity that remained cognizant during the act. Too bad that part of him wasn't in control. No. That was another sex-fiend part of him that enjoyed every ass-kicking minute of pleasure.

Their fucking might have been rough and primitive, but was it only sex? The need to scratch a primal itch? Wasn't that all Lincoln was interested in? Carson had heard enough about Lincoln's twinks— Taylor had filled Carson in on that definition—to know Lincoln didn't do relationships.

After the bonding Carson overheard Doc and Max talking about the possible and current consequences from Lincoln's blood. For the first time in hours, Carson pulled up the sleeve of the sweatshirt he'd been given. Yup, still there. Symbols and foreign text, black and finer than any tattoo job, as if he'd been born with it. Was he even a vampire anymore? Would whatever lurked inside take over completely? The questions made his head ache and his gut roil, yet despite the fear and the doubt and the unknown, lying with his arms wrapped around Lincoln, the connection strong, unbreakable, he'd never felt safer.

The door opened, and Doc stepped in. As always he wore his white coat with his stethoscope draped over his neck. The tentative yet bemused look on his face unnerved Carson. Doc sighed and closed the door. The sigh he couldn't figure out, but he was relieved the brigade of people who were in his room earlier wasn't following him.

Doc approached the bed, but not without some hesitation. Carson would be wary too.

"He's sleeping... I hope." Carson's voice trembled, belying the confidence he wanted to convey.

"And you? Are you in a place where I can examine him without fear of being attacked or, in the best case scenario, growled at?"

Carson lowered his eyes, his cheeks heating. His protective feral side hadn't allowed anyone close to Lincoln. He actually growled at Doc like a fucking dog. "I'm sorry. That wasn't me. Or maybe it was some part of me I usually have better control over."

"Did you feel out of control?"

Carson huffed. "Someone was driving, but it wasn't me. I was totally controlled by my urges."

Doc raised his eyebrows, and his face paled. He looked to Lincoln. "I never thought.... Did you bite him?"

Carson's heart kicked into overdrive.

He didn't... he couldn't....

No.

CHAPTER 13

CARSON PANICKED for about thirty seconds. There were short pockets of time where he didn't remember fully his actions. Still, he didn't have to check every inch of Lincoln's body to conclude he didn't bite him. Carson knew without a second thought Lincoln was completely safe with him. Also there wasn't the coppery aftertaste in his mouth.

"No. I didn't bite him." *Thank fucking gods.*

The sigh of relief from Doc settled the tension in the air.

Doc pulled the stethoscope from around his neck. "Can I?"

"Please." Carson needed some reassurance he hadn't hurt Lincoln.

Doc listened to his heart and lungs. Shined that annoying light into his eyes. Lincoln didn't even flinch. Checked his reflexes. Did a BP check. Still no reaction from Lincoln.

Carson's heart tripped and sputtered and then raced again. "What's wrong with him? He didn't even react to the light?"

Doc lost the worry lines around his eyes and on his forehead. "He's going to be okay. He's in a regenerative sleep. Bonding requires an immense amount of energy. His body is sort of rebooting itself."

Another mention of bonding, but Carson had a more pressing question. "Then why am I awake?"

Doc pursed his lips and nodded slowly. "I'm wondering the same thing. It could have to do with the transformation you experienced."

Carson snorted loudly. "Transformation into what? What the hell am I?"

Doc seemed to mull over his answer. Was the truth that bad?

"I don't know, Carson. Really, this—" He waved his hand over Carson's torso, covered with the ill-gotten tattoos. Funny thing was he'd always wanted a tattoo. *Be careful what you wish for.* "Well, this is beyond me. Lincoln was speaking with Jameson, trying to get more information, when you *needed* him."

A partial smile cracked Doc's face but quickly faded. His silence was only interrupted by Lincoln's gentle breaths. Carson had so many questions, most he feared asking. His mother had told Carson to find Jameson. The answers were with the creepy man who could walk through locked doors and disable security systems.

Lincoln stirred again. Unease filled Carson, but the discomfort didn't come from Carson. Lincoln's energy continued to bombard him. Carson tightened his hold and whispered in his ear, "It's okay. I'm right here."

A long, drawn-out sigh escaped Lincoln, who seemed to melt into Carson. The action overwhelmed him, and he closed his eyes, quelling the growing desire.

Doc cocked his head. "Your bond is strong. After bonding there's generally a period of adjustment, of growth. But just your touch, your words, already have a calming effect."

"Just what does bonded mean?"

Doc appeared hesitant to answer, and that pooled dread in Carson's gut. "Is it bad?" he whispered.

"No. I mean, it doesn't have to be…. It can be really… sort of…." Doc raked his fingers through his graying hair. "Lincoln should really be the one to tell you about bonding. I know the mechanics, the effects, but having never been bonded, I can't tell you much."

Carson frowned. "Well, since I've never heard about bonding until now, you know more than me. How about a crash course? Because I have to tell you, I need to understand at least one of the fucked-up things happening to me." His voice grew in timbre and intensity.

Doc nodded, seemingly unaffected by Carson's ire. "Bonding is rare. Very rare since only Sanatore vampires can create a bond with another vampire. And bonding only happens in approximately 2 percent of those who receive the blood. Special compounds in the Sanatore blood can combine with compounds in the donee's blood. The result is accelerated healing. And in certain cases, bonding."

"So Lincoln's blood healed me and threw in a bonding for free?" *Purchase this lovely pint of Sanatore blood to heal what ails you. And if you're the one hundredth caller, you will also receive a free bonding. That's right, a free bonding.*

Carson soaked in the words. "How rare *is* the bond?"

"You have a better chance of winning the lottery twice and being struck by lightning in the same day."

"That rare, huh?" Carson was a rare vampire with a rare bond and an even rarer case of tattoo-itis. "So two people bond. What does the mean?"

Instead of answering Doc asked, "What does it feel like?"

Carson tried to pinpoint exactly what he felt. "It's like a connection, but deeper. Not like that connection with someone you're close with or in love with. It's almost physical, for lack of another word, drawing me to him. It's a need unlike anything I've ever felt. Not just a need for physical contact, but a mental connection.... Gods, this sounds crazy."

"Sounds about right. The first few weeks are like a roller-coaster ride of spiking emotions and physical chaos as the bond completes. There's an intense need to be close, the need to physically touch as that happens. Much of what you're feeling will mellow out, become less intense."

"For something so rare, you seem to know a lot about this." More than he hinted at knowing.

Doc fidgeted with a button on his lab coat, appearing to avoid eye contact. Doc pursed his lips as if he was stopping words from escaping. That couldn't be good.

"What aren't you telling me?"

Doc stuffed his hands into his pockets. "Lincoln really needs to tell you the rest. He should sleep for a few hours, and I suggest you get some sleep as well."

Without waiting for a response, Doc turned and abruptly left the room. That was one way to keep from answering a question. Carson felt there was more to Doc's hasty exit than avoiding questions about the bond. What that was, Carson wasn't sure.

He massaged his pulsing temple while running his fingers over the skin of Lincoln's stomach. Although he'd been lulled into an illusion of safety by the bond, he knew better. He was screwed big-time.

LINCOLN LICKED his dry lips. His head spun, his body ached, and his ass.... His ass felt as if someone had pounded him with a massive dildo for hours.

Carson.

Not a dildo, then. The bonding.

Lincoln held his breath, hoping to head off an overreaction. Hard to do when dread scratched at his insides. He'd bonded with Carson. Or should he say Carson bonded with him. That was one way to bottom for the first time. He couldn't deny the intensity of the pleasure once he passed the initial pain. Nothing had ever come close to the ecstasy he'd experienced. His bonding with Luke didn't hit even a fraction of the pleasure and power he felt with Carson.

He would have questions. What did your blood do to me? Why was I half-crazed and out of my mind? Why did I attack you? Did you know this would happen?

Yeah, that last one. Lincoln could say he had no clue what would occur. Such a lie. He knew, even though he sequestered the truth in the back of his mind, he knew they would end up bonded. Then why did he donate, knowing everything that could go wrong? Would his bond with Carson follow that same path as Luke's?

Already Lincoln felt Carson's doubts and fears. They sought him out, wrapping tight around Lincoln's chest. Even in a regenerative asleep, he was aware of Carson sharing the narrow hospital bed with him, their bodies touching. Carson's methodical caresses, his whispered words, calmed Lincoln's anxiety and fears.

He remembered the exact moment Carson had left. Probably had run screaming from the room after what Lincoln did to him. Even so, Carson's absence hurled feelings of abandonment and rejection into Lincoln's reality.

Daylight filtered through the shade covering the window. After the bond with Luke, Lincoln had slept for nearly thirty hours. However long he slept this time, he felt good. Stretching his arms over his head, he checked for injuries, twisting his upper body side to side. Nothing hurt except the sides of his hips, where there were round bruises from Carson's fingers. Lincoln wiggled his butt, which only resulted in a dull ache. Physically he was okay. His mind was another story. His mind raced with the uncertainty of his status with Carson. Lincoln's life was in his hands. He had to trust Carson cared enough to take care with him.

Lincoln threw off the covers and slipped off the bed. Looking down, he was hit with the sight of his naked body. A search of the room didn't produce any clothes. Carson had shredded what he'd been wearing. Pulling the sheet off the bed, Lincoln wrapped the scratchy material around his waist.

The door opened, and Max peered around the corner. "Oh good, you're up."

"Don't sound so disappointed." Lincoln was already on the defensive.

Max entered but kept his distance. "You feel okay?"

The standoffish behavior of his best friend didn't help. "Yeah, just peachy. I need to get a shower and some clothes and…."

Lincoln stopped short of saying "find Carson." Max grabbed Lincoln's arm as he attempted to leave.

Turning, Lincoln observed the cautious expression on Max's face. "Doc took Carson for a shower and then food. He'll be back soon."

Did Lincoln look that desperate for information about his bond mate? Lincoln ducked his head to hide his vulnerability from Max. "Is he okay?"

"Seems to be. Although he didn't need to sleep after you bonded. He's actually kind of twitchy and can't sit still."

"Huh." Carson's strength and his ability to handle the energy of bonding only proved something else had changed inside of him. "Meet me in my office in thirty. We need to go over everything we have. Where's Jameson?"

Max frowned. "We put him in the lounge over in admin. He's being kept away from Carson."

Lincoln nodded and paused, wanting to say something to Max, but the words escaped him. Sooner or later the tension that grew between them would come to a head. Right now Lincoln couldn't deal with that.

THE SHOWER went a long way to clearing Lincoln's head. In the mirror he checked out the bruises from the bonding. His chest, shoulders, and hips were covered with marks. They would heal soon enough. The ache in his ass he thought was gone flared up as he walked. He'd be feeling that for the next few days—not that the reminder was a bad thing. Sucked that his healing abilities didn't work on himself.

He passed the hallway that led to Carson's room on the way to his office. He moved on, telling himself he wasn't avoiding Carson. He had work to do after his long siesta. If the bond had its way, he'd be searching for Carson right now. The bonding muddied the waters of his true feelings. With Luke they were exclusive for over three months before they bonded, four months after they met. Not quite to the love stage, but heading there. Lincoln felt something for Carson before they bonded. He'd been ready to see where that could go. Damn, Carson was special, or he wouldn't have considered a relationship with him. That left Lincoln with looming questions. Did Carson feel anything for Lincoln before the bond? Would he want anything to do with Lincoln now? Best to keep busy and avoid the answers.

He found Max and Doc in his office. Doc nodded, sprawled on the couch, reading over a file. Max shuffled papers. Except for a quick glance, he largely ignored Lincoln's presence. Maybe that blow to their friendship would come sooner than later.

Lincoln circled his desk and sat, trying to hide his confusion and anxiety from not knowing where Carson was. As he sifted through papers from his inbox, a mug appeared on his desk.

"Drink this," Doc said. "It's whole blood. You look like shit."

Lincoln raised his chin with a menacing glare, but Doc always won in their stare-downs. "Thanks."

The sweet liquid excited all of his taste buds. Whole blood was like a decadent dessert. He really needed to visit the bite—right. He didn't make it past the parking garage when he tried to go out because of Carson. Now that they were bonded, did that mean they were a couple? Did relationship rules apply?

Getting a little ahead of yourself, Linc.

Lincoln wiped his mouth with the back of his hand and set down the mug.

"So are you going to ask about him?" Doc's accusing tone couldn't be missed.

Max stopped sorting files, apparently interested in the answer.

Lincoln could play dumb, but Doc wouldn't fall for that. Lincoln exhaled. "How's Carson?" Just his name sent a hard shudder through Lincoln.

Just. His. Name.

The intensity of their bond grew by the minute, and if he was truthful, Lincoln had never been more scared in his life.

CHAPTER 14

"LINC. HEY, Earth to Lincoln."

Lincoln swatted away Max's hand, waving in his face.

"Just seeing if you're okay. For a minute there you were looking paler than Doc's coffee."

Doc huffed but didn't reply.

Lincoln turned his attention to Doc. "Is Carson all right? Max said he didn't need to sleep after the bonding."

"His blood work shows he's no longer deteriorating. He's strong, but the super vampire strength he experienced when needing to complete the bond seems to have worn off. Brain waves are still off the charts. My machines can't even measure their intensity. He's twitchy and unsettled and pacing as if he's three days off a nicotine and caffeine addiction. His body temperature, heart rate, and blood pressure are all elevated, but it's not taxing his system. It's as if his body is modifying itself, but why, I don't know. He ate his weight in food at the cafeteria. I imagine his metabolism is off the charts as well. At this rate he'll burn through five or six pints of synthetic blood a day."

"Whoa," Max muttered.

Half a pint a day was sufficient on top of regular meals for male vampires. Women tended to need less. Growing vampires more, but five pints was just… wow. Along with the strange writing and symbols, the red irises, the changes to Carson's body, and the intensity of their mating, their bonding hit the highest number on the "oh shit" chart.

"I did a CT scan." Doc's neutral expression was harder than usual. "Structurally everything is normal, except there's something I can't identify in his brain. An intense thermal anomaly. No concrete form. No origin. No explanation."

"What the fuck?" Max blurted out.

Doc shrugged.

Lincoln sat back. Doc's explanation didn't ease Lincoln's doubts about Carson's commitment to their bond. If Carson chose, he could reject it. Lincoln didn't have that option. But even if he did, he'd choose his bond mate.

Doc sighed forcefully. "You need to talk to him about what bonding means. He's confused, and with everything else going on, he's scared and unsure. I told him the basics, but I don't know enough, and frankly, this is your area of expertise, not mine. You did this, and you can't avoid him indefinitely."

Lincoln clutched the arms of his chair. "I'm not avoiding him."

Max snorted. "Yeah, and that terrified expression you've had since you woke up has nothing to do with this."

Lincoln gritted his teeth together, hoping to hold on to some semblance of control.

Truth hurts, doesn't it?

Max ignored Lincoln's reaction. "I know you're scared. Fuck, after what happened with Luke, we're all scared. Your life's in danger here. The sooner he knows that, the better."

Lincoln stood and sent his chair skittering back into the wall. "I'm not going to put this on him. You want me to tell him that if he denies the bond, then something bad will happen? He's got enough crap to deal with. He didn't ask for this. And I don't need his pity!"

Max leaned over the desk, a fire lighting his green eyes. "Don't you think he deserves to know that denying your bond has consequences? It's not as if he's deciding whether or not to accept your dinner invitation. This is fucking life or death, Linc. Your life. I watched the hell you went through last time. Watched you nearly die. If you don't tell him, I will!"

"Don't you dare say a fucking word, Max. I'm warning you." The threat did little to change the determined, pissed-off expression on Max's face.

"Okay, guys. Put 'em back in your pants. It's a tie," Doc said. "Max is right. You have to tell Carson. He deserves it as much as you do."

Lincoln wasn't ready to voluntarily seek out rejection. Not yet. "Not now. I need to get up to speed with the case." He rubbed the back of his neck with his trembling hand. "I'll talk to Carson later." In reality part of Lincoln wanted to run and hide while another part wanted to run to Carson and confess—what exactly would Lincoln confess? His undying love? He shoved the thought away.

Max and Doc seemed to understand when to back off, at least for now. Smart men.

Max pointed to some printouts on the desk. "I found Justin Masters. He wasn't easy to track down. Had to hack into some databases. The guy was listed under his mother's maiden name of Pike. He's just outside of Buffalo in a long-term care facility. Seems his mother died a few years ago. He was placed there shortly before her death."

"Catatonic?" Doc asked.

Max nodded. "He hasn't been subjected to any kind of neural programming."

"So he's a vegetable?" Lincoln asked.

"No," Doc said. "He's catatonic, in a sense. No personality, no interactions with others. I was just reading his records from the care facility. It seems he can take direction for easy tasks like brushing his teeth and eating. His self-care skills are limited based on their complexity. He doesn't speak, doesn't make eye contact, show emotion. He has no awareness of the world around him."

Was Justin still in there, trapped in his mind with no control over his body? Lincoln couldn't fathom a more terrifying hell, except knowing you had done that to someone you love.

"He's secure where he is at this point, but we all know the possibilities of what could happen if the wrong people found him. What they could do with him." Max paused. "We should bring him here."

Justin at the NVJ? "Carson couldn't handle seeing him. Look what confessing to biting the guy did to him."

"I agree with both of you," Doc said. "He can't stay in an unsecure location, and Carson can't know about Justin. Carson's mental stability is tenuous at best." Doc looked to Lincoln, paused for a second, and then continued. "Sounds as if he's low maintenance, easy to contain. We have the unused rooms in the basement. Very secure."

"I can have a team out of here by 1400 hours today." Max pushed those pesky loose strands of his hair back.

Lincoln hated the idea. Hated the potential harm to Carson by keeping Justin near him, even if that harm was only psychological. Or was Lincoln jealous of having Carson's first love—a person he freely admitted to loving—so close?

Would Carson ever love Lincoln the way he'd loved Justin?

Fuck, I'm losing my mind.

If he didn't pull it together soon, he'd have to relieve himself of duty. Ordering some people around would help. "Assemble a team. Four officers should cover it. Get me a plan of action covering all the bases. Any indication there's additional security other than the usual for that type of facility?"

"So far no. I have Dennison and Warez working on schematics and—"

"What the fuck? I suspended Dennison!"

Max raised his hands in supplication. "When I found Justin, I called in Dennison. You were in la-la land. Not even your bond mate could wake you, which put me in charge. I needed Dennison to hack into their system to see what we were dealing with. His expertise in security systems is unprecedented."

"He almost killed Carson. He ignored protocol and blew off the seriousness of his infraction." Lincoln didn't trust Dennison.

Max hardened his expression. "If you want this mission to succeed, then I need to have the best. Given the value of the asset, there's no room for mistakes."

Lincoln knew Max was right, but Lincoln didn't have to like it. "He's your responsibility. If he fucks up, it's your ass on the line."

"Yeah, yeah. Anyway, I looked at Justin's list of visitors. Since his mother's death, no one has been logged. Before that were a few specialists his mother had requested examine him. No doubt still looking for a way to cure him. Once she passed away, there's been no one."

Lincoln turned to Doc. "Set him up in the four northernmost rooms in the basement. No one outside of our team is to know we have a guest. Use the security elevator and change the clearance access to cover only staff who absolutely need it. They're going to sign a confidentiality waiver. They talk about Justin to anyone who's not on that list, and they're going to spend a long time in jail."

"You got it." Doc left to carry out Lincoln's orders.

Max stepped around the side of the desk. Lincoln yearned to return to their previous level of camaraderie, but hadn't a clue as to the right words to accomplish that.

"We have one problem."

Lincoln huffed. "This is a Nons facility, which means they aren't going to buy a vampire is anyone's family member."

"Can't we use a halfie? I know we have quite a few on the other teams."

Max shook his head. "Being half human they'll pass, but none of them have the experience needed to pull this off. If they fuck up, that place is going to be shut down quicker than Taylor can eat a steak."

Lincoln ran his hand over his mouth, moving down over his chin. "You got pics of the residents?"

"Yeah." Max picked up one of the folders he'd set on the desk. "Here."

Lincoln took the folder and perused pictures that must have been taken upon admission. Quite a bleak bunch. When he came to the picture of a teen, he knew he could do the job.

Lincoln picked up his cell phone, found the number, and hit Send. Hearing the deep voice brought a smile to his face.

"Lincoln. I'm touched. You remembered my birthday."

Shit. Was it… "You lying son of a bitch. I'm not falling for that again. You only get one a year. You still owe me back for all of those beers I bought you last time."

"Cry me a river. You never call for no reason. What do you need?"

Lincoln picked up a pencil, tapping it against the picture of the teen. "You wanna play?"

"I'll be there in thirty." The line went dead.

Lincoln hung up, and Max smirked. "What did Dwayne say?"

"Thirty minutes."

Max snorted. "Crazy bastard. I'll have the team prepped and ready to leave in two hours. We'll set up surveillance on the building for a while before sending Dwayne inside. Dennison will hook him up with a camera and hopefully sound. And maybe he can speak with some of the staff."

"Good idea. Just make sure the team understands Dwayne was never there, as usual. Don't want him, or me, to lose our jobs." The amount of times they'd used each other on a case would probably land them in jail for life.

Max nodded and shifted. He stuffed his hands into his pockets. Damn, the tension was still there between them.

Lincoln wiped his hand over his mouth. "Max, about Grace—"

Max raised his hand, cutting Lincoln off. Max lowered his head and was silent for a moment. When he looked at Lincoln, Max's harsh stare was painful. "I get it, Linc. Really I do. She was only half vampire, and Sanatore blood doesn't cure cancer in vampires. And the whole bonding thing could have happened. I just... I just wanted more time, you know?"

"I know." Lincoln studied Max's face. His eyes were weary, his face taut, his clothes wrinkled, and he hadn't shaved for a few days. He wasn't taking care of himself. Lincoln tried to think how long that could have been going on. Grace had been gone for a couple of years. This was something recent.

Lincoln cocked his head. "Everything okay, Max? I mean besides this."

Max crossed his arms. "Yeah, why?"

"You look like shit. You sleeping?"

Max fiddled with the stapler on the desk. "Things have been a little crazy lately. Been crashing here some nights."

Something hovered behind those eyes. Max's body language screamed "back off," so Lincoln did. "Okay. Work on the team and report before you head out. When you get back, get some rest."

"I will if you will. You're starting to look like an old man. I mean, is that gray hair?"

Lincoln quirked a smile and batted away the finger Max pointed at his head. "Hey, I'm only five months older than you."

"Yeah, and don't you forget it." Max grabbed Justin's info and headed out the door.

The steel ball of tension shoved under Lincoln's breastbone started to shrink until he thought of Carson and their need to talk. Why was his life one fucking hurdle after another?

CARSON SAT at the corner table in the cafeteria, ignoring the stares and whispers of those around him. If these people were supposed to be trained officers, their covert skills sucked. Carson was too busy scarfing down obscene amounts of food to care much. Maggie Wright had escorted him to the cafeteria as if he were five. She talked with a red-haired woman.

Her tailored blue suit, long red nails, and coifed hair told Carson she wasn't an officer. Maybe a spy?

Nearing the end of three full meals and two desserts, Carson pushed away from the table and released a manly burp. Maggie smirked, having heard him from two tables away. She raised a finger, indicating she was almost done. Carson gave her a half smile and patted his rounded stomach. Full for the moment but he'd be back there in about two hours, eating just as much.

He wondered if Lincoln had eaten. He wondered where Lincoln was. Carson wondered if he'd pushed Lincoln away forever. Everyone who ventured into Carson's room was questioned about Lincoln's whereabouts. Each time Carson received the same answer—in his office, working. After about his seventh inquiry and the resulting looks of pity, Carson felt like an unwanted crush. One of those annoying people who didn't get the hint. Was Lincoln's absence the hint? Carson's experience was limited to one relationship, which was anything but normal.

Relationship?

Whoa, slow that train down. And…. *Oh shit.* He told Lincoln how his last relationship ended. How he essentially killed his boyfriend. Well, wasn't that just a red flag to stay away? Run. Flee. Disappear. Just as Lincoln had.

Fuck.

"Carson?" Maggie slid into a seat across from him. "Hey, you okay? You look a little pale and… sad."

Carson didn't do well when people asked how he was. He didn't do well with people at all. Especially those he didn't know. His social skills were pretty much nonexistent.

"I'm okay." He avoided her piercing gaze. In his periphery she eyed him critically, drumming her fingers on the table. Her silence was enough to bring his lunch back up.

"You ready to head back to your room?" she finally asked.

Carson stood quickly in answer, and she chuckled. He followed close on her heels, eyes downcast, avoiding everyone. If he ever had to get back to his room alone, he'd get lost.

Many people said hello to Maggie. She seemed well liked. Carson figured it was good to be liked. He rubbed his stomach as they walked, the slight nausea increasing. He'd made a pig of himself, but he'd eaten even more at breakfast without any ill effects. His body had become a foreign entity to him. He was never sure how it would react. He wished Lincoln was with him. He couldn't deny the comfort and calm Lincoln brought to the chaos thundering through his body. Again Carson wanted to know where Lincoln was, what he was doing, what he was thinking about. Was it him? Carson felt like a schoolboy with a crush. Next he'd be passing notes.

Tia, could you slip this note to Lincoln? Don't tell anyone I like him. So grown-up.

An officer stopped Maggie as they passed her desk, asking her to look something over. Carson hung back, keeping his focus on the floor. His stomach roiled, and he burped. He covered his mouth and looked around, but no one seemed to hear. The churning in his stomach increased as a cold sweat broke out across his skin. He really needed to get back to his room and lie down, feeling as if he'd been spun really fast and had to keep his balance. The blood rushed to his head. He lowered his chin to his chest. His mouth watered, and in seconds, he was surely going to lose his lunch all over the floor. He needed a bathroom fast.

As Carson reached out to tap on Maggie's shoulder, a pain lanced his stomach, running straight through into his back.

"Fuck." He bent over, hands on his knees. The room spun faster.

"Hey, Maggie. Is he okay?" he heard someone ask.

"What? Shit, Carson? Carson, what's wrong?" Maggie knelt before him and looked up at him.

"Gonna be sick."

She disappeared from Carson's vision, yelling for someone to get Doc and Lincoln. *Yes, Lincoln, please.* Carson fell to his knees. Nausea washed over him, running hot and cold over his skin. Did he have the flu?

Just as he heaved, a waste can was shoved under his head. What was so tasty going down was a lumpy, acidic, bile-flavored nightmare. Over and over he heaved as his stomach forced every ounce into the waste bin. Holding tight to the rim, he swayed. When his heaving ceased, the spinning continued. His vision came in and out of focus. Carson narrowed his eyes, trying to focus to see if Lincoln was coming. For a second his eyes cooperated. Jameson stood off to the side. Before Carson's world spun out of control, he swore he saw Jameson smile.

LINCOLN ROUNDED the corner and found Carson lying on the floor. Doc was checking him over while two nurses raced up the hall, pushing a gurney. Lincoln froze, watching two officers hoisting Carson's limp body onto the stretcher. The sight of Jameson hovering nearby brought Lincoln back to his commanding persona.

"What the fuck is he doing out here?" Lincoln roared. "Is anybody doing their job?" Everyone stopped, looking at Lincoln and then at Jameson. Two officers from another squad quickly removed him. Lincoln rushed to Carson's side. His skin was a pallid shade of white. His lips had taken on a bluish tint.

"What is it, Doc? What happened?" Lincoln looked to Maggie. "Were you with him?"

She nodded, eyes wide as she stared down at Carson. "He ate lunch and we were on the way back to his room. He was fine, and then he was throwing up and passed out."

"Get him back to his room. I want blood drawn, stat. Get Casey down here. We're going to need some rapid testing."

Lincoln raced behind the gurney as they headed down the hallway. His heart pounded against his ribs, and his vision tunneled to Carson. Doc's expression did little to comfort Lincoln. As they turned the corner into the room, the fear of losing Carson slammed into Lincoln like a two-by-four to the gut. He couldn't… couldn't….

He gasped for breath, trying to take in enough air. Oh gods, if he lost Carson….

"Someone get him into a chair before he falls down," Doc yelled.

Maggie tried to guide Lincoln to a chair in the corner. "Come on, Commander. Sit."

He allowed Maggie to guide him as he focused on Carson. Beautiful, vulnerable Carson. Lincoln was supposed to protect him. Keeping Carson safe was Lincoln's job, and he'd failed miserably. He had to pull himself together, be the strong one in their relationship. He chuckled morosely. Again he thought of a relationship, and he hadn't a clue if Carson even wanted him. Well, he didn't give a fuck. He was going to be there whether Carson wanted him or not.

Lincoln almost sat, but motioned Maggie away and went to the bed. Carson looked so small, so sickly. Lincoln pushed the hair from Carson's clammy, sweat-soaked forehead.

Lincoln leaned close to Carson's ear. "Please, Carson. Don't leave me."

Lincoln caught Doc's attention as he hooked an IV bag on the pole. Doc dipped his chin, as if understanding Lincoln's pleading expression. *Save him.*

A nurse raced into the room and handed Doc a sheet of paper. He glanced at the sheet, swore, and then started barking orders. He turned to Lincoln. "He's been poisoned."

Lincoln blinked. Had he heard right? "Poisoned?"

"Yeah, and the dose is large enough to kill a regular vampire. I think the only reason he's not dead is due to whatever is messing with his body."

Someone had tried to kill Carson.

My Carson.

No fucking way!

"Warez! Lock down the building. No one gets out or in!" His roar filled the room and expanded. Around him people flinched at the noise, but he didn't give a fuck. Whoever did this to Carson was going to pay with their life.

LINCOLN PACED the room as Carson slept. Two hours had passed since he was poisoned. Doc assured Lincoln that Carson was out of the woods and would probably suffer no ill effects from the poison. *Probably.* Lincoln rubbed his hand over the back of his neck. The possibilities of who'd done this ran through his mind. Doc confirmed the poison was ingested orally. Someone laced Carson's food with a mixture of noxious plants. The number of poisonous plants on the results from the lab was astounding. How Carson survived was mindboggling. Currently teams were scouring every inch of the building, reviewing security footage of the kitchen and cafeteria. Max and his team, along with Dwayne, had left to retrieve Justin, so Lincoln needed to call in backup teams. Whoever hurt Carson was going to be very sorry when Lincoln was done with them.

A cough caught Lincoln's attention. Carson stirred in the bed. Lincoln rushed to his side and took his hand. A whimper escaped Carson's throat.

"Carson, honey. Open your eyes," Lincoln pleaded.

Carson's eyes fluttered as if the effort was too great to hold them open. Carson rolled to his side and pulled his legs to his chest.

"Carson. It's Lincoln. Please look at me." He needed to see Carson's eyes, know he was going to be okay.

"Linc," Carson muttered. "Feel like shit."

"I know, but you're going to be okay. I promise." He rubbed his thumb over the back of Carson's hand. The action stopped him from physically shaking Carson and forcing him to open his eyes.

"Can you open your eyes for me? I need to know you're okay." His attempt to sound confident and strong was pathetic.

Carson turned his head up and forced his eyes open. Still red. Lincoln could swear the color had deepened. Despite that, Carson was beautiful.

Lincoln smiled. "I'm sorry I wasn't there. I should have been with you."

Carson crinkled his brow. "Why would you be there?"

Lincoln needed to come clean. Needed to know where he stood with Carson. Crappy timing, but….

Lincoln gripped Carson's hand tighter. "Because we're bonded. I need to protect you."

Carson pulled back, a fire burning in his eyes. "Is that what bonded means? You *have* to protect me? I suppose you *have* to be here too. Well, where were you all day? Where were you when I was sick?"

Carson's drowsiness faded quickly. The mixture of anger and pain on his face yanked a hole in Lincoln's chest.

"I-I didn't…."

"You didn't what? Didn't want to be bonded to a loser like me, so you decided to cut your losses? Don't feel sorry for me now just because I'm sick. You can leave. I don't need you here."

Carson rolled over, giving Lincoln his back. Lincoln backed off and sat in a chair. And waited. He waited as Doc and his nurse came and went. When Carson woke, he looked at Lincoln and rolled away again.

He had to fix this. He stood and laid his hand on Carson's shoulder, but he pulled away. Lincoln hated that Carson shut him out. Time to fix his stupidity. Hopefully Carson would listen. Once he told Carson everything, he might be the one rejecting him.

Steeling his resolve, Lincoln said, "I was bonded once before."

CHAPTER 15

CARSON'S SHOULDERS flinched, but he didn't say anything.

Lincoln cleared his throat. "I was seeing this guy named Luke, a vampire, who worked as a bartender at a club I liked to go to. I had just moved to Utica and joined the force with Max. I was pretty sure of myself, cocky, and Luke, he was…. Well, I thought he was perfect. He was built, took care of himself, but he wasn't conceited. You know how some guys are. He was actually one of the first men I asked out on an actual date. We went out to dinner, the whole nine yards. It was… really nice."

Lincoln didn't want to rub another man in Carson's face, but he had to make Carson understand his wariness to get close… to love. Carson remained on his side. However, he turned his head slightly, as if listening.

"Anyway, we started seeing each other on a regular basis and spending time at each other's apartments getting… um… closer. I started to think it was going to be a long-term thing."

Lincoln closed his eyes as long-buried feelings of lust and desire and love and pain and grief threatened to drown him. Taking a steadying breath, he forced himself to continue. He'd buried this nightmare long ago, never to be resurrected—until now. When he opened his eyes, Carson had shifted onto his back, eyes intent on Lincoln.

"About six months after we'd started dating exclusively, I was waiting at the club for Luke's shift to end. Being a bouncer, Luke had his fair share of angry drunken patrons he had to toss. Well, before the end of his shift, this one loud and obnoxious Non was harassing a blond-haired kid who was waiting tables. Luke had warned the guy over and over to keep his hands to himself, but the guy kept at it until Luke had to toss him out. The guy was pissed for sure, but they always were, the assholes."

Lincoln sat on the edge of the bed, his back to Carson as the memories made his legs go weak. "When Luke's shift was over, we headed to my car. I had to park a few blocks away because it was a busy night. As we walked past this alley, two guys jumped us. One guy whacked me with something hard in the back of the head. It fucking hurt…." He rubbed the back of his head, recalling the bone-jarring pain that rendered him useless to help. "I went down hard, but I wasn't out. I could only watch as… as the other guy…. He stabbed Luke in the gut over and over." Lincoln swallowed hard against the bile creeping up into his throat. He closed his eyes as Carson laid a comforting hand on his back. "They… um… they left us there, but somehow I managed to call Max. I thought… I thought Luke was dead…."

Carson rubbed circles over his back. Lincoln exhaled slowly, tension leeching from his muscles. The warmth of the tender touch sent a shiver across his skin. The pull, both physical and mental, to take Carson into his arms was immense.

"Did you give him blood?" Carson asked in a hushed voice.

"Yeah, once he'd been stabilized, I did. It saved him. We ended up bonded, like you and I are."

The bed shifted. Carson moved closer, his hand still on Lincoln's back.

"But it sounds like something went wrong?" Carson asked.

Something went wrong, all right—epically wrong. "Luke… he refused the bond."

There was silence from Carson, and then he spoke. "He refused? I don't understand."

Lincoln rubbed his hands together, attempting to return feeling to his body. Anything besides the hollowed-out husk he became as the memories assaulted him. "The bond is physical and mental, but the person a Sanatore bonds with can reject the bond if they choose. I guess it's like a failsafe. Or maybe it's the way the bond forms in the person receiving the blood that allows the rejection."

"But I thought bonds were rare, and you don't know when they'll happen?"

Guilt assaulted Lincoln. In his gut he knew he was going to bond with Carson. Gods, he couldn't tell him that, though. Carson would definitely hate him. "Yeah, but I guess for the times that it does happen, there's an out for the other person." Seemed unfair to Lincoln. He didn't have an out, not that he wanted one with Carson. He'd come to mean so much to Lincoln in a short period of time.

"So you can reject our bond?" Lincoln heard a shake in Carson's voice. What was he afraid of? He could reject the bond, and Lincoln had given him a how-to manual.

Lincoln shifted back toward Carson, seeking his comfort, his safety.

"No, I can't. Only the person who receives my blood can reject the bond." Gods, he prayed Carson didn't make that choice, and not just because of the consequences. Lincoln wanted Carson in his life, wanted Carson with every fiber of his being.

Carson stopped rubbing. "So you healed Luke, saved his life, and he rejected the bond?"

Was the disgust he heard in Carson's voice real or imagined?

"Yeah. Said he hadn't agreed to bond with me. He didn't want to be stuck with one person for the rest of his life, and he went on his way." Tore Lincoln's heart out and kicked it before he left too.

Carson slipped his arms around Lincoln's chest, rested his cheek on Lincoln's shoulder, and whispered, "I'm sorry, Linc."

The contact, the connection, the hope was overwhelming, and Lincoln's heart swelled. But his tale wasn't finished.

"You see, the thing about bonding for a Sanatore is the consequences of rejection. Once the bond has formed, my mind can't function without that connection. Like I said, it's not only physical, but emotional. When I was rejected, I… um…." He so didn't want to lay this on Carson, didn't want him to stay out of fear of what might happen to Lincoln. He wanted Carson to stay because he wanted to, because *he* couldn't live without Lincoln. "My body goes into a kind of withdrawal. When Luke rejected me, I went a bit… crazy." That was an understatement. The pull to be with Luke, Lincoln imagined, was a thousand times more powerful than an addiction to heroin.

"Was it bad?"

Lincoln raked his fingers through his hair and blew out a breath. "I was crazed with need, and my body took over. I guess you could say I was feral…. Shit, my entire focus was on finding Luke and reclaiming him, owning him, never letting him go." The need controlled every thought and action. His hands shook with the memory. "I don't remember much about what happened when I finally found him… but I was told that I attacked him, tried to…." Lincoln couldn't get the words out. He choked, then cleared his throat. "I tried to fuck him without his consent." That was putting it mildly. "Luckily my friend Dwayne, who is a Nons cop, got to me first after someone called Utica PD for a disturbance. He called Max, and the team came out and were able to restrain me and get me back to Doc. If it had been anyone else, another team or any other Nons police, they would have shot me because I wasn't going to stop. Shit, I was so far gone…."

No matter how hard he clasped his hands together, the shaking wouldn't stop. It would have been better for everyone, Carson included, if they *had* put him down.

Carson climbed off the bed and stepped in front of Lincoln. Carson held Lincoln's hands. He could only stare at those small hands in his. That contact raced soothing calm through him. The touch was like an answer to everything he'd questioned.

"What happened?"

"Doc put me into a medically induced coma, hoping the bond would fade given time. They moved Luke off somewhere, I didn't know where, so if I did get free, I couldn't find him. I fought the sedation for two weeks, broke the restraints, tried to escape, and each time was given higher doses of drugs. I only remember bits and pieces of that time. After that—nothing. Another two weeks in a coma, another four weeks sedated, and eventually the bond weakened to the point I could function and start to live without the drugs. Max and Dwayne were the only ones I trusted to help me during that time." A total of six months of his life was living hell, and he still couldn't bring himself to blame Luke.

"Is that why you stayed away after we bonded? You were scared?" There was something in Carson's tone… maybe hope?

"Terrified. Still am, but I didn't tell you this so you'd feel sorry for me and choose my bond. I told you this because I need to know if you're going to reject it, because if you are…. I won't allow myself to hurt you. I will go to Doc now before the need gets bad. Maybe then when he puts me under—" *Or they kill me….*

Lincoln chanced a look at Carson, prepared for disgust or fear. Or at the very least nothing. He wasn't prepared for the compassion in Carson's eyes, the softness, the relief.

"I thought you didn't want me. When you disappeared I asked everyone where you were, and they said you were working. But you stayed away. I thought I'd hurt you, or scared you when we bonded. I was so out of control, so I understand, Lincoln, about some of what you went through with Luke. And I don't care about the bond except that it has brought us here, to this point, together."

Lincoln blinked but didn't say anything. What was Carson telling him? Maybe Lincoln heard what he wanted to hear. When Carson pressed his hand against Lincoln's cheek, he closed his eyes. The warmth went right to the icy coldness that had been building when he thought he'd lost Carson.

"Lincoln. Look at me."

The quaver in Carson's voice was unnerving. Lincoln raised his chin and was struck by the open expression on Carson's face, the desire in his eyes. "I'm not going to reject our bond, I promise."

He couldn't promise that. The commitment was too large. Carson hadn't been given the choice. Someday he might despise Lincoln. "You're young and haven't even lived in the real world. What if you think I'm what you want, then you meet other guys and feel like you're missing out? You don't have to do this."

Carson crossed his arms and narrowed his eyes. "If you don't want to be with me, just say so, because I'm a big boy and I can take it."

Lincoln shook his head and grasped Carson's thin hips, pulling him between his thighs. Burying his head against Carson's stomach, Lincoln soaked in the heat, inhaling the scent unique to Carson. He let his actions speak his intentions. Carson wrapped his arms around Lincoln's shoulders and rested his cheek on top of Lincoln's head with a sigh. Lincoln held his doubts about Carson wanting to be with him, trusting Carson not to hurt him as Luke had. Gods, what if Lincoln fucked this up?

CARSON WAS going to fuck this up. Any rational person, or should he say any person not so desperate, would be pushing Lincoln away. Or run, which would make him no better than that Luke guy. But he went and told Lincoln he wouldn't reject the bond. Damn his mouth, always blurting out what he wanted. It was nice being held, as if he mattered, as if he were loved. And he could fall in love with Lincoln. Too bad it might get Lincoln killed.

Carson tensed with that thought. Lincoln pulled back, gazing up at him. Those blue eyes, so trusting, so willing to give him a chance, made Carson's legs shake. If he ever did anything to hurt Lincoln, he wouldn't forgive himself.

"What's wrong?" Lincoln rubbed Carson's stomach. He squirmed and tried to keep the smile from his face. Lincoln cocked a quizzical eyebrow. "You wouldn't happen to be ticklish, would you?"

Carson felt his eyes widen as he tried to step away, but Lincoln wrapped his arm tight around his waist. *Oh shit.* The mischievous smirk on Lincoln's face could only mean one thing.

"Don't—" was all Carson managed to say before Lincoln tossed him onto the bed and proceeded to tickle him relentlessly.

"Oh… no…," Carson gasped out between laughs. "Lincoln… sssstop…." He couldn't draw in a deep breath. He batted at Lincoln's hands, trying to squirm to the top of the bed, but Lincoln lay on his legs, pinning him down.

Lincoln's boisterous laughter filled the room, blending with Carson's gasping pleas for mercy.

"What will you give me if I stop?" Lincoln asked, continuing with the tickle torture.

"Anything!" Carson gasped. There wasn't enough air, but hell, it felt good to laugh again.

"Anything?"

"Y-yes… anything!"

Lincoln ceased his tickling and lay in the vee of Carson's legs, his chest on Carson's stomach. As their eyes met, Carson's heart fluttered.

"How about forever?"

CHAPTER 16

CARSON'S STOMACH flipped, and his wide smile faded. *Forever.* Lincoln wanted him. Did he dare to love him forever?

Tears stung Carson's eyes. He blinked them back. He could do this. With Lincoln he could do anything. Carson whispered, "Yes."

The relief that passed over Lincoln's face told Carson his answer mattered and he'd made the right one.

Lincoln lunged and attacked Carson's lips, demanding entry. Carson granted Lincoln access as he grasped the sides of Lincoln's head. He needed Lincoln, craved him with his body and his heart. All of Lincoln was too much and not enough all at once.

Lincoln rocked against Carson's erection. The gasp that escaped him was swallowed between them. They were wearing too many clothes. Carson blindly grabbed at the back of Lincoln's shirt and tried to pull it over his head while continuing their kiss.

Lincoln broke away. He yanked the shirt off, tossing it onto the floor. "I want you to make love to me."

After what happened earlier, the trust Lincoln gave meant everything. "I don't want to hurt you again."

"You won't. We'll go slow. Enjoy it this time."

Carson nodded as Lincoln rose off the bed. He unbuckled his belt as he went to the door and clicked the lock. Carson pulled his shirt off. Lincoln unlaced his boots and pulled them off followed by his socks. He climbed onto the bed and ran his rough palms over Carson's stomach, leaving a trail of tingling across his skin. Carson's cock throbbed madly and leaked precum into his underwear. Lincoln moved farther down the bed. Hooking his fingers into Carson's waistband, Lincoln pulled Carson's sweats and underwear off. Carson let his legs fall to the side, opening wide for Lincoln.

Lincoln perused Carson's body, moving up until their eyes met. The flush to Lincoln's face, his hooded lids, the increasing rise and fall of his chest, the large bulge in his jeans only pushed Carson's desire. Lincoln wanted Carson as badly as Carson wanted him. The thrill of that knowledge was as arousing as a hand on his dick.

Carson held out his hand and Lincoln placed his palm against Carson's, then twined their fingers together. Carson yanked him forward, but Lincoln managed to fall to the side and not crush Carson. Before Lincoln had a chance to react, Carson flipped him onto his back and straddled his groin, grinding his ass against Lincoln's erection. Lincoln flexed his neck, his muscles cording as he groaned and pushed up into Carson.

Carson bent over and ran his tongue over Lincoln's nipple, feeling the pec beneath quiver. Sucking the brown disc into his mouth, Carson held the nipple between his teeth and rubbed his tongue over the nub.

Lincoln arched his back and hissed loudly. "That feels good."

Lincoln tried to grab Carson by the arms, but he slipped from Lincoln's grasp. This time Carson was going to give Lincoln pleasure, bring him to the edge until he begged for Carson to let him come. Carson moved to Lincoln's other nipple, sucking and biting. The whimpers and moans from Lincoln spurred Carson to suck and bite harder. He ran his tongue down the hard muscles of Lincoln's stomach. Not an inch of Lincoln was soft, and Carson loved the contrast between their skin colors.

He followed the trail of hair beneath Lincoln's navel and across the skin above his waistband. His stomach fluttered as Carson popped the button on Lincoln's pants and pulled down the zipper. His breath caught, realizing Lincoln was commando. Fuck, that was hot. Carson's cock pulsed, wetting his underwear.

He could practically feel the heat radiating from Lincoln's groin. The anticipation was intense as he shimmied Lincoln's jeans down his legs. Once freed Lincoln opened his legs wide, his large cock and heavy balls framed perfectly at the top of his meaty thighs. Perfection.

Carson licked his lips and leaned over. Just before his tongue made contact with Lincoln's hard shaft, he looked up from under his lashes, the connection electrifying as their gazes locked. Without breaking eye contact, Carson touched his tongue to the base of Lincoln's shaft. He sucked in a lungful of air, and his stomach twitched. Carson slowly ran his tongue to the large head, then sucked gently. Lincoln moaned, lifting his hips. Carson increased his sucking, pushing Lincoln's cock to the back of his throat.

Lincoln settled his hands on Carson's head, carding his fingers through Carson's hair.

"That's it. Suck me, hon. Oh... gods...."

The gravelly voice, the heated command, the endearment spurred Carson to go faster, but he wasn't feeling as confident as when they started. Justin's was the last cock in his mouth six years ago. Fears of screwing up and disappointing Lincoln tried to distract him. He focused on doing what he remembered felt good. Lots of tongue action, tight suction, long, steady pulls.... Oh, and massaging those heavy balls.

"Fuuuuuck yessss," Lincoln hissed and bucked his hips. He clutched Carson's hair, the pulling spurring Carson on.

He smiled around Lincoln's cock, hearing the sounds of pleasure he wrung from him. His big, beautiful, hot man. *His* man. How did he ever get so lucky to have someone like Lincoln?

Eventually you will kill him too.

Carson jerked back, Lincoln's cock sliding from his mouth. Lincoln ran his finger gently down Carson's cheek. "You okay?" he asked.

Carson swallowed hard and nodded, forcing a smile. He didn't trust his voice. Instead he licked Lincoln's ball sac, placing his hands on the backs of Lincoln's thighs and pushing his legs toward his chest. He trailed his tongue down Lincoln's taint and then brushed it over the tight hole. Lincoln's breath hitched and started to come faster. Carson massaged and licked and nipped at the opening. Only in his pornographic dreams had Carson so thoroughly pleasured a lover, been so involved in the act of sex.

The throbbing in his balls pushed out into his groin and into his belly. If he wasn't inside Lincoln soon, he'd come all over the bed.

As if reading his mind, Lincoln handed him a tube of something. Carson raised an eyebrow. "What's this?"

A nasty, wicked grin spread across Lincoln's face. "I may have heard from someone in the medical field that this is a good substitute for lube."

Carson barked a laugh. "Doc? Seriously?"

Lincoln nodded. Shit, Carson wasn't going to be able to look Doc in the eye again.

After flipping open the tube, Carson coated his cock, ready to pop just from the feel of his own hand. He stretched a whimpering and groaning Lincoln with his lubed finger. Without halting his prep, Carson braced himself over Lincoln, kissing him deeply, fucking him hard with his fingers. Lincoln pushed his hips down, meeting Carson's thrusts. Carson's entire groin was on fire. He could have gone on until he made Lincoln come, but Lincoln grabbed Carson's wrist. Heat and desire and need intensified the color of Lincoln's eyes. Carson swallowed hard.

"I'm ready. *Now*."

Carson settled on his knees between Lincoln's thighs. Lincoln grasped his thighs and lifted his leg, granting Carson access. Carson pushed his stiff cock down, panting hard, pushing the head against Lincoln's opening. With a steady pressure, Carson watched, mesmerized, as the tip of his cock disappeared, followed by the mushroom head. Lincoln's muscles clamped tight around his shaft. Carson had to close his eyes, overwhelmed by the thought Lincoln wanted this from him, was allowing Carson to enter him and… *love* him? This was more than a meaningless fuck, more than just a hollow encounter.

Carson opened his eyes. The blue of Lincoln's irises had disappeared except for a thin ring around his enlarged pupils. What clenched Carson's gut, tugged his heart into their lovemaking, was the soft openness of Lincoln's expression, filled with need and desire and heat.

Carson pushed his cock deeper until his balls touched Lincoln's skin.

"Come here," Lincoln whispered. "Want to kiss you."

Carson placed his forearms under Lincoln's knees, pushing forward until Lincoln was bent in half. A gentle brush of their lips led to a languorous joining of their mouths as Carson thrust lazily into Lincoln. Carson drew his hips back until the flare of his corona met Lincoln's tight hole. Their kiss went on, their mouths rising and falling, exploring, tasting, caressing with their tongues. Carson never knew kissing could be so erotic.

Chests heaving, Carson broke the kiss. Lincoln ran his palm down the side of Carson's face, making his skin tingle. Eyes locked, Carson pushed in slowly, the urgency of their last joining absent. The deliberate pace burned as hot as a frenzied need. The slide of Lincoln's muscles over the sensitized skin of Carson's shaft, Lincoln skating the tips of his fingers over Carson's skin, sent a shiver through him. He sat up on his knees. The change in angle released a moan from Lincoln.

"Feels so good." Lincoln exhaled. His chin rose as he arched his back, exposing his neck. Carson ran his tongue over the tight skin, then sucked up a mark on the sensitive skin behind Lincoln's ear.

Lincoln panted, running his hands down Carson's back, then squeezing his ass. Still Carson kept his thrusts slow and steady, allowing the pleasure to build gradually. He could stay there forever, loving Lincoln forever.

"Don't stop," Lincoln murmured into Carson's neck.

Carson sucked, thrust, and marked Lincoln's skin, bringing him closer to climax and strengthening their bond. The tangibility of that bond grew with each minute Carson was inside Lincoln. His heart fluttered, and a hard knot filled Carson's throat. His heart belonged to Lincoln already. It was undeniable.

Carson took in the blissed-out expression on Lincoln's face, the red flush on his cheeks, the slack jaw, the overwhelming desire in his eyes.

"Do you feel it?" Carson had to know Lincoln felt their bond.

Lincoln cupped Carson's cheek with a gentleness that stung Carson's eyes with tears.

"I do. It's our bond. The strength… it's amazing."

Carson nuzzled into Lincoln's palm as he held Lincoln's gaze. Lincoln wrapped his legs around Carson's waist, pushing up to meet his thrusts. Their skin slapped together, the sound increasing steadily. Lincoln cried out. His eyes rolled back into his head. His breath hitched, his body tensed, his chest froze. He clenched his teeth, and tendons popped out along his neck as he fisted his hands in the sheets. With an intense moan, warm semen spurted onto their stomachs. Bliss covered Lincoln's face. The expression sent a flare of pleasure blasting across Carson's groin.

"Oh gods." Carson's balls clenched. The intensity of his orgasm scrambled his thoughts. His heart thumped rapidly and echoed in his ears. He seemed to float as he lay on Lincoln's chest, their chests heaving against one another. The cum between them was warm and slippery, as was their skin, slick with sweat.

Carson sighed contentedly, his body practically melting, having never been so relaxed. Lincoln kissed the top of Carson's head and rubbed small circles over his back. The tenderness of the two gestures brought the tears he'd held at bay. He couldn't help himself. His torrent of emotions covered such a large range that the only thing he could do was shed tears. He didn't want Lincoln to see him weeping after sex. That would be awkward. He lowered his chin so Lincoln couldn't see his face.

Lincoln rolled them onto their sides and entwined their legs together. Carson tucked his face under Lincoln's chin. They were sweaty and covered with cum, but Carson didn't care. Lincoln grabbed the sheet and covered them. Lincoln encircled Carson with his strong arms and pulled him tight to his chest.

"It's okay, love. I'm here, and I won't leave you." Again Lincoln kissed him on the head.

Carson sighed heavily and drifted off to sleep.

CHAPTER 17

A HAND on Lincoln's shoulder woke him from the best sleep he'd had in years. He clutched Carson tighter. He missed waking with someone in his arms, someone who wasn't a convenient fuck or a one-night stand. Carson was his bond mate, and he hadn't rejected the bond between them.

Not yet, at least.

Lincoln shut down that thinking. If he doubted Carson, didn't believe his words, he would end up wrecking what they did have. He'd give Carson space, try not to crowd him or push too hard. If this was all they would have, it was more than he had a few days ago. One thing for certain: they'd be sleeping in a larger bed. This gurney had them plastered to one another. On second thought, it was perfect.

"Lincoln?" Carson whispered.

Still not fully awake, Lincoln replied, "Yes, love?"

A snort filled the room. "Aww, I never knew you cared."

Lincoln's eyes popped open, realizing Carson hadn't said his name. Tommy Dennison stared down at him. John Dennison's little brother. *What the hell?*

Lincoln sat up, carefully shifting the sleeping Carson off his arm. Lincoln scrubbed at his face and blinked away the drowsiness. His skin chilled without Carson sprawled over him.

"Tommy, what the fuck are you doing here?"

He was a NVJ commander in Buffalo, last Lincoln knew. Tommy was ex-military and some kind of tactical genius. The genius part did nothing to override the stupidity-inducing Dennison attitude.

Any amusement in Tommy's face died. A pinched, pained look crossed his face.

John.

Max.

Lincoln scrambled for his watch on the bedside table and squinted at the dial. Six o'clock.

"That's 6:00 a.m.," Tommy said, interpreting Lincoln's confusion.

If Tommy was there, something must have happened to Max's team.

"Fuck. What went wrong?" Lincoln jumped off the gurney, not giving a shit that he was naked. He snatched his pants off the floor and stuffed his legs in. "Why the hell didn't anyone wake me, fucking dammit!"

Carson stirred and opened sleep-filled eyes. "What's wrong?"

Lincoln leaned over Carson, forcing a gentle smile. "Nothing, love. I overslept. Gotta make a living, right?"

Carson's expression remained neutral as he searched Lincoln's face. Finally he nodded. His wariness was understandable given Lincoln's disappearing act earlier.

"I'll be in my office. You get some more rest, and when you're up, find Doc, and he will bring you down to visit."

A smile threatened Carson's lips. "Really?"

"Yeah, I'd really like that. Now can I have a kiss to carry me over until I see you again?"

A beautiful red flushed Carson's cheeks, and he smiled. Lincoln brought their lips together, letting Carson guide the kiss. When Carson placed his hand on the back of Lincoln's neck and deepened the kiss, Lincoln's heart beat harder.

Reluctantly Lincoln pulled away from the sweetness of those soft lips. "I'll see you soon."

Carson bit his lower lip and nodded.

Lincoln ushered a smirking Tommy from the room. "Heard you bonded *again*. Seems this one's working out better than the last. By the way, what's up with the tattoos? Kid got a fetish or something?"

Lincoln shoved Tommy against the wall. No one would talk bad about Carson. "That's my bond mate you're talking about, so watch it."

Tommy raised his hands. "Okay. Sorry. Touchy."

"You don't talk about him. Now what the fuck happened?"

Tommy's expression changed from cocky to worried. "John's team is missing."

Lincoln's stomach dropped like a stone. "Max?"

Tommy nodded.

"Why haven't I heard about this?"

Tommy shrugged. "I just got here. John called me around seven o'clock last night. Said all of their transmissions to Coms had gone unanswered for hours. I tried to call here, e-mail, text, the red phone, nothing. I called Rome NVJ, and they tried and got nothing. It was as if no one was home. They sent a unit here and the place was locked down like Fort Knox. Nothing could override the system, so I had to drive out here. Took me two hours to regain control of enough systems to get the door open. By the way, no one here knows what the fuck's going on."

Lincoln frowned and took off down the hallway, Tommy hot on his heels. Entering his team's area, he found Maggie and Tia at their desks.

"Hey, Linc," Tia said with a smirk. "How about those Knicks?"

He ignored their usual banter and turned his attention to Maggie. She stiffened.

"Why wasn't I updated on the situation with Max's team?" The timbre of his voice vibrated through the room.

Maggie continued to look perplexed as she stood. "Max checked in last night at 1700 hours, stating the mission had been cancelled. He said the orders had come straight from you. The target was unattainable, and they were returning last night."

Lincoln looked to Tommy, who shrugged. "I told you what John said."

Tommy quickly reiterated to Maggie and Tia what he relayed to Lincoln. Both officers sat at their computers, fingers flying over the keys.

Maggie leaned toward her screen and frowned. "The entire system was locked down at 1818 hours, no one in or out, no transmissions. Total emergency lockdown. But how's that possible? The entire building would have been put on alert."

Tommy powered on the computer at Max's desk. Lincoln wanted to tell him to get his hands off but stopped himself. Lincoln ran his hand over his hair. "Maggie, you said Max called. Did you talk to him?"

Maggie shook her head. "Coms took the call, and the message was relayed here."

"When did you come on?" Lincoln asked Tia.

"Last night at 1730 hours… sir," she quickly added.

What a goddamned mess. Max was missing, along with his team. "I need an entire system check run right now. I want to know who the fuck locked down the system. And then we need to—"

"Uh, Lincoln... you're going to want to see this." Tommy didn't look away from the monitor as Lincoln rounded the desk. He peered at the security footage on the screen, time stamped October twenty-first, 1810 hours. Yesterday. Minutes before lockdown.

Lincoln furrowed his brow and leaned closer. "What the...?" Jameson stood before a computer screen, hands raised, eyes closed. His mouth moved, but there was no sound.

"Sound?"

"He's not saying anything. I mean, the sound's up. His lips are moving, but nothing's coming out," Tommy said. "Who is this guy?"

Lincoln ignored the question. Jameson had waltzed into the building through locked doors, disabled the security system, and commanded computers by thought. Jameson, who was there because of Carson.

Lincoln's chest constricted until he couldn't breathe. He bolted down the hallway toward Carson's room.

Please be in bed. Please be in bed.

Lincoln skidded into the door, just managing to grab the handle and throw it open. The bed was empty. Lincoln spun around. The room was empty. Tommy ran into the room and knocked into Lincoln.

"Where is he?" Tommy asked.

Before Lincoln could answer, Maggie and Tia joined them. "Jameson's gone. The two guys from beta team guarding his room are unconscious and unresponsive," Madison said.

Lincoln clutched at his hair and gasped for air. *No. No. No.*

"Hey, man. Are you okay?" Tommy asked.

No, he wasn't fucking okay. Carson was gone. Lincoln grabbed a tray of medical supplies and flung it at the wall. The metal tray clanged against the cinderblock wall and banged onto the floor.

"Oh shit." Tommy backed up, eyes wide. "You aren't going to lose it like last time, are you?"

The door to the bathroom opened, and a wide-eyed Carson peered out. "What was that noise?"

Lincoln reached out and grabbed Carson, pulling him tight to his chest. "Fuck, you scared me."

Carson pushed at Lincoln's chest, but he refused to let him go. Carson, probably realizing he fought a losing battle, relaxed against Lincoln and rubbed his arm.

"Hey, big guy. I'm okay. Just taking a piss. That's all."

Lincoln chuckled, squeezing Carson tighter. He was never leaving Lincoln's sight again. Lincoln's heart couldn't take it.

He loosened his grip, and Carson looked up. "What's wrong?"

Lincoln signed heavily. Where did he even begin?

CARSON SAT on the couch in Lincoln's office, overwhelmed by the activity in the small room. People he'd never seen before came in, handing over information, giving updates, and receiving orders from Lincoln. Seeing him in full-command mode was quite a sight. Forceful, dominant, cunning—and hotter than hell. Carson worked to keep his libido in check because watching Lincoln pooled heat in his groin. So much power. Carson needed a distraction before he humped Commander Samuels on his desk. Not appropriate at a time like this.

From what Carson had pieced together, Max took a team somewhere to bring back someone and didn't check in. They were all currently missing. Carson wasn't sure what that meant, but from the ensuing chaos, missing wasn't good. Add Jameson to the missing too. Everyone seemed to be freaking because they didn't know where he was. What unsettled Carson most was he might have had something to do with the entire mess. If he was dangerous, why had his mother told him to find Jameson Merrick? Dangerous or not, her letter stated Jameson knew something about who or what Carson was. Maybe now he'd never find out that info or what the heck he'd become. As much as Carson wanted it to be true, the tattoos and the red eyes weren't a side effect of the bonding.

A loud voice echoed in the hallway, and Doc rushed into the office, about as pissed off as a wet cat.

"Where were you?" Lincoln scowled. He did intimidating well.

Doc stopped at the desk and planted his hands on the edge. Apparently Doc wasn't easily intimidated. "Locked in the basement all night with Lopez from security and Simpson from research."

Lincoln raised an eyebrow. "What were you doing in the basement with them? My orders were clear that only certain alpha team members were to have access to that location."

Doc's entire body stiffened, and his near growl rated on the scary scale. "We were in the elevator, coming from the second floor to find you, when the elevator dumped us in the basement and locked down."

Lincoln rubbed his neck, an action Carson had come to equate with increased stress levels. "The entire building was locked down last night. We have surveillance footage that indicates Jameson is responsible. By the way, he's missing."

"How convenient, considering he's the one who poisoned Carson."

CHAPTER 18

CARSON GASPED and felt his eyes widen. Jameson had tried to kill him? His mother said Jameson was supposed to help him.

"Jameson tried to kill Carson?" Lincoln asked.

"Security footage from the kitchen," Doc said, his body language appearing less lethal. "Jameson was in there right before Carson showed up to eat. And before you ask, I ordered special nutrient-dense meals to be prepared for Carson, so that's how his food was targeted specifically. How in the heck Jameson snuck past the kitchen workers is beyond me. No one recalls seeing him."

The tall red-haired woman Maggie was speaking with in the cafeteria yesterday entered the room. Once again her hair and makeup were done to perfection. She wore a crisp, well-fitting gray pantsuit. Even Carson had to admit she was pretty. Everyone looked to her as if she were their answer to everything.

She tipped her chin. "Commander. Dr. Reynolds." When she approached Carson, he nearly jumped off of the couch. "Mr. Locke, I'm Dr. Simpson. You're looking better than the last time I saw you."

Carson furrowed his brow. He saw her in the cafeteria while shoveling food into his mouth. He hadn't looked well? "Thanks?"

She smiled. "I'm sorry. It was after you were poisoned. You were still sleeping, so you wouldn't remember. I'm a professor and researcher of vampire history at Syracuse University, and Dr. Reynolds asked me to come and look at the writing and symbols you've developed."

Developed. Good way to put it.

"Anything, Sheila?" Doc asked.

Dr. Simpson sauntered up to the desk in a graceful, commanding manner. "If you remember your history, the vampire race has its origins in that southeastern part of Central Europe, mainly where Moldova, Romania, Bulgaria, and Slovakia are today. Facing persecution as demons, they migrated south into the area of Bosnia, Croatia, and

Albania, and fled farther to the new world. They settled in unpopulated areas in the mountains of Peru and Bolivia. The writing on Carson is an ancient language with roots in Slavic, Thrac—"

Lincoln raised his hands in supplication. "No offense, Dr. Simpson, we all remember our history lessons and the origins of our ancestors. What we need to know is if you can tell us what the writing says? As well as the meaning of the symbols."

Her arched eyebrows rose up her forehead. "As I was saying, Commander Samuels, it's a combination of Slavic, a Thracian tongue, Latin from Europe and Quechua, and the missing key, an unknown ancient language only recently discovered in 2008 in the ruins of a Spanish church in Peru, yet to be fully translated."

Doc snorted. "You could just have said no."

Dr. Simpson smirked. "I never just say no, Dr. Reynolds."

Carson wasn't sure, but something appeared to pass between them in their respective expressions.

Lincoln chucked a file onto his desk. "So nothing, then." His shoulders nearly touched his ears, his forehead creased, his lips a thin line. Lincoln's tension and frustration poured into Carson, putting him on edge.

"I know he's a shaman, but that just means he goes on spirit walks and talks to 'spirits'"—Lincoln did the air quotes, disbelief plastered across his face—"and in riddles. Burns herbs and stuff. It doesn't mean he can walk though locked doors, knock out officers without touching them, or mess with an entire building's security system."

Carson had missed some of the conversation, but clearly they were back to Jameson. The man who tried to kill him. What if Jameson had killed Carson's family when his mother trusted Jameson?

Flashes of his mother, the blood, the knife.... If Jameson were responsible, Carson would kill him. Anger hit him like a bat. His body flushed, and power radiated out from his gut. He fisted his hands, breaths increasing.

"Carson." Lincoln stood before him, appearing partially concerned and confused. "You okay?"

Carson exhaled. When he unfisted his hands, they shook slightly, the residue of the energy burning off in his muscles. What the hell was that?

Nodding, Carson smiled. "Yeah. I'm good."

He knew Lincoln wasn't totally convinced, but he nodded and went back to his conversation.

"Commander, don't underestimate the power of Jameson Merrick. Manashan shamans possess mental and psychic abilities that are beyond that of any known vampire. The Manashan are descendants of a powerful Thracian tribe of vampires called the Besins, with origins in blood magic."

Lincoln grunted. "Are you saying he's using some kind of ancient magic?"

The amusement on Lincoln's face showed his disbelief. Carson totally believed in magic. Just look at his new tattoos and red eyes, which had appeared out of nowhere.

Dr. Simpson clasped her hands behind her back. "If you want to call it that. In theory shamans use the elements of nature and the spirit world to draw in energy to perform their rituals and magic—for lack of a better term."

"So he can disable security systems and lock down computers with his mind?" Lincoln actually snorted, which Carson found strangely endearing.

"It's not out of the realm of possibility, Lincoln."

"Just fucking great." Lincoln threw his pen down on the desk, but it popped up and flew onto the floor.

Tommy entered the room next. Man, it was getting crowded in there. Carson wanted them all to leave so he could spend time alone with Lincoln.

Tommy tossed a file onto Lincoln's desk, which already overflowed with files and papers. How his bond mate found anything, Carson hadn't a clue. He smiled. *His* bond mate. That filled his chest with warmth.

Lincoln raised a challenging eyebrow at Tommy, who merely pointed to the folder. Lincoln opened it, and as he scanned the contents, he tensed and his eyes widened. He wiped his hand over his mouth.

"Can I speak with you in the hallway?"

Tommy nodded, and Lincoln left the room with him. Doc approached Carson and asked how he was doing.

Carson's eyes were on the door where Lincoln had just exited. "I'm fine." He turned to Doc. "What's going on?"

Doc shrugged and continued to assess Carson visually. Carson felt like a rat in a cage. He tried to ignore Doc and the tension and uneasiness that flowed into his body, no doubt coming from Lincoln. A sinking foreboding clutched Carson. Something was really wrong. Gods, how could things get worse?

After what seemed like forever—in reality only about ten minutes—Lincoln and Tommy returned. When Carson saw Lincoln's guarded expression, the hair on Carson's body stood on end. Lincoln handed the file to Doc. He looked through the contents and came away with an expression similar to Lincoln's. He took the file back, then tapped it against his palm, either contemplating something or stalling.

Carson gripped the edge of the cushion as Lincoln approached. He knelt on one knee next to Carson's leg and placed his hand on Carson's knee. The gesture would have been overtly romantic if not for the unease flowing from Lincoln.

"Not planning on proposing, are you?" Carson forced a chuckle. Anything to clear the fog of seriousness.

Lincoln's eyes heated but quickly flashed back to his previous wariness. He cleared his throat and placed the folder on the cushion next to Carson, who eyed it with the same wariness.

"Can I ask you some questions about the day your family was killed?"

"Murdered. They were *murdered*." Carson added more force than he meant to.

"I know," Lincoln said in a quiet voice. The softness in his eyes was as calming as the thumb he rubbed over Carson's thigh.

"I told you everything I know."

"Yes, you did, but you only talked about finding your mother. What about your brother and uncle? Where were they in the house?"

Carson tensed with the questions. He swallowed hard repeatedly until he thought he could answer. "I didn't see them. I found my mother first. She said that... she said that the person who... st-stabbed her... said he'd killed them already. I... didn't look for them because my mother said to get the letter in the box on her dresser and get out. She didn't know where the man had gone."

"Did your mother say who had stabbed her?"

Carson shook his head. "I didn't ask."

Lincoln nodded. "That's okay."

He had something to tell Carson and hesitated for some reason. Lincoln picked up the file as if it were dangerous and then looked to Carson. His forced smile sent a shiver down Carson's spine.

Lincoln handed the folder to Carson. Inside was a photo of Caden and Uncle Graham. His breath hitched. The picture was grainy, as if the image were taken at a distance and then enlarged. A lump the size of a cantaloupe formed in his throat, and tears stung his eyes, seeing his little brother.

"Caden," he whispered.

"This is your brother and uncle?" Lincoln rubbed his palm over Carson's knee.

"Yes." Carson ran a finger reverently over the image of Caden.

"This photo was taken from a surveillance camera outside of a bank in Oswego five days ago."

"Five days ago? No, that isn't possible. They're dead. They were murdered."

Lincoln shook his head, as did Tommy. Doc continued to give Carson that rat-in-a-cage look.

Lincoln squeezed Carson's knee. "No. They're very much alive in this picture. A bank teller reported that your uncle withdrew a large sum of money. She stated that he was highly agitated and nervous, as was the teen with him. She reported the incident to the bank manager because she feared your brother was with your uncle against his will. She said she had a *feeling*. The bank manager called the local Nons police."

An icy chill crept over Carson. He blinked, trying to focus on what Lincoln was saying, trying to understand what…. Caden was alive? His brother wasn't dead?

"Caden… he's not…." His voice broke on the words. He lowered his head, taking in several deep breaths, willing his head to stop swimming. This couldn't be real… could it?

"Carson?"

Carson raised his chin. The dire expression on Lincoln's face told Carson there was more. But oh gods, Caden was alive. His brother. His best friend.

Lincoln licked his lips and grasped Carson's hand. "We did extensive background checks on your family. We looked at everything…. Acquaintances, activity, financial records…." He paused.

"Just tell me," Carson gripped Lincoln's hand.

"The account your uncle withdrew the money from has received monthly deposits from a dummy corporation for the past twenty years. A significant amount of money. That corporation has been linked to Manny Monrovia."

Carson frowned. That name. Where had he heard it before? Probably his uncle. Carson shrugged, not understanding the connection.

Lincoln's expression seemed pained. Carson rubbed his thumb over the back of Lincoln's hand in a soothing gesture. That seemed to spur him on.

Lincoln sighed deeply. "Manny Monrovia is the person responsible for your kidnapping. He's the man who forced you to bite Justin."

Carson could have sworn time stopped. A sheet of white had fallen over his vision. The raging beat of his heart and rushing blood and gasping breaths blocked out all sound. Something sped through his veins, filled his muscles with sparks of power and hunger and need. Gods, *it* needed…. What, he didn't know.

Visions flashed of fire, chanting, pain, and screams and blood, so visceral he could smell the burning wood mixed with a sweet sulfurous odor, feel the never-ending searing pain of needle pricks on his skin, hear his own screams and groans and… ecstasy?

Not his memories, but their familiarity spread and opened an entirely new part of his mind. A foreign dialect he'd never heard spoken spilled into his head. The memories intensified. Justin appeared before him. Sweet, innocent Justin tied to that table, eyes haunted and bitter and way too forgiving as Carson leaned over him. The salty taste of Justin's skin, the pulse of his jugular beneath Carson's tongue, the resistance as his fangs punched through the skin. What he hadn't remembered? Groaning as the sweet blood hit his tongue, grinding his hips into the side of the table, knowing he should stop sucking, but the bliss was too addicting. And then he came… came from sucking away Justin's life through his blood.

A mournful howl filled his ears. He swore his heart had been ripped from his chest, leaving him cold as his blood leached out of the gaping hole.

Screams and alarms sounded around him, but nothing could save him from the devastating sorrow emanating from his soul. His uncle. The rage crushed the sorrow like a bug in its palm. His uncle, the man who cared for them, had a hand in what happened to Justin, possibly killed Carson's mother, took his brother.

Caden.

Misery and pain swelled with the anger, a rush of endorphins, and the white before his eyes bled into red as his mind turned to revenge. Cold, calculated justice for those he loved. His uncle would pay, and so would Manny Monrovia. With the strength surging through Carson's veins, he knew he could render that justice. Everyone involved would pay dearly.

LINCOLN CROUCHED behind his desk, his hands clamped over his ears, and still the howling, painful wail from Carson penetrated his head, vibrating the marrow in his bones. The air in the office pulsated, and every hair on Lincoln's body stood on end. The anguish, and the anger from Carson were like physical blows to Lincoln's mind. He tried to rise but was continually knocked back. He had to get to Carson and stop whatever the hell kind of onslaught he'd unleashed.

Behind Lincoln on the floor, Tommy was out cold. Lincoln was sure he'd find everyone else in the same state *if* he could move. Pieces of his heart broke off with each howl from Carson. Gods, the pain and misery and anger. He prayed Carson gained control, or the NVJ would take drastic measures. His life was in danger. The alarm was on yellow alert, level one. That would change. Lincoln knew the drill. Assess the threat level, devise a tactical response, assemble a team, attack. Carson would be considered red alert. The attack would be an all-out assault to "contain" the threat, including death.

Shit, even Lincoln didn't know if Carson was a danger to anyone.

The alarm changed to orange alert.

Carson, you have to stop, please?

NVJ officers would kill him without hesitation. He had to get through to Carson. Lincoln crawled forward, his forehead against the floor. Creeping along, he peered round the side of the desk at Carson. Lincoln froze. *Holy shit.*

A red aura surrounded his body. The writing and symbols glowed bright red. His eyes were glowing red orbs. Carson was eerily still as he stood, still howling out his pain and anger. Tight bands cinched Lincoln's chest. Carson was caught in some inescapable hell. Was he being harmed, or was something taking him over?

"Carson!" Lincoln was immediately swallowed within the relentless noise. He shuffled forward, still unable to remove his hands from his ears or risk busting an eardrum.

Red alert.

Metal shutters slammed shut over the windows of the office. Fuck, that was bad.

Carson, please stop. They're going to kill you. Oh gods, I can't lose you, please.

The wailing moan ceased, leaving only the unrelenting alarms. Carson turned his head toward Lincoln, his focus far off, as if he were blind.

"Carson!"

Nothing.

Carson?

Carson's head tilted to the side. Had he heard what Lincoln thought?

Carson, love, can you hear me?

Carson turned, facing Lincoln.

If you can hear me, Carson, talk to me, please. You're freaking everyone out. You need to come back. Please talk to me.

Carson moved closer, his chin tilted down as if he could see Lincoln. Maybe he could.

Lincoln?

Fuck yes, Carson. You have to stop now. We've hit red alert. They see you as a threat, and things are going to get bad. Can you stop?

My uncle... he has to pay for what he did. I have to get Caden. I can't....

Carson dropped to his knees. The red glow still covered his body and his eyes.

I can't... it's too big... too strong.... I don't know what it is.

Lincoln crawled the distance between them. Tentatively he placed his hands on Carson's shoulders, ready for anything to happen. The heat coming from Carson was too hot, yet Lincoln forced his hands to remain. He counted on the physical connection to bring him back.

Fuck. An unknown behemoth, still in its infancy, incubated within Carson's core. Lincoln's mind couldn't comprehend the potential power of what could only mature into something behemoth. What would become of Carson? What the fuck had Lincoln's blood done?

Fight it. I can feel it coming from inside of you, and it's strong, but you're stronger. I know you're hurting and angry, but this is only going to get us all killed. Please, I can't lose you....

Lincoln... help me.

The office door was busted in, and a tactical team of officers in full riot gear, weapons ready to kill, trampled inside. Lincoln lunged, wrapped his arms around Carson, and did the only thing that might save them. He put his back to the officers, protecting Carson with his body. They'd have to go through Lincoln.

"Stand down! Situation under control!" Lincoln's desperation belied his usual authoritative tone.

"Back away from him, Commander. Orders are to kill." The officer tried to get a bead on Carson with her laser sight. More of the red dots were on the wall behind Lincoln. If Lincoln moved, they'd fill Carson with bullets.

"Stand down!" Fear unlike anything he'd ever known had him close to hyperventilating. If he blacked out, no one would save Carson. "Please! He's my bond mate. Don't shoot!"

"Move, Commander!"

Lincoln pushed Carson backward, seeking protection behind the desk. "It's okay, love. I won't let them hurt you." He ran his shaking hand over Carson's back, trying to calm the growing rage in him. "Stay calm. It'll be okay. I promise. I promise. Just stay right here."

Carson looked up at Lincoln. His eyes no longer glowed, but his tattoos still raged with a fiery red. He lifted his hand and wiped his thumb over Lincoln's cheek. Wet. Lincoln hadn't even known he was crying. Carson cupped Lincoln's cheek and a pleasurable warmth soaked through Lincoln. Love.

"Commander, you have ten seconds, and then we shoot." The NVJ wasn't fucking around.

I won't let them hurt you.

Abruptly Carson jumped to his feet, shoved Lincoln back, and he went down hard onto the floor. Carson faced off with the officers.

"Fire!" the woman commanded.

CHAPTER 19

LINCOLN LUNGED at Carson's feet as the gunshots exploded but failed to knock him to the floor. He watched helplessly as Carson flailed back into the wall.

An endless tortured scream erupted from his throat. "Noooooo! Carson, no! Carson, no!"

Lincoln couldn't breathe. Couldn't think of anything but charging the officers and killing every one of them, but he had to get to Carson. Lincoln got to his knees, eyes blurred with tears. A massive cramp in his stomach caused him to double over. He retched violently, shaking, crying, coming apart as he heaved the contents of his stomach onto the floor. The spasms racked him relentlessly until his stomach was empty. He crawled away from the putrid stench and collapsed onto the floor from fatigue.

Blood. The smell brought another retch. He swallowed hard. Tears and snot covered his face. Sobbing, gasping, muscles clenched. He couldn't....

A hand on his back startled him, but he refused to look up. Refused to see Carson dead. He wanted to die, wished for a bullet to end him.

"Lincoln."

Lincoln shook his head. He couldn't do this.

"Lincoln, look."

Lincoln shuddered. No. It couldn't be. He lifted his head, blinking away tears, only to start sobbing again. He lunged up into Carson's arms. Alive. He was alive.

"I'm okay, baby. Don't cry." Carson gripped Lincoln tight to his chest.

Lincoln gasped as uncontrollable sobs wracked his frame. "I... thought you... were dead."

The pain still had his heart in a vise. Any second he feared Carson would appear dead at his feet. Was he trapped in an alternate reality, thrown out of his head to save his sanity? "You can't be real. They shot you," he whispered, calm enough to speak.

"No. I'm real and I'm here. I don't know how, but I knew the bullets wouldn't hurt me."

The waver in Carson's breath helped Lincoln quell his sobs. Jesus, he had to get it together. He pulled back enough to place his hands on the sides of Carson's head. Fear and uncertainty shined bright in Carson's eyes, which no longer glowed like red orbs. Lincoln rested his forehead against Carson's and sighed.

"I was so scared," he whispered.

Carson cupped Lincoln's cheek as he had earlier. "I said I wouldn't leave you. I promised."

Lincoln closed his eyes, chin still quivering. "I don't ever want to lose you. You're mine." He brushed a gentle kiss over Carson's lips.

A groan came from across the room. Doc roused from his state of unconsciousness. Tommy also stirred. Every member of the tactical team was sprawled on the floor.

Oh fuck. "What did you do? Are they dead?" If they were dead, Carson wouldn't live through the hour.

Carson shook his head. "No. Unconscious and unharmed. I don't know what I did. I just wished they would stop, and they fell." His face paled, eyes wide and glazed with what looked to be shell shock. Lincoln feared he was about to pass out. "They were going to kill you because of me. They thought I was dangerous enough to kill."

Carson slumped against Lincoln, and within seconds, Lincoln was holding him up. "What's wrong, love?"

"Lower him to the floor. Looks like he's in shock," Doc said.

"I'm going to lay you on the floor. You know Doc. He's just got to check you out. Okay?"

Carson chuckled softly into Lincoln's chest and nodded. Lincoln lowered him gently, cradling the back of Carson's head until he was on the floor. Doc knelt and placed two fingers against Carson's neck.

"Lincoln." Carson looked at him with a dull, glazed look. "I need to find Caden."

"I know, and we're going to get him, just as soon as you get some rest."

Carson shook his head, but he didn't try to get up.

"Is he going to be okay, Doc?" Lincoln rubbed the back of his hand over Carson's cheek.

Doc looked at Lincoln with an "are you fucking kidding me?" expression, but said, "Yeah. Whatever… happened took a lot out of him." Doc sighed as he scanned the room. "The shit's gonna hit the fan over this. You know that, right?"

Lincoln nodded, but his attention remained on Carson. Whatever happened next, he would protect the man he loved with his life.

LINCOLN RUBBED his hands over his face, wishing the nightmare would end. The NVJ regional director for Western New York State, Anthony Feith, from Rochester, sat across the table from Lincoln. Next to the director was Tommy. For two hours they played the irritating game of repeatedly asking Lincoln the same questions. One of the techniques in Lincoln's interrogations toolbox, but only effective if you were new to the game. Lincoln wasn't. It really pissed him off Director Feith treated him like a suspect.

Doc wasn't kidding. The shit hit the fan, all right, all the way to Washington, DC, and straight up to the director general Carina Williams herself. Nothing good would come from the NVJ bigwigs having eyes on the Tabula Rasa. That type of interest generally meant someone disappeared—for good. Lincoln's dread clenched his fists. Carson had to get away from the NVJ and hide. That was if he was even still in the building. What if they had shuttled him away already? Lincoln had to get out of that room and find him.

"Commander Samuels. Please answer the question," Director Feith said in his usual clipped tone. Lincoln never cared for the man. "How did the Tabula Rasa come to be in your custody?"

"For the fifth time. Carson was arrested trying to steal blood from a VBM. When I was discovered that he was a Tabula Rasa, he was brought to medical on my command, sir." He gritted out each word through his teeth.

The sour expression on the director's face told Lincoln he didn't care for his manner of answering. "And you thought it wasn't imperative that an unregistered Tabula Rasa be brought to the attention of your superiors?"

"As I said earlier—several times—the immediate concern was for his health and the threat on his life due to the reported death of his family."

"What about the team you sent out to retrieve"—the director glanced down at the papers before him—"Justin Masters. Just what was the purpose of that mission?"

Out of the corner of Lincoln's eye, Tommy shook his head minutely. He didn't want Lincoln to reveal the truth about Justin?

Lincoln shifted in his chair. Shit, what was that about? Another shake of Tommy's head, and Lincoln said, "It was reported that Justin Masters was a vampire being held in a facility against his will."

The director narrowed his eyes. "And why can't I find any information about this man or the orders to retrieve him?"

No paperwork or information? What had Tommy done and why?

"It was filed. I did the paperwork myself. It was loaded into the computer."

The director sat back and sighed. "Yeah, well, the system is one fucked-up mess, Commander."

Lincoln raised his eyebrows, and Tommy covertly smirked. "I don't know why that is, sir."

The director pulled the papers on the table into a pile, placed them into the folder, and then closed it. "Frankly this whole operation has gone to hell in a handbasket. As of now, Commander, you are relieved of duty until a full investigation can be launched into the incidents of the last few days."

"You can't do that." Lincoln knew he should have chosen his words more wisely as soon he spoke.

The director scowled. "I can, Commander, and my word is law here. You will remain in this building until my investigation is complete. Until then you are to have no contact with the Tabula Rasa. You will both be under guard, and Commander, if you try to see him, you will be hauled off to a place much worse than this."

Lincoln had to see Carson. Already his body itched, his thoughts centered on his bond mate, needing desperately to touch his skin. He imagined it felt similar to a drug. A new bond required the two vampires to stay close, connect physically often. Lincoln swallowed hard and almost said something to that effect, but refrained. Tommy raised an eyebrow but remained silent.

"What will happen to Carson?" Lincoln asked the director with a choked voice.

"A detail from the Center for Vampire Advancement will be here at 2000 hours to collect the Tabula Rasa. He will be brought to a secured location."

No! He'd never see Carson again. They would lock him away where he would be a guinea pig to be studied, treated as a thing. They wouldn't give a damn about any bond.

Lincoln, what's wrong?

Lincoln sat upright and looked around. The director spoke with Tommy.

Lincoln, I can feel your fear. What's going on?

Carson?

Yeah. Are you okay?

Where are you? Lincoln tilted his chin down so the director didn't see him doing anything weird.

Yeah. I'm with Doc.

Thank gods. Lincoln's fear went down a few notches. He had to calmly tell Carson what he needed to do without scaring him.

Listen to me carefully. I need you to tell Doc exactly what I tell you. Can you do that?

There was a moment of silence. *Only if you tell me you're okay.*

Lincoln chuckled to himself. *I'm okay, love, but if we don't get out of here, things are going to get bad. I don't want to scare you, but after what you did.... Well, you caught the attention of some very powerful people in the NVJ. Do you understand?*

I'm sorry about what I did. I really fucked this up.

You didn't ask for this. We'll figure this all out, but first we have to get out of here. Now listen carefully.

CARSON RELAYED Lincoln's directions to Doc, who wrote them from across the room. As far from Carson as he could get. He didn't blame Doc after what Carson did earlier, but Carson believed he had whatever "it" was under better control. The longer he lived with it in him, the more it became part of him he could control.

Lincoln's fear nearly had Carson in a panic. Doc didn't suggest a sedative, to Carson's astonishment, but a sort of guided meditation. Hard to do when the world was about to end. Carson calmed and then focused on the connection with Lincoln. Carson nearly fell off his chair when Lincoln answered.

The writing on Carson's body glowed again. From the way Doc stared at Carson, his eyes were probably glowing again as well. Assuring Doc nothing bad would happen didn't make much difference in his hesitation. Carson couldn't blame him after seeing a room full of people rendered unconscious. Carson hadn't figured out how he'd accomplished that one. His burgeoning mental abilities wigged him out as much as everyone else. Now it appeared he'd caused the same reaction in a shitload of other people. Really important people.

"Lincoln says a detail is coming from the CVA?"

Doc's sharp intake of air couldn't mean anything good. Whatever the CVA was snapped Doc out of his fear of Carson, because he was now standing next to him.

Have Doc get you into the basement, and I have a new code for the elevator.

Why the basement? And you're kind of freaking Doc out.

Carson heard Lincoln's mental snort.

Doc's as tough as nails. He'll take care of you. Now tell him. And you need to write down the new code Tommy changed.

"He says you need to get me into the basement. Tommy changed the codes. Give me a piece of paper."

Doc handed Carson a pad and pen from his coat pocket. Carson wrote the numbers Lincoln told him, and Doc took the paper. The following silence from Lincoln unnerved Carson. Lincoln's nervous energy held steady.

Lincoln? Are you safe?

I'm here. Yes, I'm safe where I am. Listen, love, very carefully. You and I are being watched very closely. They want to take you away from here. They... they want to separate us. I won't let that happen.

Carson shook his head. He couldn't leave Lincoln. He couldn't even imagine being without him. *How can they do that?*

I don't know, but it doesn't matter. I'm getting us out of here, but I need you to do something for me.

Even through their bond, Carson heard something that alarmed him. *That depends on what it is.*

Lincoln chuckled. *You are a spitfire. Damn, I can't wait to get to you. But that won't happen if we don't do things right. If I don't come to the basement by 2100 hours, that's 9:00 p.m., you're to leave with Doc. There's a secured evacuation tunnel that will use the same code I gave you. No one else can access this. Do you understand?*

Carson let his defiance flood their bond. *No. I am not leaving you here. I can come and get you. I can try to do what I did in your office. I can control it better now. It's how I'm talking to you. Please let me help.*

Another silence and Carson started to panic.

No, Carson! They are coming to take you, and they'll have ways to deal with you. Get out of here with Doc, and I'll catch up with you. I promise. For now, know I'll be there if I can. Nothing will keep me away from you. Nothing. If you don't get out of here, you can't find Caden.

Carson closed his eyes. His brother was alive. That fact was hard to hold on to when he'd been mourning his little brother for weeks.

Okay, but you promise me that you'll be there, Lincoln, and if you can't then you'll find me.

I will. I promise. Be safe.

You too. Don't do anything stupid.

You got it. Now you and Doc get to the basement. I'll see you soon.

CHAPTER 20

CARSON ENDED the connection. The red glow of his skin dissipated. Doc gazed at him expectantly, a pair of socks in one hand and shoes in the other.

"Put these on. I have an idea about how to sneak you to the elevator. I'll be right back."

Doc left the room. Carson slipped on the socks and shoes, which were a little big but worked. He leaned forward, elbows on his thighs, lowered his head, and took in a deep breath. So much had happened in such a short time. His once boring and lonely life was thrown into chaos, dragging him like a runaway horse. His mother dying, fleeing his home, nearly getting arrested, bonding with Lincoln, his body turning into something unknown, finding out Caden was alive, his uncle.... All of it the tip of some massive iceberg. He'd continue to change, gain more power, maybe more abilities. An anomaly, or maybe a monster. He sank deeper into the fear of what he knew, knowledge without origin.

Doc returned, his lips pursed and brow furrowed. He closed the door. "Get up on the bed and cover up. I'm taking you for a short ride. Don't say anything. Just lie there and leave it to me."

Carson lay down and covered himself. Doc raised the metal side rail, and it clicked into place. Going to the head of the bed, Doc popped the brake and moved the bed toward the door. He stopped and opened the door. Outside a man of medium build, with a brown mustache and a black hat and vest with NVJ letters, greeted them.

"Let me help you there." The guard grabbed the end of the bed and pulled it through the door. "Which way to the CAT scan?"

"Left and then right." Doc guided the head of the bed.

How were they supposed to get away with a guard? Carson looked up at Doc, who gave him a quick nervous glance, then looked ahead. Once they made two turns, they stopped at a closed door. The guard turned the knob and walked backward, pushing the door open as he helped with the bed. They were in the CAT scan room. Confused, Carson kept quiet. What he wanted to do was jump off the bed and run to the basement. What if Lincoln already waited for him? Carson had to trust Doc, but the delay in being able to touch Lincoln, hold him, raked over his nerves.

"I'll need to wait outside. This machine gives off radiation. The scan will take an hour, so don't come back in here before then," Doc told the guard.

He looked hesitantly around the room, then nodded, seemingly satisfied with what he saw, and left. Doc raised his finger to his lips when Carson tried to speak.

"Okay, Carson. I need you to lie on the table," Doc said as Carson rose from the gurney.

Doc actually wanted him to lie down. Carson hopped up and stretched out. Doc leaned down and whispered, "Lie here. I'm going to start the CAT scan. Don't move. When the coast is clear, I'll come and get you."

Carson nodded. He thought about contacting Lincoln, but his skin would start glowing again. What if he couldn't make it stop? Best to wait.

A loud clunking noise startled Carson, and then a hum filled the room. Carson raised his head and peered over his feet. Doc sat before a computer monitor behind a large window. In less than a minute, Doc emerged and motioned for Carson to follow him. They circled the thumping machine to a door not visible to the rest of the room. Emerging into a small hallway, Carson held his breath, sure any moment they'd be caught. Doc led Carson to another door and into another hallway. Stopping at the end of the hall, Doc closed his eyes and exhaled. He opened his eyes and looked around the corner.

"This way," he whispered.

They came to an elevator. Gods, this had to take them to the basement, because his heart was ready to explode in his chest.

Doc punched the code Lincoln gave them into the keypad, and the doors opened. He pushed Carson in and punched in more numbers. The doors closed, and the elevator started its descent.

"Holy shit." Doc wiped at his forehead with his sleeve. "I'm getting too old for this shit."

Carson was about to say something when the doors opened into another hallway.

"We're safe. No one else can get down here without the codes. We leave in less than an hour. We were prepping this level for a visitor, so there's food down here, as well as clothes that should fit you."

Carson tried to appear as relaxed as Doc appeared, but until Lincoln was with him, that would be impossible.

LINCOLN PACED the room where he'd been sequestered. A NVJ officer with a nametag that said Henderson silently guarded the door. Seemed the director came prepared with his own cadre of officers. Lincoln definitely outranked her, but his orders were now null and void. Carson should have been in the basement by then. He trusted Doc as much as he trusted Max to protect his bond mate. Doc would get Carson into the basement, then get him out of the NVJ and protect him with his life. Lincoln didn't want that to become necessary.

Tommy was gathering the files and information he removed before the director arrived. At least someone was thinking because Lincoln was all about Carson and making sure he was okay. If it came down to it, Carson was all that mattered. He needed to get away safely, and if that meant going without Lincoln, then it would have to be. He wouldn't rest until Carson lived without the fear of anyone trying to use him again for what he was or was becoming.

The door opened, and the officer stepped back. Tommy walked in and told her to wait outside, and she complied. Lincoln never imagined he would miss giving an order. Tommy motioned Lincoln toward the other side of the room.

"We don't have long," he said in a hushed tone. "There are more NVJ officers loading in here by the minute. The director is tearing the place apart. I have the files and information in a utility closet near the elevator in the north wing."

Lincoln pursed his lips. "Any chance I can get out of here with Carson?"

Tommy smirked. His mischievous expression reminded Lincoln of Tommy's nickname, "boy genius."

"I'm working on something big. You'll know it's happening when you hear it. Just be ready to bolt for the elevator. Don't let anything stop you." Tommy stopped, and when his eyes met Lincoln's, they were hard. "If you don't get out of here tonight, you won't ever get out."

Lincoln understood. If he didn't get out, he was a dead man. "If I don't make it out of here, I need you to find Max. I need him to take care of Carson."

Tommy nodded and chewed on his bottom lip. "And if Max is unavailable?"

In other words if Max was dead. Lincoln didn't even want to consider the possibility. He closed his eyes, and when Tommy's hand landed on his shoulder, he flinched. "I'll make sure Carson's taken care of if you don't get out of here, but that's not going to happen. I'm sure Max and John are fine. I have a few people on their trail. Just waiting for them to report back."

Lincoln blew out a deep breath. "Yeah. I hope so." For all of their sakes, Tommy had to be right.

Tommy glanced at his watch. "You've got ten minutes. Be ready."

Lincoln nodded. Tommy left. The guard returned to her post. Whatever Tommy planned had to be big enough.

CARSON STOOD by the entrance to the tunnel, unable to stop pacing. Ten minutes. Lincoln still hadn't appeared. Doc leaned back against the wall. To all appearances cool as a cucumber. Any second Carson would start climbing the walls. How could he leave Lincoln there? What if they wouldn't let him leave? What if they punished him for Carson's escape?

"I can't...." Carson pushed his fist into his gut, trying to counteract the pain growing there.

Doc walked over to him. "What's wrong? You're pale and sweating. Are you sick?"

How could he tell Doc the panic from the thought of leaving Lincoln was making him sick? He shook his head. "I can't leave him." Carson looked into Doc's eyes. The blue gray had darkened.

"You're right. We can't leave him," Doc said.

Carson blinked. Not ten minutes ago, Doc had insisted, Lincoln or no, they were leaving on time. "Really?"

Doc scowled and shook his head. "No. I didn't mean…. We have to leave no matter what. There'll be a diversion in"—he looked down at his watch—"five minutes. Lincoln has ten minutes to get here. If not we go."

Carson grabbed his hair and clutched it tight. He battled with the need to contact Lincoln, but Doc put the kibosh on that idea. Carson could only contact Lincoln in an emergency because Doc still got that wary PTSD look whenever Carson mentioned the idea.

"I don't think I can be away from him. It's already tearing at my insides." A clawing need worked through his body and threatened to take over any rational thought he had.

Doc eyed him warily. "Maybe I could give you a light sedative. Just enough to take the edge off."

That was the last thing he wanted or needed, and the suggestion angered him. "No! No more fucking drugs."

"No more drugs." Doc agreed to the idea easily, and then he bit his lip.

Carson cocked his head. Doc was anything but agreeable. Carson focused on Doc, on his thoughts and feelings, trying to catch anything. Recalling how he connected with Lincoln, he followed a thin silvery line, a connection into Doc's mind. A sudden wave of doubt and confusion smacked him hard. Was that Lincoln?

No, this felt different.

"What if I said I wasn't going to leave without Lincoln, no matter what you say?" Carson asked, bracing himself.

Doc's angry scowl, accompanied by a blast of anger, knocked into Carson. "You'll do what I say, or you're going to get us both killed."

Carson reversed the connection, sending rather than receiving. What happened next nearly floored him.

Doc pursed his lips, as if thinking hard. "You know what, I think you're right. We have to wait for Lincoln. We can't leave him here. I love him."

Carson snorted. *Holy. Shit.* He'd planted his thoughts in Doc.

He shook his head. "What the fuck? I didn't—"

Doc's panic overwhelmed Carson. He sent calming thoughts to Doc, and his body appeared to relax, as did his expression.

"I didn't mean I love him. I meant—"

The confusion on Doc's face was priceless. Carson nodded. "No, you didn't."

Carson contemplated what he'd done. Had he actually planted a suggestion in Doc's head? He had repeated word for word what Carson was thinking? Fuck, what if he could.... What if he had some kind of mind control over others? No, the idea was too far out there.

The door to the room flew open. Carson spun around. Tommy ran in, a bag tossed over his shoulder. Not Lincoln. Crap. Carson focused on Tommy. A confusing array of emotions battered Carson—excitement, guilt, satisfaction, and at the tail end, a smidgen of fear.

Again the connection was there for Carson to enter Tommy's mind. *Stop!*

Tommy skidded to a halt. His brow furrowed as he looked around with a dazed expression.

He gave Carson a puzzled look, which cleared quickly as he looked at his watch. "Take cover. We've got about thirty seconds before all hell breaks loose."

Carson intercepted what Tommy intended to say and made a suggestion. "Once it does, Lincoln has got exactly... um... thirty minutes to get here."

"You mean ten minutes." Doc looked to Carson, who turned his head quickly, trying to make that move appear nonchalant.

Tommy looked between the two of them and shook his head. "I wanted to say ten, but.... Damn, I don't know why I said thirty."

Doc grabbed Carson's arm, his mouth open, but before he could say anything, an explosion rocked the building. They all hit the floor.

CHAPTER 21

THE ENTIRE building shook. Alarms blared, glass shattered, and concrete crumbled. Lincoln covered his head as chunks of ceiling tiles fell on him. Fucking Tommy. Nothing subtle with that guy. Henderson hit the floor as well and had her head tucked under her arms. That was Lincoln's chance. Scrambling from the floor, he lunged for Henderson's gun and ripped the weapon from her holster. He rolled up onto his knee, pointing the weapon at her. His hand trembled. Being away from Carson did a job on his nerves. Henderson raised her head. Her eyes widened, seeing her gun in Lincoln's hand.

Shit, he was officially a criminal.

"I'm sorry. I can't let them take Carson away from me. They're going to use him, and I can't let that happen." He felt the need to explain himself despite the lack of time.

Her green eyes clouded and became glassy. "They took my son from me. He's a Sanatore, and I haven't seen him in over two years. They said it was for his own good, but they used his safety as a way to keep me in the NVJ. To do things I'm not proud of. Oh gods, why did I let Feith use me like that?"

Well, shit. What the fuck was that all about? He didn't have time to figure it out. Seven minutes. "I have to get out of here. Do I need to tie you up?"

She shook her head and rose from the floor. "Take me with you. Use me as your hostage."

He was about to shake his head, then thought of getting to Carson. He pushed her out the door. "Go left. Run!"

They sprinted down the hallway as people shouted and alarms blared. Turning the corner, he ran into Henderson as she backed up. She mouthed, "Feith."

A group of NVJ officers scrambled about as Director Feith barked orders into his phone. Behind them someone shouted, heading their way.

They were so going to get shot. He grabbed Henderson's arm, and they ran down an adjacent hallway. He had to find another way.

"Do you know where you're going?"

"The long way around. Just follow me," Lincoln said, mapping the building in his mind. Two lefts, and another left, and Henderson collided with someone and went down.

Lincoln skidded to a halt and turned back, drawing the gun on the officer on the ground.

"Fuck, that hurt!"

"Wright!" Lincoln helped her up.

Maggie's eyes widened, and she lunged into Lincoln's arms. "What the fuck, Linc? The director wouldn't tell us where you were. Did you hear that explosion?" She stiffened upon seeing Henderson, and then stepped back. "I mean, sit rep, Commander?"

"Sit rep is we're getting our asses out of here now." Henderson grabbed Lincoln's arm, urging him to move.

Maggie gave him a puzzled look.

"The Center for Vampire Advancement is coming for Carson. I'm getting him out of here. He's with Doc and Tommy at the northwest escape tunnel. I've got about three minutes before Doc and Tommy get him out of here."

"What do you want me to do?" Maggie called after them.

Lincoln shook his head. "You never saw us."

Maggie pulled something out of her pocket and tossed it to Lincoln. He caught the metal object and turned it over in his hand. A USB drive.

"I was going to find a way to get that to you. Information about Monrovia and Jameson. Also there's a link to a secure line to contact me and Madison. I'll be your eyes and ears here. Good luck, Commander."

Lincoln closed his hand around the USB drive. With a salute to Maggie, he ran to catch up with Henderson.

As he turned the corner, he heard Maggie yell, "He's headed toward the east wing."

Lincoln grinned, grateful for her loyalty.

As they skidded around the corner, the elevator door came into sight. "There." Lincoln pointed, trying to control the shake in his hands as adrenaline overloaded his system. A red light flashed when he punched in the code. Fuck.

"Come on." Henderson looked behind her. "I think I hear someone coming."

Lincoln rubbed his hands together and blew out a breath. He punched in the code again. The green light flashed.

"Freeze!" a man yelled down the hall.

The elevator door opened. Lincoln shoved Henderson inside, crowding her into the corner by the doors as a volley of bullets hit the back wall.

Lincoln stabbed the key to shut the door repeatedly. Officers were getting closer. He could hear their boots hitting the floor. "Close, damn it!"

The doors closed just as the first officer reached them. If Lincoln's heart didn't explode, it would be a miracle. Their labored breaths filled the small space. Henderson threw off her cap and wiped her forehead.

"Fuck, that was close." Lincoln slumped against the wall.

Henderson ripped open a Velcro pocket in her cargo pants. She withdrew something in a small piece of plastic. Grasping Lincoln's wrist, she pulled up his hand and put the item in his hand. A photo of a smiling young boy, maybe eight, with large green eyes and a large gap where his front teeth used to be.

"If something happens to me... his name is Manuel. They took him from me just like they took his father. I tried to hide him, but the bastards found him. Please, promise me...." She choked on a sob and then schooled her features. "Promise me you'll find him. There're things going on in the NVJ that no one knows about, things that aren't right."

Things going on?

"I promise."

The doors slid open, and Henderson rushed out. Lincoln tucked the photo into his pocket and exited the elevator. Lincoln took the lead as they ran down the hall, glancing at his watch. Five fucking minutes late. Carson would be gone. No matter what, Lincoln would catch up with him. He wished he could initiate contact....

Around the corner he found Carson staring at Doc and Tommy. Both of them stood silently.

"Carson!" Lincoln sprinted to his lover. He'd convinced himself he'd never see him again.

"Thank gods, Lincoln!" Carson jumped into Lincoln's arms.

Lincoln closed his eyes, soaking in the feel, the smell, the touch of Carson, who shook like a leaf in his arms.

"I knew you'd be here. We just had to wait. I knew you wouldn't let me leave alone," Carson whispered into Lincoln's neck.

Lincoln ran his hand over Carson's hair. "No, love. No way. We're a team. You and me."

"Too bad your team is about to be dismantled."

Lincoln set Carson to his feet and stepped in front of him. Director Feith stood at the entrance to the room with a group of officers, their guns drawn and aimed at them.

"Use me." Henderson held up her hands. "Don't shoot. The perp has a gun."

Momentarily confused, Lincoln looked down at the weapon still in his hand. He stepped behind her and pointed the gun at her head. "Don't move, or she dies."

The director cocked an eyebrow. No one moved. Carson grasped the back of Lincoln's shirt tight in his fists. Carson's fear was palpable. They'd come too far to fail now. Lincoln had promises to keep.

The director smirked and said, "Officer Baker."

The officer next to the director fired. Henderson's chest exploded in a shower of blood. A searing pain burst in the side of Lincoln's chest. The force threw him back, landing on the floor, his arms still secured around Henderson's waist. He quickly rolled her off. He knew she was dead by the unblinking stare of her eyes.

The pain seized his chest and stole the breath from his lungs. A red stain expanded across his shirt. Fuck.

CARSON COULDN'T move. So much blood. They'd killed that poor woman. And Lincoln....

"No, Lincoln!" Carson dropped to his knees. His shirt was soaked with blood.

"It's.... I'll be okay." Lincoln coughed, his face twisting in pain. His blood pooled on the floor by his side. "Go," he whispered.

The gurgling sound he made threw Carson back in time. His mother. In those last minutes, blood had filled her throat and spilled from her mouth, as she died on the floor right in front of him. She'd asked him to take care of Caden. He would keep that promise.

"Yeah, not without you. And not until I take care of these guys." They'd fucking shot his bond mate.

Carson stood and turned on the group of officers. Director Feith smiled smugly. Carson let loose his rage of losing his mother, of believing his brother was dead, of seeing Lincoln suffering and bleeding. The writing and symbols flared brighter than ever. Stunned expressions passed around the room. A few officers lowered their weapons, mouths gaping. A few, well, they were terrified.

A crackling sound grew in intensity, like a motor speeding up. The deeper Carson dug, the more primal the power. Carson opened channels into each of their minds. Fear, loathing, guilt, hate. Carson gathered the power in their emotions, but he pushed them away.

"Drop your guns." Every gun hit the floor.

The director's eyes widened. "Pick up your weapons now."

"If he dies, I will find you and you'll pay. Now you're going to let us walk out of here."

The director nodded. "Of course. You're all free to go."

"Tommy. Doc. Open the tunnel and get Lincoln out of here."

"Carson, come." Lincoln's voice shook.

Carson crouched and touched Lincoln's forehead.

"Right behind you, babe. Hang on."

TOMMY AND Doc lifted Lincoln from the floor. The agony on his pale face was terrifying. Carson kept an eye on them and the officers behind him while Doc and Tommy disappeared into the tunnel with Lincoln. Carson turned back to his captive audience.

"You've never heard of Carson Locke and… um… you've sent Commander Samuels off on a long-deserved vacation and… you'll remember shooting Officer Henderson and take full responsibility for her death."

The director merely nodded.

Carson backed toward the tunnel, then paused. "Go to sleep."

The collective group collapsed. Carson picked up the gun Lincoln had been carrying and shoved the cold steel into his waistband. He prayed he didn't accidentally shoot himself in the ass. Avoiding the dead officer, he jogged into the tunnel. He hit every button on the keypad, but the door didn't close. He concentrated on the circuitry inside, the mechanisms to the door, the power.

Close. Close.

Nothing.

Apparently minds were his thing. He retrieved the gun and put some distance between himself and the keypad. Point and shoot, right? Squeezing the trigger, the sound of the gunshot exploded through the tunnel. The kickback shot pain through his hands and up to his shoulders. His hands stung. And he'd missed the keypad. Aiming again, he fired until the gun only clicked. Alarms in the tunnel blared. Fuck it! He chucked the gun and ran.

He immediately opened up his mind and found Lincoln still alive.

Hold on, babe. I'm coming.

CHAPTER 22

LINCOLN GRITTED his teeth. Pain pulsed and radiated from his chest into his arm and shoulder and jaw. He had been shot in the leg about three years before. Hurt like a bitch. But this… this was excruciating. Bile rose in his throat, mixed with the coppery taste of blood. His head throbbed and his thoughts faded in and out. Carson was coming. Lincoln could feel him. Hopefully he would survive long enough to see him again.

You will not leave me. Do you hear me? You fucking hold on, and that's an order.

Lincoln snorted at the gruff and commanding Carson, who not too long ago had been meek, scared, and starving. He toughened up quick. Life had a way of forcing that shit on a person.

Doc scowled above Lincoln, opening packages of gauze. "Something funny about getting shot? You're just lucky we keep a fully stocked first aid kit in company vans."

Doc pushed the pile of gauze against the wound. Stars flashed in Lincoln's eyes, and he couldn't suppress the whimper that escaped. He was cold and tired, and he wanted to sleep, but he knew it wasn't sleep trying to take him. Vampires might have the ability to heal a little faster than humans, but this wound was life-threatening. Damn, why couldn't anything go smoothly?

The doors to the van flew open, slammed shut, and then Carson appeared above Lincoln. "Go, go, go!"

Within seconds Tommy had them speeding from the precinct. A teleporter would have been more helpful at that moment.

Carson gripped Lincoln's hand, and his return squeeze was weak. He tried to focus his eyes on Carson's face, but a hazy vision was all he managed to produce.

"I'm going to give you a local. The bullet pierced the lung and it's filling with blood. I need to drain it."

Sounded fucking painful, so Lincoln focused on Carson. The tears in his eyes added to Lincoln's pain.

"It's gonna be okay." Carson kissed Lincoln's forehead. "You're going to be okay."

He grasped Carson's hand. Lincoln couldn't breathe. Panic reared up, stole more of his air. His vision faded in and out. He needed to tell Carson now, but trying to speak only produced a hissing sound. He was going to die, and Carson would never know.

"Hold him still while I numb the area," Doc said.

Carson leaned down and touched their foreheads together. "Focus on me," Carson whispered.

Warmth expanded through Lincoln's mind. The searing pressure in his chest faded. There was calm, pleasure. Euphoria lifted Lincoln above the pain, the burn in his lungs, the panic. He was aware of Doc pushing and prodding on his chest, but there was a disconnect between his brain and body. Was this what dying was like?

Just float here with me. Feel my arms around you, holding you.

No, this was Carson. Lincoln closed his eyes, adrift in the cocoon of something warm and wonderful. He squeezed Carson's hand. Gentle stroking on his cheek. Carson's warm breath on his face. Lincoln had to tell Carson…. What had he needed to tell him?

That's it. You're safe here with me. There is no pain. Now, you're going to sleep, and when you wake up, I'll be here. Sweet dreams.

Lincoln barely managed a nod before he was swept away into sleep.

CARSON'S BODY shook from the massive amount of pain he'd taken on for Lincoln. The burning pain in his chest, the nausea and fear, were almost too much.

"Carson, stop!"

Doc had been yelling at him since Lincoln had slipped into unconsciousness. Carson was unsuccessfully fighting to break the link. Even though Lincoln wasn't conscious, his body continually messaged the pain signals into his brain, into Carson's brain. He opened freely to the pain that came with power. He screamed with the agony, twisting his mind around the power. Mentally he yanked free of the bond and fell onto the hard metal floor of the van. Clutching at his chest, he rode out the pain, terrified knowing Lincoln had suffered so badly. But Carson was able to take that pain from him and bring him relief. The entire day, week—hell—month had exhausted him, and he fought to stay awake himself.

"Jesus Christ. What the hell was that?" Doc's hands were on Carson, checking everywhere.

He pushed Doc away. "No. Lincoln."

Doc frowned but went back to care for Lincoln. Carson pulled himself up and leaned against the wall, chasing his breath. Fuck, not being able to breathe was some scary shit. Lincoln's chest now rose and fell rhythmically. Doc had cut into Lincoln's chest wall and inserted a tube, which he taped into place. He gave Carson sideways glances periodically as he dressed Lincoln's wound.

Doc yelled up to Tommy. "Where're we headed? The sooner we can stop, the better. I need to do some delicate work and can't do it in a bumpy van."

"Safe house," Tommy called out. "Owned by someone I know. We can hole up there and regroup. We're about an hour out. Best I can do."

Doc looked down at his bloody hands and arms. "If it has a shower, I'll kiss you on the mouth."

Tommy barked out a laugh. "Sorry, Doc. You just don't do it for me."

Doc smirked. "Same here, dickhead."

Carson threaded his fingers through Lincoln's limp ones. He closed his eyes, grateful Lincoln was alive. If Carson had anything to do with it, Lincoln would live a long life. Carson's powers were evolving quickly. So far he'd spoken telepathically, rendered a room of people unconscious, influenced the behavior of others with his thoughts, and routed Lincoln's pain into his own mind. What else could he do if he tried? Lincoln's blood had the ability to heal. That blood was the catalyst to the changes within Carson. Maybe if he tried, he could accelerate Lincoln's healing. Once he got some rest and some food, he'd try. He was starving. Damn his new metabolism.

"What did you do?"

Carson's eyes popped open. Doc stared at him again with that same ready-to-bolt uneasiness.

"I took his pain," Carson stated matter-of-factly.

Doc's eyebrows practically touched his hairline. "You did what?"

A wave of panic hit Carson. He shifted nervously and tightened his grip on Lincoln's hand. Should he tell anyone what he could do? He wished Lincoln were awake to tell him what to do. Lincoln groaned in his sleep, and his legs moved restlessly. Shoot, had he pushed that thought to Lincoln? Quickly Carson closed his eyes and sent Lincoln the calming beta waves of sleep, and Lincoln settled again.

Opening his eyes, Carson was waiting for Doc to demand an explanation. "I… um…. He was in pain, and I wanted to take it away, so I did. I took it inside of me and sent him back calm, peace, pleasure. And then I put him to sleep like I did the men back there."

Doc narrowed his eyes and assessed Carson for so long he thought Doc's questions had ended. Not a chance.

"What did you do to me and Tommy earlier?"

Carson lowered his eyes and rubbed Lincoln's hand. "What do you mean?"

"Don't play dumb with me, kid. Earlier it was as if you were…." He looked unsure about what to say.

"Like I was making you say what I wanted to hear?"

"Yeah, exactly." Doc looked as if he was two seconds away from throttling Carson.

"I didn't know I could do that. It started with you and… then I tried it with Tommy, and it worked." He shrugged.

"Are you saying you can make people do what you want?"

"It seems like it." Carson didn't want to have this conversation. He was sure nothing good would come from others knowing what he could do. But if Lincoln trusted Doc….

Doc shook his head. "No way."

Time to freak Doc out. "I want a Big Mac."

Doc frowned. "We aren't stopping to eat."

Carson connected with Tommy, planting his desire for a Big Mac. While Carson was starving, food was the last thing he wanted. Just a demonstration.

Tommy glanced over his shoulder. "Hey, guys, we need to find a McDonald's. I really need a Big Mac."

Doc eyed Carson as if he were part of a carnival sideshow. Carson looked away until he heard a chuckle. Doc appeared to be relaxed. He was smiling and laughing?

"Oh man, the fun...." Doc shook his head, looking to Tommy. Something was up between them.

Carson frowned. He couldn't imagine using his ability for fun. And using it for your own agenda had to be wrong. But didn't he do just that when he convinced Tommy and Doc to wait, even though it was dangerous? He could have gotten them killed.

Shit.

"I'm sorry. I made you do something that you didn't want to do. You told me that waiting for Lincoln was dangerous, and I didn't listen. I was only thinking about myself. I won't do it again, I promise."

The corners of Doc's lips lifted. "For a young kid, you're pretty smart. And you're right. Using this... this thing you can do to benefit yourself isn't okay. It's deceitful, and it's an invasion of privacy. Going into other people's heads without permission, it's.... Well, it's a violation of someone's body."

Carson pursed his lips. How would he feel if someone pushed into his mind, planted ideas, and made him bend to their will? It was like raping someone's mind. He shuddered. Oh gods. What if it happened when he wasn't trying? What if the ability got stronger, and he started trying to take over people's minds and use them as puppets for his bidding? He'd become a monster and....

He tried to catch his breath. He was hyperventilating.

"Hey." Doc knelt beside him. "Calm down. It's okay. You didn't mean to do it. You were just scared."

Carson shook his head. "I... I...."

"Put your head between your knees and breathe." Doc laid a hand on the back of Carson's neck. The weight helped to ground him. He'd been a danger to others his entire life, and now he felt like a ticking time bomb. When would he finally go off?

CHAPTER 23

CARSON PULLED his knees up to his chest. He sat in a chair next to the bed Lincoln slept in. Doc had asked that Carson keep him under for a while longer. When he questioned the violation of Lincoln's mind, Doc's drawn-out conversation about want versus need, and dire situations, became a morality lecture. Carson appreciated the advice, but it did little to comfort him about his new abilities.

Tommy's safe house was an old farmhouse in the middle of nowhere. Carson wasn't sure if there were other residences around since they arrived after dark. It was now six in the morning, and Carson had sat up the entire night making sure Lincoln didn't suffer. Carson struggled to keep his eyes open, and each time his head fell forward, he was startled awake.

"Go to bed, kid." Tommy leaned against the doorjamb. He wore a T-shirt and jeans. His feet were bare. He resembled his brother with that same surly, superior attitude. At least Tommy hadn't tried to kill Carson. That was a plus in his book.

"I have to keep him asleep. He'll be in pain if he wakes up." Carson dropped his feet to the floor, resting his elbows on his knees. He sniffed near his armpit. What he really needed was a shower. His new high metabolism really cranked out the sweat.

"It's gonna happen anyway when you pass out from exhaustion. Doc's coming in to give Linc some pain meds. Said he needs him to wake up so he can assess his condition." Tommy cocked his head and was silent as he surveyed Carson's arms. A shiver passed over Carson. Back to that rat-in-the-cage feeling. The fucking involuntary tattoos really registered him as an oddity.

"I remember when he bonded with Luke," Tommy said conversationally.

Just hearing the asshole's name sparked anger in Carson. If he ever saw that bastard, he had a bunch of choice words just for him. Maybe a few suggestions.

"Yeah, so?" Carson's tone was less than friendly.

"Nothing. I just mean Linc was a mess. That guy really fucked him over big-time."

The tone of Tommy's voice.... Was there a warning in there somewhere? Carson stood on shaky legs, puffing out his chest. His strength had to hold up long enough to tell Tommy off.

"Yeah, well, I'm not him, I *am* here, and I've *been* here since we bonded. And you count on it that I'm *not* going anywhere. He's my bond mate, and I lo—"

Carson sucked in a breath. His heart rate kicked up. He loved Lincoln.

He fucking loved him.

Tommy appeared thoroughly amused. "What was that?"

Carson closed his eyes. Such a revelation should have caused him more joy. Maybe if everyone he loved hadn't ended up dead. No. Caden and his uncle were alive.

"Don't blow a gasket, kid. Your secret's safe with me. You've got some big balls there. You'll need them to deal with the crap he throws at you." He clapped his hands and rubbed them together. "Well, all right. Let's get this show on the road." He looked over his shoulder. "Hey, Doc, you want to get your ass in here sometime today?"

"You want to suck my dick, Tommy boy?" Doc yelled back.

Tommy's eyes widened. A rush of lust hit Carson. Tommy quickly scowled and rolled his eyes. Was Tommy turned on by what Doc said?

Tommy's cheeks reddened, and he averted his eyes. Doc stepped up behind him. "So I'm here. Care to get your big ass out of my way?"

"You been looking at my ass, Doc?" Tommy asked, moving into the room.

"In your dreams, Romeo." Doc passed by Tommy, then set the first aid kit he carried onto the bed. He had lost his lab coat.

Carson looked between the two men, and damn if they weren't lusting after one another. Carson grinned. He wasn't invading anyone's privacy. Their covert desire bombarded the room. Were they secretly screwing? Or was this want disguised with a layer of hate? Or—

"Carson? You okay over there? You look like the cat that swallowed the canary." Doc held up a syringe, drawing liquid from a vial.

"Huh? Oh yeah, I'm good."

Carson went to the bed and watched Doc press the needle into Lincoln's arm. Without thinking, Carson blocked the pain. He hissed and covered his arm.

Doc looked up at him. "He wasn't going to feel it, you know?"

Carson shrugged and didn't respond.

Tommy's eyes widened. "So it's true, what you said in the van. You can take away pain. I heard you say it, but it's just… unbelievable."

Carson sat on the bed next to Lincoln. "Yeah, unbelievable," Carson murmured. "I think I can accelerate his healing."

"And just how're you going to do that?" Carson's claim apparently offended Doc's medical sensibilities.

Carson wasn't sure how, but he had a feeling he could heal. Something spoke to him, told him he could help. "I don't know, but I received his blood, and he's a healer. I mean, it was his blood that changed me, right?"

"Possibly… I don't know…. Most likely, but I still don't know how that happened." Doc scratched his head.

Carson's desire to crawl in and lie next to Lincoln's warmth, to be enclosed in his arms, was like an unquenched thirst.

"I have to try." Carson lightly rested his palm over Lincoln's wound.

The heart beat strong and steady. Without thought Carson rested his other palm on Lincoln's cool forehead. He closed his eyes, searching for the channel to enter Lincoln's mind. The path was familiar, like coming home, and peace settled across his nerves. The pain that overwhelmed Carson in the van was now vague. Lincoln was truly resting, his thoughts quiet.

Carson willed his energy past the mind-body barrier and to filter down into the wound in Lincoln's chest. The energy patterns there were fragmented, disjointed. Carson worked to realign the energy, which snapped into place like pieces of a larger puzzle. He marveled at the cooperation, the ease to rebuild what was injured.

Lincoln's heart rate increased as his body pumped blood into the damaged area. When the energy patterns were repaired, Carson withdrew into Lincoln's mind. He gave Lincoln a mental nudge akin to waking a sleeping person.

Lincoln's eyes fluttered open, unfocused and drowsy, no doubt from the narcotics. When Carson saw those blue eyes, his heart wavered.

Lincoln turned his head and blinked, inhaling deeply and then exhaling, as if testing his lungs.

His eyes focused, and he lifted the corner of his mouth. The blue of his eyes seemed to lighten. "Hey," he whispered.

Relief brought a smile to Carson. "Hey yourself. How you feeling?"

He placed a hand on Lincoln's stomach. Lincoln immediately grasped it. He licked his lips and frowned. "I was shot."

Not a question, but Carson nodded anyway.

Lincoln blinked several times, as if trying to bring lucidity to his mind. Yet when he looked into Carson's eyes, the clarity was striking. "I thought I was going to die. I had to tell you, but... I couldn't talk. I need you to...." Lincoln took their hands, fingers entwined, and laid the back of Carson's over the bandage on his chest. Over his heart. "I love you."

Carson's heart fluttered, and his throat tightened. He swallowed and managed to croak out, "I love you too." He ran his fingers over Lincoln's forehead and through his hair. Carson was so elated he believed he could fly.

Lincoln grinned wide, grasped the back of Carson's neck, and pulled him down for a gentle kiss.

"Okay. Easy does it. The man was just shot."

Carson sat up, and Lincoln refused to release his hand. "Don't you think I know it, Doc?"

"How you feel?" Tommy asked.

Lincoln rubbed over the site of the gunshot wound. "Not feeling too bad for having a hole in my chest." He put his elbows down on the bed, still awkwardly holding Carson's hand, and pushed up. Carson supported Lincoln's back and helped him to sit.

"Take it easy. Any pain? Light-headedness? Nausea? Do your legs or arms hurt at all?"

"He was shot in the chest, Doc." Tommy shrugged when Doc scowled his way.

"Pain in the arms or legs can be an indicator of blood clots."

"No pain. Could use some water."

Carson grabbed the cup on the bedside table and helped Lincoln drink. When Lincoln was done, Carson returned it to its former place. Lincoln coaxed Carson to lie against his side. Carson inhaled deeply and exhaled, melting against Lincoln. He could breathe finally, and now that Lincoln was healing, Carson could crash.

Before he drifted off, Carson murmured, "I love you."

LINCOLN HELD Carson, grateful for the second chance. "Love you too," he whispered into Carson's hair, but his bond mate's breathing had already evened out, steady with sleep.

Lincoln raised questioning eyes to Doc.

"He sat up all night and refused to sleep. He wanted to make sure you weren't in pain."

Lincoln rubbed his palm over Carson's back. Feeling him cured all of his ills. "Isn't that your job, Doc?"

Doc rubbed the back of his neck and opened his mouth as if to say something, but he just sighed in exasperation.

Tommy had no trouble answering. "Your boy's got some mad skills."

"Skills?" Lincoln tightened his grip around Carson. He had a feeling Carson's "mad skills" weren't going to thrill him as much as Tommy. Probably push his guilt even higher since his blood had changed Carson, putting him in greater danger.

"Yeah, let me fill you in on some of what's happened since you've been incapacitated." Tommy launched into a convoluted story of mind control and pain-wrangling and finished with accelerated healing.

"With his mind and his hands? No blood?" Lincoln was speechless.

"Yeah, and took him about two minutes. I bet he—"

Doc cut him off. "He got you to where you are, but you're still healing. And for all we know, this might wear off and you're back where you started."

Healed without blood. What had he done to Carson? Made him a target ten times greater than the Tabula Rasa he had been—or still was, that's what.

"Doc, what do you think?" Lincoln asked.

"I don't know what to think, Lincoln. I've never seen anything like it. I have a feeling Jameson's the one who has the answers, maybe, but he's vanished along with everyone else."

Lincoln reached under the covers and dug into his pocket, relieved to find the USB drive from Wright still there. He pulled it out and tossed it to Tommy. "This might have something useful on it. Maggie gave it to me before we left. There's also a link to a secure transmission channel that will get us in touch with the members of my team left at headquarters."

He winced as he thought of Max missing, along with Tia, Taylor, and John. More guilt. He was so caught up in Carson that he'd ignored his responsibilities as commander. What if Max or all of them were...?

Lincoln shook his head. Thoughts like that wouldn't get him anywhere. Until they heard differently, there was still hope.

Doc, no doubt seeing the war of emotions on Lincoln's face, asked, "You okay?"

Lincoln steeled his expression. "I'm good."

Giving Carson one last nuzzle and kiss on the head, Lincoln gently laid him down. Carson snuffled, turned his head into the pillow, then settled. Throwing his legs over the side of the bed, Lincoln winced at the pull in his chest.

"Just take it easy. You're healing quickly, but don't overdo it."

Lincoln grunted. "Doc, we're in a heap of shit here. We're fugitives harboring a level—I don't think there is a level for Carson at this point—and they're looking for us." They'd all die before they touched Carson.

"So what's our next step?" Tommy asked.

Lincoln slowly stood. He had to admit, for almost dying, he felt pretty damn good. He waved them out of the bedroom to allow Carson to rest. The living room they entered was sparsely decorated with furniture and accessories stuck in the seventies. So much aqua and orange. Other doorways led to different rooms or outside. The two doors that were closed made Lincoln uneasy. He hadn't been able to secure the location. He'd have to trust Tommy on that one.

"Where are we?" Lincoln looked out the window. The house was by large fields edged by woods. Not a house in sight. Good private location.

Tommy parked himself in front of a laptop that was on the gold coffee table. His fingers flew over the keyboard. From what John and others in the NVJ told Lincoln, Tommy was past dangerous with his skills.

"We're outside of Cazenovia. This house belongs to a great-uncle of a guy I knew from childhood. No one can link me to him or the house. No one knows we're here. I think we're good for a couple of days."

Lincoln nodded. "Anything useful on the USB?"

Tommy frowned and sat back. "There's a clear connection between the uncle, Graham Winters, and Manny Monrovia through that bank account. The records here are more detailed. There's about a million dollars in there."

Doc whistled. "Damn."

"Every month on the first, five thousand dollars is deposited into the account. Always the same, and not a month missed for twenty years. Each month two thousand was transferred to...." He clacked the keys some more. "First Niagara Bank into a joint account with the names...." Tommy's breath hitched and his brow rose. "Graham Winters and Carson Locke."

"What about me and my uncle?"

Lincoln spun around. Doc jumped. Carson stood behind him.

"You're supposed to be sleeping." Lincoln wasn't sure what to think. Had Carson been using money from Monrovia? Why would he after what had happened? There had to be a good reason. However, Lincoln's training honed in on the discrepancy. "Do you have an account with your uncle at First Niagara Bank?"

"Yeah. Man, I forgot all about that. Why?" Carson crossed his arms.

"Did you ever withdraw money from that account?" Lincoln didn't want to sound so detached, but it was easier.

"No. It was my uncle's account." Carson narrowed his eyes.

Lincoln continued to push. "What did he use the account for?"

"I didn't think he did. He told me he'd set it up in case something happened to him. He wanted me to have access to the money so I could take care of my mother and Caden and keep the house. Like I said, I'd forgotten all about it."

Tommy looked up from the screen. "It says here the account was initially opened in 1993."

"It started out as one of those 'in trust for' accounts. When I turned sixteen, a man from the bank came to the house. I signed the papers for a joint account with Uncle Graham."

Lincoln wiped his hand over his mouth. He let his mind run away with just one unknown fact, allowing himself to doubt Carson. Some lover he was.

"Do you know how much money is in that account?" Tommy asked. Carson shrugged. "No clue."

"Four hundred and sixty-seven thousand dollars."

Carson's eyes widened, and his face paled, but he didn't say anything. Tommy looked at the screen again. "1993. That's the year your father mysteriously disappeared and your uncle came into the picture."

"Wait." Lincoln turned to Carson. "You said your father—"

"My father died in a car accident after I was born. That's what my mother told me. Why would she lie?"

"Reports from the NVJ state that Carl Winters was reported missing and never found. No suspects or witnesses." Tommy looked up from his computer. "Your mother's maiden name was Locke?"

"Yes."

Confusion and pain flowed from Carson, and Lincoln refrained from going to him. "So possibly the uncle got rid of his brother so he could step in and… do what? Have access to Carson? He was receiving money from Monrovia for what?"

"For keeping Carson safe until he reached puberty and his full powers came into play."

Lincoln spun around. Jameson stood before the front door.

CHAPTER 24

"WHAT THE fuck?" Lincoln reached for his gun, forgetting he no longer had the weapon in his waistband.

He charged Jameson, hands stretched out to grab him. Jameson stayed still, that crappy grin on his face. Something akin to an invisible fist punched into Lincoln's gut. He stopped short and doubled over in pain.

"Lincoln!" Carson stood by Lincoln as he forced air into his lungs. With Carson's touch, the pain subsided. Lincoln rose to standing.

"Commander Samuels, you should know better by now. I'm not here to harm anyone. I'm here to help you."

"You poisoned me!" Carson pushed toward Jameson and hit that invisible wall.

Jameson tutted. "I didn't poison you. What you ingested was a mixture of herbs that broke through the last barrier to your powers. Once that happened the powers bestowed on you hundreds of years before your birth came to fruition. You, my boy, are the first and only Salutem vampire."

"What the hell does that mean?" Lincoln asked.

Carson only stared at Jameson, who smiled. The gesture was smug and arrogant, and Lincoln had to refrain from throttling him.

"It means that Carson's creation, his path, was set generations ago. In his past life, Carson was a vampire chosen to return and bring salvation to all vampires... save them from their own self-destruction."

"His past life? As in reincarnation?" Doc asked.

Lincoln knew Doc didn't believe in anything without yards of scientific proof attached.

Jameson ran the braid through his hand over and over, no doubt an unconscious gesture. "Yes. Reincarnation. Is it so hard to believe that we are reborn many times before our souls move on to the afterlife? Some are reincarnated shortly after death while others are suspended in stasis before the Great Spirit returns them to our realm."

"Well, if that isn't a bunch of horseshit," Doc said. "And I suppose you had something to do with this?"

"Not me exactly. I come from a long line of shamans who have passed along the knowledge of the birth of the Salutem for over three hundred years. What a joy it is that he has come in my lifetime." Jameson stepped closer to Doc. "And Simon, you are very much a part of this prophecy, as is everyone in this room. You all have a role to play."

Doc scowled. "Yeah, and what's my role?" He waved his hand across the room to the others. "What's their role?" Doc dared the shaman to share his information.

"To complete the steps to bring us to this point in time. To create what Carson has become."

All fine and good. Yet Jameson had piqued Lincoln's interest with one word. "What did you mean, *self-destruction?*"

Jameson's grin faded. "Right now in the vampire community, there are those who are very powerful, taking what is not theirs and coveting powers that should be protected. They're using those powers to gain position and wealth. The balance is tipping drastically to one side. Vampires are being used and abused, and their lives are being controlled by those in very powerful positions."

Henderson's son, Manuel.

Lincoln pulled Manuel's photo from his pocket. "Officer Henderson said her son had been taken, as well as her husband. That the NVJ was using her son as leverage to keep her doing what the NVJ asked of her, which she said wasn't always moral or ethical. She asked me to find him if something happened to her."

Carson took the photo from Lincoln, who couldn't look away from the smiling boy. His stomach clenched thinking of Manuel, and others, being used for nefarious purposes.

"Yes, they take indiscriminately, without regard to families or the welfare of the individual. You've no doubt heard the rumors and dismissed them as easily as others have." Jameson pursed his lips. "And to answer your question about roles. You wanted to know roles here, Simon?"

Tommy shifted nervously, catching Lincoln's attention. Tommy paced and wiped his forehead, pacing some more, and then finally settled next to Carson. The position boxed Carson between Lincoln and Tommy, increasing his protection.

Doc folded his arms over his chest and nodded.

"Simon, you were instrumental in recognizing the need for Carson to receive Lincoln's blood. Your tenacity would not have allowed you to rest until Carson was cured. Lincoln, you were the key to unlock the powers. I predicted you would be the one over ten years ago, and worked to guide you to the correct placement to meet with Carson."

What? "You fucked with my life?" No, every decision Lincoln had made concerning his life was his own. He never questioned himself, always felt what he chose was the correct path—except with Luke. Others always marveled at his self-confidence in his choices. He always made the right decision and….

Jameson raised an eyebrow. He nodded as if he was privy to Lincoln's thoughts. Lincoln felt like a puppet on a string and that Jameson had pulled every single one. That wasn't possible.

A surge of rage came from Carson. His face twisted in a scowl, and he glared daggers at Jameson. "Did you kill my mother? Are you in this with my uncle?"

Jameson didn't even bat an eyelash at the outburst. "No, Carson. I didn't have anything to do with the death of your mother. I was, however, in constant contact with your uncle."

Carson flew up and grabbed handfuls of Jameson's vest, the markings on his body glowing red. "I'm going to kill you."

Lincoln and Tommy both stepped forward. Jameson raised a hand to stop them. Lincoln growled as Jameson rested his hand on Carson's shoulder. "Don't touch him."

Jameson removed his hand. His expression softened like that of a grandfather gazing at his grandson. "Carson, your uncle made some poor choices many years ago. He did move in with you once he found out what you were and struck a deal with Monrovia. For some unknown reason, he hated his brother, your father. You were to be his revenge. The deal was your uncle would turn you over to Monrovia when you turned sixteen. However, your uncle came to love you and your mother and brother."

Carson loosened his fists around the fabric. He dropped his hands. The red glow muted and then disappeared.

"So what? The uncle killed the mother and kidnapped the brother. The money he withdrew was money from Monrovia. Apparently his love of money was stronger. He's a murderer and the cause of all of this shit." Tommy's voice sounded stressed. Beads of sweat coursed down Tommy's cheeks. Something wasn't right.

Jameson focused on Carson. "In all actuality Graham tried to keep Monrovia away from you, feeding him false information about your status and abilities. He refused to turn you over at sixteen. That was the motivation for kidnapping you and Justin. Monrovia wanted proof your powers existed. He forced you to bite your friend. Graham contacted me when you went missing. We found you both. Too late for Justin, though."

Carson was silent, staring at Jameson, not one muscle twitching, his chest barely moving. And the strange thing was Lincoln couldn't feel anything from him, as if Carson had shut down his feelings completely.

"Neither I nor your uncle killed your mother." Jameson looked to Tommy. "But you know that, don't you, Tommy?" Jameson cocked his head inquisitively at the officer.

Before Lincoln could react, Tommy had his arm around Carson's neck and yanked him away. When Lincoln reached for Carson, Tommy placed a gun to Carson's head whose eyes grew wide as he stared at Lincoln.

Lincoln swore he was seconds from a heart attack, seeing the gun at Carson's temple. In Tommy's eyes was a wild desperation. Lincoln had seen that look before, just before a person lost it and took out everyone around them.

THE COLD steel pushed painfully into Carson's temple. Lincoln's expression was part scowl, part terror. Jameson remained calm and collected, but at least he wasn't grinning anymore.

"Tommy boy? What the fuck are you doing?" Doc tried to approach him.

"Doc, Stop! Don't come any closer. I will shoot him."

Bewildered, Carson looked at Lincoln, who appeared to be assessing the situation, possibly running scenarios through his head. Lincoln had to come up with something before Carson's brains were scattered around the room.

Tommy's arm tightened around Carson's neck. He reached up and grasped Tommy's forearm, but the effort was futile. Carson's head swam with the lack of oxygen, but he had the advantage. He closed his eyes and sought an opening into Tommy's mind. His internal heat rose, signaling his tattoos were glowing. Tommy's body tensed behind him.

The arm around Carson's neck loosened. He felt Tommy's warm breath on his ear. "You don't want to do that, kid. The house is wired with explosives, and I have the trigger."

Carson's eyes popped open. Tommy waved the hand of his arm around Carson's neck. Indeed he held a black box with a red button in his hand. Classic.

"You won't blow yourself up." Lincoln called his bluff.

"Won't I?" Tommy's voice quavered. "If I don't bring Carson back to Monrovia, I'm dead, and so is John."

Lincoln frowned. "He has John? What about—"

"Yeah, Max too. The entire team. I didn't want to do any of this."

"Then why did you?" Lincoln looked angry enough to break Tommy in half.

"I was young and stupid and just got back from Iraq. I... I was messed up. Half of my platoon had been killed, and I was self-destructive. I needed some quick cash. This guy I knew in high school hooked me up with Monrovia. I've never met the guy. Talked to him mostly on the phone, and messages from private couriers. I did some small shit for him, computer work mostly, and then I pulled out. Told him I wanted to get my life back together. John helped me. Moved me to Rochester and got me set up with the NVJ. I thought I was out... until...."

"Until he had John. You didn't lock down the building, did you?" Lincoln asked Jameson.

"I was trying to obtain information about Carson's condition since no one would share that information with me. Once I found that the building was being locked down, I had to leave or be trapped with all of you. That's some powerful magic you have access to, Tommy."

Tommy flinched. "I... I didn't want to use it. Monrovia gave me the ritual. I had to."

"Are you sure John's still alive? That any of my team are alive?" Lincoln's voice had wavered at the end.

Carson prayed they hadn't been killed because of him.

"Yes. Carson, get my phone from my left front pocket of my pants. Don't be stupid, or I might pull the trigger." Doubt appeared with the myriad of other emotions from Tommy. Carson reached behind him, found the pocket, and nearly fumbled as he extracted the phone.

"Swipe the screen."

With a shaky thumb, Carson swiped the lock. A picture of John popped onto the screen tied to a chair. Both eyes were black and blue, his lip bloody. "Show them."

Carson turned the phone for all to see. "Swipe it again."

Carson turned the phone back and swiped his thumb, and the next picture popped up before him. He sucked in his breath. Max sat on the floor, back against the wall, and there was a man pulled tight to his chest. Carson stopped breathing and clutched the phone tight. It couldn't be... no....

Justin.

CHAPTER 25

LINCOLN REACHED for the phone, but Tommy stepped away, yanking Carson with him.

"Stay back!"

"It's Justin," Carson said, to stop Lincoln from coming forward. "And Max."

He turned the phone and showed them. Lincoln's jaw clenched, and his fists balled at his sides.

"If I don't call in every thirty minutes, he starts killing them." Carson heard Tommy choke on a sob. "Including your brother and uncle."

Carson swallowed hard. "Where's Caden?" If Monrovia had Caden, then Carson had no choice but to do what the evil man wished. He'd never allow harm to come to his brother.

"Next picture."

Carson's hand shook. He managed to swipe the screen. There was Caden, wide-eyed and terrified, a gun held to his head.

"You do realize you've made a pact with the devil," Jameson said to Tommy. "Not only will Monrovia kill John and the rest of the officers, he'll kill all of us and then force Carson to do whatever he desires. He knows how deadly Carson can be."

"I won't let you out of here with Carson."

"You don't have much of a choice, do you, Linc? He said the first person would be Max. He knows.... He knows you're close to him. He friggin' knows everything." Tommy had nearly sobbed the words. His conflict was evident in his words and thoughts, had become too strong to block out.

"I have to go with him." If Carson went with him, then Lincoln would be safe, and Carson could face Monrovia alone. He was strong, and as Jameson said, he was deadly. "We have no choice. If you don't let me go, Monrovia will kill Max and… Caden."

"Tommy boy, please." Doc said, the pleading look on his face was heartbreaking. "Don't do this. We can get John back. We can get all of them back and stop Monrovia. Taking this route, you're a traitor and a coward, and that's not you. I know it's not you."

Those conflicting emotions kicked up an internal storm. In the middle of the chaos, Carson felt a strong emotion.

"You love him. Listen to Doc," Carson said.

Doc's mouth dropped open.

Tommy's breaths increased, and a whimper escaped his chest.

"Is that true, Tommy? Do you still love me?"

Tommy was silent. The trembling of his body vibrated through Carson. Tommy nodded.

A blur of movement to Carson's right and then he was hit hard in the side. Tommy's arm was ripped from around Carson's neck. Pain burst in his shoulder as he hit the floor. He rolled onto his back, then scrambled to his feet. Lincoln was on top of Tommy and managed to snag the gun and trigger.

Lincoln turned a fiery glare on Carson, then jumped up and grabbed hold of him. Carson held on tight.

"I've got you," Lincoln whispered.

Doc shouted and yanked Tommy from the floor, fists in his shirt. "Why didn't you tell me, you stupid son of a bitch?" An angry twist to his face, Doc pulled back and punched Tommy in the face. His head snapped to the side, but Doc held him up. "That's for not coming to me with this shit!"

The sadness in Tommy's eyes was immense. "I'm sorry. I messed everything up."

Doc smacked Tommy upside the head.

"Owww, what was that for?"

"For not telling me you still loved me." Doc smashed his lips onto Tommy's. He flailed and then wrapped his arms around Doc and returned the kiss.

Carson bent down and picked up the cell phone. He tapped on Doc's shoulder. Doc pulled back. Carson handed the phone to Tommy. "Call Monrovia and tell him you're bringing me in."

Lincoln sputtered. "W-what? Fuck no!"

"Lincoln, we don't have any other way. He's going to kill them. Max. Caden." Carson couldn't lose his brother again. Nothing would stop him.

Lincoln's jaw clenched, his blue eyes hard. Carson expected him to put up fight. "We plan every step. And I go. No discussion."

Carson hated the idea. Didn't want Lincoln near the danger. "Nothing I say will change your mind?"

"No." Lincoln's expression was stern, but his eyes showed his love.

"Okay. Tommy, does he know what I've become? Aware of my new powers?"

"No."

Carson grinned nervously. "Then he's in for a big surprise."

Jameson, who had remained strangely quiet, nodded his silent approval of Carson's idea. Too bad Carson hadn't planned any further than going in with Tommy. From there, he'd have to rely on his intuition and the situation. He was terrified, but his brother's life, as well as Justin's, was at stake.

He was going to come face-to-face with one of his worst nightmares. His chest tightened and his stomach roiled. He took comfort in Lincoln, laying his head on his bond mate's shoulder. He had to keep it together. He was going to get them all back, and Monrovia was going to pay.

LINCOLN HELD Carson close as he dozed next to him in the back of the van. Tommy and Doc sat up front. Jameson sat across from Lincoln and Carson. They hadn't wasted any time packing up and heading out once Tommy had contacted Monrovia. He'd been delighted with Tommy's ability to capture the Tabula Rasa.

Lincoln clenched his teeth at the thought of the man who had wanted Carson for most of his life. What perplexed Lincoln was why Monrovia had waited seven years between the first kidnapping and the attack on his family. Monrovia had sent someone to take Carson, but they'd failed. How had his uncle and Caden escaped, and why had they left Carson behind? The questions plagued his thoughts, and the lack of answers ached his head.

He pulled Carson closer and kissed the top of his head. Once this was over, he would take Carson away from New York and anyone who would use him.

"He has a duty now. He must stay and fulfill his destiny," Jameson said, as if he'd read Lincoln's mind. "That's his purpose in this life. It's like breathing air. He can't avoid it."

Lincoln wanted to swear at Jameson, tell him to shut up. Instead, he said, "He didn't ask for this."

Jameson shrugged. "Despite our thoughts to the contrary, most of our lives are beyond our control. That's an illusion. We're all moved and played like pawns on a chessboard. Carson is no different."

Lincoln was unwilling to believe he'd been pushed and pulled by the will of someone or some force.

Jameson shrugged. "You may want him to be safe and hidden, but what does Carson want? Have you asked him?"

Lincoln hadn't. What would Carson want? He'd been hidden away from the world his entire life. This could be his chance to gain freedom, to live. But what kind of life would he have? And what would he have to do to fulfill his purpose?

"What did you mean by his 'purpose'? Are you talking about taking vampires with special abilities?"

"Among other things," Jameson said. "Soon all will be clear, Commander Samuels."

Jameson closed his eyes and said nothing further. Lincoln didn't trust the man, or Tommy, as far as he could throw them. And he was going into a dangerous situation with both of them as backup. He'd contacted Maggie before they'd left. The entire NVJ in the western part of the state had mobilized to capture them. She'd fed false intel, sending out a reported sighting at a gas station south of Rochester. They had passed Rochester and were heading to Buffalo. In another hour, they would arrive at the location where Tommy had arranged to meet Monrovia. Their plan was simple. Crash the party and let Carson work his mojo. Lincoln couldn't rid himself of the feeling this was all going south despite the apparent advantage they had.

He settled back, enjoying the warmth of Carson as he tried blocking out his racing thoughts and questions. He soon fell into a light doze with the feeling that Carson had given him a little push to get him there.

THE VAN jostled and pulled Lincoln from his sleep. He blinked. Jameson's eyes were still closed. Probably communing with the universe or something.

"Where are we?" he called up to Doc and Tommy. He smirked when he saw they were holding hands between the bucket seats.

Tommy looked over his shoulder. "Five minutes out."

Doc unbuckled his seat belt and moved into the back. Carson stirred and stretched, rubbing his eyes. Lincoln had gotten used to the red irises, but what about Monrovia? The tattoos could be covered with clothes, but the irises would be hard to hide.

"I could wear sunglasses." Lincoln raised his eyebrows. "You were thinking about Monrovia seeing my irises."

"How did you hear that? You're not glowing."

Carson looked down at his body and shrugged. "I don't know. I just did."

"His powers are growing, becoming easier to access." Jameson finally opened his eyes.

"That's a good thing, right?" Lincoln heard the slight nervousness in Carson's tone.

"Yes, it is, love." He had no clue if it was or wasn't.

Lincoln pulled out a sheet of paper with a rough schematic of the building. "Carson will go inside with Tommy, against my better judgment. Jameson will cut off the security system."

"Won't take but a minute. I'll also interfere with the incoming and outgoing communications, in case we're spotted. Anyone reporting won't be able to contact anyone on the inside." Jameson gave Lincoln that confident trademark smile.

Lincoln eyed Jameson, grateful the shaman was on their side. "Once they're inside, we get everybody out. Then we regroup and go after Monrovia."

"It's not too late to back out." Lincoln ran his finger down Carson's cheek. Their bond was strong. Lincoln loved him, and letting him walk into that building was killing him. How could he tell him no? Carson was an adult, and so fucking powerful.

I love you and you're right. It's my decision. I will be able to talk to you. I'll be careful.

Lincoln smiled and nodded, placing his forehead against Carson's.

"You two are doing that telepathic shit again, aren't you?" Doc asked with a wistful tone.

Carson smirked.

"I'm pulling into the driveway. Everyone stay down. Lincoln, tie Carson's hands behind his back for show." Tommy slowed the van and turned into an empty parking lot.

Carson wrapped his arms around Lincoln's neck. Their lips touched, and Lincoln opened for him. Within that kiss, Lincoln conveyed all of the love and hope and happiness he could. Memories of their last lovemaking session filled Lincoln's mind. He ran his hand down Carson's back as the intensity of the arousal increased. Another nudge, there were images of him and Carson, sitting on a couch, cuddling, watching TV, cooking, laughing, walking hand in hand. The future…. Carson showed him visions of what their future could hold.

Lincoln broke the kiss, breathing heavily, wishing they had more time. "We'll have all of that. I promise." He'd promise Carson the universe.

CHAPTER 26

LINCOLN GRASPED Carson's hand as their cheeks rubbed together. The smoothness of Carson's skin juxtaposed against Lincoln's stubble.

A throat cleared. "Men. The good-byes are over. It's time for battle," Jameson said in his eerily calm tone.

Lincoln hadn't even realizing the van had stopped. He grinned, seeing Doc and Tommy sucking face. When the two pulled away, Doc's face lit up redder than Carson's eyes.

He placed one more chaste kiss on Lincoln's lips, then smirked. He turned and clasped his hands together. "Tie me up, Commander." Carson waggled his eyebrows, and a vision of Carson tied to a bed slammed into Lincoln.

"Not funny," Lincoln groused. He picked up a length of rope from the supply kit and tied it loosely around Carson's wrists. Leaning over his shoulder, Lincoln placed a kiss on Carson's cheek. Tommy handed Lincoln a pair of sunglasses, and he placed them on Carson's face.

"See you soon." Lincoln patted Carson on the ass.

Carson mouthed the words "love you" as Tommy led him out of the van. The doors slammed shut. Lincoln watched through the front window as Tommy led Carson into the front of the building. If Tommy turned on them again, Lincoln was prepared to rip Tommy's intestines out through his nose.

"Is he going to screw us over again?" Lincoln asked Doc.

Doc chewed on his bottom lip for a second and then shook his head. "He was scared for his brother, and Monrovia has him totally freaked out for some reason. What it is, I'm not sure. Tommy had some major issues stemming from his stint in the army. I mean deep-seated, buried issues. Something huge happened to him and his platoon over in Iraq, I could never get him to talk about it. It's the reason we didn't last." The pain in

Doc's eyes said he wasn't sure if their relationship could ever last. "He will do what he said he would."

"If he hurts Carson, I'll gut him."

"He knows that," Doc said.

"It's time to go." Jameson cut off further speculation as to Tommy's current allegiance.

Lincoln secured his gun in his waistband at the small of his back. All three of them crept from the back of the van. Dusk hadn't turned into night yet, so the cover of dark wasn't with them. Hopefully, everyone inside was focused on their captives. The sooner they took those hostages out of the equation, the more leverage they'd have.

At the back of the building, Jameson closed his eyes and placed his hand on the wall. Lincoln looked to Doc, who shrugged. They waited for the go-ahead from Jameson. Lincoln's patience shortened by the minute. Finally, the shaman opened his eyes and nodded.

Lincoln struggled with the rusted screws of the grate leading into the basement. When the grate was removed, Jameson and Doc climbed in, followed by Lincoln. The basement was dark and dank, and reeked of mold. Doc pulled out a small flashlight, and they moved to the stairs. Quietly, they ascended. At the top, Lincoln carefully turned the knob. He cracked open the door and peered out. The well-lit hallway was empty. He motioned for Doc and Jameson to follow. Once they were in the hallway, two men emerged from an adjacent doorway, holding rifles trained on the three of them.

Lincoln contemplated his options, then noticed the NVJ lettering on their rifles. If he hadn't handled dozens those weapons, he might have missed the marking.

He scowled. "Those are NVJ weapons."

"Gentlemen, I'd like to introduce you to Lieutenant Wilson and Lieutenant Anderson, formerly of the NVJ. My first and second-in-command." Jameson motioned to the men.

"Traitors?" Lincoln scowled at the men, itching to take them down.

Jameson smiled smugly. "Most every man and woman has a price."

"You working for Monrovia?"

Jameson got a hearty laugh out of that. "Oh, Commander Samuels. You have no idea who I am."

Someone moved behind Lincoln, but before he could turn around, pain exploded across the back of his head and everything went black.

CARSON FOLLOWED the tall guard who met him and Tommy at the door. Carson was more powerful than anyone in the building and still terrified. Tommy's hands were on Carson, guiding him in his role as kidnapper. Carson felt the slight tremble and pushed a calming thought to Tommy, hoping to settle him because he needed his help. Lincoln, Doc, and Jameson should have been in the building and working to free everyone.

Carson opened his mind to get an update from Lincoln.

Lincoln?

Nothing.

Lincoln, where are you?

Again nothing. He was nearby, but he wasn't answering.

Carson glanced back over his shoulder at Tommy but couldn't chance saying anything because of the guard. Tommy frowned and cocked his head as they walked down a narrow hallway. Carson shook his head minutely.

At the end of the hall, the guard opened the door and led them into a small room. There was a couch, a table with chairs, and a minikitchen. The space resembled a break room for workers. The guard motioned them in with his gun.

"The boss will be here shortly. I'll be right outside the door, so sit down and wait." With a scowl he slammed the door and the lock clicked.

Tommy nodded confidently, but once the guard left, he sighed heavily and wiped his forehead with his shaky hand. "What's wrong, Carson?"

Carson paced frantically in the small space. "Lincoln isn't answering. I can feel him, but he isn't saying anything." Something was wrong. The only logical conclusion was Lincoln wasn't conscious. "Shit," Carson rubbed his hands together.

"Let's not freak out just yet. Once Monrovia gets in here, you can do your thing and take him down," Tommy said as if it were as easy as all that.

Carson gave a short nod. He continued to reach out to Lincoln, with no reply. He took deep breaths and shook out his hands, keeping his head in the moment, avoiding imagining the worst. He'd come to depend on the connection with Lincoln. Without that link he felt totally alone. He needed a distraction.

"So you and Doc, huh?"

Tommy frowned through his initial surprise. "Yeah, so what?"

Touchy. "Nothing. I could feel your attraction. Whenever you two were together, I wanted to tell you to get a room." Carson went for the joke, hoping Tommy would relax.

There was a hint of a smirk at the corner of Tommy's lips, which quickly disappeared. "It's complicated, with a past full of crappy shit that got in the way, including our age difference. We may love one another still, but it doesn't mean it's going to work. I'm surprised he didn't gut me after what I pulled today." Tommy's crestfallen look was painful to see.

Carson blocked out Tommy's pain. The skill was getting easier. His learning curve with this shit was high, which was a plus for all of them.

"He understood why you did it. Pissed him off that you didn't trust him enough to come to him for help. You're going to have to do a lot of groveling to make that up, but... I can safely say that he really cares for you."

Tommy ducked his head. "Sometimes caring isn't enough."

Carson gave him some space. Lincoln still wasn't answering. Sweat popped out on his skin, and a wave of panic washed over him. Lincoln's mind was quiet, yet his body was in distress, in pain. Carson doubled over and grabbed his head.

"Fuck," he muttered, as the pain hit hard and fast.

"Carson, what's going on?" Tommy knelt before him.

"He's in pain. His head." Carson gritted his teeth.

"Stop connecting with him or... whatever you do. You need to be able to concentrate on Monrovia."

Carson forced his mind to close the connection. The feat was monumental. Lincoln's mind seemed to be holding him there, unwilling to let go. They were in a mental tug of war, Lincoln refusing to let go and Carson prying himself loose. He tried to send calming thoughts to Lincoln. The pain continued to beat against his brain.

"Hurry up," Tommy whispered. "Someone's unlocking the door."

Carson was helplessly tethered to Lincoln's mind, as if he wanted Carson to know he was there. He understood that. However, what was Lincoln accomplishing by holding him hostage?

Lincoln, let go. Someone's coming.

There was no response, but the connection severed. Carson reeled back and fell on his ass.

The door opened. The guard frowned at Carson on the floor. He motioned to them. "Come on. Boss is ready for you."

FUCK. LINCOLN'S head pounded out a drumbeat, pulling him back to consciousness. Damn, he'd really wanted to stay in the warm darkness with Carson. He'd been reluctant to allow Carson to leave because.... Why? He'd wanted… no needed, to tell him something… about…. The incessant throbbing jumbled his thoughts, roiled his stomach. Someone shook him. He struck out against the hands.

"Lincoln."

Not Carson….

"Linc, open your eyes, you son of a bitch!" More shaking, and there was a stinging blow against his cheek.

"Stop."

"Lincoln, I swear to the gods, I'm gonna twist your nipples until you open your fucking eyes!"

Only one person ever used that threat to get Lincoln's ass out of bed after a night of drinking and debauchery. Lincoln groaned and forced his lids open. One bright bulb in the ceiling knifed his eyeballs. He forced himself onto his side.

"Lincoln. That's it, man. Come on. Talk to me." The face before Lincoln's was blurred. Blinking, he forced his eyes to work together… just focus….

"Max."

CHAPTER 27

LINCOLN REACHED out and a well of panic threatened to choke him when he couldn't reach Max's solid form.

"Max?" Lincoln tried to rise, but the room tilted and spun. Oh man, he was gonna hurl.

Hands grabbed Lincoln's shoulders, pulled him up, and then he was crushed into a hard chest.

"Fuck, Linc. They dumped you in here about an hour ago. What happened?" Max whispered into Lincoln's hair.

Lincoln wrapped his arms around Max, mostly because he was glad to see his best friend. Partly because the world spun too fast. Max was there. He was alive.

"Thought you were dead, asshole," Lincoln mumbled but clutched Max tighter.

"Yeah, well, we're even because I thought the same, fuckhead."

Lincoln snorted, ignoring the pain even breathing caused. Lincoln used Max for leverage and made it onto his knees. Max supported his weight until Lincoln could stay upright.

"You got a huge knot on the back of your head and—"

A whimper filled the air. Max scrambled backward. Lincoln squinted and focused on the man plastered to Max's side. Short reddish-blond hair, slim build, white skin with freckles, dressed in a thin black T-shirt and gray sweats. His feet were bare. Max stroked the guy's hair and ran his hand over his back.

"It's okay. It's just Lincoln. Remember I told you about my friend who was coming to get us out of here? That's him." Max rocked the man who shook in his arms.

"Justin?" Lincoln whispered to avoid scaring him further.

Max nodded. "They took him from the long-term care facility. He was in this room when we were dumped here."

Lincoln fought irrational feelings of animosity toward Justin. Mentally he wasn't even a man, but a small, scared child. Justin calmed as Max held him close.

"How'd you get here?" Max asked.

As Lincoln's vision focused, he noticed deep-purple bruises on Max's face. One of the lenses in his glasses was cracked. He had stripped off his black NVJ jacket and top and only wore a white Under Armour shirt caked with dirt and blood.

"First, are you okay?" Lincoln asked, knowing Max would deny any injuries.

Max pursed his lips and nodded. "I'm good. Whoever's responsible for this knew where we would be and what we were doing. We were at a total disadvantage. Took the whole team down." Max grinned, but the smile didn't make it to his eyes. "But we didn't go down without a fight."

Max was a spitfire and no doubt would take on an army if need be. Lincoln grunted. Was Tommy responsible for revealing the location of the team? Shit. Tommy had broken laws that could get him thrown in jail for the rest of his life—or worse. Not that Lincoln hadn't broken a few of his own.

Lincoln glanced around the small room that looked as if it had been used for storage. Stained concrete floor, cinder block walls, and an exposed ceiling with pipes and ductwork covered with dust and cobwebs. Charming. The thick metal door was a monstrosity they wouldn't be able budge. Not that Lincoln could even stand to walk over there.

"Where's the rest of the team? We got a pic of John tied up but alive. Pic of you and Justin. One of Caden."

"John was in here with me until this morning, when they yanked him out. No clue where he is now, or the others. We all walked in here, though I think Taylor broke his collarbone when one of the bastards rammed him with the butt of his gun. Tia may have a broken wrist. She wouldn't let go of some guy's balls, and another guy stomped on her arm. Man, did that guy screech like a girl when her hand was yanked off his balls." Max chuckled morosely. "Haven't seen them since we were forced in here."

Lincoln smirked. His team was Grade A. Now he had to get them all out of there in one piece.

"Does he talk, say anything at all?" Lincoln motioned to the huddled mass of man practically sitting in Max's lap.

Max's eyes softened and then furrows of worry crinkled his brow. "No, but he's terrified and seems to be becoming more aware of things around him. Until a while ago, he just sat there, staring off into nothing, flat effect, nonreactive, almost like... there was nothing. But earlier, I don't know, it's like he woke up and started to show emotion. Yesterday he couldn't have cared less if rats were crawling on him, wouldn't have moved a muscle. His eyes were vacant, nothing there. But earlier he turned and looked right at me as if he saw me...." Max chewed on his lip. "Like suddenly someone was in there."

Well, shit. "He's been catatonic for over seven years and now.... What? Suddenly he's waking up?" If Justin were literally waking up, then had he been locked away and unable to get out? The thought chilled Lincoln to the core. What he'd done to Justin haunted Carson. Knowing he'd locked Justin in his own mind would probably shove him right over the edge.

"Where's Carson?" Max asked.

Justin whimpered again. His breathing increased, and he pushed closer into Max.

"Did he just react to Carson's name?"

Justin answered by trembling. Max murmured words to Justin Lincoln couldn't hear. If he recognized Carson's name....

"He's here. And from what you're saying, it sounds like Justin's turnaround coincided with his arrival." Why was beyond Lincoln. They could ponder that later. "Jameson is behind this."

Max's eyes widened, and then he narrowed them. "Son of a bitch."

The pounding from Lincoln's head had spread down into his neck. He was totally useless at this point. "That's just the start." Lincoln spilled every detail. Jameson, the poisoning, Carson's newfound powers, Henderson and her son, fleeing, the gunshot, Carson healing him, Monrovia, Tommy's betrayal and redemption, NVJ guns, Jameson's betrayal, and the tap to his head.

Lincoln knew Carson had tried to contact him while he was unconscious, but where was he now? Carson wasn't answering. The connection seemed to only work one way. If Carson didn't have his end "on," then apparently nothing got through.

"So is Jameson working with Monrovia? I mean, what's there to gain? And NVJ officers are in on this? Are they voluntary, or blackmailed like Tommy? You said NVJ had that officer's kid and husband. Just what the fuck has been going on in the NVJ?" He huffed. "And Doc and Tommy? What's next? Flying monkeys and forty days of rain? Fuck!"

"Be careful what you wish for." Lincoln nodded, regretting the action as the room spun. He groaned and hung his head in his hands.

"Sounds as if we're running out of options here. Jameson knows about what he can do. He wouldn't take him without a way to control him, would he?"

Lincoln's vision doubled. That couldn't be good. His stomach roiled, not just from his head wound, but from one thought that had plagued him since he woke.

"Jameson has everything needed to control Carson in this building." Lincoln was confident he was going to pass out or puke, or both.

Max looked at Justin again and then at Lincoln. Max's eyes widened. "Oh fuck, he's got…." Max's words died out.

"Everyone Carson has left in the world."

Lincoln fell onto his hands and lowered himself to the floor, praying Carson was okay, praying he'd survive if Jameson killed everyone he loved.

CARSON AND Tommy followed the guard again. Once they'd left the small room, Carson feigned needing to use the bathroom so he could try to contact Lincoln once more. What was disturbing was Carson felt the connection, but Lincoln's words were jumbled and didn't make any sense. Maybe the connection was short-circuiting. Maybe his powers were going, which meant they were all in a shitload of trouble.

Back in the hallway, their journey was short. They stopped before a door. Carson steeled his spine before he gave into the urge to crumple into a heap on the floor. The guard pushed open the door. In the center of the room, Lincoln was strapped to a table. Carson did almost collapse. Lincoln's eyes were closed. Jameson stood by the table, a fucking annoying grin plastered on his face. Carson ripped off his sunglasses and threw them to the floor.

Tommy knocked into Carson to get into the room. "You did this? Where's my brother? Where's Doc?" Gasping, Tommy charged into the room. Doc was tied to a chair, face mottled with dark bruises, his mouth gagged. There were two other guards. The one with the evil sneer stopped Tommy, then blocked the wild fist Tommy threw at him. He slammed the butt of his gun into Tommy's gut, and Tommy fell onto his knees, groaning. Doc gazed blearily at Tommy as he struggled with his restraints, to no avail.

Carson narrowed his eyes at Jameson. "You're not Monrovia."

As long as Carson drew in breath, he'd never forget the beady-eyed man who forced him to bite Justin. Jameson chuckled smugly. "Of course not. Monrovia's long dead. I killed him when I rescued you. He was a two-bit hustler trying to work his way up in the vampire world. I didn't need an idiot like him messing up my plans. Justin's grandfather was the one who sold you off to Monrovia for money. I removed those threats quite readily."

Carson knew Justin's grandfather disappeared after the kidnapping. The case was never solved. Who else had he taken care of?

Carson was concerned Lincoln wasn't moving. Carson gave his brain a super hard nudge. Lincoln's eyes fluttered several times.

"Those powers of yours are amazing. I have to say I am more than pleased with the outcome," Jameson said, glee evident in his voice.

A few blinks and Lincoln's eyes stayed open. Carson was relieved to see the recognition in them. Lincoln struggled against the ropes, but there was no getting out of the mess without a knife.

It's okay, Carson assured Lincoln again and turned to Jameson. "What are you doing? My mother left me a message asking me to find you. She said you knew the truth about me, but she couldn't have known everything." No way she would have sent Carson to a stark raving lunatic.

Jameson steepled his fingers. "No, she did not. The prophecies were written hundreds of years ago and passed along through each generation of Manashan. When you were born, those prophecies were set into motion. Believe me, I helped them along the best I could. I've worked for nearly a quarter century to assure that the correct pieces fell into place. No one person possesses the power needed to complete such tasks, so I had to borrow from many different kinds of vampires. You see, under another name, I run the Center for Vampire Advancement division of the NVJ. So many resources and opportunities to research vampires. No oversight and unlimited money. I could take whatever I wanted. And I did."

CHAPTER 28

CARSON GASPED. "You're responsible for taking that boy and his father? Who else have you ripped away from their families?" All of this pain and misery, so Jameson could do what? "But you said I was supposed to clean up that mess. The corruption. That's what I was here for." With the shock wearing off, anger took over Carson.

Jameson chuckled. He was way too amused with himself. "Originally maybe. However, your talents lie better in the realm of vampire domination. The current leaders are shortsighted, working for justice and equality for vampires. Hitting their heads against Nons society. While the Nons give lip service to that equality, they will never allow vampires to attain the same power they have."

Movement caught Carson's eye. Tommy inched slowly toward Doc. The guard above Tommy stomped down on his hand. Carson swore he heard bones cracking. Doc flailed at Tommy's scream, his yells muffled by the rag in his mouth. He practically tipped his chair over trying to get out of the restraints.

Jameson shook his head and sighed at the interruption. "If he moves again, shoot him in the head."

The black-haired guard balked at the command while the blond-haired one grinned with anticipation.

Doc pleaded with his eyes, no doubt imploring Tommy to remain where he was.

"Anyway, to continue. Hundreds of years ago, a group of very powerful vampire shamans predicted the eradication of the vampire race. The dominant human species will one day wipe vampires from the map. These shamans chose one from among them with the ability to erase the minds of other, a Tabula Rasa like yourself. This shaman was set on a path for rebirth many generations later. By combining the powers of a Tabula Rasa and a Sanatore, the spirit of that shaman was set free. You're the reincarnation of a vampire who lived hundreds of years ago.

Your power will allow me to balance the power between the Nons and the vampires."

Carson scowled, rage brewing in his gut. "Why is it that every plot comes down to power and one bunch of jerks wanting to take over another bunch of jerks?" Carson bunched his fists at his side. "I swear to the gods and on my mother's grave that you'll never get help from me."

Jameson narrowed his eyes, then waved with his hand. The blond guard walked across the room and waited by one of the many doors. A malicious sneer marred Jameson's face.

"Would you swear on the life of your brother?"

The guard opened the door and pulled someone into the room.

Carson's chest tightened. "Caden!"

His brother's head snapped up. Upon seeing Carson, his mouth dropped open as relief and fear crossed his face.

"Carson! Carson!" Caden tried to get away as the guard held him firm. "Let me go! Carson!"

Relief brought tears to his eyes. "Caden!" He was alive and so close.

Carson hastened around the table, needing to hold Caden and know he was truly okay. Jameson stopped Carson from passing. He let loose the immense power within him. His tattoos glowed bright red as gasps filled the room. No one would keep him from Caden. *No. One.*

Jameson raised his hand toward Caden. His scream sent an icy chill down Carson's back. Caden grabbed his head. The screams increased as he dropped to his knees.

"I'll kill him slowly," Jameson warned, a steely determination on his face that Carson couldn't discount.

Caden screamed, and Carson struggled to pull back his power. The sight of his brother suffering overrode his control.

"Car-son, s-stop," Lincoln muttered.

Carson connected with Lincoln's mind.

C-calm… d-down… ho… honey.

Even Lincoln's thoughts were disconnected. He was hurt worse than Carson had thought.

The glowing red of the marks on Carson's body faded as he gained control. Whatever Jameson had been doing to Caden ceased. He fell onto his hands on the floor, panting.

"Don't hurt him." Carson scrambled for a plan to get them out of this mess.

He searched for a path into Jameson's mind, then planted the suggestion to let them all go. Jameson frowned and then cocked his head as if he heard something. He moved closer to Carson, a contemplative look on his face. Shit, the suggestion was working. Jameson opened his mouth. Instead of speaking, a slow, heartless grin crossed his face. Carson didn't see Jameson's hand until it struck him across the cheek. The pain exploded through Carson's head. He stumbled back, hitting the table where Lincoln was tied down.

Caden shouted to Carson. Lincoln's anger rose exponentially, pushing into Carson's mind. He rubbed his aching cheek, glaring at Jameson.

"I'm not some weak vampire you can manipulate with your parlor tricks!" Jameson showed his first real hint of anger. "Don't try that crap on me or else…." Another raise of his hand, and Caden was writhing in pain, again.

"Stop! Okay, what do you want?"

Carson could go along with Jameson until he could get Caden away from him. Carson had to stay calm, not panic and *never* underestimate Jameson. He was powerful, and he'd manipulated events and people to get what he wanted. He was fucking dangerous. Carson got that now.

Jameson lowered his hand, and Caden's screams stopped. "Good. Now, hopefully, you clearly understand that I haven't spent a quarter of my life assuring this moment occurred and not taken great pains to guarantee all variables were under my control. Lieutenant Anderson, could you bring in my last piece of insurance that Carson will cooperate?"

If Carson hadn't been leaning against the table, his buckling knees would have dropped him onto the floor. Blood rushed his head as his heart kicked into overdrive. A sick roll of his stomach and his mouth watered, the room tilted. He knew who was coming, yet nothing could have prepared him for who'd come through the door.

He'd convinced himself he hadn't seen him in the photo. The reddish-blond hair, the creamy white skin, the freckles. The man's head was buried against the chest of a very disheveled and beleaguered Max. He assessed the room, eyes narrowing as he saw

Lincoln tied to the table. Yet Carson's attention was pulled to the man who no longer had the body of a boy, but of a man. Carson was staring straight at...

"Justin," he said in a choked whisper.

Tears flooded his eyes and didn't hesitate to course down his cheeks. A trembling wended through Carson, and his hands visibly shook. Beside him, Lincoln struggled against the ropes. All Carson could do was send calming thoughts to Lincoln's confused mind. He tried to push something through to Carson, but he shut him out, fearful Lincoln would experience the terrifying anguish eating Carson alive.

Behind Max and Justin, Carson's uncle entered, his short gray hair mussed and dirty, his lined face smudged. He had a thick growth of beard. His uncle was a consummate shaver, even twice a day some days. Bruises covered his cheeks, along with a few blood-crusted scratches, but he still held his usual stoic expression. The appearance of his uncle brought Carson's doubts to the surface about his hand in Jameson's scheme. Carson wanted to believe his Uncle Graham innocent. However, the evidence was incriminating.

Carson's uncle quickly moved to Caden, still on the floor, and cradled his nephew. Caden clung to him. Not until his uncle looked up, did he see Carson. The stoicism faded, his mouth twisted, and his lip trembled.

"Carson?" he asked as if he couldn't believe his own eyes.

Carson swiped at his tears. He hated Jameson Merrick with his entire being for messing with his family, his entire fucking life.

"Uncle Graham, did you... are you...?" Shit, Carson didn't want to know the truth if it wasn't what he wanted to hear. "Did you help him?"

His uncle shook his head violently. "No, no. I love you boys, and I loved your mom more than my own life. And your dad too, but... I was angry with your father for a stupid inheritance I thought should have been mine. I was young and stupid, and when your father died, I took your mother's offer to stay at the house. She always said she saw something better in me than I showed the world. But back then I couldn't see it and was going to help Monrovia. I did until I fell in love with you all so I lied to him. I never touched his money, not until...." His uncle turned a spiteful glare at Jameson. "Until the supposed Monrovia contacted me and ordered me to bring Carson to him." Uncle Graham huffed. "I told him to go to hell."

"That was your first mistake." Jameson ran his hands over that fucking braid Carson wanted to cut off. "If you'd complied, Carmen would be alive now and you and your nephew would be free. Actually, everyone here is here because of your refusal."

"You told me you'd taken Carson and Carmen! I don't understand. They weren't in the house when I searched, so I took Caden. I was going to find Monrovia, and kill him myself."

Carson had been on the back of the property. He wasn't supposed to leave the house without telling them. Fuck.

"Too late. Monrovia's been dead for seven years. And since you'd refused to hand Carson over, I chose other means to get him."

His uncle wasn't involved in what had happened, hadn't killed his mother. Carson swallowed against the hard lump burning his throat. "Why did you kill my mother? You didn't have to. I would have gone with you."

Jameson actually looked distressed. Maybe that was a lie too. "I never wanted harm to come to her. Your uncle was to be out of the house, so the man I sent could take you and your brother. I needed some leverage to get you to cooperate. I hadn't bargained that your brother would go with your uncle, or that your mother would resist and the fool would harm her. He then fled without you, fearful he'd go to jail. Believe me, when I got my hands on him, he pleaded for jail."

Caden jumped off the floor. "It doesn't matter what you intended to do! You killed my mother even if you weren't the one who stabbed her!"

The hard edges of Jameson's face returned, but he didn't react to Caden's outburst. "It was an unfortunate event that can't be changed. But your destiny, Carson, has been so ingrained into your lifeline, the prophecy has played out without further assistance from me. You received Lincoln's blood. You've become what was intended."

Fuck destiny.

"Enough!" Jameson's impatience filled the air. "Are you prepared to cooperate with me? Or should I order my men to execute your entire family right here in front of you?"

Carson gritted his teeth. What choice did he have? Everyone he cared for was in that room. With Carson's stunted nod, Jameson cracked a smile.

"Wise boy." Jameson circled the table and stood by Lincoln's head. "However, a slight nod does little to convince me of the sincerity of your cooperation. There's only one thing that will allay all doubts of your loyalty to me."

Jameson placed his hands on either side of Lincoln's head. He tried to shake the hands off, but Jameson gripped harder. Even blocking the connection with Lincoln, Carson felt a surge of panic from Lincoln. Carson touched Lincoln's leg to calm him. Jameson turned Lincoln's head far to the left, exposing his neck...

Carson's heart rate tripled. A veil of white haze coated his thoughts. Panic reached icy fingers through his body. Cold sweat clung to his skin. Jameson became Monrovia, and the person strapped to the table wasn't Lincoln but Justin—beautiful, sixteen-year-old Justin. And they were in that room with the dingy white walls and aged medical equipment—the abandoned hospital where Monrovia had taken them.

Tears flowed from Justin's eyes, tracking down the side of his face, disappearing into his short hair. He tried to put on the bravest face for Carson, but the pain from the bullet hole in Justin's leg prevented any truth to the façade. He was going to die because of Carson's refusal. Monrovia held Justin's head to the side, waiting for Carson to comply. Monrovia had threatened to shoot Justin in the face. If Carson complied, Monrovia would get Justin medical treatment for the wound in his leg. Carson wouldn't. How could he do that to Justin?

"I-it's okay, C-Carson," Justin whispered. "G-gonna ki-kill me anyway."

Carson shook his head, not wanting to hear. A loud and malicious cackle came from Monrovia as he pulled out the gun and shot Justin in the other thigh. Carson and Justin both screamed as blood gushed from the wound.

"Screaming isn't going to help. Bite him. Bite him now!"

Carson's entire body shook, moving to Justin's side. Monrovia grinned. Then it was Jameson grinning. The person on the table was no longer Justin but Lincoln, the man he loved with his entire heart and soul.

"Bite him, Carson, or suffer the consequences."

CHAPTER 29

CARSON'S BREATH stuttered from his chest as he tried to say no, but nothing came out. Carson looked to Justin who trembled in Max's arms, his gaze darting around the room. Carson needed him to formulate some sort of a fucking brilliant plan. Justin was terrified, and Carson was right there with him. Gods, did he know what was happening? Did he understand? Whether he did or not, Max would protect him, just as Carson's uncle would protect Caden with his life. His uncle, their protector, had wrapped an arm over Caden's shoulder. His little brother, who'd always made Carson's pathetic life more bearable, stared at Carson, eyes wide and pleading. His family, his friends, his lover—all trapped there by a madman.

"This is your last warning, Carson." Jameson still held Lincoln's head to the side. Deep red blood stained Lincoln's hair at the back of his skull.

Lincoln tried to look at Carson, but from that angle, Carson knew Lincoln couldn't see him. Carson moved into his line of vision and connected with those brilliant blue eyes. The eyes he'd fallen in love with, that had grabbed his heart from the start. Lincoln had risked everything to save Carson. And now Carson was being forced to sacrifice his bonded mate.

Fuck no!

"Carson, it's okay." Lincoln slurred his words, but they were clear enough to slice into Carson's chest, carve out his heart, and crush it dead. Those blue eyes pleaded and, at the same time, reassured Carson.

He couldn't kill Lincoln. *Couldn't.*

"*Speak* to me," Lincoln said, his voice rising.

Carson stared, only seeing an empty existence without his mate. But if he didn't bite Lincoln, *everyone* would die. His brother and uncle and Justin…. He'd just gotten them back.

"Make a decision." Jameson's tone was ripe with impatience.

Carson gasped, and his mouth moved, and nothing came out.

"Your choice. Shoot the uncle."

The guard with the blond hair smiled ruefully and pulled up his gun. Carson shouted, and before he could react, the gun went off.

Doc screamed through his gag.

"You stupid idiot!" Jameson glared at the guard. "That's not the uncle." He pointed to Tommy on the floor and then to Uncle Graham. "That is."

Carson's uncle stood before Caden in a protective stance.

The guard shot Tommy! Doc fought against his bonds, screaming and bucking until his chair fell over with a *bang*. Even that didn't stop him.

He shot Tommy.

Oh gods, was he dead? Carson couldn't see him from where he stood. "Stop!" Carson screamed. "I'll do it. Stop!"

Max pushed Justin behind him, then rushed toward the guard, who was about to shoot Carson's uncle. Max jumped the guard, and they wrestled on the floor. Lieutenant whatever his name wrapped his arms around Max. The other guard jumped in and they both pinned Max to the floor. Poor Justin huddled in the corner, shaking and hugging his knees. Doc did anything he could to free himself and get to Tommy, who had a bloody hole in his shoulder. Nothing was going right.

JAMESON CONTINUED to hold Lincoln's head to the side, opening prime real estate on his neck. *Fucking son of a bitch.* Tied down, Lincoln was helpless. His attempts to prod Carson into communicating with him had fallen short. All of his attempts had failed. With his head spinning, his thoughts had been broken up like letters in alphabet soup. His message hadn't gotten through. Carson had to know about Justin, that he'd started waking when Carson had arrived. It could buy them time, possibly save them all. Hopefully, it wasn't too late for Tommy. Damn, Dennison would end Lincoln if his little brother died on Lincoln's watch—if Dennison and the rest of the team were still alive somewhere in the building.

Carson had to agree to bite Lincoln, or Jameson would make sure his uncle was shot next time, then Caden. But if Carson bit Lincoln, he wouldn't know he might be able to reverse the effects and would believe he'd killed Lincoln. He couldn't allow his bond mate to suffer that horror, again.

Carson wrung his hands. Beads of sweat covered his pale face. He chewed his bottom lip and his eyes darted around as if… as if he were making a plan.

"Carson."

He didn't even react to Lincoln but spoke to Jameson. "I'll do what you say, but you have to let Doc help Tommy or I won't do it."

Jameson snorted. "And if I don't?"

Jameson's hands moved off Lincoln's head, allowing him a limited view of the room. The only people he could see were Carson and two of the guards.

"Then I won't do it." Carson showed a steely repose, but Lincoln felt anxiety and fear pouring from him.

What the fuck is he doing?

"Carson. Stop." Lincoln tried any movement to loosen the restraints, but his arms and legs were numb. If he didn't get out soon, his limbs would be useless. "Carson!" Pain shot through his skull.

Carson jumped and whirled toward Lincoln. He was a big pile of nerves, and Lincoln had to calm him down quick, or they were all going to die.

Jameson barked orders at the guards to let Max up to tend to Justin, and to right the chair Doc was tied to. Was he seriously going to listen to Carson? Then Jameson directed them to untie Doc.

Lincoln took the opportunity to get through to Carson. "*Talk* to me, Carson," Lincoln said in a quiet tone. He raised his brows, hoping Carson would understand.

Carson was partially distracted by the activities in the room. But then he turned and his eyes widened.

Carson, talk to me, please.

Lincoln… I can't… I don't know what to do. He's going to kill them. Oh, gods, they shot Tommy.

Oh yeah, he was hanging off the edge and ready to fall.

Listen to me carefully. I want you to look at Justin.

Carson's eyes widened almost comically, and then his guilt flooded into Lincoln.

You have to look at Justin. Just look, please, love.

Carson slowly turned in the direction of Justin. Max had pulled Justin to his feet and talked to him in a low voice. And damned, if Justin wasn't looking right at Max, as if he were cognizant of what Max said, as if he understood. Lincoln made out Max saying "okay" and Justin nodded back. *He nodded back.* Well, shit. Lincoln prayed Jameson didn't notice the dramatic changes in Justin. If he did their plans might backfire.

Carson's hand covered his mouth. When he turned to Lincoln, his eyes were glassy. *But... how?*

Since we came here, he's changed. Since you *came here. Max has seen it. Somehow you're healing him just by being here. I think we can use it as a way to stall what's happening.*

Jameson yelled at a guard to get a first aid kit. His barking tone was far from the serene calm he generally projected. Lincoln had to get through to Carson, and fast.

You think he's like this because I'm here? Carson looked far from convinced.

I do. And I think if you bite me that the same thing will happen. Give Jameson what he wants. Buy us time, because if you don't, he'll kill Caden, your uncle, Justin, everyone, including me.

Jameson came around the table, his jaw clenched. He grabbed Carson's arm, all patience gone. Dragging him along, Jameson pushed Carson on top of Lincoln and then shoved Carson's face into the crook of Lincoln's neck. Despite the direness of the situation, having Carson touch him was comforting.

It's okay, Carson. Really, love. Everything will be all right. Do what he wants, and then we can figure out a way to get out of this. I love you. I know you won't hurt me.

A sob broke free from Carson, and his warm breath fanned over Lincoln's neck. He shivered.

"Bite him." Jameson pushed harder on Carson's neck.

Lincoln felt the warmth of Carson's lips on his jaw. A gentle kiss. Lincoln closed his eyes as his heart broke from the aching pain sloughing off Carson. He wished he could hold him.

Trust me, Carson.

"Bite him now!"

Lincoln felt the shudder run through Carson, felt his fear kick into overdrive. A searing, hot pain struck Lincoln's neck and spread out like an exploding star beneath his skin. Carson gripped Lincoln's shoulders hard enough to bruise. The intense pain diminished with each pull from Carson's mouth. The warmth spread into Lincoln's chest, his gut, his groin. He panted and groaned with pleasure as his dick filled and lengthened. The blossom of pleasure expanded, infiltrating every empty space. Lincoln had bitten many willing people, but he'd never been on this side of the bite. Fuck, he was a pain slut too.

His head clouded, and Lincoln swore Carson fed him pleasure through their link. Lincoln was in danger of coming in his pants. The long pulls from Carson's mouth, his wet lips on Lincoln's neck, Carson's hard cock pushing into Lincoln's thigh....

Carson moaned low in his throat and sucked harder and faster. Lincoln's head swirled. Every vein burned as if molten lava flowed through them.

Carson, fuck, honey.

Carson groaned again, his fingers kneading the flesh of Lincoln's shoulders. Carson rubbed his hard bulge over Lincoln's thigh. Fuck, this was supposed to be... to be...

Lincoln's thoughts jumbled. He tried to catch anything resembling a coherent word or sentence. Anything. But he twirled around on the edge of reason. He had risen so high on a wave of ecstasy, and now he dived fast, submerged within the pleasure. He couldn't find which way was up. And he was cold. So fucking cold and tired and all he wanted to do was sleep.

THE HEADY rush was nothing short of erotic. Carson had never experienced anything as arousing, anything as delicious as biting into Lincoln and drinking. He sucked and bucked and writhed on Lincoln. Nothing else existed at that moment. Or anyone except the two of them. Around him, Carson heard muffled shouts and a scuffle, but he was lost in a land of bliss with Lincoln. He wanted to stay there forever and ever...

He felt the moment their connection was severed. A cold shiver ran over his skin and settled in his muscles. So fucking cold and...

Lincoln?

Nothing. Carson stopped sucking on the bite and frantically licked at the puncture holes to stop the blood flow. Lincoln's body had gone slack. Where he'd been hard, his muscles tense, and panting just seconds earlier, he was now still, breaths shallow and not answering.

Carson looked at Lincoln. His eyes were closed, his expression flat, showing nothing. Carson grasped Lincoln's chin and turned his face toward him, trying to stop the speeding train of panic from smashing him into a million pieces.

"Lincoln?" Carson gently shook Lincoln's head. "Lincoln, babe, open your eyes, please," He choked out in a sob.

What have I done?

CHAPTER 30

BEHIND HIM, Jameson chuckled. "Well done, Carson. Well done. You've proven your loyalty."

Carson ignored the ire rising in his gut. Lincoln... he couldn't have....

Carson tried speaking through their bond. Lincoln needed to answer him, reassure Carson that he was okay, that Carson hadn't...

"Not again," he whispered. His hands shook as he released Lincoln's jaw. The tremors ran up his arms, and soon his entire body had joined in. Lincoln remained motionless, not a twitch, the only movement the rise and fall of his chest.... Just like Justin had been after Carson had bit him. Gone.

Something cracked in his mind, revealing something looming and terrifying he'd been holding back, something he hadn't allowed to come forth out of self-preservation. Now he couldn't give a fuck.

He stumbled back from the table. The screaming sound of that speeding freight train deafened him. His chest heaved as the panic and pain and anger gripped tight around his ribs and squeezed his heart until it was a mere small, aching muscle in his chest.

He was a murderer.

He'd killed Justin. His mother. Lincoln—the one person who meant the world to him, loved with every fiber of his being.

A cold-blooded murderer.

Muffled shouts again. Carson looked at Max, who struggled against the black-haired guard. Max's face twisted in rage, and his mouth moved, screaming words Carson couldn't hear. Max looked as if he wanted to kill Carson. And he should. He should take him out before he hurt anyone else. Carson had drained Max's best friend of everything he was. Carson was too dangerous to live.

A gleeful Jameson practically vibrated from Carson's ability to follow directions. Carson gritted his teeth and pulled all of the panicky fear and heartache, all of the pain from his entire life, the emptiness, the loneliness, the hopelessness into a ball of power as black as coal, sitting where his heart should have been. A rush of adrenaline fueled his efforts. The symbols and writing on his body lit into a fiery red glow, brighter than ever. What happened was beyond Carson, beyond a Tabula Rasa, or a Salutem vampire, beyond being a brother, a nephew, a son… a lover.

Jameson narrowed his eyes. "Stop now!" Carson heard the words this time. A shaky command from a man who no longer had the upper hand.

With Lincoln's blood once again coursing through his veins, Carson was strong, and he would get his revenge. Sweet, satisfying revenge. His survival meant little to him.

Carson drew power from that black orb of power, a pulsing, living entity that expanded in chest. He willed that power out of him, nothing he'd even been aware he was capable of doing. Jameson stumbled back. The shaman's face twisted in a vicious scowl. He faced Carson head-on. A maniacal grin split his face as he raised his hand. Not only did Caden's screams fill the air, his uncle's did as well.

"You will stop this nonsense now. You don't want harm coming to your family and friends." His grin turned into a determined sneer. He flicked his hand, and screams filled the room to capacity.

The roaring in Carson's ears became deafening as he crashed through every barrier in his mind, uncovering energy unlike anything he'd ever encountered. Twisting and twining through him, hot waves licked at his nerves, fired neurons at supernatural speeds, endowed him with ancient powers. Primitive words were chanted in his head, a chorus igniting each word and symbol, melding into a brilliant, fiery orange as if Carson's skin was on fire. He was high on the power.

Fuck yeah!

Carson focused on a channel into Jameson's mind but was quickly shut down. Another, and that was shut down as well.

Jameson cackled, continually shutting Carson down. "You're fucking with the wrong man, son! I have the power of hundreds of vampires. Powers most people have never seen before. I have the power of your own father, who held on right to the very end."

The stony glint in his gray eyes raised Carson's hackles. His father, his mother. Jameson had stolen them, murdered them. He wouldn't get what remained of his family. Carson drove another jolt at Jameson, effectively severing the connection Jameson had with Caden and his uncle Graham. Their screams ceased.

A blast of heat hit Carson square in the chest. He stood his ground. *Fucking asshole.* Can't get in one way, try another.

Carson grabbed hold of the energy Jameson unknowingly fed him as more blasts hit him square in the chest. Carson's black ball expanded to fill organs and bones and muscle, and the hair on his body stood on end. The mass was solid and heavy, weighing on his limbs as if gravity had doubled. He struggled to remain on his shaking legs, threatening to give. Fear flooded the room from every mind. Even the guards were wide-eyed and terrified.

"Give it up, Carson! You can't possibly win here. You're only going to die!" The quaver in Jameson's shouts told Carson something important. Jameson struggled to hold his ground. Carson's time had come.

"I'm counting on it."

Jameson's stunned expression was priceless. *Didn't expect that, did ya, prick?*

"No!" Caden tried to get to Carson, but his uncle held him. With pleading, sad eyes, they begged Carson to stop. But Lincoln was gone and Carson didn't want to live without him.

Carson aimed dead center for Jameson's heart, ready to unleash a world of hurt on the man who'd destroyed his life. But a movement caught his eye.

Did Lincoln's eyes open?

The distraction was enough for Jameson to get in a few good hits. Carson stumbled back, unable to look away as Lincoln's eyes fluttered open. He stared off into nothing. Stared as Justin had, unseeing, a body no longer inhabited, dead inside.

When Lincoln turned his head, Carson was unprepared for the clarity, the direct eye contact, the fucking smirk. "Carson."

Carson's breath seized. Jameson bombarded him with hits of energy, battering Carson's body. Bone-breaking pain poured through him. He was able to thrust a wall of energy before him, warding off the strikes momentarily.

Carson's plans had changed.

He searched the amalgam of powers that mingled and coursed through his head. He grasped familiarity, the one that would enact his revenge. Death was too permanent for Jameson, too kind for a motherfucker like him. Jameson would suffer the remainder of his life trapped in his mind. Carson drew on the power of the Tabula Rasa, now ten times stronger than before Lincoln had changed him.

The ground beneath Carson shook. Plaster fell from the ceiling. The blast was going to be huge. Carson imagined an invisible hand, reaching out and wrapping fingers tight around Jameson's throat. The shaman's eyes widened as he clawed at the invisible grip.

Carson pushed out his power and the guards went down, out cold on the floor.

"Untie Lincoln! Get everyone out!"

Jameson made a last ditch effort. A surge of power hit Carson with hurricane force winds, but he held tight to Jameson. Searing agony stomped on every nerve in his body, and his jaw clamped down involuntarily. Oh, fuck, he was burning from the inside out.

"Carson!" Lincoln struggled to free himself as Max sliced through the ropes binding him.

Get out, while I end this. It's gonna be huge!

"Carson, stop! You don't need to do this!"

Free of his restraints, Lincoln slid off the table, but his legs gave out. He crumpled helplessly to the ground. The pain on his face was almost too much for Carson to bear.

Yes, I do. He won't stop! He's fucking powerful... too powerful. Now get your ass out of here and protect my family! I'll be right behind you! Carson severed the connection, but not before adding, *I love you.*

Carson focused on the task he'd been destined for. The threat to the vampire world he'd been fated to eliminate was Jameson himself.

He fought to hold back long enough for those he cared about to clear out. The rumbling beneath his feet grew in magnitude, shaking the walls, crumbling concrete, and quaking every muscle in his legs. Carson's jaw clenched tight with the effort.

Doc carried Tommy out with the assistance of Caden and his uncle. Max threw a loudly protesting Lincoln over his shoulder. Lincoln's trepidation and anger were front and center as his eyes connected with Carson, and then he was gone. He could scream at Carson all he wanted later.

Jameson fought a losing battle, while feeding Carson his energy and pinned beneath Carson's invisible hand. Terror for what he'd help create froze on Jameson's face.

With a feral grin, Carson forced every molecule of energy he possessed out in radius around his body. The sonic wave distorting the air, rippling outward, flipping the heavy metal table, exploding lights, and blowing Jameson across the room. Windows exploded, doors busted open. The wave disappeared into the walls and ceiling. A low groan followed as the building shuddered and plaster rained down.

Oh, shit!

The walls undulated and crumbled. The ceiling shifted as the metallic sound of tons of bending, twisting beams collided with the sounds of air rushing through the room. Carson sprinted for the open door and then the entire ceiling came down.

AN EXPLOSION rocked the right side of the two-story building. The force hit Lincoln where he lay on the ground with Max wrapped tight around his legs. Fucking jerk had tackled him when he'd tried to go back into the building—the building now collapsing piece by piece. Carson still inside. Lincoln's fear was exponential and belted him hard in the gut.

"Quit kicking me! You'll get killed if you go in there." Max tightened his grip on Lincoln.

He dug his fingers into the dried grass, trying to pull himself toward the building, to no avail. "Let me go! I have to get Carson!" Sweat poured from Lincoln's face as he watched the horrifying scene before him.

A roar louder than a jet plane filled the air. The ground shook as the entire side of the building fell in on itself. A huge cloud of dust and debris mushroomed into the air and blew outward, hitting Lincoln in the face. He covered his head.

No! No! No!

CHAPTER 31

"Carson!" Lincoln kicked until Max let go. He barreled past Doc, who leaned over Tommy, struggling to keep him alive. Lincoln had no clue where the rest of the team was. He hoped they hadn't been in the section that had collapsed.

Lincoln tore into the portion of the building still standing. A thick fog of dust blocked his vision. The dry mist clogged his throat and burned his lungs. He coughed and pulled his shirt up to cover his mouth and nose. He tried to yell for Carson, but more hacking coughs cut off his words. Feeling his way around a corner, he rammed into a hard body. Grasping at the person's shirt, Lincoln read the NVJ logo.

"Dennison? Where are the others?"

"Right behind me."

John coughed and seized Lincoln's shoulders. "Fuck, Samuels. We have to get out of here!"

Lincoln struggled to breathe. "Carson. He's in there!"

When Lincoln tried to pass John, he held tight to Lincoln. "You can't. It's too dangerous!"

Lincoln shoved John hard, and he stumbled back, releasing Lincoln.

"Commander, the building is unsafe!" He hadn't seen Dwayne behind John. He held Tia against his side, guiding her through the dust. They both held pieces of cloth over their faces. A makeshift sling made from Tia's outer NVJ shirt held her right arm.

"Everyone go straight to get out. Go!" Lincoln coughed.

Lincoln stepped around Dennison, who practically hacked up a lung. That's what he got for smoking. Behind Dwayne and Tia, Myers walked stiffly up the hall, leaning heavily against the wall. His arm had been wrapped tight to his body to support his broken collarbone.

"Move it, Myers! Keep going." Lincoln pointed toward the faint light at the end of the hall as he passed.

"Commander, the building's unsafe." Taylor spoke through gritted teeth.

Lincoln ignored his warning and continued into the darkness trying to cover his mouth and nose.

Lincoln bolted blindly down the hall, eyes gritty from dust. Up ahead the light brightened. Then he was faced with the aftermath of the room they'd been in. He pushed back the panic that threatened to bring him to his knees. How could anyone survive that?

Stop. Focus on finding Carson.

A breeze through the massive holes in the walls cleared most of the blinding dust. Lincoln pawed mindlessly through the rubble, throwing large chunks of cinder blocks and plaster. Beside him, Dwayne and John appeared and started to help. Lincoln gave them each a grateful nod.

"Carson!" Lincoln cleared a path, moving what he could. Twisted metal from beams weighing thousands of pounds blocked much of their access. Lincoln wouldn't give up. Even if....

Carson, love, talk to me, please.

Tears stung his eyes. He grabbed anything in his way, tossing it aside. His hands bled as jagged pieces of concrete and metal cut into his palms. He ignored the pain. This wasn't right. They were supposed to beat the enemy and love one another for the rest of their lives.

"Lincoln!" Dwayne waved his hands frantically. "Help!"

Lincoln's heart rose into his throat as he climbed over a pile of plaster, slipping and losing his footing. He scrambled to the spot where John was helping to dig. "Is it him?"

John didn't have to answer. The top of Carson's head, coated with white plaster, his face battered and bruised, his eyes closed.

Dwayne gritted his teeth as he lifted a large piece of rubble. With a mighty push the metal crashed to the side.

Please, gods, please, no!

"Carson?" Lincoln slammed onto his knees and cradled Carson's head. His head rolled to the side. John and Dwayne worked to clear the rest of the debris. "Carson, come on, wake up, please. I found you. Please."

Tears flowed freely as Lincoln wiped the dust from Carson's face. He searched his neck for a pulse as his fingers shook, but he couldn't locate one. "Dwayne, I don't think he's breathing," Lincoln said in a shaky whisper.

Dwayne knelt next to Lincoln. "Let's ease him out. John, give us a hand."

Lincoln pushed his hands under Carson's shoulders and wrapped his arms around Carson's chest. John lifted Carson's lower body as Dwayne supported his middle. They pulled Carson's limp body from the rubble. His arms flopped around like dead weight. Once they'd reached a cleared space, Lincoln sank back, cradling Carson against his chest. A sob tore from Lincoln's throat, followed by another and then another. Carson had deserved a much better life, and now he was fucking gone. An inhumane sound ripped out of Lincoln's chest, and heart-shattering sorrow clawed at his insides, rendering deep gouges, permanent wounds left to bleed for all eternity.

"Lincoln!"

Lincoln blinked a wall of tears from his vision. Doc knelt before him, his hands gripping Carson's shoulders, that interminable scowl on his face. "Let me help him."

Lincoln frowned. How could he help? No one could help.

Dwayne grasped Lincoln's chin and lifted his head. "Linc, buddy. Let Carson go. Let Doc work."

Lincoln looked down into the swollen and damaged face. A large cut marred his forehead, but Carson was still beautiful. Lincoln loosened his hold and lowered Carson to the floor. Doc checked the pulse in Carson's neck and then his wrist. Next, he pressed his fingers against the inside of his upper thigh.

Dwayne's hand was heavy on Lincoln's shoulder, no doubt holding him in place. Lincoln swore he stopped breathing while waiting and praying....

"He's got a faint pulse." Doc immediately leaned over and tilted Carson's chin back and blew into his mouth, then started chest compressions.

"Lincoln. He needs blood."

"Huh?" Lincoln snapped out of his daze and sat up with renewed energy.

"Open a vein and put it against his mouth."

Lincoln checked his pockets. "Knife! I need a fucking knife!"

"I got nothing." John looked around them.

"Me neither," Dwayne said.

"Fuck it!" Lincoln grabbed a jagged piece of metal and tore open a vein in his wrist. The searing pain ripped through his arm. Lincoln laid his wrist across Carson's open mouth and let the blood seep in, praying his blood healed him.

"Swallow, Carson, come on." If this didn't work.... Lincoln wouldn't make it, didn't want to.

Doc stopped compressions and placed two fingers on the side of Carson's neck. Lincoln looked up to see the concentration and—was that fear? Were they too late? Lincoln rested his forehead against Carson's as he continued to feed him blood Carson didn't swallow. He could feel the effects of giving blood again so soon, but he'd drain every ounce to save his bond mate.

A faint thumping noise pulsed through the air, increasing in speed and growing faster. The wind kicked up dust as two choppers hovered over the ruins of the building. Lincoln closed his eyes. He threaded his fingers through Carson's hair. Just as he'd thought Carson was gone, his mouth moved, and he swallowed.

Lincoln lifted his head. "Yes! That's it. Drink." Tears dropped from Lincoln's chin onto Carson's face, running through the dirt and dust on his skin. Lincoln weakly lowered himself to the floor, not once removing his wrist from Carson's mouth. Carson swallowed again, and Lincoln let out a chuckle that quickly morphed into a sob.

"Go and lead them in here!" Doc yelled to John over the thumping beat of the chopper blades.

Lincoln's adrenaline dropped sharply. He laid his head next to Carson's, whispering words of love and promises for their future as he floated. Peace blanketed his body. He couldn't fight the pull any longer and let himself go.

A BRIGHT light flashed in Carson's eyes. He tried to turn his head, but the light followed. The intensity burned as he struggled to get away from the fucking thing. Everything hurt, and the incessant light yanked him out of his cathartic slumber, exacerbating the aches in his arms and legs.

His chest burned with each breath. His face was a throbbing mass of pain. Carson groaned and tried to shift around.

"Carson, love. Calm down." That deep, honeyed voice reached in and calmed Carson's racing heart. Strong, familiar hands ran over his arms, soothing and stroking. The light finally disappeared, to Carson's relief.

A hand took hold of his, and then warm lips pressed against his for a moment. The sweet scent of his bond mate embraced Carson. He tried to smile. Even that hurt.

"I'm right here. You're going to be fine. Rest, love. I'm not going anywhere."

Carson tried to open his eyes to see that Lincoln was okay. See for himself that he wasn't dreaming, but suddenly the bed tilted and his world went black.

The second time Carson woke, he opened his eyes to dim light in the room. The white institutional ceiling, cinder block walls, and constant beep of the heart monitor told him he was back at the NVJ in Utica, probably in the same room he'd previously occupied. When he tried to recall how he'd come to be there, a hail of memories assaulted him—visions of Lincoln screaming as he'd been carried from the room, the attack on Jameson, the building coming down. Had he made it out?

Carson squeezed his eyes as pain throbbed in his muscles, his bones, and worst yet his head. He tried to connect with Lincoln, but pain spiked in his temples. Panic-laced dread had him struggling to get out of bed.

"Hey, Carson, relax. You're still injured."

Carson stilled. A blurred figure stood next to his bed. His vision cleared enough to see Doc pointing to a bag of blood hanging from the pole. "Lincoln's blood. In a few short hours, you'll be good as new." He smiled, but truly he looked exhausted.

"Lincoln? Is he okay?" *Please be okay, please.*

Doc rested his hand on Carson's arm in a comforting gesture. "Lincoln's perfectly fine. Worried about you, but after he gave more blood, I banished him to a nap."

Carson's body gave a collective sigh, and he sank back into the mattress. His eyelids fought his will to stay awake.

"I know you're afraid to fall asleep and miss him, but he's going to be out for hours, and you need your rest too. I promise, the minute he wakes up, I'll send him in. By then you should be ready for him."

Carson's protests failed to surpass the fatigue. Knowing Lincoln was okay, would return to him soon, allowed him to float and give in to sleep.

CARSON WAS pain-free when he woke. Lincoln's blood had worked its magic. He was no longer hooked to the IV and other machines. He didn't have long to wonder where Lincoln was since they currently shared a bed. Doc must have given Lincoln the green light, or he'd ignored Doc's orders.

Carson turned onto his side and faced Lincoln. His lover was pale, but other than that, he looked healthy and very much alive. Carson rested his palm against Lincoln's cheek, and instinctively Lincoln nuzzled it in his sleep. Grinning wide, Carson sought out their link. A peaceful contentment filled Carson, chasing away the cold that had taken hold since he'd faced Jameson.

Carson closed his eyes, savoring how safe he felt. Lincoln's hand caressed Carson's cheek, and he relished the roughness, the gentleness. Carson opened his eyes. A glassy-eyed Lincoln gazed back. Carson smiled. When Lincoln smiled back, Carson threw himself into his arms.

"Oh, love," Lincoln whispered. Carson squeezed him tighter. Lincoln chuckled, running his hands over Carson's back and into his hair. "How do you feel?"

Carson was ready to purr like a cat from his touch. "Believe it or not, I'm perfectly fine. Your blood did the trick."

Lincoln sighed. "When we found you, you weren't breathing…" He swallowed hard. "But we're here, and I'm never going to let you out of my sight again. I love you."

"Love you too. I was so scared. I thought I'd killed you," Carson whispered as memories of biting Lincoln crushed his chest.

Lincoln kissed Carson's temple. "You just took too much blood, and I passed out for a few minutes. We're bonded. Nothing you do could hurt me. I'm sure of that now."

Carson shuddered and placed his hand on the back of Lincoln's neck. With wonder-filled eyes, Lincoln gazed back, and for a few minutes, they soaked in the sight of one another. Carson leaned in and placed a gentle kiss on Lincoln's lips. He'd kill anyone who ever dared to take Lincoln from him again.

Carson caught his bottom lip in his teeth. He just wanted to forget everything, but that was impossible. "Jameson?"

Lincoln frowned. "Dead. Killed when the building came down."

The man who'd tried to take everyone he'd loved was no longer a threat, but did Carson still have everyone he loved? "Caden and my uncle?"

Lincoln's face softened. "Here, and they're both perfectly fine. Caden's like a mother hen around you. Your uncle had to force him to get some rest. They both love you very much."

Carson smiled, but it faded quickly as he thought of his mother. A lump jammed up his throat, and he shook his head.

"I'm so sorry you lost your mother, Carson."

The warmth and love was enough to help buoy him against the pain. "I miss her." A tear escaped his eye and he smiled again. "She would have loved you. Anyone who would do what you did to save me? Yeah, you would have been number one in her book."

Lincoln beamed. "I wish I could have met her. But I know she was a good woman because of the son she raised."

Carson tried not to mourn the past too much. His mother's death would always be a painful memory, but his future was right before him. Despite Jameson's fucked-up plans, and his meddling in the course of their lives, he'd led Carson to Lincoln. Damn, how screwed up was it that Carson was thankful to the evil man because he'd brought them together?

"I'm grateful too," Lincoln said.

A loud noise in the hall shot through Carson, bouncing off every nerve. He was still jumpy. He peered over his shoulder to the door.

"Don't worry. I locked it." Lincoln waggled his eyebrow, running his hand down Carson's arm, then his thigh.

Carson shivered hard. He buried his face in Lincoln's neck, and the smell of sweat and blood sent a wave of heat that hit him hard in the gut. Carson licked at the pulse beneath his tongue, and sense memories of biting Lincoln were better than any aphrodisiac. A groan escaped

Lincoln. He pulled Carson tighter to him. Arousal flowed freely between them, feeding their desire. Carson needed reassurance that they were both okay, that life would go on, that they were still alive. He needed Lincoln, now.

CHAPTER 32

LINCOLN COULDN'T get enough of Carson suckling the skin on his neck. He tilted his head, letting Carson know he enjoyed every friggin' minute of it. Carson ground his dick into Lincoln's hip. He writhed and groaned. Lincoln grasped Carson's ass and ground him harder against his leg. Carson rubbed his palm over Lincoln's thick bulge. Needing to take back some control, Lincoln rolled onto his back, pulling Carson on top of him.

Lincoln kneaded Carson's ass as their ragged breaths filled the air. The excitement and need rolling from Carson overwhelmed Lincoln's senses. "I want you to make love to me and then I want you to bite me." Lincoln moaned as Carson nipped at his neck. "Shit."

"Anything you want, babe."

Carson quickly divested Lincoln of his T-shirt, sweats, and boxers, and then licked a line from the base of Lincoln's dick to the tip. The tingle ran down his shaft and filled his balls. Precum leaked from his cock, and Carson lapped up each drop. When Carson finally took the head into his mouth and tongued the slit, a wanton moan escaped Lincoln.

"Feels so good, love." Lincoln raked his fingers through Carson's hair. He pushed his hips up, feeding more of his cock into Carson's mouth. He pushed Lincoln's cock into the back of his throat. Lincoln panted as Carson held his head still and allowed Lincoln to fuck his mouth.

Carson pulled off and pumped Lincoln's cock from root to tip. Carson wet his finger and then massaged Lincoln's opening lightly. Carson placed his mouth over the head of Lincoln's shaft. As Carson's finger pushed inside, Lincoln tightened his grip on Carson's hair. Lincoln gasped from the burning invasion, which vanished when Carson crooked his finger. White-hot sparks shot up Lincoln's spine, and his chest heaved.

Carson's talents never failed to amaze Lincoln. Carson moved down and sucked on Lincoln's balls, Carson's tongue running over the hairy sac that pulled up tighter. He fed another finger into Lincoln's hole, stretching and scissoring and relaxing the opening. His tongue trailed up his shaft, teasing the head relentlessly. The sensations magnified until Lincoln was sure his chest was going to explode. Too much too fast.

Lincoln pawed at Carson's head. "Stop.... S-stop... shit... gonna come. Not yet."

Carson removed his fingers and replaced them with his tongue, lapping at Lincoln's entrance, wetting the hole, driving Lincoln out of his mind with need. Growling, Lincoln grabbed Carson and pulled him up until their noses nearly touched. A wild feral gaze stared back at Lincoln from eyes eaten up by black pupils. Lincoln stripped Carson of his sleep pants, and Carson pulled off his T-shirt.

Carson settled between Lincoln's legs and caressed his cheek. Lincoln was sure he couldn't love anyone more than he loved Carson. Lincoln kissed his bond mate, their tongues tangling and moans swallowed between them. Their connection pulsed like a living, breathing being that seared and sizzled across every one of Lincoln's nerves. Carson pulled back from the kiss, leaving Lincoln's lips cold. He pointed to the tube of lube on the bedside table. Carson cocked an eyebrow, and Lincoln shrugged with a smirk. Carson grabbed the tube and coated his cock. He pushed his coated fingers into Lincoln, and he gasped.

Carson's skin had flushed red, and a sheen of sweat coated his forehead and the planes of his chest. Carson's beauty only increased with his arousal. Lincoln reached for Carson. Lincoln couldn't believe he'd become such a dedicated bottom.

"You ready?" Carson asked.

"Yes."

Carson lined up with Lincoln. Every inch of Carson's cock burned upon entry. Lincoln bore down, easing the way, eyes never wavering from Carson's. He pulled out and pushed back in quickly. The pleasure mitigated the pain.

Carson leaned into Lincoln's thighs, folding him in half.

"Lincoln," Carson whispered. "Open your eyes."

He didn't realize he'd closed them. Opening, the uncensored expression of love on Carson's face squeezed his chest painfully. The pleasure flowing through their bond filled Lincoln's mind to capacity, and he was sure he'd combust.

"Love you." Carson grunted as he plowed into Lincoln over and over. Lincoln reached for his cock, but Carson growled, batting his hand away.

Lincoln's balls were on fire with his need to come. He exposed his neck to Carson. He moaned and ran his tongue over the rapidly pulsing vein in Lincoln's neck. He shuddered hard.

Carson's hips slapped against Lincoln. He grasped Carson's biceps, ready to fly. "Bite me."

The stabbing pain forced Lincoln to clamp down on Carson's shaft. In response, Carson increased his thrusts, pushing Lincoln's euphoria to astronomical heights. He cried out and grasped the back of Carson's head to prevent him from pulling away. Carson sucked, and it burned and felt amazing at the same time. The onslaught of pleasure from Carson's cock in his ass and the sucking on his neck grayed his vision. His heart smashed into his ribs at a rate too high to count.

"I-I… fuck. Carson… I love you!" Lincoln screamed as his balls squeezed painfully, the muscles in his stomach contracted, and the air froze in his lungs. Carson moaned and slammed him harder until Lincoln wasn't able to string a coherent thought together. Blood rushed from his head, as his chest seized and locked up. He couldn't draw in a breath. He clutched Carson's head, willing him to suck harder and faster. He was right there, so ready….

Come for me, babe.

Pleasure fired every neuron in Lincoln's brain at once, and cum shot from his dick, splattering across his face and chest. A blinding white light flashed in his vision as he fought to pull in enough breath. The slide of Carson's cock against his highly sensitized hole threatened to fill his dick again. Carson removed his fangs and licked at the wounds, driving Lincoln crazy.

"Come on, love. Fill me."

Carson threw his head back. He thrust deeply. His entire body tensed, suspended, and he roared his release to the ceiling, filling Lincoln with his seed. Carson collapsed onto Lincoln. Their chests pushed against one another, desperately seeking air. The sweat clinging to Lincoln's skin cooled, dousing the raging inferno burning inside.

"Holy fuck." He panted. "I think… you killed me." His heart pounded so hard all of his veins pulsed.

Carson remained spread over Lincoln, limp as a rag doll, face tucked under Lincoln's chin. "I think I'm paralyzed from the neck down. That was… fuck me. I may need a week to recover."

Lincoln chuckled. With his remaining energy, Lincoln wrapped his arms around Carson and rolled them onto their sides. "A week in bed with you. Count me in, love."

"Thank you, babe."

Lincoln rubbed his chin over Carson's hair. "For what?"

Carson was silent, and Lincoln thought he'd fallen asleep. "For loving me."

A sob pushed into Lincoln's throat. His eyes burned. He was the lucky one. "I didn't have a choice, love. You had my heart at first sight."

They spent a few bliss-filled minutes nuzzling cheeks together, and then Lincoln drifted off, sated and more confident than ever that Carson had been destined to be his, forever.

CARSON GRIPPED Lincoln's hand as they walked to the conference room of the NVJ. Why he was so nervous, he hadn't a clue. He'd been told that he'd slept for nearly four days while healing. He had yet to see his uncle and Caden. They were in the conference room. There were also some important people from the NVJ who wanted to talk to them. His fear of what would happen, to not only him but Lincoln, his family, and Justin, was barely under his control.

Lincoln nudged Carson's mind. Lincoln grinned like a fool. He'd been nudging Carson all morning nonstop.

"You're really enjoying the fact that you can initiate our link, aren't you? What's that, like the ten billionth time today?"

Lincoln shrugged, but the pride in his expression told the truth. *I love being able to talk to you whenever I want, no matter where I am.*

And that was definitely true. After their earlier sexcapade, Carson had nearly tripped over his own feet on his way to shower when Lincoln's voice had popped into his head. Both of their abilities were growing and changing. Where would they stop?

They stopped before the closed door to the conference room, where their futures were to be decided, probably for them.

"You ready?" Lincoln asked. He raised their joined hands and rubbed Carson's knuckles across his soft lips.

Carson smacked down the iron butterflies pounding their wings against his stomach. He nodded tentatively.

"I'm right here, okay? Remember I told you, no matter what, they won't separate us. And you will be with your family."

Carson wanted to be as sure. "I believe you."

Carson pecked Lincoln on the lips. He opened the door, revealing the people already inside.

Carson stepped inside. Caden stood across the room at the window, his back to Carson, but whirled around when he heard the door close. Caden's body went completely still, so odd for the boy who'd been in perpetual motion since birth. A wide grin lit up little brother's face. In a flash of arms and legs, he launched himself onto the long conference table separating them. He ran down the length and flew into Carson's arms. He barely caught his hundred-and-eighty-pound little brother without either of them going down.

"Hey, bro!" Caden squeezed him tight, and then more arms surrounded both of them.

Uncle Graham smiled tremulously.

"Hi, Uncle Graham." Carson was relieved they were finally together.

"Hey, buddy," Uncle Graham whispered. His lower lip trembled, and Carson knew if his uncle cried, he'd lose it too. "Your mother... I'm sorry I couldn't protect her. I tried to keep you all safe. I really did."

Carson patted him on the shoulder. "I know you did. I know." A burning lump wedged into his throat. His uncle had lost someone he cared for as well. "I'm just glad you're both okay."

Uncle Graham nodded, and the three of them remained in their embrace, unwilling to let go. Carson caught Lincoln smiling at him from across the room. That's when Carson saw him.

Justin.

He sat on a small sofa next to Max. His head was bowed, and he appeared to be staring at the floor. Was the awareness he'd exhibited earlier with Jameson still there? Carson released his brother, unable to look away from his former friend and lover.

"He's getting better," Caden whispered.

Carson felt his eyes widen in surprise.

"He's more aware of things around him. I think he recognized me, but things still seem pretty jumbled in his brain. It comes and goes. Max seems to be the only one who can calm him down when he gets upset."

Caden swallowed hard. "Does he remember... what... that I...." Shit, he couldn't say the words aloud.

Caden squeezed Carson's shoulder. "I don't know."

Carson crossed the room to the boy—now a man—he'd once loved. Intense jealousy smacked him. Lincoln's attention was pinpointed on Justin.

Carson couldn't help feeling smug, knowing Lincoln was possessive of him. *Babe, you're the only love in my life now. The only one for me.*

Lincoln continued to scowl in Justin's direction despite Carson's assurance. Just when Carson was sure he wouldn't relent, Lincoln's jealousy receded. Carson gave him an encouraging smile, which he returned. With a steadying breath, he took the final steps to stand before Justin and Max.

Max looked up with a leery expression that confused Carson. Ignoring Max, Carson crouched down in front of Justin.

Licking his lips, Carson forced a shaky smile. "Hey, Justin."

Justin tensed and clasped his hands together in his lap. Warily, he raised his head until their eyes met. A frown of confusion marred his face. Those steel-winged butterflies worked their way into Carson's chest, pounding furiously against his ribs. He rubbed his sweaty palms against his jeans.

"It's me, Carson."

At the sound of Carson's name, Justin's eyes widened. He pushed back against the couch, scrambling to get away from Carson. The terror on his face spoke volumes.

"No!" He tried to climb over Max to get away.

Carson fell back onto his ass, unable to tear away from the fear in Justin's eyes. Justin, who'd once promised to protect Carson from the world and never feared anything, even death, was now terrified of

Carson. He wanted to pull Justin to him and promise him he wouldn't hurt him. But for now only Max could get through to him.

Arms slipped under Carson's, dragging him away from his past. Years of suppressed guilt and mourning surfaced, clinging to every surface of his body. He wanted to beg Justin to forgive him, but he wouldn't hear Carson, might never hear him. Lincoln pulled Carson to his chest while he watched Max soothe the man he'd permanently damaged.

"He's afraid of me," Carson whispered. The truth was hard to take, but why wouldn't Justin fear him? Carson had pretty much killed everything he was.

"It's not your fault. You were forced to bite him. If you hadn't, Monrovia would have killed Justin. At least now, he has a chance to recover. A chance at a life."

Carson recognized the truth behind what Lincoln said. He wasn't sure his self-imposed blame would ever disappear completely. He could only try his damnedest to find a way to bring Justin back to the person he'd been.

"I have to help him."

"We will. We'll get him whatever he needs."

Thank you.

Max held Justin close. Justin clutched Max as if his life depended on the connection. Justin's breathing slowed. The twitching in his muscles ceased. A hand on Carson's shoulder startled him.

His uncle stood next to him with an encouraging smile. "He'll be okay, Carson."

"I know. It just hurts to know I was the cause."

Uncle Graham tousled Carson's hair. They would all help each other heal… if they got the chance.

The door to the room opened, and several men and women entered. Many dressed in business attire, others in NVJ uniforms with weapons in holsters on their belts. Lincoln tensed and moved in front of Carson, on high alert. Were they in danger?

Doc followed the group inside. He nodded to both Carson and Lincoln as he passed and made his way over to Max and Justin.

Who are they?

Bigwigs from the NVJ. By the way, I put in my resignation today. I won't work for a corrupt agency.

You what?

Lincoln glanced over his shoulder at Carson. *I swore I'd take you away where no one would hurt you ever again.*

Carson smiled.

A woman with short silver hair, and what looked to be an expensive gray designer suit, stopped before Lincoln. "Commander Samuels." She nodded eloquently and extended her hand.

Lincoln didn't hesitate to shake her hand. "Deputy Director Stewart."

Carson placed his hand on Lincoln's back. *What's going on? You're scared.*

I don't know. Just stay close.

That didn't sound good.

"Shall we?" Deputy Director Stewart waved her hand toward the table.

Her entourage seated themselves around the long table. Lincoln directed Carson to the opposite end. Doc settled into the chair next to Carson. The man looked as if he'd aged ten years and had been defeated every single day of those years.

Carson leaned close to him. "How's Tommy?"

Doc's lips formed a thin, tight line, highlighting the lines around his mouth. He shook his head. "He's not good. His family is with him now. He isn't…"

Carson gripped the arms of the chair, waiting, but Doc merely shook his head.

"Maybe I could help. Try to heal him." Maybe he could heal Tommy as he had Lincoln. His blood was useless from anyone other than Carson. Once a Sanatore bonded, their blood only healed their bond mate.

"I'm willing to try anything."

Carson needed to try to heal Tommy, if only for Doc's sake.

Deputy Director Stewart cleared her throat and opened a folder on the table before her. She looked to Lincoln and Carson.

"I am Deputy Director Alana Stewart, here under direct orders of NVJ Director General Carina Williams."

Shit, even Carson knew that name. Carina Williams held the highest position in the NVJ and was a member of the president's cabinet.

Deputy Director Stewart leaned forward and clasped her slender hands on the table. "On behalf of the entire New Vampire Justice system and the director general, I am here to extend a sincere apology to you, Carson Locke, as well as you, Commander Samuels, and your entire team, for what you have endured at the hands of Jameson Merrick. He was the acting Director of the NVJ Center for Vampire Advancement under the name of Fredrick Mason. As this investigation continues, it has come to our attention that several NVJ officials were privy to at least some of Mr. Merrick's dealings and activities. As a result of bribery, coercion, or through their own will, they either aided Director Mason or turned a blind eye to his activities."

Carson shouldn't have been shocked that others in the NVJ had been part of Jameson's scheme.

"As they say, we're searching a stack of needles for a piece of hay, and it's going to take time to sort out the extent of the corruption and damage wrought by this man." She shook her head. "The fact that this man was able to infiltrate and operate within the NVJ without detection for over twenty years does not speak well for the NVJ. In fact, it's a blow to our very core and what the NVJ stands for.

"So that brings me to the other reasons we are here." She pulled several sheets of paper from the folder and laid them on the table in neat piles.

Lincoln's tension increased. He leaned back in his chair, and that's when Carson spotted the gun that rested on his thigh, his finger on the trigger. Only the table obscured its existence to the rest of the room. Carson looked to Lincoln, who was expressionless.

Lincoln? What are you going to do?

Lincoln kept his attention on the room's occupants. *Just follow my lead, no matter what.*

Carson looked over his shoulder at Max. He'd moved from the couch and stood at parade rest. His face wore the same expressionless mask as Lincoln. Max wore something in his ear, like a listening device. He was in on whatever Lincoln had planned. Doc shifted in his seat and looked as pensive as they all did. *Jesus, tell me what's happening? I can help.* He was ready to rain down a shitload of power if need be.

If I need you, you'll know it.

"Let's get started," the deputy director said.

Carson's stomach rolled into a tight ball, and he swore it tried to wedge itself behind his liver. The anticipation was too much.

"Under the authority of the NVJ, I have been vested with the power given to me through a document signed by the Director General of New Vampire Justice, Carina Williams, and carrying the New Vampire Justice seal. First, Commander Samuels."

She picked up a paper before her and passed it to a man in a blue suit beside her. He proceeded toward Lincoln, the paper held in front of him. Lincoln tensed and braced his hand on the table, a steely determination on his face.

Lincoln, don't shoot anyone.

I won't let them take you away from me.

What?

They couldn't separate them after the hell they'd gone through, after what they'd done to stop Jameson. A fiery buzz crackled beneath Carson's skin as his panic hit a new crescendo. Heat flared in the markings on his body. Any second, he'd start glowing like a Christmas tree.

The man stopped next to Lincoln. If Lincoln shot him, the officers would kill him on the spot. Carson was prepared to knock out everyone in the room—if it worked again.

"Commander Samuels, Director General Williams respectfully declines your resignation. I am authorized to promote you to the newly created position of Director of Special Operations for the NVJ."

Carson blinked repeatedly. *Director Samuels?*

Lincoln stared at the woman as if she'd just revealed she was an alien from outer space. He looked down as the man in the blue suit practically forced the paper into his hand. He took the paper, scowling as he read the contents, his anger evident not only to Carson but everyone else in the room.

Lincoln, calm down. I think we should hear what she has to say.

Lincoln turned to Carson, and his face softened.

Please.

Reluctantly, Lincoln nodded. *She'd better say something pretty spectacular.*

"Commander Samuels, if you accept, you will report for duty in two weeks to Washington, DC, where you will head a task force created to clean up twenty years of corruption and locate some three hundred vampires whose disappearance is thought to be connected to Jameson Merrick."

Lincoln's face blanched. Carson's mouth fell open. Three hundred vampires.

"Please wait. Before you decline… Carson Locke."

Eyes wide, Carson watched as she handed off another paper to her delivery boy. Carson's heart stopped as he waited. Everything could still go to hell in overdrive.

"Mr. Locke, you've been granted full protection under the auspices of the NVJ. From this date forward, you're protected from any form of testing, abuse of power, or coercion. Your status of a Salutem vampire will become classified level-one information. Anyone releasing that information will face the most severe of penalties. The NVJ has no interest in using you for any means. You're free to live your life as you see fit. Your family will receive the same protection, as well as Justin Masters."

The man presented Carson with the paper. He reached out slowly, as if it would disappear. "Thank you." The man smiled curtly and returned to the head of the table.

Carson looked to Lincoln, who stared at the paper with the same disbelief as Carson.

"Well, shit." Lincoln wrapped his arm around Carson's shoulders, pulling him close. Their shared relief expanded, settling Carson's fears. He rested his head on Lincoln's shoulder. His family was safe.

"Now, Commander Samuels. May I ask for your decision regarding the deputy general's offer?"

Carson thought he saw a slight upturn at the side of her lips.

Lincoln took Carson's hand. *What do you think, love?* Doc startled Carson when he spoke. "They're just communicating telepathically. Give them a minute." Doc rolled his eyes.

The deputy director, who'd appeared puzzled, now looked stunned. "Oh… okay… um…" Her brow furrowed, and she leaned over the table, cocking her head at Doc. "Seriously?"

"Yeah, seriously, but they're harmless."

Carson snorted. So far from the truth. The deputy director along with her entire group passed uneasy looks amongst themselves.

Well. I'm not doing this if you don't want to. It's your turn to choose what you want to do with your life.

Director Samuels? Sounds hot.

Lincoln huffed. *Pervert.*

You love it.

Lincoln grinned. *I do.*

Carson chewed his lip and then took Lincoln's hand. *I think we need to finish what we started.*

So do I.

Carson sat forward. "Deputy Director Stewart. We accept your job offer."

"We?" she asked, but her smirk was knowing.

"Yeah, we do," Carson said.

"Glad to hear it. Dr. Simon Reynolds."

Doc, who had been staring down at his hands, his mind no doubt on Tommy, appeared confused. Carson helped him out by pointing in the direction of the deputy director.

"Dr. Reynolds, you're hereby appointed as the new Director of the NVJ Center for Vampire Advancement. You've got a big job ahead of you."

The man delivered the paper to a stunned Doc.

She patted a pile of papers. "In this stack, I also have appointment letters for each member of your team, to be assigned to your task force, as well as one Sergeant Dwayne Simpson of the Utica PD, who said, and I quote, 'I'll play.'"

Lincoln chuckled.

"Gentlemen, it's time to clean up the trash and take it out. I'll see you all in Washington, DC, in two weeks. I know I won't be disappointed."

With that, the deputy director and her entourage cleared the room. No one spoke, or even seemed to breathe, while attempting to comprehend what had happened.

They won, right? Carson turned to Lincoln and nudged him in the ribs with his elbow.

"Director Samuels," Carson growled.

Lincoln looked at the paper in his hand and then burst out laughing. That laugh was beautiful and a sign that they had indeed won, for now. Carson joined in, and that laugh was the best of his life.

"We're moving to Washington, DC. Awesome!" Caden exclaimed.

Carson raised his brows. "You want to move there with me?"

"Bro, you can't get rid of me. Plus, I can go to college there and meet lots of women!"

"I wouldn't mind a change of scenery," Carson's uncle said, clapping Carson on his shoulder.

Carson chuckled.

"Sounds like we're all moving to DC." Max had a hint of a smile on his face. "And don't even think that I'm calling you Director Samuels. Your head is big enough."

The twitch at the corners of Max's mouth wrecked his attempted frown. He pulled Justin close again. Justin easily rested his head on Max's chest as he played with a button on his shirt. Carson had an idea who Justin would live with in DC. Did Max understand what was happening between him and Justin? Max had been married to a woman, but when Max looked at Justin... something in his gaze caught Carson's breath.

"You'll call me Director and you'll like it." A wide grin covered Lincoln's face.

Damn, he's gorgeous.

His smile turned lecherous. "You're pretty damn hot yourself, Carson Locke." There was no hiding his thoughts from their bond.

The door opened, and the rest of Lincoln's team flooded into the room. Hugs were shared and congratulations given, but Carson only had eyes for one person—the man who'd saved him, the man he'd saved. The Tabula Rasa in love with the Sanatore.

Exclusive excerpt

A Chance for Us

New Vampire Justice: Book Two

By Jake C. Wallace

Love between a young vampire with a broken mind and the jaded officer who cares for him might be all that stands between a human-vampire war....

Justin Masters is stuck in a nightmare. Waking after seven years in a catatonic state, he falls desperately in love with the straight NVJ officer who saved him. Between that and dreams of being tortured and taking pleasure in the pain bleeding into his waking hours, Justin's sure he's starting to crack.

The growing unrest in the vampire world should be Max Kincaid's focus, but Justin's struggle, along with Max's confusing feelings for his ward, have him reeling. When Justin's attacked, his resulting needs might be more than what Max can provide, but he'll be damned if anyone else will touch Justin.

As the NVJ investigates humans missing from a high-end bite club, they uncover a deeper plot that traces back to Justin. If those who want him have their way, there will be bloodshed. Justin and Max are in a fight to save Justin not only from those who would use him, but from his own mind.

Coming Soon to
www.dreamspinnerpress.com

CHAPTER 1

JUSTIN MASTERS needed something to clear his spinning head. He was having another bad day, one of the worse he'd had in weeks. He clutched his knees to his chest, arms squeezing as tight as they could, the pressure against his chest making it hard to breathe. His fingers were knotted together and ached. His need to feel anchored, tethered to the earth, was like a hard lump rising in his throat. He bit hard on the inside of his cheek, the pain cathartic and needed. Any moment, he was sure he'd be stuffed back into his head, trapped and helpless as he had been for over seven years.

Those years held only memories of fear and anxiety and pain. If you were to ask him where he'd been and what he'd done, he couldn't answer, but ask him how he'd felt and the words would be incongruous with one another. While he recalled fear and pain, he also recalled warmth and safety. Now, he struggled every day to keep from returning to that vaguely remembered version of hell.

Until five months ago, he'd been nearly catatonic, a prisoner in his own mind, drifting, fearful, mindless, knowing he was alive in some reality, but not having a coherent thought to make sense of anything around him. Then he'd woken up. Slowly, painfully, he'd come back to reality in a body seven years older than he'd last remembered, to the fact that his mother had died while he'd been away, and to Max, a vampire.

Like a newborn babe opening his eyes, Justin recalled his first clear vision of Max, the New Vampire Justice Lieutenant, with the kind blue-green eyes, round wire-framed glasses, shoulder-length wavy blond hair tied messily in a ponytail, and a smile that immediately had warmed the coldness of Justin's last seven hellish years. The man Justin currently awaited to enter the room where he spent every day, useless and cast aside. Justin wasn't on top of anyone's list. Just a collateral human the vampires had rescued in their battle with the evil Jameson Merrick, the man who'd tried to use Justin's former boyfriend, Carson Locke, to gain the power to rule the vampire world.

Just the name "Carson" sent a shiver of fear and confusion through Justin. At sixteen, he'd fallen in love with the reclusive, beautiful Carson, the Tabula Rasa vampire whose bite could erase a mind, turn a person into a mindless, reprogrammable husk. But six short months later, they'd both been kidnapped. Justin could still recall the moment when Carson had been forced to bite him, which sent him into those seven years trapped in purgatory.

Justin rubbed his palms over his thighs. The constant, dull ache that increased when walking was a relentless reminder of the gunshot wounds he'd endured in a bid by their captives to force Carson to obey their command. Justin closed his eyes as visual memories of the searing agony and terror of knowing he was going to die ramped up his anxiety. He'd loved Carson and had felt responsible for their situation. The pain in Carson's eyes, his tears as their kidnapper commanded he bite Justin or allow him to die, still haunted him daily.

"I-it's okay, C-Carson," Justin had whispered. "G-gonna ki-kill me anyway."

Justin knew he'd given Carson permission to bite him, knew that acquiescence had meant he'd die, and at that moment, he'd been ready. The pain of two gunshots had taken his will to live, and he'd just wanted to make everything okay for Carson. But Justin hadn't died that day. What had happened was worse than any death he could have imagined. No one knows why he woke up after all that time, but it had something to do with Carson entering the building he'd been held in. That had started another version of hell.

He gasped in a breath. Fuck, he'd done it again. Max was going to be pissed. Justin had allowed himself to get lost in his head, lost in the nightmares of his past, and now he was too far gone to get back on his own. At that point, only physical pain or being wrapped up, restrained until he couldn't move, would work to center him and bring him back to reality.

He'd forgotten everything he'd been taught in therapy with his counselor, Walter—breathe deep, distract himself, use the worksheets to work out his thoughts and emotions. But when his mind raced, and he couldn't focus on anything, not even a single thought, all of those tools were useless. He was supposed to control these escalations on his own, had worked on this with Max and Walt, because Max felt Justin had become too dependent on him. Max, who'd taken Justin in, who'd held Justin whenever he'd been ready to shake apart, who'd stayed by his side as he'd learned to do everything again, including make a meal and doing his laundry and, fuck, even go outside without falling to pieces. Max's concern that Justin be able to make it on his own, to stop relying on him, was like a knife to Justin's chest, because he'd fallen in love with the man. But to Max, Justin was like a little brother—a needy little brother—and despite being only two years younger than Max, Justin was essentially still a teenager in a man's body. He was a scared and needy kid who couldn't make it through a day without clinging to Max. What kind of life was that for a straight man who wasn't even related by blood to Justin?

The tightening in Justin's chest pushed his rate of breathing higher. Something horrible was going to happen, and it wasn't his own death as he would hope. He couldn't breathe, couldn't think, and was going to lose it big-time, again.

MAX KINCAID shuffled through the papers on his desk, searching for the report of a missing human. He was dead tired. Sleep had become a commodity during the last five months. His usual good mood was in the crapper, and he needed a vacation. Fat chance of that. His team had been appointed by the director of New Vampire Justice, Carina Williams, who was also a member of the president's cabinet, to clean up the corruption left by the former Director for the Advancement of Vampires, Jameson Merrick. Some three hundred vampires had been discovered missing and linked to Jameson. Their job had been to find those vampires.

Lincoln's entire team, which included a half-dozen NVJ officers, had moved their lives to Washington, DC, which Max hated with a passion. He was knee deep in political bullshit and people—fucking people everywhere crammed into a sixty-three-mile area. He'd grown up outside of Utica, NY, which could be considered large for a city, but Washington was just too much. And if it was too much for him, he knew it had to be terrifying for Justin.

Thankfully, Director Lincoln Samuels—Max still had to laugh at the title his best friend had acquired—had taken it upon himself to move the New Vampire Justice Headquarters from the center of the city to southwest DC on the Anacostia River. The building had been part of the deal Lincoln had made with the NVJ for moving the entire task force. The building housed the NVJ, the new Center for Vampire Advancement headed by Simon "Doc" Reynolds, and separate apartments for everyone on the task force. The building was a fortress and a sanctuary for both Max and Justin.

Max pulled off his glasses and rubbed at his eyes. If a minute didn't go by that he was worrying about Justin, it would be a fucking miracle. After five months, the man had made incredible strides coming out of a body on autopilot, which had definitely been a lights-on-but-no-one's-home scenario. The first time Max had seen Justin after their retrieval team had been held hostage, he'd been taken aback by how handsome the man was, especially in that cinder block hole of a room they'd been shoved into. Justin had that creamy clear skin you rarely see and small freckles all over his nose and cheeks, which matched the color of his sandy-red hair. His greenish-hazel eyes had been dull, lifeless, as he'd stared out into nothing. Not an emotion showing, he could have been mistaken for a statue if he hadn't been breathing.

Max could remember the moment those eyes had focused on him, blinking rapidly as if just waking from a long sleep. Max had been holding Justin close, trying to share warmth because the man was shivering. Justin frowned, his gaze never wavering from Max's face. When Max said his name, Justin's frown had deepened, but then he'd rested his hand on Max's chest. The gentle touch had caused Max's heart to skip a beat. Max muttered soothing words in a low tone to Justin to let him know he was safe, and Justin sighed and scooted closer, resting his head on Max's chest.

Since then, their lives had been a roller coaster of good, bad, and worse times. The further Justin emerged from his comatose state, the more scared and clingy he'd become. Max felt for him. The days he was steady and appeared happy were interspersed with days riddled with panic and fear. Happy, steady days Max could handle. It was the outbursts of anger, rage, and the irritability that were hard to deal with. He had to remember what Walt continually told him. Justin wasn't in control of his emotions, and only time would change that.

Unfortunately, Max wasn't sure how much more time he could give Justin. His life was on hold, and he needed to move forward, to what he wasn't sure. What scared him most? There were times he wasn't sure if he wanted Justin to stop depending on him, and he didn't know why.

The ringing phone gratefully saved him from his distraction. "Kincaid."

"Hey, princess, we're all in the conference room. Think you could join us?" Lincoln Samuels asked in a sickly sweet, faux tone.

"Waiting for my engraved invitation, sweetheart."

Lincoln snorted. "Consider this your invitation. Drag your ass."

Max hung up the phone and rummaged through the files, finally locating the one he wanted. Grabbing a cup of synthetic blood, he sauntered down the hallway. No way was he rushing for Lincoln. He might be a director in the NVJ, but to Max, he was still the skinny kid from down the road that Max could beat up. That wasn't so true anymore since Lincoln towered over Max, but Max wouldn't go down easy if they tussled.

Entering the conference room, all eyes were on him. Doc smirked knowingly from where he sat near Lincoln, wearing his usual white lab coat. Max chuckled to himself, envisioning Doc sleeping in his coat. Next to him John Dennison wore his usual scowl. The rest of the team were seated around the table: Taylor Myers, Maggie Wright, Tia Warez, Dwayne Simpson, the newest human member… and lab technician, Casey Daley. Shit, Max hadn't expected her to be there. She smiled sweetly at him, and he nodded, maybe a little too sharply, because her smile wavered. Her innuendos about starting their relationship again had increased recently, and his excuse that he needed time to adjust to the move and Justin were wearing thin.

"Thanks for joining us." John scowled deeper. "Some of us do have shit to do."

Max overcame the urge to give the finger to the uptight man. He was a good officer but a shitty vampire. How his wife put up with him, Max would never know.

"Yes. Try to be on time." Lincoln pushed a folded piece of paper down the table. Max reached out and pulled it close but didn't bother to open it. He knew what it said. The last time he was late, Lincoln had bet Max he'd be late again. He now owed Lincoln beer and wings.

"Okay, let's get started." Lincoln opened a folder before him. "We're getting more cases and have very little manpower to handle them. I've brought on three new hires, vetted by Max and myself. Here's their information." He dropped a pile of papers into the center of the table, and everyone grabbed one. "They have excellent backgrounds. Two are currently NVJ, one from Buffalo, the other from Charleston. The other is ex-military."

Heads went up at that last bit of info.

"You hired a human?" Tia asked. It was no secret that she harbored no love of the Nons, a vampire term for humans. Seemed her entire family were anti-Non. Not unheard of but most vampires had assimilated into human culture and lived peacefully. They weren't allowed all of the rights as humans, like serving in the military or holding office, but they were gaining civil rights inch by inch. Humans and vampires were segregated in other ways. It was illegal for human doctors to treat vampires and vice versa. At least the segregation wasn't as bad as it had been in the past with blacks. Physically, the only tell between them were the elongated canines, which were nowhere near the length seen in movies and images of killer vampires. The greatest difference between humans and vampires was diet. Vampires ate all of the foods humans ate but also required a steady diet of blood. And not even human or, yuck, animal blood. The synthetic stuff was sufficient, and most vampires had never tasted human blood, which was illegal to drink outside of sanctioned bite clubs.

"Hey, human here." Dwayne waved his hand at Tia and smiled wide. He loved to push the Nons racism button with Tia. He had it bad on both fronts. He was a human and black.

She looked him over. "Yeah well, I don't think of you as human. You're just Dwayne."

That got a laugh from some around the table. Apparently, he'd broken through her prejudices, which Max knew were learned.

Lincoln narrowed his eyes at her. "Yeah, I hired another human. You got a problem with that?"

Tia was probably gritting her teeth, but she wasn't going to mouth off to Lincoln. He was some scary shit when he got pissed.

"No, sir."

"Good. Keep it that way. We were brought here to clean up Merrick's mess, the corruption, and find the missing vampires. In five months we've located or confirmed the deaths of three-quarters of them, took down a dozen or so of Merrick's conspirators, including politicians and influential leaders, and we've reestablished the NVJ as a by-the-book agency."

There were a volley of snorts and covert laughs around the table. Not always so by the book but close enough. Lincoln glared at them, then smirked.

"We've still got work to do, and we need all the help we can get. We're getting more requests from the Nons police. I've got three calls just today from Metropolitan PD, asking for help on crimes involving vampires. I feel having human team members will be an asset in dealing with some of the precincts that are more vampi-phobic. It's a different cultural climate here than in Utica. Back there, we had a general acceptance between vampires and humans, but here, it seems the sides are always clashing." Lincoln leaned back and sighed, throwing down his pen.

"Why do you think that is?" Maggie asked. Out of all the team members, Max found her the most personable and stable. They all had their issues, some more than others. She was the one he'd want to take with him when there was trouble.

John grunted. "Power. There's so much of it here in the capital, and everyone wants a piece. Many of the people here would sell their mother to boost their standing and make more money. It's the culture, and for some reason, now, the vampires are moving in and looking to get their share."

Max shot Lincoln a look of surprise and got one back. Jameson had sought vampire domination, claiming that while the Nons gave lip service to equality for vampires, they would eventually seek to destroy the vampire race. And he'd nearly done so by unleashing an ancient power inside of Carson. There was no denying the racial tension was increasing. Over the past twenty years, the population of vampires had nearly tripled to around 25 percent of the population. Growth that fast could be seen as a threat to humans, given that a small percentage of those vampires had some kind of powers. Lincoln was a Sanatore vampire capable of healing other vampires, possibly humans (no one had ever tested that theory) with his blood. Healing Carson had bonded them and changed Carson from a Tabula Rasa into a Salutem vampire, never seen before. He was one big mystery, and if word of his capabilities got to the humans, there could be problems.

Was this increasing violence between the vampires and humans the start of that predicted downfall of the vampires?

Max looked down at the folder before him. A report concerning a missing human at an exclusive bite club dead center of DC on 1432 Pennsylvania Ave SE. This was the fifth human missing from the club in less than a year. Humans weren't strangers to the bite clubs. Masochists and pain sluts frequented the bars where biting was supervised and the perfect scene for BDSM. Biting a human outside of the bite clubs was a crime even if consensual, and biting through force anywhere was punishable by death. Vampires law was clear-cut on biting since fear by humans of being bit was what kept vampires lower in society.

To control this, bite clubs had been formed for both containment and safety. Because vampire fangs were only slightly longer than human eye teeth, they were only effective in accessing veins near the surface of the skin. That meant the jugulars and veins in the wrists and hands were most effective for feeding. The jugulars were out since damage to those could kill a person. Since feeding wasn't the goal of biting, most vampires just pierced the skin, bit down, enough to pool the blood and sucked. Max had heard of tourniquets, like those used when drawing blood, as a way to pop out larger veins, but he'd never seen that used.

Max had never bit anyone and had only tasted synthetic blood. He couldn't imagine drinking human blood, or even animal blood, as some vampires were into that fetish. Wasn't for him.

"Max?"

Max looked up and saw Lincoln pointing to the door. Turning, he saw a young NVJ rookie standing by the door, her eyes wide. "Lieutenant Kincaid. You're needed upstairs."

"Fuck," Max muttered as Lincoln gave him that knowing gaze.

He didn't care what Lincoln thought of Justin. He was a responsibility that Max had to see to the end.

JAKE C. WALLACE started writing from a young age, but took a break for marriage, kids, and college (in that order). A few years ago, he rediscovered his passion for writing stories and ventured out into the brave new world of publishing. He has published several novels and short stories. Recently, his novel *Jerricho's Freedom* was a finalist in the Rainbow Book Awards.

At night and on the weekends, Jake writes about all things men, believing there is nothing hotter than two men finding and loving one another, whether for a night or forever. An avid reader of M/M romance, Jake loves a good twist of a plot, HEA, HFN, or tragic ending, and has over two thousand books in his library. He also writes what his best friend calls HUNKs (Happy Until the Next Kidnapping). In his daytime hours, Jake works with individuals with autism and behavior issues. He is owned by a beautiful partner, three kids, and two grandchildren. He lives in Northern Vermont.

Website: www.jcwallacebooks.com
Facebook: www.facebook.com/jcwallacebooks
Twitter: @jcwallacebooks.com
E-mail: jcwallacebooks@gmail.com

Soul
Seekers

JAKE C. WALLACE

Nineteen-year-old college student Levi Reed has spent his life with hollow emotions and a darkness so deep that he's convinced he's losing his mind. He'd give anything to feel something, anything, real.

When a mysterious stranger appears, Levi is convinced the man is trying to kill him. When he's near, Levi experiences head-crushing pain and something surprising—real emotions for the first time. Jeb Monroe is arrogant, self-assured, closed-off, and handsome, but he isn't the harbinger of doom Levi assumed. Jeb's mission: help Levi find his missing soul.

Levi is pulled into the secret world of Seers and Keepers, those born with the innate ability to manipulate souls and tasked with balancing the negative energy they can produce. Levi learns he possesses a rare gift, and he's in danger. As Jeb and Levi grow closer, they discover a group of zealots who want to harness Levi's power to cleanse the world of damaged souls. Everyone Levi cares for is threatened unless he agrees to become their tool of death. But agreeing could spell the destruction of humankind. With no one to trust and nothing as it appears, it's up to Levi to save them all.

www.dreamspinnerpress.com

Also from Dreamspinner Press

www.dreamspinnerpress.com

Also from Dreamspinner Press

ANOTHER
HEALING
BOOK TWO

DEPTH OF
RETURN

M. RAIYA

www.dreamspinnerpress.com

Also from Dreamspinner Press

TA MOORE

DOG DAYS

www.dreamspinnerpress.com

Also from Dreamspinner Press

www.dreamspinnerpress.com

FOR **MORE** OF THE **BEST GAY ROMANCE**

PRESS

dreamspinnerpress.com

www.ingramcontent.com/pod-product-compliance
Lightning Source LLC
Chambersburg PA
CBHW051632260626
47170CB00004B/1138